# SHAYDE

## BOOK 1 – BEGINNING

JASEN R. DOBSON

# BLURB

Drayel Shadow Walker, a powerful Warlock & leader of the Warrior's Guild, is trying to eliminate the King whose ban on magic has caused a rift in the kingdom and the people are suffering. With the Guild chipping away at the King's armies, Drayel's victory is imminent. But at what cost?

The King, desperate to stop Drayel, sends an emissary to try and persuade the Warlock from his course. Their meeting will change the course of history forever.

In this fast paced, riveting offering, Jasen R Dobson creates an engaging story of a world on the edge of war-- and the people that will save or destroy it.

*Shayde: Beginning is Book 1 in a 5 part series.*

# CHAPTER 1

## BEGINNING

*T*HE FIRES BURNED LOW ON THE BATTLEFIELD AND THE SCREAMS of the injured or dying could be heard over the few remaining swords clashing together. This battle was over.

Drayel Shadow Walker observed the field with eyes still glowing bright green from the harnessed power coursing through his body. The Gods Eye Medallion, still warm from the energy that had been flowing through it, was now tucked safely away inside his shirt of enchanted Mithril armor. Drayel let his arms drop wearily down to his side and relaxed for the first time since the battle had begun at sunrise. It seemed like days since the fighting commenced, but the sun directly overhead told him that mere hours had passed.

"Drayel!" came the sound of someone joyously shouting his name nearby.

He turned toward the caller and smiled when he saw his friend, Korin Silver Steel, jogging the last twenty or thirty feet between them. The two men could not be more different in appearance.

Drayel was just over six and a half feet tall, thin and muscular, with long black hair that flowed like a shining dark river across his shoulders.

His eyes were an emerald green that he made glow constantly to remind everyone of the power contained within him. Very few ever saw him when he wasn't fully clothed, but the few that had told stories of the man's tanned skin being tattooed from his shoulders to his feet in glyphs written in the ancient language of the mystics.

Tall, dark, and brooding, the Warlock was not an approachable person by design.

He could tolerate very few humans, especially those that practiced tenebris magicae, or dark magic. He'd found they were easily corrupted by the limited power that dark magic afforded them. Those with the innate ability to harness it found dark magic was much more malleable than light magic.

Light resisted malevolent commands and desires where dark only sought to fulfill the wielder's desires, good or bad. And, as in nature, dark magic was also generally weaker than light magic.

Korin Silver Steel had discovered upon his eighteenth birthday that he was able to summon a small amount of light magic. He'd used it to help turn his father's quaint weapons shop into the best in the kingdom. Swords imbued by Korin would never rust, never dull, and were generally perfect in their craftsmanship. Hence Korin took on the namesake of his work, Silver Steel.

Korin could have used dark magic in greater amounts and created a larger number of lesser blades, but he took pride in his work, and the gleaming blades wielded by the Guild were rightfully feared on the battlefield.

Korin paused to catch his breath. A polar opposite of Drayel's tall, wiry, and dark figure, Korin was a large-framed man packed with muscle from long hours pounding on the molten metal in his father's forge. Sandy-haired and brown-eyed with fair skin, Korin was light to Drayel's dark. And where Drayel was likely to glower and send people running in fear, Korin's smile pulled people to him with natural ease.

"Give me a second to catch my breath." Korin panted while bent over bracing his hands on his knees. The big man was sweating profusely and was covered in brackish-smelling blood and vile. He had been one of the first onto the field and had fought viciously from beginning to end.

Drayel had no doubt that stories would be told of the muscled warrior's almost poetic battles witnessed on this day. For someone so large and heavy the warrior was fluid on the battlefield and moved with the grace and speed of a man much smaller in stature.

Today many enemies had misjudged the big man's speed and skill and paid for it with their lives.

That being said, the man was exhausted and was making a conscious effort to keep the smile on his face.

"You know, if you'd spend even a portion of your time training specifically on your cardiovascular system, you wouldn't be frothing like a horse, my friend." Drayel said with what he hoped was a straight face.

Korin flashed him a very vulgar hand gesture in response.

"I seem to remember the last time you and I crossed swords in the training circle it was your skinny butt that needed to sit down when we were through my Lord." Korin gazed up at Drayel with a lopsided grin.

Drayel felt his heart warm at the sight of his friend's smile. It was true. Drayel was an accomplished swordsman, but when it came to skill at arms Korin was unmatched.

"Luckily for me, Lord Silver Steel, I only use my sword while my magic replenishes. I..." Drayel's words filtered away as his gaze caught another person flickering toward himself and Korin.

The man strolling toward them was not a welcome sight to Drayel, even if he was mostly considered an ally.

Tallon Grey Cloak was a powerful Warlock in his own right. But he lacked any sort of code when it came to killing. And it didn't help that he was little more than a lackey for Maricin Cor Render, the second most powerful person in the Warrior's Guild. Tallon had no ambition beyond serving at her feet and did her bidding with a disturbing amount of zeal.

"Drayel, Korin, my Lady Maricin Cor Render bids you join her at the Guild in order to celebrate today's victory over the King's pawns." Tallon said with a smirk.

He knew that Maricin "summoning" Drayel would annoy the Warlock and current leader of the Guild.

It was well known that Maricin believed she should be the one guiding the Guild's movements. It was her frequently voiced opinion that Maricin was certain that if she possessed the God's Eye Medallion, along with the Dark Heart Medallion she currently held, she would easily surpass Drayel's power. The message was also a jab at Drayel from Maricin in that she had already returned to the Guild before the battle was over. Drayel had ordered Maricin to hold a crucial pass through the hills surrounding the Guild that could have been exploited by the King's troops to get behind the Guild's forces and box them in.

In her arrogance, she'd simply assumed that once she destroyed the first wave of troops that came through the crossing, no more would make the attempt.

She had left halfway through the battle and returned to the Guild to bathe and send messages to emissaries of the Guild claiming "her" victory over the King's forces.

She had disobeyed Drayel's orders and subjected the Guild to a potential loss and damning defeat had they been flanked and ambushed.

Her smaller slights and displays of disrespect could be overlooked, but placing the entire Guild in danger just to snub Drayel would not be allowed to stand.

Drayel smiled.

"Yes, Tallon, let's do go pay a visit to my dear second. Please, lead the way." Drayel gestured with a swoop of his arm toward the horses Tallon had brought with him. Something in the quick acceptance and tone of his voice told Tallon that the visit would not go at all as Maricin had planned.

# CHAPTER 2

## MARICIN

M**ARICIN** C**OR** R**ENDER HURRIED ABOUT HER TASK.**

Not out of any sense of danger or need, but simply out of vainglorious pride in what she believed was an important step in removing Drayel from his seat at the head of the Guild.

She had sent out messages to all the Guilds in Tor'Amal, the capital city of Ka'len. If she could gain the support of even half of them, then she could continue her plan to ascend to the leadership role without fear of reprisals from the other Guilds.

Unseating Drayel was dangerous in its own right. Doing so without the support of the Guilds would just result in her being ousted before she could ever warm the throne in the Citadel's main chambers.

She could not hope to defeat Drayel in direct combat, he was much too powerful for her alone.

But if she had the support of their Guild, the Warriors Guild, then he would have no choice but to step down if she was duly elected to lead them as Drayel had been. So, she undermined him at every turn.

She sent out intentionally vague or incorrect orders from Drayel to their Soldiers. She'd hoped to undermine their confidence in him as a leader.

But that damned Korin Silver Steel that Drayel had positioned as his General was always quick to identify and correct her slightly altered versions of Drayel's orders. And had thus far thwarted her plans to undermine his leadership.

However, after defeating the first round of troops at the pass this morning and seeing the way the battle was turning in Drayel's favor, she'd quickly left her post and returned to the Citadel to send messages of "her" victory and gain the confidence of the other Guilds.

She'd never hesitated to leave the pass and was certain that her destruction of the King's men would be sufficient to deter any more from trying to come through.

She was only half correct.

No more men came through the pass, but only because the ten Warriors sent with her had held their positions when she rode off.

All ten of them had died fighting, though their efforts stopped the King's men from getting through.

But Maricin did not know that.

She'd sent Tallon out to find Drayel and summon him back to the Guild.

She knew that with this battle won that it was only a matter of time before the Guild took the King's Castle in Tor'Amal and claimed it for its own.

The Warrior's Guild would rule Ka'len and Maricin Cor Render would be a queen.

She heard quick footsteps approaching the massive double doors that separated the main chamber from the entry hall.

They were left open these days as the King's army was the only threat they faced since no other Guild would dare attack them, and the King's army was all but defeated. The battle today being the nail in the coffin of the King's defenses outside of the castle.

Maricin turned toward the approaching individual and found one of the servant boys waiting patiently at the door with his feet spread comfortably apart and hands clasped loosely behind his back.

"My Lady, Master Drayel, Lord Silver Steel, and Mister Grey Cloak are approaching. I was told to inform you upon their arrival." The lad bowed and turned to go.

"Wait." Came the low and hostile command from Maricin.

"I believe you meant MASTER Grey Cloak, correct? I wouldn't want to think that you would intentionally disrespect your betters, boy." Maricin glowered at the now terrified child.

The boy was staring at the Dark Heart Medallion that she always wore on display for all to see. It had begun pulsing with a red-tinged black light that was growing faster and starting to extend from the medallion toward the boy. Everyone in Ka'len knew that medallion and what it meant to be struck by it.

The boy was no doubt imaging his flesh being seared to his very bones as so many before him had been.

Maricin herself was imagining that very thing.

It wasn't that she cared about Tallon at all. She just could not or would not tolerate any disrespect to her, or those under her, like the boy had just accidentally done.

She would kill him and make sure that every servant in the house knew that Tallon was to be referred to as MASTER Grey Cloak, not Mister like some common mortal.

The child had turned white with fear and had lost control of his bladder, evidenced by the growing puddle at his feet. He could not move as he was paralyzed by fear. He could only watch with growing horror as the light from the medallion began to reach for him.

Maricin raised her arms in front of her, palms outward and fingers toward the sky, and began uttering her command to the Dark Heart Medallion.

Almost as if in anticipation of the command, its pulsing sped up and the darkness emanating from it began to coil like a snake around the black crystal. The boy's legs gave out at that moment, and he sat down hard upon the cold stone floor. He tried weakly to push back toward the open door but was unable to summon the strength to move.

Maricin pulled her lips back from her teeth in a horrid grin and started the last line of the command that would send the coiled beam of black light across the room and end the child, now openly sobbing on the floor in front of her. With sadistic glee, she uttered the last word of the deadly command, or tried too.

Before the last syllable could form on her lips, a blinding white light tinged with green streaked across the room and knocked Maricin from the dais she was standing on.

Maricin slammed into the wall behind the throne and slumped to the ground beside the chair she so coveted. Through blurry eyes, she saw a distorted Drayel bending down to help the boy stand.

The cursed Silver Steel bastard had Tallon shoved against the wall with his long and murderous sword pressed to poor Tallon's throat. He must have tried to aide her when he saw Drayel preparing for his cowardly sneak attack. Drayel held his hand to the child's forehead and uttered an arcane phrase. The fear in the boy's eyes diminished greatly. Drayel whispered something low and urgent to the child who nodded quickly and fled the room.

Drayel stood up, tall, strong, and obviously angered.

"Maricin Cor Render, You have violated the trust placed in you by myself, and the members of this Guild. Not only have you attempted to openly undermine the leader of the Guild, but you also placed the entire Guild in danger by leaving your post. In addition to these crimes, you have violated our most sacred trust by trying to murder one of our own INSIDE this sacred place." Maricin was slowly becoming terrified herself.

Drayel Shadow Walker was not one to raise his voice or scream in anger. His cold deadly tone carried enough threat to bring the strongest and bravest of Warriors to their knees groveling for their lives.

That was the tone he was using now with her.

Maricin knew she had erred. And now she would die for it.

"The members of this Guild, if offered nothing else, are given protection and a home inside these walls. While we fight to unseat the coward on the throne, I will not have anyone fear for their lives from you or anyone else that calls this place home."

Drayel paused briefly as he considered his judgment of Maricin's actions. She mistakenly took his brief pause as indecision and thought to speak and defend herself from whatever Drayel decided for her punishment.

"Drayel, if I may...." She started.

"SILENCE."

The command came from Drayel low and firm.

The power and warning in that single word stopped Maricin from uttering the lies and half-truths that she'd been formulating while she sat on the floor beside the throne.

Drayel crossed the floor in an almost leisurely manner and climbed the dais. He stood tall, strong, and foreboding before Maricin as she attempted to push back against the stone wall behind her.

"Maricin Cor Render, for your crimes of insurrection, your failure to protect this Guild and all in it, and the attempted murder of a future Warrior of this house, I, Drayel Shadow Walker, banish you from the Warriors Guild. I banish you, Maricin Cor Render, from Tor'Amal. I banish you from the country of Ka'len. As I will soon rule all Ka'len I will have Warriors posted at every port and entryway into Ka'len. Should you ever decide to return to this place it will be upon pain of death. You have until the rising of the sun tomorrow to leave this place. And you may take MISTER Grey Cloak with you on your way out."

Drayel turned on his heel smoothly and efficiently to walk away from the now infuriated Maricin.

She'd thought Drayel would have ended her right then and there. But the audacity of the man to send her away from the Guild that she'd helped build? To force her to leave her country? Simply because the great Drayel Shadow Walker said so? Oh no. Her pride would not allow it.

Lord Drayel, Master Drayel, Leader of the Warriors Guild. Maricin was sick of it. And to tell her she MAY take Tallon with her? As if she was a commoner that had to beg favors from his future majesty? Never.

She would die before she was spoken to that way by any man. As Drayel walked toward Korin, and the now utterly defeated-looking Tallon, Maricin rose to her feet. Before Korin could shout a word of warning, Maricin completed the spell that had been building to kill the child. The black streak shot across the room toward Drayel's defenseless back. She'd done it!

Maricin crowed with laughter as the black light streaked unhindered toward the great Drayel Shadow Walker. Tallon's eyes lit up with joy and anticipation as Korin's face fell at the sight of death soaring toward his friend.

Drayel simply smiled.

With a casualness brought on by a multitude of battles Drayel simply raised his left hand up and behind him to catch that horrid black beam that had caused the deaths of so many.

It was then that Korin noticed the glow emanating from beneath Drayel's floor-length black cloak.

As he'd turned away from Maricin he'd anticipated her cowardly attack and had been rapidly filling the Gods Eye Medallion with his power. When he heard Maricin finish casting her spell he'd simply channeled the power from the medallion into the palm of his hand creating an impenetrable shield.

The black beam broke easily against the light held in Drayel's hand.

Drayel smiled and with that same casual and effortless manner, he reached out with the Medallion and wrapped Maricin up in a blanket of light, leaving only her face uncovered.

With a slight hand gesture, Maricin was floating defenseless five feet off of the floor. Drayel turned and started walking away while she was dragged along behind him. When Drayel reached Korin and Tallon he looked at the man now standing quietly and openly glaring at Drayel.

"Mister Gray Cloak. It is well known to myself and the Guild that you supported my former second's attempts to usurp my authority. However, as we are in the middle of a war, and your abilities are not without merit, I am inclined to forgive you of your transgressions. Assuming, of course, that you swear fealty to myself and the Guild." Drayel watched Tallon's face as he turned to look at Maricin, floating trapped behind him.

Tallon noted an almost imperceptible nod of her head in the affirmative. He would have preferred to have left with her but assumed that she had her reasons for wanting him to stay here in the Guild with Drayel, so he nodded as well.

Drayel saw the exchange between the two and picked up on Tallon's affection for Maricin.

Fool.

"Very well Grey Cloak. You will be allowed to stay. Your penance will be to work in the kitchens alongside the boy this witch almost killed. And if he ever shows a talent for magic, you shall instruct him. Are we clear?"

Drayel knew this proclamation would not sit well with Tallon. The prideful warlock could stomach working in the kitchen for a brief period of time, but when a Warlock takes on a student then he is responsible for that student for as long as he lives. He could only pray the boy was completely mortal and had no power of his own.

Tallon nodded again.

"Korin, see Gray Cloak down to the kitchen and ensure he follows the boys every command to satisfaction. I myself will be removing this vermin from our halls."

He nodded back over his shoulder to the still imprisoned Maricin who was glowering at him as if she'd kill him right then and there.

"Right away, Lord Shadow Walker." Korin said with a grin.

Korin and Drayel were friends, but Korin still respected Drayel's position within the Guild and referred to him by his proper title from time to time.

Usually when it would serve to aggravate him since Drayel himself hated being called Lord, Master, or anything other than his name alone.

Korin disappeared down the hallway with Tallon in tow.

Drayel followed them until they turned off to the left and down a long set of stairs located halfway down the hallway. He continued straight on toward the portcullis that served as the front door of the large stone castle.

The sentries stationed there saw Drayel coming with his strange package in tow but did not ask questions. They simply raised the gate and cleared the way for their leader. Drayel walked about one hundred yards from the front door and deposited Maricin unceremoniously on the ground.

He pulled the God's Eye Medallion from under his Mithril armor and placed it in plain sight. Fully charged and glowing deep emerald green.

Where Maricin's power coiled around the outside of her medallion like a snake, the power within the God's Eye stayed firmly inside the green crystal. It swirled around in a tight circle that looked like green flowing water with occasional lightning strikes inside. The ornate silver housing was fashioned by dwarves thousands of years ago when the medallions were first gifted to man and looked like a set of eyelids encasing a green eye with a white center when the lightning flashed inside of it. Its power, when wielded by one capable of doing so, was virtually limitless. As it was now.

Drayel dropped the controlling light from around Maricin and allowed her to stand. He'd picked this spot for their final confrontation because of its proximity to the battlefield.

The crows and vultures had already begun descending on the corpses left out in the sun to rot. As they would soon do to hers.

"Maricin, I attempted to show you mercy by not ending your life when you so richly deserved it. You repaid that generosity by trying to murder me from behind like the coward I always suspected you were. I'm now giving you the chance to kill me, face to face, in a duel. Your death, whether it deserves to be or not, will be honorable. And when you are dead I fully intend on destroying that cursed artifact you wear. Nothing good, or worthy of the Guild, has ever come from the wearing of that particular medallion." Drayel said matter-of-factly.

Maricin looked about in a panic. She knew she could not hope to defeat Drayel in single combat. No one could.

A new plot came to mind as she surveyed her surroundings.

She steeled her nerves and calmed her rapidly beating heart. Maricin rose to her feet and brushed the dirt off the back of her long black dress.

Now beginning to feel more confident, she began to slowly walk in a circle around the patiently waiting Drayel. With minor effort, she forced herself to laugh to cover up the overwhelming fear that she was about to meet a sudden and violent end.

"Oh Drayel, Drayel, Drayel. You make it sound so easy. As if it is a foregone conclusion that you will easily dispatch me. But I think not. This Medallion that you seem so eager to destroy, is second only to the one you now possess. I wouldn't think that you, who values power even more so than I, would be so willing to destroy it. Or so stupid as to underestimate it!" She finished with a scream.

A group of Warriors on horseback had come charging across the field behind Drayel, whooping and celebrating their decisive victory over the King's army. It was them she targeted with her blast. Drayel, sensing correctly that he was not the intended target, spun quickly to throw up a protective shield around the approaching Warriors.

With his back to her, Maricin sensed an opening. Drawing the long, thin, rapier from its sheath beneath her robe she charged across the small space between her and Drayel.

She reached him just as the last of her attack against the riders was dispelled and Drayel's shield diminished. She saw the usually bright green glow in his eyes was slowly fading away.

He'd used a large amount of magic on the field today. Then again in the throne room, imprisoning her, and finally to stop her attack against the riders. Drayel was exhausted. He would not be able to use magic against her until he rested. Unfortunately, neither could she. She had reached her limit as well.

So, swords it would be.

Drayel spun away from her lunge causing her to overextend and miss her mark.

Barely.

Maricin was no novice when it came to swordplay.

As a member of the Guild, she'd trained with Korin as well.

And as much as she hated the man, his skill was undeniable. So, she'd listened, watched, and learned well.

His sudden spin put her off balance, but only for a moment. She dropped her shoulder and rolled away from Drayel, bringing her thin blade up to catch and deflect the overhead chopping motion she knew would follow her roll.

She grinned when she felt Drayel's blade connect and slide down the rapier. She lost her smile when she felt his blade turn to catch under the crossbar and bite into the metal.

She respected Korin's teaching, but would not allow herself to carry one of his blades. Most of the Warriors in the Guild wielded Korin's blades. As did Drayel.

Drayel recognized her roll and the familiar high block and deflection that Maricin practiced so often in the training circle. He knew that she would attempt to misdirect his clumsy chop with it. He also knew that she used a blade made by a respected vendor. But that vendor was not Korin Silver Steel.

Drayel's edge cut neatly into the weaker sword's handguard and found purchase.

A quick step to the side, coupled with a roll of his wrist, and the sword was ripped from her grasp and thrown across the field toward the now dismounted group of Warriors. Drayel completed the maneuver by spinning away and retracting his blade to a ready position.

As quickly as he'd spun away he now lunged, swift as death itself, and plunged his blade into Maricin's chest.

Her eyes went wide with shock and pain as she fell backward, sliding off of his blade to collapse upon the muddy ground.

The Warriors in the background came to attention and raised their swords toward the sky while repeating their common oath, "For the good of the Guild."

Drayel nodded at them, releasing them from their duty to observe the battle and ensure that it was as fair and even as possible. They sheathed their swords and mounted their waiting horses to return to the Citadel and relay the news of Maricin's death.

There would be an inquiry, but it would stand as a fair duel.

Drayel knelt beside Maricin to take her hand. She tried to roll away from him out of fear or instinct. Drayel simply pressed down on her shoulder and held her still.

"Maricin, why could you not simply flee this place? You knew that you stood no chance against me, and still you fought. Your anger, rage, and pride brought you to this. You could have ruled at my side when we take Tor'Amal. But it just wasn't enough for you was it? I will not mourn your death. Nor will you hold a place of honor in the great hall. Your body and your memory will fade from this world until both are no more than dust."

Drayel stood to leave while Maricin's mouth and lips worked to find words to spit back at the Warlock. She was unable to do so.

At last, she let her head drop back into the mud and was still.

# CHAPTER 3

**D**RAYEL WAS AWAKENED JUST AFTER SUNRISE THE FOLLOWING DAY by the sound of a Guard knocking lightly on his chamber door.

"What is it?" Drayel grumbled in a less than pleasant voice. He was not a morning person.

"My Lord, the sentries at the front gate have reported a commotion this morning just before dawn. It's being said that Maricin Cor Render's coven came for her on horseback. They were glamoured to blend into the darkness of the morning. So, they were not seen until they dismounted and secured Maricin's body. They took her along with the Black Heart Medallion."

The Guard took a step back from Drayel's chamber door as if expecting the Warlock to lash out at him. When in truth he was cursing himself.

He should have thought to take the medallion after killing her. It never occurred to him that Maricin's coven would even want her body. Or that anyone would have been brave enough, or fool enough, to venture onto the Guilds grounds so brazenly and take them both. Damn it.

Now he would have to decide whether it was worth dispatching a battalion to chase the witches and recover the medallion, or to continue pressing forward and take the King's castle at Tor'Amal.

The King first he decided.

Once Drayel ruled Ka'len he could devote the full might of the Warriors Guild, as well as the rest of the Guilds, to locating and retrieving the medallion from the witches. Then he'd kill them all for the audacity of coming into his home and taking something that belonged to him. He rolled over onto his side and raised himself halfway out of the bed, bracing his left arm underneath him at an angle.

"Is that all? Or do you have more wonderful news to greet me with this morning?" He asked with a sneer and just a hint of sarcasm. The Guard looked noticeably nervous and cleared his throat before proceeding.

"My Lord, the emissary from Tor'Amal is at the portcullis requesting to see you."

The Guard braced for Drayel's response then dove into the hallway to avoid the lamp that smashed into the wall where his head had been only moments before.

Drayel's eyes flared green, bright, and powerful. He was fully recharged after his night of rest. And angry.

He'd warned the smarmy little cretin that the coward king had sent that if he ever returned to these lands that he would not leave.

Drayel threw the covers back and vaulted from the bed. He dressed quickly. Putting on the same black cloak he'd worn on the battlefield the previous day, his sword, and the Gods Eye Medallion.

He started to pull his hair back but decided he'd let it stay free for dramatic effect. These puppets never came alone. So, when this one's companions ran home to their master he wanted them to have a grand story to tell.

As he left his room he let power seep from his pores. He illuminated himself in soft white light with a green tinge and made his hair flow behind him as if moving in a strong wind. His eyes glowed fiercely, and he was confident that his overall demeanor would be utterly terrifying to the little peon that was no doubt waiting outside of the closed portcullis with his tiny entourage.

Drayel stormed down the hallway, cape and hair flowing, power surging through and out of him, to find the portcullis standing wide open.

No sentries at the door and no signs of a struggle. Just as Drayel concluded that they were under attack he heard the sound of raucous laughter coming from the sitting room. Drayel stormed into the room, hand on his sword, ready to eviscerate the King's men and scold his sentries for leaving their post.

What he saw stopped him cold.

His hand dropped from his sword as he allowed his power to ebb and return to a less imposing state.

He kept the glow in his eyes and the medallion charged though.

For sitting in the largest chair in the room was a woman that was simply unlike anyone he'd ever seen.

There was no armed entourage. She wore no weapons, no armor, but seemed completely at ease sitting in the midst of four armed enemies. She also had not flinched in the slightest when Drayel had stormed into the room. Even the most hardened Soldiers would cower in the face of his rage. But this woman seemed to be completely at ease.

Who was she to have no fear of him?

Drayel, Lord of the Warrior's Guild, ender of Armies, Kings Bane, and the most powerful being in all of Ka'len.

This incredibly ordinary-looking human had persuaded his sentries to open the gate, leave their post, and practically bring her tea and cookies while she waited.

At that particular moment, a kitchen worker politely stepped around Drayel to bring in a tray of tea and cookies.

Drayel saw red.

Had his Guild members been so easily fooled? Had they learned nothing of bewitchment and enchantments over the years?

Maricin may have been a traitor, but she had trained them all in the ways of witches. That was the only solution as to why this woman was sitting in his home eating cookies and drinking tea instead of being made to wait safely outside of the gate.

Drayel tapped into his power and scanned the room looking for charms or signs of a spell emanating from the woman. To his amazement, he found nothing. Surely she was not able to simply charm his highly trained sentries into opening the gate and allowing her to pass.

He crossed half of the distance between him and this enigma and took a long look.

Small framed, but not tiny, she was almost six feet tall. Her hair was blond to the point of being almost silver and hung down past her shoulders. The same length as Drayel's.

Her eyes were a brilliant sapphire blue and hinted at some type of power or deviousness behind them. Light skinned, toned musculature, and with skin free from any blemishes or flaws she was quite possibly the most beautiful woman he'd ever seen. He'd called her ordinary-looking earlier, but there was nothing ordinary about her.

"Shall I help you retrieve your jaw from the floor Lord Shadow Walker? Or would you prefer to let it rest there?" She asked with a slight smile and a hint of mischief.

Drayel shook his head mentally and bit back the cutting retort that had formed on his lips.

"Leave us. Now." He ordered his guards and the kitchen worker that had lingered in the back of the room after leaving the tray of food. "And Guards, If I ever find that you've left my door standing wide open and unsecured again..." He leveled his gaze on the men and allowed his eyes to flare with that menacing dark green, "I promise you it won't be tea and cookies you find yourself rewarded with." The men bowed hastily and fled the room.

They knew Lord Shadow Walker would not kill them, but they'd all seen the type of damage he could inflict on the battlefield. And that thought alone was sufficient to keep their imaginations active enough to where he would never have to actually touch them to keep them in line.

"Who are you and why are you in my home?" Drayel asked with more than just a little hostility. "I was told the emissary to the coward king had returned to darken my door once more. I'd rather hoped I would have had the chance to break him in fun and ever more creative ways. But instead, I find, you." Drayel paused to give her a chance to respond.

The blond enigma rose from the chair, brushing cookie crumbs from her simple white dress. Two thin straps hung the soft silk material from her shoulders with a simple silk belt about a hands width wide tied around the middle of her trim waist. The dress hung down and barely covered shapely legs that....Drayel stopped. What was this woman doing to him?

There had to be some kind of enchantment at play here. Drayel had bedded scores of women over the years, but none had ever distracted him in such a manner.

"My Lord Drayel Shadow Walker, I am Elisa Cor Sanctus. Emissary to King Mannock Blackspear, First of his name. As well as the future Matron of the Cor Sanctus coven. My mother is Varna Cor Sanctus, the current Matron. I was sent to serve King Mannock when I was a child as a peace offering between my Coven and the Crown following the war for the Omni plains." She said with practiced ease.

Though Drayel detected a sense of sadness in the last few words she spoke.

He remembered well the "battle" for the Omni plains. Many years ago, the coward king had decided that the plains, renowned for the giant rock formations carved out to look like demons and other malevolent beings by the Cor Sanctus witches that inhabited the plains, would make a wonderful game sanctuary and had ordered the peaceful witches to abandon their ancestral home.

The witches, who had lived in peace with the previous kings for centuries, rebelled at the King's orders. They had fought briefly, but the peaceful witches had no wish to harm humans and surrendered instead of slaughtering the human army.

Drayel thought they'd been fools.

For now, they were forced to wander the mountain ranges and take refuge where they could. And for all of the trouble to gain their lands, the King's game sanctuary had failed. Someone, or something, was killing the animals as fast as the King's game wardens could bring them in. But even so the king would not return the land to his formerly loyal subjects. One of the many reasons that Drayel had determined that the king needed to be removed from power.

"His majesty received the report from the battlefield last night. And he was told his official emissary would willingly hang before returning here again. So, he sent me." Elisa said with a small smile gracing her lips. "I suppose his majesty would rather lose a witch boarded at the castle than a well-bred emissary from Tor'Amal."

"It would seem so Mistress Cor Sanctus..." Drayel started.

"Elisa. Please. No titles, just Elisa." she asked.

"Elisa then." Drayel started over. "Elisa, what exactly did the coward king send you here to ask of me? Did I not make my position clear to that tiny little worm that was here last? Your king will not be long seated on the throne of Ka'len. He is simply keeping it warm for me until I arrive." Drayel said with an insincere smile. "Shall I show you to the door?" He asked.

"My Lord Shadow Walker..." She began.

"Drayel. If I am to call you Elisa then I expect you to return the favor and drop the Lord and Master titles. I am now, and have always been, Drayel." He said with a hint of authority in his tone.

"Drayel then." Elisa let that wisp of a smile grace her lips again. "Drayel, his Majesty sends me with a request and a gift.....a gesture of goodwill as it were."

"I'm listening. But be forewarned, I doubt that I'll be very receptive to anything your temporary king has to offer." Drayel said.

"He said you would probably say that my Lor.....Drayel." Elisa said with a slight bow of her head. "His Majesty is now convinced that it is only a matter of time before you and your Guild take the castle. He no longer has illusions of his invincibility, or that he can win this war. However, he rather likes his head being attached to his shoulders, so he offers the following terms. In return for your calling off the attack on the palace and saving thousands of innocent lives in Tor'Amal by doing so, his Majesty offers to return the Omni plains to my people, give you a lordship over half of Ka'len, and grant you a seat on his council. He feels that if he is doing such a terrible job ruling this country, then maybe your educated insight could help steer him in a direction that is best for everyone involved. What say you, Drayel?"

Elisa stood quietly when she finished speaking and watched Drayel's face for any sign of what his answer would be, she did not have to wait long.

Drayel laughed.

Elisa took a small step backward as the sound of the Warlocks laugh was a deep baritone that did not match the man's demeanor at all. She'd expected him to become angry, to lash out, anything other than laugh.

Drayel turned slightly and gestured toward the large couch situated against the twin floor-to-ceiling windows facing the east where they would catch the first rays of sunlight.

Elisa hesitantly walked with him to the couch and used the small table sitting in front of it as an excuse to walk away from him and toward the farthest end of the dark green velvet settee.

She did not care for the tone of that laugh. It did not sound joyous or filled with humor. It was arrogant, angry, everything a laugh should not be.

Drayel noticed her less than subtle attempt to place distance between them and understood completely. She was finally starting to see that he was not some trivial Lord or Councilman to be played with and manipulated.

"All of this and you have yet to tell me what the ever so gracious king request of me. How could I turn down his wondrous gift of HALF of the land that will be mine before the winter moon rises without even knowing the price I must pay to earn this oh so generous offer." He smiled mirthlessly.

Elisa could feel that Drayel's hospitality was reaching its end and that she'd soon be escorted out of the castle. But she was bound by her childhood oath to the king to carry out his wishes. Elisa steeled herself before responding. She knew now that coming here had been a fool's errand. She also knew that if Drayel didn't kill her that the King might very well do so for her failure. But either way, she would complete the task that she had agreed to. Then she would return to Tor'Amal and face her fate.

"Drayel, in return for being given control of half of Ka'len, my home-lands returned, and a seat on his council, His Majesty ask that you and the Warriors Guild travel to the Omni plains and determine what has been killing the animals kept there. He fears that whatever is killing the animals would be a threat to anyone that inhabits the land."

Drayel sat in stunned silence looking at the woman seated across from him. The sheer audacity of the king to assume that he would not only accept half of what he planned on simply taking but to put a price tag on it that might cost the lives of Guild Warriors was madness.

And why should he care if Omni was returned to the Cor Sanctus witches by the King? Could he not simply do the same when he ruled this land? It would seem that the only ones that would benefit from the King's "gift" would be the king himself and the people of Tor'Amal that would inevitably be caught in between the Guild and the castle garrison when Drayel finally came for it.

"The old fool has truly lost his wits. Why? Why would I risk my Warriors to take back land that will be mine? What concern do I have for the homeland of witches that would not even fight to keep it? No, I will not accept your King's terms. I will rule all of Ka'len, or none of it. I will not sit on his council and listen to his group of ring kissing doddering old fools pat him upon his sweat-stained back and tell him he is a worthy leader. All while he sits on his ample backside growing fatter and more complacent." He said in a rush.

The anger getting the better of him as he went over the king's pathetic offer over and over again in his mind.

"Drayel, please, don't dismiss this so quickly." Elisa begged. "I know the King's terms aren't ideal. And maybe you're right. Maybe my people should have slaughtered the humans that came to drive us from our land instead of being merciful. And Isolde knows the humans have been less than thankful. But still, for all their faults, many of them are kind and good. If you attack Tor'Amal many humans will be killed before they can flee the city. And the king will close the gates surrounding the city beyond the castle walls to slow your advance. I'm well aware that you could simply bring the castle down around him. But in doing so you would destroy the prize you seek and kill many people within the castle that are either forced to work there or work there to feed their families. They are not all Soldiers. Please Drayel. Take some time to consider this."

Elisa was shaking when she finished speaking.

The emotion in her voice was not contrived. She had grown up with the staff within the castle and the children in the city. There truly were good people there. Even some of the Soldiers within the walls only served because work was impossible to find while the king fought Drayel.

Being a Soldier was merely a way to feed their families during the war. And most could care less who ruled Ka'len as long as it meant the end of the war.

"Elisa, I fear you have traveled very far for a very short visit. I can hear the passion in your voice, and I believe that you feel that the King's offer is fair and just. However, the Warriors Guild is founded upon strength and skill in battle. Ruling Ka'len is the ultimate display of power. I have outmaneuvered your king on every front. My armies have annihilated his at every battle. Your king thinks only of himself. This is evidenced by the land he took from your people. The taxes he imposes to build his monstrosity of a castle. Using his own subjects as cannon fodder between himself and his enemies. The castle walls should protect the people, not fence them in to act as a human shield. I shall never bow to such a man. So again, no. I reject your King's offer. Before the first snow falls my battalions shall surround and take his castle. Then it, along with all Ka'len, will be mine."

Drayel stood to call out to the Sentries and have them escort Elisa to the gate. When he looked down he was surprised to see the formally well-composed woman had tears streaming down her face. Drayel was not used to seeing a woman express emotion openly. Such things were discouraged and trained out of Guild men and women at a young age. It was unsettling.

"As you wish, Drayel." Elisa stood up to her full height and pulled her shoulders back proud and strong.

She wiped away the tears running down her face and looked at him with hostility for the first time. Her own eyes showed flecks of lightning, so similar to the God's Eye that it was concerning to Drayel. He wondered just what sort of power this future Matron truly possessed.

"But just know, your ambition will see you on the throne. But yours will not be a peaceful kingdom. The people dislike the king, but they tolerate him because he is not always cruel. The kingdom was at peace until you began attacking the King's men. He HAS gotten better as he ages. You? You the people will hate and rebel against at every turn. You and your men have killed their fathers, brothers, and sons in a senseless battle for a throne that none of them care about. The common people of Tor'Amal just want to live their lives in peace! But you MEN! You men with your egos, and your pride, and your insatiable need to prove who has the biggest......sword. You will see thousands of innocents die so that you may sit upon a cold stone chair in a cold stone castle with your cold stone heart. You don't have to throw me out LORD Drayel. I can see myself out." Elisa tossed her hair over her shoulder and stormed past a shocked Drayel.

No one had spoken to him that way since he was a child. By the time he recovered enough to respond the portcullis was slamming back into place and her horse was throwing up dirt and mud as she headed North back toward the pass and the road to Tor'Amal.

# CHAPTER 4

## CHANGE OF PLANS

*E*LISA RODE HARD FOR THE PASS. SHE'D LET HER ANGER GET THE better of her. She had not done that in ages. What was it about that arrogant bastard with his deep green eyes and gorgeous hair? Wait, what?

What did it matter what he looked like? He was cruel. He was rude. And yet, try as she might, she could not stop thinking about him.

She kept thinking that she should have punched him in the face before she left. Maybe then she would have had something better to report to Mannock. The bastard. Drayel again. Isolde!

What was it going to take to get him out of her mind?

It started raining again just as the pass came into sight. It was treacherous at best when dry and the sun was bright overhead. But after the heavy rains of the previous moon, it had become slick, and her mount had trouble finding footing among the slippery stones and muddy ground. On the way in it had been bad, it was even worse now.

Elisa knew that Drayel himself had rent the very hills to create this passage. He'd designed it to intentionally slow the approach to his citadel and make it harder for an approaching force to come through in large numbers.

Unfortunately, she did not have one of the Guilds mounts that had been raised and trained to find footing here. Her horse slipped and stumbled so many times that she was forced to dismount for fear of the animal injuring itself or her with it.

They were less than a furlong into the pass when she heard an unsettling noise. There was a cracking noise coming from high upon the passage walls. She looked up and froze in fear.

The King's men had been hard at work before initiating the attack on the citadel.

They had dug a long gap along the passages about halfway up the walls as far as she could see ahead of her.

The top of the gap had been braced with large round shoots of bamboo and boards from horse carts to keep it from collapsing. She saw the barrels of explosive powder set every so often along the gap and tied together with a rope soaked in pitch so that it would burn from one to the other.

This was how Mannock's army had meant to cover their retreat if need be. They'd never gotten the chance to use it.

Now the rain that was pouring down in sheets was washing out the hastily placed supports. The top of the hill was beginning to push down and bow the bamboo braces that remained. The cracking sound she'd heard was one of the braces up ahead giving out followed by a slow stream of mud and rocks rolling into the pass in front of her.

She realized to her horror that all of the braces were about to give.

Elisa screamed in rage and defiance. She turned her mount back to the citadel. It was their only hope. She slapped the horse on the backside to set it running.

The horse was not a military mount. It belonged to one of the castle staff and had

been lent to her for the trip. As the horse turned to run it slipped and kicked backward trying to regain its balance. In doing so it struck Elisa soundly in the chest, knocking the wind from her.

Elisa fell to the ground gasping. She had little time left. Elisa raised her hands to the gash in her chest and pulled the torn material from the wound. She whispered a brief incantation that made her blue eyes blaze and the lightning in them move faster and faster. Her hands began to glow with a soft blue light. She held them to her wound and winced as the icy cold magic rushed from her hands to the damaged skin. It itched as it healed, but the pain was leaving, and the bleeding had stopped.

The time she had used to heal herself had cost her though. Several of the braces further down the path had already failed. She could see the mountain of mud and rocks that had already filled the pass and that was growing larger as it rushed toward her.

Elisa ran.

She cursed her heritage as she did. In Cor Sanctus covens, only the Matron holds the Isolde's Soul Medallion that allows her to fly. In theory, all Cor Sanctus could fly, but over the centuries they'd gotten out of practice and had lost the ability to summon flight without the medallion to focus their energy.

So, she ran.

Her heart raced and breathing became harder and harder. She slipped and fell several times on the slick stones. She cursed Drayel and his damned pass. She cursed the king for sending her here. She cursed herself as she felt the fear taking over her.

She could feel the rumble of the pass giving way behind her. She could see flecks of mud, water, and stone flying past her head. And there, just ahead, the exit. If she could just make it a little further she would be fine.

She never felt the large chunk of stone that struck her in the back of her head, knocking her unconscious well short of the end of the pass. The mud, dirt, and debris continued to roll toward her with the force of a hurricane. As the mud arced over her prone body, preparing to bury her alive, a green and white light shot out of the dark from the direction of the Citadel. She didn't hear the hoof beats as the rider approached and dismounted. She didn't see the massive display of power as the rider approached the pass and forced the tidal wave of mud and rocks to break against the shield wall he willed into place.

When the danger was no more, he stepped over to her and lifted her head, listening for sounds of breathing. He wasn't sure if he was relieved or not when he heard a sharp intake of air from the blonde-haired witch, but he did know that he'd seen her heal herself with that blue light.

And healers were always welcome at the Citadel.

Drayel lifted her easily and placed her across the saddle of his horse. He tied her hands and feet to the stirrups on either side of his mount. Not at all comfortable, but it would keep her from falling off while they returned to the castle.

# CHAPTER 5

TRAPPED

$E$LISA AWOKE IN A STRANGE BED WITH DAYLIGHT STREAMING IN through the windows. She knew instantly where she was. The twin windows matched the ones in the sitting room that she'd left, yesterday? How long had she been here?

She looked around the sparse room and found very little in the way of furniture or decoration. She did see some soft-looking leather shoes and a clean white robe laying across the desk in front of the windows. She looked down and realized with shock that she was completely naked.

Isolde!

Had Drayel seen her naked? Surely not. She would die from mortification. But that wasn't her most pressing issue at the moment. Her head still ached fiercely. She continued her scan around the room and found a glass of water and some bark from a white wood tree that was known to help alleviate pain.

Fortunately, she had a faster way of doing that.

She did not take using magic lightly. She'd learned quickly as a child that humans feared all forms of the craft. Even if it could be used to help them, as her coven had done for centuries before the current king. Now it had been almost fifty years since magic had been allowed to be practiced freely in the kingdom. It was still done, but mostly in secret.

Only the eldest of the humans remembered a time when the Cor Sanctus were welcomed in Tor'Amal. Now they were considered no better than their Cor Render witch cousins. Whereas the Cor Sanctus witches worshiped the Goddess of Healing, Isolde, and practiced peaceful ways over violence, the Cor Renders were completely opposite.

They worshiped Illyian, the goddess of death and giver of the Dark Heart Medallion. To be considered the same as a Cor Render witch was a serious insult to the Cor Sanctus.

But the distinction was one they could ill afford to fight the humans over at the moment.

So, Elisa raised her hands again, summoning the innate power that lay sleeping in her body. She always felt it building around her heart first, then it would flow outward through her hands to whatever she was touching.

In this case, she held the back of her own head and neck. The pain was gone instantly. Replaced by the icy cold of the magic. There was very little itching this time. She supposed that whatever had struck her had not done an excessive amount of damage. That was good. She could heal almost any wound, but if it was severe enough, there could still be scarring.

She sighed when the healing was done and lay back on the pillows that had been provided for her. The room was sparse but the bed, at least, was comfortable. Healing always left her tired. The more power she expended the more exhausted she felt. This time she felt like a short nap would be just right to recharge her power stores. But that was not meant to happen. Drayel charged into the room without bothering to knock. A minor look of annoyance on his face.

"My Guards were supposed to inform me as soon as you awakened. How do you feel?" he demanded.

He stood there at the foot of the bed staring down at her. Elisa was suddenly very aware of her nakedness under the thin sheet she'd woken under. She self-consciously pulled it up higher around her shoulders while glancing down to ensure that the sheet was not revealing anything it shouldn't be.

"I'm feeling very well, thank you, my Lord." She said.

She noticed the slight narrowing of his dark green eyes at the "Lord" and remembered that he'd asked to dispense with titles.

"Drayel," she started again, "how did I get here? The last thing I recall was running out of the pass with the walls caving in around me. Then I awoke here. I'm fairly certain I was not clear of the pass before I lost consciousness."

As she spoke the terrifying memory of the world crashing down around her came flooding back. She shivered and clutched the sheet tightly in her suddenly sweaty hands. It had seemed a living nightmare. One that she was certain would be the death of her. How had she survived?

"You were found shortly after the cave in began and brought here to recover. My men have been scouring the area to assess the damage. They have found broken braces and powder kegs among the rubble. Yet no explosions were heard prior to the cave in. So, I am assuming that the King's men had the foresight to rig the pass with explosives to trigger an avalanche and cover their retreat. A shame they never had a chance to use it." He said with just a hint of self-satisfaction.

Elisa closed her eyes so he wouldn't see her roll them. Drayel continued, "I'd venture since you were almost crushed beneath the onslaught, that you were not the cause of the pass falling. Am I correct in assuming that the hastily rigged braces were washed out by the rain causing the massive mudslide?" he asked.

Elisa nodded in confirmation.

"Yes. I was not far into the pass when I noticed what had been done. I tried to run when the first brace gave but my idiot horse kicked me in the chest and I..." Elisa stopped. She had almost told the Warlock that she was a healer. She didn't know if she wanted him to have that knowledge, or what he would do with it if he did. Elisa took a breath before speaking. "And, I was knocked down and hurt my knee. So, it made fleeing the pass even more difficult." She looked at the Warlock and saw him smiling at her.

It was better than his taunting laugh the previous day, but still did not reach his eyes.

"Elisa, you are a guest in my home for the moment. Let's dispense with the lies for the time being." Drayel said sincerely.

Elisa looked at him innocently and prayed that her face did not give away the panic that she suddenly felt.

"Lies? Drayel, what lies are you speaking of?" She asked timidly.

"Elisa, please. Do not do me the discourtesy of subverting my intelligence. You were seen using healing magic on the chest wound your mount gave you, not a knee injury." He smiled with satisfaction when he saw her face blanch white. He knew that she would not like him knowing her secret. And he could guess why.

"Elisa, be calm. You are in no danger here because of your magic. In fact, this land, MY land, is a haven for those with extraordinary abilities. Users of the craft are appreciated and welcomed here. Especially healers. And so it will be when I rule all Ka'len. No one will have to hide who and what they are for fear of retribution from the King and his laws."

He said the last word with contempt. He looked at the woman lying supine in the bed before him and saw the thoughts racing behind her eyes.

He could tell she wanted to deny his claims regarding her use of magic. She wanted to run, to hide, to simply flee from this place. The secret that she'd hidden since taking up residence in Mannock's castle was now known to the most powerful, and reportedly treacherous, being in all of Ka'len. He read all of that in an instant and her deep breath followed by a sigh of acceptance confirmed it.

"Drayel, it must not get back to King Mannock that I have this ability. The king has grown less violent in his old age. But he is still distrustful of magic users. He jails them in iron cells beneath the castle. Most are treated humanely enough, but they are never freed to walk the streets of Tor'Amal again." She said with a shudder.

Her biggest fear had been realized. That her secret would be discovered and her fate be placed in the hands of another. And of all people, why HIM? Isolde!

Drayel contemplated her words for a while before responding.

"Get dressed and meet me in my private dining hall for breakfast. We have much to discuss." He commanded. She could tell by his tone that he was used to being obeyed and expected her to acquiesce.

"Drayel, what will you do now that you know my secret?" She asked hesitantly.

"We'll discuss that over breakfast. We have time, and many things to discuss." He said with stoicism.

"Time? I was under the impression that you were to march on the castle before the first winter's moon rose. That's not very long I'm afraid. So, I shouldn't think I'd be your, guest, here for very long." She said questioningly. "And I need to know if you'll tell anyone else about my magic Drayel. I have to know!" she said emphatically.

"My Lady, your secret, as it were, is safe with me for now. And as far as your time here and being my GUEST, as you so politely put it, I am not your captor. The first winter's moon rose last night. Weeks earlier than it should have. Heavy snows fell during the night blocking the second pass out of my lands. And that route would add several days to your trip under normal circumstances. With the snow and ice, it is all but impassable. I could clear it for you in a few days, assuming the snow didn't fill it right back in. But the route around the mountain has sinkholes, ponds, and other natural defenses that are formidable when the land is clear and passable. Under cover of snow, you would die shortly after clearing the gate at the end. The landscape around that area is one of the reasons I've allowed it to stay open. The pass to Tor'Amal is caved in and will take my men the rest of the winter to clear. I will help, of course, but moving a literal mountain of mud will take time and energy.

I will have to recover each day and the work will be slow. My men do not enjoy the protection from the cold that I am afforded. Their exposure must be kept to a minimum. So, you see my Lady, you are free to leave. You just simply can NOT leave." Drayel, having said all he wanted to regarding their current situation, spun on his heel and stomped toward the dining hall expecting her to follow him.

Elisa lay in the bed for a few more moments contemplating his news. This was bad.

The winter months in Ka'len were extremely harsh. Drayel had been correct in his assessment that if she tried to return to Tor'Amal on her own she'd be dead long before reaching the castle.

She knew Mannock would get a report of the pass collapsing. And the snow was a natural deterrent to travel. So, surely he would forgive her for the delayed return. And maybe, just maybe, she could use this time trapped in Drayel's castle to change the stubborn Warlock's mind regarding attacking the castle when the passes cleared, and the snow went away.

If he didn't kill her first.

# CHAPTER 6

REVIVED

**S**HE AWOKE WITH A GASP IN A DARK CAVE. HER FINGERS SPASMED and flexed as she tried in vain to grab the cold stone floor and arched her back in an attempt to rise.

She found she was very weak and unable to achieve even a sitting position.

But she was not dead.

She should have been. His sword had pierced her heart and been driven out of her back. How did she now live?

She saw movement from the corner of the cave nearest the entrance and made a feeble attempt to scramble away by pushing her feet against the floor. She could find no purchase and soon gave up the endeavor. It was pointless to try and run from whoever was coming toward her. She could not fight. If she died here, it would not matter.

She had died once already; it wasn't that bad.

"Still running from your problems girl?" The old crone cackled.

Maricin took a deep breath. No, death would have been a favorable alternative to facing the old witch that now meandered toward her.

So, she'd chosen to wear the glamour of a weak old woman for this.

That figured. Maricin knew that under the guise before her the real appearance of her mother was stunningly beautiful. She chose the weak old hag form often to distract her victims and make them underestimate her.

Maricin knew better.

"Hello, mother." Maricin said haltingly.

She would do nothing to anger Matron Celeste Cor Render. She was already on thin ice for having abandoned the coven to join Drayel after discovering his power exceeded hers and her mother's. But now she was back home and lying on the floor of the cave she was born and raised in, along with all of the other children belonging to the Cor Render coven.

"Oh, so you DO remember your dear old mother, child? You were gone for so long I was starting to think you'd forgotten me!" She said with a low and ominous laugh.

Matron Celeste walked deeper into the shadows surrounding the firelight and emerged her true self. Tall, at just over six feet, with crimson red hair that hung below her firm and shapely buttocks, dark brown eyes that appeared black at first glance, and a toned abdomen that had more than a few scars to decorate the clearly defined muscles of her core. Her toned, and rather impressive Maricin thought, body was barely covered by the V neck dress she now wore.

The slit up the side of both legs went from her foot to her midsection, then split again going up to her shoulders. The tiny belt that held it together resulted in an outfit that left very little to the imagination. But that too, like so much about the Matron, was simply a game of distraction. To misjudge her and lose yourself in her beauty was to lose your very life.

"Of course, mother. I could never forget you. Although, I am surprised you saved me." Maricin admitted.

Celeste threw her head back and howled with laughter. The sound was warm and welcoming, but somehow terrifying in its own right.

"Saved you? Oh, dear child NO!! Never was that my intention.

Illyian! Why would I go out of my way to save you? You abandoned us for that, that, Warlock!"

She spit as she said the last word just for emphasis.

"No dear, we felt your life force ebbing from you the moment he plunged his blade into your heart. We came on the mounts that Illyian blessed us with, swift and silent as the dead. Well, because they ARE dead...but Illyian brought them back to us. Much like she did for you dear daughter."

Celeste laughed and continued her slow circuit around her prostrate daughter. Showing no emotion or other sign of her intentions but watching Maricin's face to see how she responded to the news.

"No, saving YOU was never the plan. We came for the medallion that you stole from me when you ran off to join your little Warlock's cult. THAT is what we came for. But imagine my surprise when I arrived to find you not only breathing but healing from your wounds. That should not have been possible. Cor Renders have never been healers. But there you were. Lying there in the mud. Covered in your own blood and filth. The Black Heart Medallion burning into your skin. Melding with you. Of course, I TRIED to take it back but the cursed thing resisted me. Burned my hands when I touched it. I wanted to take your head and see if the medallion would release you then. But the Oracles that were with my little recovery effort suggested that you might be Illyian blessed. And thus, are untouchable by us. By me especially. As Matron I have to follow the will of Illyian."

Celeste said, venom dripping from her every word.

So, that's it Maricin thought. That's why I'm still alive and resting by the fire on the floor of my childhood home. Instead of being down in Celeste's demented playroom where she tortured her victims before killing them at her leisure. Thank Illyian for the busybody Oracles. Always finding Illyian's will in everything. This time they had inadvertently saved her life. But something was nagging at her.

Had Celeste said that the medallion had melded with her? She lay back on her back and rolled toward the fire so that the flames illuminated her upper body. She slowly pulled up the black tunic that the Cor Render witches favored until she saw it. Maricin almost screamed but summoned all of her will to not do so. She would not give Celeste the pleasure of hearing her scream.

But by the Gods.

The damned medallion was buried deep inside her chest. She could see it just underneath her skin. Pulsing in time with her own heart. Had Illyian really saved her? Or had the medallion acted on its own? She assumed she would not know the answer in this life. But she dreaded the idea of owing Illyian a life debt.

She dared not think of what the Goddess might demand in return. But she lived.

Maricin lay back on the floor and relaxed completely. Her mother would not go against the Oracles. To do so would invite the wrath of the entire Coven. And none of the other Witches would invoke the wrath of Illyian by harming her.

Maricin laughed. Soft and quietly at first. It built into a laugh that was more a scream of exultation. She lived. She would heal.

And she would have her revenge.

# CHAPTER 7

BREAKFAST

Eʟɪsᴀ ʀᴏsᴇ ғʀᴏᴍ ᴛʜᴇ ʙᴇᴅ ᴀғᴛᴇʀ ᴇɴsᴜʀɪɴɢ Dʀᴀʏᴇʟ ᴡᴀs ᴛʀᴜʟʏ gone. He'd left the door standing wide open during his swift departure.

Giving her no privacy and showing again his complete absorption with himself.

Elisa huffed and walked quickly across the warm stone floor, keeping the blanket wrapped tight around her. The warmth of the floor was a testament to the designers of the Citadel. The kitchens below the castle were rumored to have huge ovens that vented through the walls and aquifer-like passages beneath the floor. Thus, warming the entire castle on its way out of the chimneys in the tallest spires.

Elisa shut the door quietly and let the blanket drop away from her. She enjoyed the warmth of the room and appreciated it even more when she looked out of the twin windows and saw snow that was threatening to reach the top of the exterior curtain walls.

A man standing on horseback would still be covered by that snow.

She shuddered at the thought of the biting cold. Her own room back in Mannock's castle would be almost unbearable right now. The cold floors and drafty windows were great in the summertime but were absolute misery in the winter. She shook the thought from her head. No, she would not enjoy her time here. Mannock's castle was home. She was just a visitor here.

Drayel had insisted that she was a guest, not a captive. So, that was something at least.

She slipped on the leather shoes and found them soft and warm. The robe was silk on the outside and lined with something like rabbit fur on the inside. It was incredibly warm and comfortable.

She searched the desk and found a small piece of ribbon left by the room's previous inhabitant and used it to pull her hair back. As she did, she caught the fresh scent of saffron soap on her hands and arms. Had someone bathed her while she was unconscious? She supposed they had. She would have been covered in mud and Isolde knew what when they brought her back here. The staff would not have wanted to place her in a nice clean bed like that. So, she had been tended to and treated well it would seem.

Elisa walked back to the door and opened it slowly. She found two of Drayel's sentries waiting outside of the door. They both turned and looked at her in unison. The one on her left had two bars sewn onto his cherry red service tunic. He stepped to her side and offered her his non-sword arm.

She hesitated but decided that good manners dictated she take the man's arm and allow him to perform the task that he'd obviously been assigned.

"My Lord Shadow Walker has requested that I escort you to his private dining hall for breakfast. It is my pleasure to escort you, Lady." The Guard said sincerely.

Elisa smiled at the Captain. He was making every attempt to be polite and friendly. She could do no less.

"And I appreciate your taking the time to guide me there. This castle is fairly large, and I fear it would have been time for the mid-day meal before I ever found Lord Shadow Walker's table." She smiled brightly at the Captain and was pleased to see it returned.

They walked in companionable silence for a few minutes. As they turned a corner they were nearly knocked over by a male of average height, sandy blond hair, a sharp nose, and flat brown eyes. The man wasn't ugly by any means, but something about him just FELT wrong to Elisa.

Her escort took the brunt of the blow and managed to deflect the smaller man away from them. The man stopped in the middle of the hall and spun back toward them letting his hands glow bright red. Elisa realized that the man was also a Warlock like Drayel. She let her hands drift to the front of her robe and palmed a small amount of blue light in between them. It would not injure the man but might distract him long enough for her and her escorts to dodge any attack the Warlock hurled their way.

The Captain saw the faint glow in her hands and stepped subtly in between her and the angry Warlock.

"My apologies Lord Gray Cloak. I was so entranced with the loveliness of our guest I was not paying attention to where I was going. I beg your pardon, my Lord." The Captain said with false sincerity.

Elisa bristled.

They had done nothing wrong. It was this pompous Lord Gray Cloak that had hurtled around the corner blindly and crashed into them. Elisa took a step to go around the Captain and let Lord Gray Cloak know the truth of the matter when she saw the Captain's hands were behind his back frantically waving side to side in a stop motion. The second Guard, who up until this point had been a ghost, stepped next to her and politely took her arm in his hand, and gently squeezed. Not aggressively but pleading with her to be still.

"Fools. The lot of you. Watch where the hell you are going or I'll burn you alive where you stand! Gods! Why Drayel insists on...."

Tallon Grey Cloak continued his tirade as he walked away rapidly. Head down and barreling along like a spooked horse.

Her escorts let out a collective breath she hadn't realized they'd been holding.

The Guard holding her arm let go immediately and stepped back, embarrassed at having touched her. The Captain just turned back to her and raised his hands in front of him.

"We apologize if we offended or mishandled you, Lady Elisa. But that man, Tallon Grey Cloak, is an exceedingly powerful Warlock. He could have killed the three of us at a whim if he so desired. He is only held in check by fear of Lord Shadow Walker. Had you confronted him I fear he would have harmed you and we would have been powerless to stop him. Thank you for holding your tongue, Lady. It is appreciated." The Captain said.

"Captain Sandler, if you'd pay more attention in the training circle perhaps you wouldn't be so afraid of that blowhard." said a deep baritone voice from behind them.

Captain Sandler flushed red with anger until he saw the teasing smile on the face of the new arrival.

"My Lord Silver Steel, not everyone is blessed with the skill of our weapons master. Well met Sir." Sandler said. "May I introduce Lady Elisa Cor Sanctus of Tor'Amal. Lady Elisa, please meet Lord Korin Silver Steel."

"Lord Silver Steel, your reputation precedes you. Your father's shop produces some of the finest blades in Ka'len. It's a pleasure to meet you, my Lord." Elisa said with a small nod of her head. Korin smiled and inclined his head.

"Ahh, a lady of refined taste I see. It's been too long since this place had a little class and elegance in it I say!" Korin said with that same beaming smile on his face.

"Captain Sandler, would it cause you any undue distress if I relieved you of your escort duties and took Lady Elisa the rest of the way?" He asked.

Captain Sandler looked reluctant to release his charge into another's hands. And had it been anyone other than Lord Korin Silver Steel, he would not have. But he knew well of the friendship between Drayel and

Korin. And Lady Elisa could find no finer protector to defend her and escort her to her destination.

"Of course, my Lord. I should go and see how the preparations to begin clearing the pass are proceeding. I leave her in your capable hands, my Lord. Lady Elisa, it has been a pleasure. I bid you good day."

Captain Sandler took her offered hand and kissed the back of it before turning to walk back in the direction that Grey Cloak had gone earlier.

"So, you are what all of the commotion has been about the last day or two. I can see why." He said with a sly smile. "I haven't seen Drayel so flustered over a woman in years." He chuckled quietly.

"Flustered? Drayel? I hardly think that Lord Shadow Walker is at all concerned with me or my well-being. I believe he'd kill me at the slightest provocation. Why should he be flustered?" She asked.

Korin looked at her with humor in his eyes but changed his tone to a more serious one when he spoke.

"You say he isn't concerned with your well-being and would see you dead? Then tell me this Lady Elisa, if that were true, why did he fly down from his balcony, steal a Sentry's horse, and go thundering across the valley when he saw you in danger? The power he used to stop that mudslide could be seen for miles and was twice that he unleashed upon the King's men. I've not seen Drayel summon that much energy in a long, long, time. He halted the avalanche and pulled you from the pass. Then he brought you back here and turned you over to our healers, such as they are. He had the maidens wash you and clean your hair. Then he had you placed in the best room in the castle. He saw to your safety and care before he went and collapsed in the sitting room. He had to be carried to his chambers to rest. He arose with the sun to wait on you to awaken so that he could check on your well-being. Does that sound like a man that would kill you so carelessly?" Korin asked.

Elisa was taken aback by his revelation. Drayel rescued her? So, he must have been the one that witnessed her use of the healing magic.

But how had he known she was in danger? Had he sent someone

along to spy on her? If so he wouldn't have been able to get the message in time to have saved her. So, that meant that Drayel had been watching her leave the castle. She was surprised to find herself just slightly pleased that the Warlock that had been either stoic or angry with her during their conversation yesterday had rushed out to save her. Why should she be pleased? He was still an angry, overbearing, selfish ass of a man. But still...Elisa ended the train of thought before it took her down a path she was not prepared to go.

"Lord Silver Steel, perhaps I have misjudged your Lord Shadow Walker to some extent." She said. Elisa saw Korin start to laugh then subdue it in an attempt to maintain a serious expression on his face.

"Lady Elisa, I would recommend that you unlearn your royal training when you are with LORD Shadow Walker. Drayel does not hold to titles. He feels they are man-made constructs that only serve to provide little men with false power. He feels that real power comes in the form of magic and battle prowess. The few that he deems worthy he will address with their titles as a sign of respect for that person. Though with me, we've known each other since we were lads. So don't be surprised if he calls me Korin more than Lord Silver Steel." He finished.

Elisa shook her head in acknowledgment. Drayel had basically said the same thing during their initial meeting. So, the Warlock did have some sort of moral code that he adhered to. She was starting to form a very different picture of this man than the one Mannock had portrayed.

He had told her Drayel was a heartless, murdering, monster that would stop at nothing to achieve his goals. And while Mannock was not completely wrong, Drayel did intend on taking the castle at Tor'Amal regardless of the death toll, he was not completely unreasonable and felt he had a good reason to take the throne. So, maybe he was a monster, but maybe he could be persuaded to be more man than monster.

Elisa smiled.

"Lord Silver Steel..., or do you prefer Korin, my Lord?" She asked.

"Korin, my Lady. With my friends I prefer Korin." He said with that same beaming smile.

Elisa found the man utterly charming and quite easy to like.

"Korin then. Please, do tell me more about your childhood friend, Drayel. It would seem I've been given very one-sided information on the man. I would love to know the rest if you please." She asked sincerely.

Korin grinned.

"Elisa, if I may," he looked at her for confirmation. She nodded yes, using her familiar name would be perfectly fine,

"Elisa, I fear telling you all of the dirty details of Drayel's past would take more time than we have remaining on our journey to the dining hall. What say you to joining me for a dram of mead and a glass of white wine before dinner this evening?" He asked, still smiling.

Elisa could not refuse the man's charm and genuine likability.

He was attractive, charming, and easy to talk to. More so than the dour Drayel Shadow Walker. So, spending a few hours in Korin's company did not sound like the most displeasing idea she'd ever heard.

"Korin, it would be an honor. I would be pleased to join you for drinks and conversation." She realized with some embarrassment that she did not have anything to wear beyond the simple robe and slippers she now wore.

Her own clothes had disappeared. And she was certain that her shirt had been ruined. And her gold? She hadn't thought to ask what had happened to the meager purse she'd brought with her for the journey.

"Korin, I have just realized that I have absolutely nothing to wear to dinner tonight," she said dishearteningly.

Korin raised one eyebrow slightly and inclined his head in a roguish manner. Elisa barked a laugh at the look. She hadn't figured Korin for a fiend. But she could tell from the look on his face he was not serious. Well. Mostly.

"Do not worry about that Elisa. I'll have someone bring you some things. It looks like you'll be staying for a while. And it wouldn't do for you to wear the same robe every day, flattering though it may be." He said with a grin.

Elisa smiled back at him.

"Why thank you, my Lord. And I have to ask, among my things when I was brought back from the pass, there was a small bag of gold. Not much, but it is all that I have in the world. Would it be possible to have that brought to my room with the clothes?" She asked.

She saw Korin's jovial face darken just slightly.

"My Lady, your clothes were all disposed of last night. They were blood- stained badly. We all feared that you were gravely injured. Though the healers could only find a small laceration on the back of your head. Which does not explain the amount of blood on your clothes. We'll have to discuss that as well as it seems you are completely unin-jured this morning." He said.

She could see him looking her over. Not in a sexual manner, but merely assessing her physical state.

"The gold in your purse was taken to the vault in Drayel's personnel chambers. We don't have any thieves among the Guild. But the Thieves and Assassins Guild uses this place for their initiations. New members must enter the Citadel, take an item, and leave a silver-coated feather in its place to prove they were here. Drayel stops most of them. But a few are good enough that he lets them take a small item as a reward for their efforts. I'll see that your purse is returned in its entirety before I come by to retrieve you for our date." He said. He was still smiling, but she could tell that he was assessing her heavily as well.

They'd stopped in front of an ornate door inscribed with all manner of mystical symbols, wards, and other protective totems engraved in it. And for all of the protections that the door offered, it was standing halfway open with the smell of a variety of breakfast foods wafting out into the hallway.

Elisa's stomach growled in response. She hadn't realized how hungry she was.

"So, this is where I leave you lady Elisa. Enter when you're ready. And I'll see you later this evening. Until then, Elisa." Korin took her hand and kissed the back of it in the same manner of the Captain earlier.

If nothing else this band of killers and monsters that Mannock so feared were incredibly polite and well mannered, with the exception of that pig Grey Cloak. Elisa turned back toward the door after Korin disappeared around a corner in the hallway.

She took a deep breath to steel her nerves and entered the dining chamber.

# CHAPTER 8

TALLON

*T*ALLON LEFT HIS DOOR OPEN TO ALLOW THE BREEZE FROM THE hallway to cool his overheated room. He entered his chamber and sat down in his favorite chair before drifting off to sleep. He woke shortly after from the same dream. Maricin being dragged from the Citadel and cut down outside the gates.

Tallon was still bitter and angry with Drayel over her death. Tallon had understood the game he and Maricin had been playing was a dangerous one. He just never believed any harm could come to Maricin. She was just as powerful as Drayel Shadow Walker. His only advantage was the possession of that cursed God's Eye Medallion.

Maricin had told him, as well as others, that if she possessed the God's Eye that she would easily surpass Drayel.

And Tallon believed her. Right up until she was cut down by the Warlock outside the very gates of the place she once called home.

But now she was gone. While Maricin lived Tallon had been focused on a single goal, getting the woman he was secretly in love with into the top position within the Guild.

Now she was gone. He supposed he could focus his energy on helping Drayel unseat the king. To grow his own position and power base until he himself could stand up to and de-throne Drayel.

Although that would take years. While he was no novice, Maricin and Drayel had both been far beyond his own skills. So, no, he would not face Drayel alone. Not yet.

He had been out with the men, helping to clear the pass all morning, at Drayel's command. He had made his way back to the castle quickly when the work crews had decided to call it a day due to the cold weather.

Tallon did not believe it was that cold. He'd shifted several large boulders across the opening of the pass to keep some of the wind off of the workers. But he had also wrapped himself in a cloak of warm fire while he helped move a boulder here and there.

But now he was exhausted from using his power for most of the morning. He was looking forward to having the servant girls come to wash him. They didn't particularly like Tallon, he was cruel to them and liked to let his hands wander where they did not belong. Most would probably have tried to kill him by now, except that they were afraid of his power. And he had made it clear that, should anyone inform Drayel about his proclivities, they would be dead before the sun dawned the following day.

He walked across his chambers and kicked his mud-covered boots off in the middle of the floor. He'd just pulled off his sweat-stained tunic when movement caught his eye in the corner of the room.

Tallon's hands blazed red as he slung a ball of fire directly into the stone corner. He was shocked to see a white-gloved hand reach out and grab the fireball. The hand then squeezed the fireball until it faded from existence.

Tallon stood there in shock as a face slowly materialized out of the dark.

"Hello, Tallon." Said a familiar voice. Tallon's face went pale white. "Hello, Maricin." He said with a shaky voice.

"We have much to discuss." She said with a laugh. Tallon flinched as the door slammed shut behind him.

Maricin was home.

# CHAPTER 9

## CONFLICTION

**D**RAYEL HAD WATCHED THE WOMAN, ELISA, RIDE AWAY FROM THE castle.

She was angry, but he had understood that she did not comprehend the scope of his plan. Yes, more people would die. But when he ruled Ka'len she would still have her lands returned. But in addition to that, magic users would once again be free to roam the country without fear. And certainly without being locked up in the castle dungeons. Taxes would be reduced to the absolute minimum required to pay for keeping up the infrastructure of Ka'len.

Roads needed to be maintained, water aqueducts built or repaired, and the Ka'len military needed to build and man outposts along the ports, passes, and other entry ports of the land. Gone would be the "entitlements" of the Lords and the King. No more money going for lavish parties where food was wasted by the wagon load while people starved on the streets.

Gone would be the constant construction on Mannock's castle. The lavish clothing, all of the excess that the royals felt the people were supposed to provide for them simply because their fathers had the good fortune to be named Lord of this or that city in Ka'len.

So, she would return to Mannock and tell him that Drayel could not be moved. That in a few weeks' time he would see Drayel blow the very gates off of his castle walls, and King Mannock would be no more.

Drayel smiled at the thought.

However, the route from the Guild's castle to Tor'Amal was dangerous. Men camped out along the roadside, in valleys and on top of hills, waiting for unsuspecting prey to ride by. Drayel determined that she had made the trip to his home unmolested only due to the recent passing of the King's army. They would have cleared the route along the way looking for scouts from the Guild.

That was a fool's errand.

Drayel did not use human scouts for that very reason. He used his animal familiars as observers. They could hide in plain sight and were difficult to spot unless you were looking for them. Much like the hawk that had circled above Elisa and her mount. Drayel had bonded with the animal and sent it out from the balcony of his room overlooking the approach to the castle. It had flown in lazy circles while Drayel observed through its eyes. It would be days before the hawk tired and needed to rest. The animal was stronger than its brethren and wore an amulet around its neck infused with energy from Drayel. The silver hawk amulet was the finest silver and had detailed craftsmanship. Right down to the green, emerald eyes that held Drayel's gift of energy to the hawk.

He watched through the hawk's keen eyes as she approached the pass. He laughed a few times as her nag tried to find purchase upon the slick stones. The hawk's sharp hearing picked up a cracking sound from the pass well ahead of Elisa. Drayel willed the hawk to fly down into the pass and see what lay ahead. Drayel felt a sense of fear through his connection to the animal when it flew below one of the bamboo braces. Drayel looked through his familiar's eyes and determined quickly what was about to happen. He willed the hawk back up out of the pass and high into the air so that he could see the woman.

He saw the brace give way and the woman turn her horse free. He saw the kick and then Elisa hitting her knees. Drayel had been surprised to feel some small amount of concern for her well-being. This woman that had come to his home to ask him to be merciful to a coward king. This temptress that had coerced his guards into letting her into his home unannounced. This woman, this WITCH.

Why should he care if she lived or died? She was nothing to him.

But still...Drayel did not think. He released one eye from the hawk's view. It was disconcerting the first time he used it, but now he was well versed in the skill. He had leapt off of his balcony and floated to the ground. The Sentry that he landed beside didn't have time to protest as Drayel took the reins from his hands and was on his horse and gone before the man realized what had happened.

Drayel watched with growing concern as the avalanche bore down on Elisa as she, what was she doing? He looked hard through the remaining connection to the hawk and saw her forming a ball of energy in her hands. So, she was gifted. Interesting. He watched as she pressed the ball of light against her skin. He believed she meant to cauterize the wound. Drayel watched in amazement as the blue ball shrunk in her hands. As did the gaping wound in her chest.

A healer! That was her secret. Cor Sanctus witches were known for many years as the best practitioners of healing magic. But Drayel had thought the talent lost to the ages, as most people did.

But his amazement turned to dismay as he watched the scene play out from high above. He could now see himself riding through the dark, but he could also see Elisa struggling to make it to the end of the pass. And he could see the cursed avalanche racing toward her. She would not make it to the end of the pass before it caught her. And he would not arrive there in time to save her.

Well, if he was anyone other than Drayel Shadow Walker.

He was known as the most powerful being in Ka'len. He was about to remind everyone why.

Drayel took the leather thong he'd used to tie his hair back on the way to his chambers earlier and wrapped it through his belt and around the saddle horn. Drayel rose to his full height and stood tall in the stirrups. He locked his legs against the sides of the still galloping mount and raised his hands straight out to his sides until they were level with his shoulders.

He summoned the magic from his core and poured it all into the God's Eye while he focused his intent in his mind.

The God's Eye had felt his will through the mental link he shared with the sentient artifact. It added its own formidable power store to the effort adding the white tint that so often blended with Drayel's green power displays. When Drayel felt the power inside the Gods Eye was at its maximum he slammed his hands together in front of him in a clapping motion, then quickly flipped both of his wrists, turning palms out and fingers touching, in front of the medallion. The power ripped from the medallion and tried to take Drayel out of the stirrups.

He held on tight and squeezed his legs harder striving to stay in the saddle. His mount had whickered at its discomfort but continued to drive forward. Its pace now slowed to a walk as it fought to move forward against the onslaught of power that tried to drive it and the rider backward. When the horse could no longer advance they'd stopped. Drayel had allowed a break in the power just long enough to slip from the saddle. The leather thong had long since broken and hung limply from his belt. His feet hit the ground and he began leaning into the shield that he'd created.

It felt good to release all of his power at once. The God's Eye was warm, and he could tell through the link that the artifact was pleased with having been unleashed. The wall was massive. It covered the entire pass and had pushed the avalanche far enough back into the pass that the mud and rock had flowed back up and over the sides of the hills.

Drayel had walked up to Elisa and found her unconscious and bleeding from a head wound. He'd put her on his horse, tied her to his stirrups so that she wouldn't fall off, and returned to the castle. He had her taken to the human healers at the citadel. They hadn't done much for her other than bandaged the wound on her head. They had washed her gently, having made Drayel wait outside of the room, and looked for more wounds.

They could not believe that the head wound alone had caused her to lose that much blood. But after close inspection, they determined that there were no other injuries. They'd called the castle maidens in and had them wash her with sweet-smelling soaps and clean the mud and blood from her hair. Drayel had instructed them to take her to the best room in the castle to recover. Upon seeing her safely delivered to her room he'd turned to walk back to the sitting area.

He hadn't made it very far when the weariness of his great expenditure struck him. He would have hit the floor face first had Korin not been coming out of the sitting room at that very moment. He remembered the indignity that he'd felt when the big man had tossed him over his broad shoulders and carried him up two flights of stairs to his chambers. Too weak to protest as he normally would have, he'd allowed the servant girls to bathe him as they had Elisa. He then lay back on his pillows and slept. A deep refreshing sleep.

His nights were usually filled with nightmares and fitful sleep full of dark things in shadows and evil waiting to be unleashed. But this night he'd been at peace. Strange. Right before he'd fallen asleep he'd ordered his Guards to awaken him as soon as Elisa woke. They had not yet knocked on his door when he awakened.

And he knew.

Somehow he just knew in the back of his mind that she was awake. He'd rolled out of bed, reluctant to leave the warmth of it, but needing to check on Elisa. He'd found her well and in good spirits. So, he'd invited her to breakfast. To talk.

What had he been thinking?

What did he have to talk about with this ambassador to the king? What could he truly tell her that she wouldn't go right back to the king with? Gods, what was it about this woman that made him so damned irrational? He should have let her die. She was essentially the enemy.

He should not have brought her back into his home. And he certainly should not be eating breakfast with her! But here he was. Sitting at a table bedecked with an extravagant layout of every different type of breakfast food in the castle. On most days Drayel would have two or three scrambled hens' eggs, a piece of sausage, and dry toast. So, this was yet again unusual behavior for him. He was just about to make the food disappear and leave the room when he heard a soft knock on the open door and she walked in.

The first time he'd seen her he believed she was possibly the most beautiful woman he'd ever seen. Now, walking into his dining room in a simple robe and slippers, he knew for certain that she was. He stood quickly to greet her, banging his legs into the table and upsetting a few of the bowls filled with various foods.

Elisa had the good sense to cover her mouth with her hand rather than burst out laughing at his gaffe. Although Drayel did not miss the slight upturn of the corners of her mouth behind that hand. His first reaction was anger at the embarrassment caused by the slip, but her smile washed that away like the early morning tide washes away footprints in the sand. He calmed the rising anger inside of himself and laughed. A short bark that caused both of them to jump just a little.

He motioned to the chair at the far end of the table. Elisa nodded politely and took the offered seat. The food smelled amazing, and her stomach growled again reminding her that she had not eaten since the previous morning. All of the stress of the past two days and the expenditure of magic had left her ravenous. She maintained her composure and observed what Drayel placed on his own plate before fixing hers.

He chose a simple meal of eggs, sausage, and toast. Much like one she would have fixed for herself back in Mannock's kitchens. She mimicked his choices and sat back down to eat.

She could still feel the tension in the air between them. He was hiding the fact that he saved her life, and she still did not know WHY he had saved her or what he expected in return. Did he expect her to be a spy? Did he want her to use her magic to heal his Warriors? She dreaded the answer because thanks to the weather and the caved-in pass, she was ultimately at his mercy.

They ate in awkward silence for a few moments. When both rose to fill their plates for a second time Drayel decided that he had had enough of the uncomfortable stalemate in the conversation.

"You do seem to be fully recovered this morning. Did you sleep well?" he asked.

He mentally cringed at his poor attempt to start a conversation. Elisa noted the tension in his posture and the way that he would not quite meet her eyes when he spoke to her. He was having a hard time focusing on the cut-up bits of fruit in the bowl in front of him while casting sidelong glances at her waiting for a response. She decided to have mercy on him out of appreciation for his willingness to break the ice.

"I did my Lor.....Drayel. I slept very well, thank you," she said sincerely.

She noted the slight sag in his shoulders as some of the tension in his body went away. He nodded and walked back to his seat. He waited until they were both seated before continuing.

"So, Lady Elisa, if we're to be completely honest with each other, I was fairly apprehensive about dining with you this morning. I'm not yet convinced that I can trust you to not return to the king and divulge everything that you will see here during your, stay." He finished.

He placed both hands on the lavish chair arms and sank back into the fur- lined padding that adorned the backrest.

"I'm at a loss as to what to do with you. I can't very well confine you to your room for the months it will take to clear the pass and the snow to melt away. And I can't let you have the run of the castle either. An escort perhaps?" he asked.

Although it appeared the last part of the sentence was more him talking to himself than her. Elisa had the feeling he did that often. The man did appear quite lonely.

Elisa took a few more bites before responding. Drayel seemed to have lost interest in the food. She had not. After consuming a few more pieces of the crisp bacon and taking a sip of the cold orange juice she set her fork down and looked up at the waiting Warlock.

He now sat with his legs crossed and his chin resting on the palm of his left hand. Head slightly tilted to the left as he observed her and waited for her response. She gently dabbed the corners of her mouth with a linen napkin to brush away the crumbs before speaking.

"Drayel, I appreciate your honesty. And I, myself, was unsure of how this meal would go. If we're being honest." She said.

She wondered how far she wanted to delve into the sensitive subjects that she knew they must eventually discuss. She decided that if she was to be his captive or his guest, it would be better to get everything out on the table at once. He wanted honesty, he would get it.

"Drayel, why did you save me?" She asked.

She saw the warlock stiffen and set up straight in his chair simultaneously.

"Yes, I know it was you that saved me. I also know that you saw my use of healing magic in the pass. If you truly consider me only a single-minded agent of the king, and that my only purpose here is to spy on you, why bring me back? You could have easily let me die. Not that I don't appreciate it, I do. But I would have been buried under tons of dirt and rock. You would not have been to blame. And you could have pinned my death on the King's men, and by association, the king himself. It could have only helped your cause. But instead, you bring me back, have me tended too, and are now seated across from me in your personal dining hall. I do not mean to sound abrupt, but what is it you hope to gain from me that you would go to such efforts?" she asked.

She stared at the now flustered Warlock sitting across from her.

Drayel took a moment to think about her response. This felt like a political quagmire that he was wading into with this woman, yet it was a simple conversation.

Why had he saved her?

He SHOULD have just let her die.

Was it just the fact that she was a healer?

Or was it something else?

He wasn't comfortable getting into what something else might be, so he decided to cling to the most rational excuse he had for saving her.

"Your healing abilities are exceedingly rare." He blurted.

Not his finest declaration, but it would do. He saw her face tighten unconsciously.

Apparently, she hadn't liked his answer.

"Elisa, you say you want me to call off my taking of the King's castle because it will cost the lives of Soldiers and innocents. With your healing prowess the number of deaths could be made marginal at best." He saw she was not responding well to his suggestion. Her body language was tight, and her brilliant blue eyes narrowed taking on a sharp appearance.

"Think about it, Elisa. How many people have died in Ka'len over the last fifty years because your people have not been able to openly practice healing magic? How many of your kind have been killed at the hands of fearful men that panicked at the thought of a witch walking among them? Even though they only discovered she was a witch after she had healed one of them?" He asked. He hoped trying a more benevolent path would open her up to the request he was building toward.

"If your people were allowed to return to their homeland, peace restored to the kingdom, and magic no longer outlawed, how many people could your coven save? You say you are to be the next matron of the Cor Sanctus coven? Why not be the leader that takes them home and sees magic restored throughout Ka'len? Join us. Help me keep my Warriors alive and healthy. Save as many citizens as you can but join us. Join me." He finished in a flourish.

It was more than he had planned on saying. But once he began speaking to her he found he could not stop.

Elisa was angry when Drayel first began to speak. He had only saved her to use her! Mannock had used her for years as an emissary between him and his enemies. She was tired of it. She had almost refused to go to speak with Drayel when the king commanded it, but as she was a guest in Drayel's castle, she was more of a slave in Mannock's. To refuse the king was to risk imprisonment or death.

Drayel suggesting that she join him and eventually use the magic that she had suppressed for so long was tempting. As was the chance to save lives and heal the injured.

But why should they be injured or killed in the first place? If she could just get Drayel and the king in the same room, and ensure Drayel wouldn't kill him on sight, she felt that she could negotiate peace between the Guild and the Crown. Both sides would have to make minor concessions, but it would save countless lives.

"I will consider your offer Drayel. I cannot promise yet that I will join your cause, because I still feel there is a better way than open war but, I would like some time to think it over. Would that be agreeable?" she asked.

She saw the gears turning behind the Warlocks eyes as he processed her response. He was looking for any twisting of words or half-truths. Thankfully she had been honest and there were none to find.

"Agreed." He said after some consideration. "However, until you decide to join me, I can't let you just roam the castle at will. I noticed yesterday that you do not wear a sword, Lady. Pray tell, why is that?" he asked.

"Why ever would I need one Drayel? I am not a Soldier or one of your Warriors. My weapon of choice has always been words. And I must say I usually do quite well in those types of battles." She said with a smile. Drayel shook his head in a side-to-side manner.

"Forgive me, Lady, it is simply that your magic is not offensive in nature and can do little to protect you should you find yourself in harm's way. And if you do decide to join me then there is a very real chance that you will find yourself on a battlefield tending to the wounded. I highly doubt the King's men will spare you a second glance before cutting you down. So, with your safety in mind, I believe I have an answer to both of those problems," he said with what she could have sworn was a malicious grin.

# CHAPTER 10

CIRCLE OF DEATH

**D**RAYEL HAD STOOD ABRUPTLY AFTER HIS DECLARATION AND insisted that she follow him. She had been reluctant to leave the table full of food, as she was not certain that she'd had her fill.

Drayel removed the problem by snapping his fingers and having the food adorning the table disappear. Elisa scowled at the warlock but stood since she no longer had a reason to linger at the table.

They'd exited the room and turned to the right, walking into a section of the castle that was foreign to Elisa. They turned down several hallways and ascended and descended flight after flight of stairs. Elisa marveled at the size of the construct. From the outside, it appeared relatively small. But as they walked she saw that it was equal to Mannock's castle in Tor'Amal. Should Drayel continue his quest and win the day, he could very well rule Ka'len from here if he wished.

He also appeared to be trying to mislead her and cause her to lose her sense of direction within the labyrinth of hallways. Which was useless since she was able to see the sun rising through various windows along the way. When they finally exited the hallway through a massive stone archway she knew with certainty that she'd need to cover her eyes to protect them from the sunlight they were about to walk into.

Except the sun wasn't directly in front of them. It was behind them. How? She'd carefully observed each and every direction change and had tracked the position of the sun as they walked. Drayel saw the confusion on her face and smiled.

"Lady Elisa, I believe you'll find my home has more than one secret and that my insistence on an escort may be more beneficial than you believe." He said with a grin.

Elisa smiled back. Isolde he was cute. Elisa forced the thought to the back of her mind but caught her gaze drifting down to his belt line as he turned away and found he actually had quite a nice...figure.

Elisa blushed at the thought and quickly raised her eye line to the back of his head. He was walking toward a group of his Sentries and Warriors that were huddled in a perfect circle. Well not huddled, Elisa corrected herself. They were standing around a huge golden ring in the earth. The curved top protruded from the earth almost a foot and was equally as thick. In circumference, it was about the same diameter as a round pen used for the breaking of wild horses. And within it were four smaller circles that met in the middle and left a perfect ring about three feet wide around the outside edge. Someone had constructed a twenty-foot by twenty-foot platform in the middle of the rings. One leg in each of the four circles.

Elisa could see the fresh cut of the wood and knew that the platform was not a permanent part of this, arena? She wasn't quite sure of the purpose until she saw two men walk out from the crowd. A crowd of bruised, bleeding, and by the Gods, smiling men.

She looked again and saw one of the fighters was the man she was supposed to have dinner with later that evening, Lord Korin Silver Steel.

A quick assessment from Elisa determined that Lord Silver Steel was far less bruised and damaged than most of the men surrounding the platform.

The man walking up the other side was a good two feet taller and one hundred pounds heavier than Korin. The brute made Korin look like a child gazing up at his father.

The brute smiled at Korin before drawing a wicked-looking long blade. It was a monstrous weapon. Easily four feet long and six inches wide with a serrated edge along one side, and a razor-sharp edge along the other. He grasped the hilt in both hands before raising it, point facing the ground, up to his chin, and bowing his head to the hilt in a form of barbarian salute.

Lord Silver Steel just smiled at the behemoth before him and walked over to a full rack of weapons attached to the side of the platform.

Elisa had been concerned for his safety when she saw his opponent. Now she was concerned for his mental health.

For out of the small assortment of various styles of sharp-edged steel blades Lord Silver Steel had chosen, of all things, a wooden sword.

She looked up at Drayel and was about to plead with the Warlock to intervene and stop this horrible mismatch of fighters when she saw Drayel, like most of the men around the platform, were smiling and calling out to the bigger man to take care and quit now before he was injured.

The bigger man, she heard him called Aldron, smiled back at the crowd and displayed a crude hand sign in response to their jeering and cat calls.

What was she missing here? Lord Silver Steel was heavily muscled and appeared agile. But this Aldron was massive and had a wicked sword. While Korin, Korin was going into the duel with a stick.

Elisa looked over at Korin and found him completely at ease with the idea of the upcoming match. He moved around the platform swinging his sword around in small circles in one hand, then the other. The circles grew larger and larger until his entire arm was moving with the swing. Deciding he was warmed up enough Korin stepped to the center of the platform and touched his foot to one of the red lines painted there.

Aldron was still walking around the stage. Circling Korin while screaming insults at the crowd and cursing his opponent. When he had succeeded in whipping himself into a battle frenzy of adrenaline and anger he too stepped to the middle of the platform and placed his foot against the line on his side of the stage. Barely a foot of space separated the giant barbarian, now seething with anger and rage, and the almost bored-looking Korin Silver Steel.

One of the men in the crowd climbed up the stairs and joined the fighters on stage.

Elisa saw it was the Captain that had been her escort briefly that morning. What was his name? Sandler. Right, Captain Sandler. Elisa watched as the Captain walked over to the weapons rack and picked up a large mallet. He turned and walked to the edge of the platform where Elisa now saw there was a giant brass cymbal mounted to the side of the stage. It was flat instead of vertical which made it hard to see from her position.

"Warriors and servants of the Guild! Now comes the final battle of the tournament!" He announced over the rising cheers of the crowd.

"As you well know, you have all fought bravely, and with great skill in your efforts to become the Commander of Lord Drayel Shadow Walker's Army!"

He yelled loudly and passionately. Much like a barker at a traveling merchant's tent trying to entice buyers to enter. He went on.

"And now, here we have the absolute best of the best. After five days of battle, our remaining Warriors are standing on the stage before you. From a small nomad tribe of hunters in the far North of Ka'len, deep in the Horinthian Mountains, comes the man-eating, giant-slaying, monster from the mountains, Warriors of the Guild, let us give a round of applause for Aldron Stone Spear!!" He finished with a flourish.

Elisa was surprised to hear that the response was a lot more even than she'd have imagined. Among the boos and good-natured jeering came a large amount of support for the big barbarian. Elisa looked at Drayel and found him frowning slightly.

"Drayel, is something wrong?" She asked.

He hesitated for only a moment. Before shaking his head and forcing a smile.

"No, there is nothing to be concerned with. Stay here and watch the show. Do not get too close to the stage or the men are likely to trample you underfoot when the battle commences. They can get a little, spirited." He said before walking away at a leisurely pace.

Elisa found a wine cask sitting underneath a catwalk in the shade and chose it for her seat from which to watch the battle that was about to commence. She felt it would be a short one for Korin and that her dinner plans would be changing shortly.

Sandler waited on the cheering and booing to die down before continuing.

"And last, but certainly not least. Your current Commander, the master of Battle, the Siren song of swordsmanship, the undefeated champion, and weapon master of the Warriors Guild, Lord Korin Silver Steel!!" He announced the end, again with a flourish. The crowd erupted with cheers. The majority of the men shouted his name and pumped their swords in the air overhead. There were, surprisingly to Elisa, a few jeers and boos mixed in among the shouts of praise for Lord Korin.

When the noise had calmed to a dull roar Sandler walked back over to the brass symbol, hammer in hand.

"Warriors, as you know, there are only three ways to win the last battle. To throw your opponent from the stage, to have him submit, or kill him outright!" The crowd cheered loudly at the last proclamation. Their desired outcome clear.

Elisa didn't understand how they could cheer the men fighting on the stage so loudly, then in the same breath call for their death. Maybe if she stayed here long enough she would. But she doubted it.

"Gentlemen, when I strike the cymbal the battle will commence.

There will be no stopping of the fight once it has begun. There are no rules save one. This fight is between these two brave men. Let no man interfere in any way before the fight is over on pain of death!" Sandler shouted.

With that, he raised the mallet and struck the cymbal.

# CHAPTER 11

## GLYPHS

Drayel had been standing beside Elisa watching the two fighters enter the ring when he detected a faint red glow coming from the circle of onlookers. He had not lied to Elisa when he said his home held many secrets. And one that he held close to the vest was the glyphs and symbols that were engraved in the walls, flagstone pavers, and in some places the ceilings of the Citadel.

These glyphs were old magic that was tied to his power alone. Not overly complicated but they served one very specific task. To detect when someone in his home had murderous intentions.

He knew that Aldron would try to kill Korin, but then everyone in the courtyard, Korin included, knew that. But that was battle and would not trigger his wards.

No, someone was planning on murdering someone else very soon.

The glyphs picked up wrong intentions that the doer was intending to hide from Drayel. The stronger the glow the worse the intentions. In this case, it was fairly strong and insistent.

Now he just had to determine who among his men was about to turn against one of their own.

He would see that the person did not succeed.

Drayel was still walking toward the crowd when the cymbal rang out across the courtyard. Aldron exploded from his line, charging straight ahead while swinging his massive sword out to the side then straight up over his head, arms fully extended, and brought it down in a great chopping motion accompanied by a grunt of effort.

Drayel smiled as Korin stepped almost casually out of the way of the herculean swing. He watched as Korin stepped out of the path and swung his wooden sword around and slapped it against the back of the big man's knee causing it to buckle. Aldron went down on one knee but quickly reversed the angle of that massive sword and swung it out and around behind him in a great arching motion that was designed to take the legs out from under an opponent. Had Korin tried to block that swing with his wooden sword it would have shattered it into pieces.

Instead, Korin did something that most fighters half his size could not accomplish while wearing leg armor and a chest plate, he bent his knees slightly and backflipped over the cutting blade.

The move was so unexpected that Aldron had fully committed to the swing, sure that he was about to cut the weapons master down. Now HE was fully exposed and off-balance.

Korin rushed in, flipping the sword up so that the hilt led the way, and smashed Aldron's nose. Blood flew and the crowd cheered. Drayel looked across the courtyard and saw Elisa's hand shoot up to her mouth in surprise. Then to Drayel's surprise, she smiled. She was honestly enjoying the fight. He had not seen that coming.

Aldron dropped to both knees with his non-sword hand covering his gushing nose. He had let his sword arm drop to the stage, still loosely gripping the giant sword's handle.

Korin walked over to stand in front of the monster, but just slightly out of range of that wicked blade.

"Aldron Stone Spear, do you yield?" Asked Korin.

There was no malice or teasing in his voice. Just an honest chance for the barbarian to yield the battle. Aldron looked up at Korin from his kneeling position. Blind hate and rage filled his eyes. All sense of sanity lost. Aldron had let himself get lost in his primal instincts. Instincts developed over centuries of survival by the nomad clans of barbarian warriors. Aldron had been dangerous when the fight started. Now he was deadly.

The barbarian roared in outrage and lunged to his feet. Bringing his massive blade to bear he charged his smaller opponent swinging wildly.

Korin found himself quickly back on his heels, completely defensive. He dove to the right and rolled back to his feet only to find the enraged barbarian had already reversed course and was pursuing him with a vengeance.

Drayel watched the display of athleticism from his friend and was only slightly concerned that Korin might have made better use of one of his own steel swords instead of the wooden bokken. But for now, he had to worry more about this unknown threat and trust Korin to handle the barbarian.

Korin watched the barbarian charging around the ring after him. He knew that he could not continue to run.

The platform was too small and eventually, Aldron would pin him in a corner or force him from the platform. Korin smiled, though the exertion of dodging the wild and frequent swings made it appear more of a grimace. He knew what he had to do.

Korin worked toward the nearest edge of the platform, enticing his opponent with the prospect of driving him off of the platform. Aldron rushed in, sword held out in front of him in both hands. He attempted to lunge and stab Korin through the chest. As he did so Korin planted both feet and tried to dive toward the middle of the stage as he did earlier.

This time though one of his feet slipped on the wooden surface causing him to land flat on his stomach. The crowd groaned at the slip and some stood with their mouths open in shock. Few expected the weapons master to fail.

Drayel looked up at the stage when the crowd groaned in unison. He was expecting to see Aldron flat on his back or flying from the stage. He paused when he saw Korin laying on his stomach and gasping as if the wind had been blown from his lungs. He watched as Korin struggled to his knees in an attempt to get back on his feet.

Aldron did not miss the opening. With a mighty roar, he pulled his leg back and kicked Korin in the stomach as hard as he could, causing the weapons master to curl into a ball and roll away from his nemesis.

Aldron raised his sword in one hand high over his head and roared at the skies. Taking the massive blade in both hands he raised it over his shoulder and rested it like a woodsman carrying his ax. Korin Silver Steel struggled back to his hands and knees. His grip now weakened to the point he could barely hold his sword.

Aldron stalked ever closer. When he was within striking distance of Korin he leaned forward and grinned with bloodied teeth.

"Do YOU yield, LORD Silver Steel?" He asked. His voice full of venom and anger.

He smiled again when Korin turned his head away from him coughing. Aldron could barely make out Korin's response of,

"Never."

Drayel turned and looked at Elisa, who now had both hands covering her mouth and genuine fear in her eyes. She locked on to Drayel's eyes and mouthed a silent plea.

"Help him." She said.

Drayel shook his head. He could not. If Korin did not win this match unaided then the men would never respect him, and he would lose the title regardless of the outcome.

It was entirely up to Korin.

Although it would appear that Aldron did not share Drayel's devotion to morals and tradition. There were several of his kinsmen in the crowd that day. They were all grouped together and cheering their kinsman's impending victory.

Drayel smiled viciously when he saw the small metal tube in the largest of the barbarian's hands. Aldron's younger brother, Ulrich, held the blowgun to his side in a poor attempt to conceal it.

Drayel knew well that the northern barbarians were not above using darts tipped with the deadly nectar of the Blood Rose for assassinations.

The Blood Rose appeared to be a common red rose, except it had no thorns, and on the inside of the blossom was a small pouch that held the deadly nectar. In liquid or dried form, the smallest amount of the nectar would kill the largest of animals, or men, and leave no trace when its work was complete. The barbarians had initially used it to hunt ogres and trolls that threatened their tribes. But had eventually adapted it to combat applications and used it fairly effectively.

It appeared that they now intended to use it for an assassination. Drayel quickly determined that should Aldron begin to lose, Ulrich would fire the small dart into Korin, quickly weakening him so that Aldron could kill him and claim victory.

Drayel thought not.

When Korin had answered Aldron smiled and turned to his brothers. He spread his arms out wide to his side and roared again. This time turning back toward the still kneeling Korin and raising his blade high overhead, he mimicked his first attack from the battle.

Chopping straight down toward Korin's neck, Aldron roared with exaltation over his forthcoming victory.

Korin moved.

Dropping his left shoulder and knee he rolled in toward Aldron's legs, and inside of the swing. Quickly spinning out from under the huge barbarian's chest he came out standing directly beside his opponent, whose gigantic sword was now buried in the stage where Korin had been only seconds before.

As he completed the spin he saw Eliza, from the corner of his eye, throw both hands into the air in celebration as she realized his ploy.

Korin quickly brought his sword up over his head and chopped downwards in a blow very similar to that of the barbarians. The wood cracked against the back of Aldron's head like the sound of a child striking cherry pits with a wagon board, and the barbarian lost his grip on the massive sword.

Korin struck again and Aldron's eyes glazed over as he fell to his knees, head now even with the edge of his serrated blade that was still stuck in the stage.

Drayel watched as Ulrich realized that his brother was all but done. Ulrich tapped the barbarian closest to him and whispered something. Drayel saw the man nod and begin poking the others and nodding in the direction of the stage. All six of the barbarians surrounding Ulrich were suddenly very invested in their kinsman getting back into the fight. They yelled and screamed encouragement to the downed man. They raised their arms in the air and pushed or shoved everyone in the vicinity causing quite a disturbance and also opened up a small area in the middle of them where Ulrich stood alone with a clear shot to the stage.

The younger barbarian was raising the tube to his lips when up on the stage Korin had grabbed a fist full of Aldron's hair and now had his neck pressed against the serrated edge of his own blade.

"I'll only ask this once more, Aldron Stone Spear, do you yield?" He asked as he not so gently forced the barbarian's thick neck down onto the points of the blade. With a simple downward shove, he would rip open the big man's throat and end this battle. But again, he gave him a chance to maintain his honor.

Drayel saw Aldron look over toward Ulrich and mouth "Do it." Ulrich smiled and pressed the tube to his lips.

Korin Silver Steel was no novice when it came to battle. He'd fought in this army or that one since he'd been old enough to hold a blade. Over the years, as his battle prowess increased, so did his sense of what was going on around him in the midst of battle. That sense was now telling him something was wrong. He looked down at his opponent and saw him

mouth the silent command. Korin turned his head in the direction Aldron was looking just in time to see Ulrich bring the pipe to his lips.

There would be no time for Korin to dodge the flying needle that would soon be streaking his way.

Korin smiled at Ulrich. He had no fear of death. If he was to die then he would take Aldron with him.

Ulrich read the intent in Korin's eyes and saw red. Or more accurately, green. A sudden blinding green light had enveloped him and held him completely paralyzed. He tried to scream for help but found his kinsman equally encased in the binding light.

Korin followed the flowing stream of green light back to a very angry Drayel Shadow Walker. Drayel looked back at Korin and nodded. An unspoken command and answer to the question that passed between them. With a shove, Korin opened the carotid artery in Aldron's neck before releasing him to bleed freely onto the platform.

The crowd normally would have erupted in cheers for the victor, but they all saw the group of barbarians encased in their Lord's power. It didn't take long for the seasoned veterans standing around the platform to see the blowgun pressed to Ulrich's lips and determine the truth of the matter.

Most immediately began calling for the heads of the barbarians. Drayel kept them under the spell as he walked up onto the platform and stood next to Korin. He looked over and saw Elisa staring at the still twitching body of Aldron with a look of horror on her face. It was clear that death was not something she was accustomed to. That was something that would change quickly if she stayed with him. Them. Stayed with them he meant.

The momentary distraction irritated the Warlock and he growled at his lapse of concentration. He growled and looked for Captain Sandler.

"Captain, come up here and do your duty." He snapped.

The Captain quickly mounted the steps and stood beside Korin. Taking Korin's non-sword hand in his own he deliberately raised it high in the air.

"Warriors of the Guild! I give you your commander. The still undefeated, Lord Korin Silver Steel!" He screamed the last part to be heard over the cheers of the crowd.

When the raucous celebration had calmed to a dull roar Captain Sandler released Korin's hand and bowed stiffly at the waist before practically running from the stage.

The crowd grew quiet and looked again to the group of barbarians still held in Drayel's power.

"Warriors of the Guild. When the battle for Commander first began, the rules were made clear. That there was to be no outside interference from anyone during the match." Drayel stated in a booming voice that carried far further than it should have.

"The man lying on the platform at our feet was a coward and a cheater." He said in a voice laced with venom. "He enlisted the help of his kinsmen to help him should he be unable to defeat Lord Silver Steel. These men together plotted to distract you and kill Lord Silver Steel with the dart in the blowgun still pressed to Ulrich's lips." He said as he pointed toward Ulrich. The weapon was still raised to his mouth for all to see.

"Warriors, I ask you, does anyone here see this another way? Were the Stone Spear clan's actions this day honorable? Or would you say they violated the honor of combat as well as the trust the Guild placed in them by allowing them to join in our fight?" He asked the men surrounding the platform.

Shouts of guilty and dishonor, cowards, and kill them were returned in force. Drayel looked out across the crowd but did not see the small band of men walk past Elisa and through the stone archway into the castle, led by Tallon Grey Cloak.

"What say you, Warriors? Has Aldron's blood paid the debt? Or does this crime demand more?" He asked.

He looked at Ulrich as he finished speaking. His intent was clear to those watching. He heard various cries from his men. Some asked for him to kill the entire group of conspirators, some called for the death of Ulrich alone, and some said the debt was paid.

Drayel was angry about the attempt to murder Korin. But in the end, it was Korin who was wronged. Drayel knew that if he made a decision regarding the barbarian's punishment that it could cause a potential rift between the men. He decided the best course of action was to let Korin make the decision.

"Lord Silver Steel, as the aggrieved party, do you feel that the death of Aldron satisfies the rule against interference, or do you yet demand more blood? I shall allow you to make the decision regarding the fate of these fools. And shall abide by your wishes, whatever they may be. So shall we all." He said with finality.

Korin nodded his head in acceptance.

He turned and surveyed the crowd, his eyes landing on Elisa. She was still sitting on the wine cask where she had been sitting during the fight. She was still very pale but was snapping out of the shock caused by Aldron's death. She was shaking her head no and mouthing "No more. Please, No more" over and over.

Korin considered the situation. The men of the Guild were supposed to feel safe and protected within these walls. If rules were broken with no punishment, then there would be no incentive for the men to follow them. As much as he understood Elisa's request, he could not allow Ulrich to live, having broken the rule about outside inter-ference.

"Warriors of the Guild, I, Korin Silver Steel, commander of the Army, and weapons master of the Guild, have decided that the six conspirators in this cowardly act shall be imprisoned in the cells beneath the castle until such time as they can be returned to their clan in the North. They shall not be harmed, but their hair will be sheared to the skin before they leave these walls."

Several men laughed at the proclamation, while others shook their heads in disappointment. They still wanted blood. The oldest of the group understood Korin's intent clearly. A barbarian's hair was a symbol of his strength and bravery in combat. The longer the tribesman's hair, the more honor he held. To be returned to their tribe with shorn heads was the ultimate disgrace. And it was likely that the fighters among their tribe would kill them for allowing their heads to be shaved without fighting to the death. So, even in mercy, there was a chance that the men would die at the hands of their kinsmen. But the Guild would be held harmless since they did not draw their blood themselves.

"Ulrich Stone Spear, however, is guilty of attempted murder most foul. While breaking the one rule of the tournament, he attempted to interfere in the final match and aid Aldron when it became clear that he would lose. Our rules and laws stand for one reason. To maintain safety and good order within the Guild. If we do not enforce the laws, and the will of our Lord Drayel Shadow Walker, then we will lose our discipline and honor in short order. It is with that in mind that I sentence you, Ulrich Stone Spear, to die. Sentence to be carried out immediately." Korin said solemnly.

The crowd became silent and every eye turned toward Ulrich and the barbarians. Drayel motioned to a group of waiting Sentries. They walked over and took the six conspirator barbarians by the arms and removed their weapons.

Drayel dropped the controlling green light from them but kept it around Ulrich.

When the Sentries had escorted the group of barbarians away from Ulrich and through the stone archway into the castle, Drayel placed a hand on the God's Eye Medallion. There was a crackle in the air like lightning before it strikes. Drayel's power was suddenly infused with the white light from the medallion.

Ulrich's feet lifted from the ground until he was high overhead, where all could see. Drayel guided Ulrich over the stage and had him levitating directly over the top of the now still form of Aldron. Korin looked at Drayel and saw his intent. Korin calmly walked down the steps from the stage and began having the men nearest the stage step away.

When everyone was clear of the main ring, Drayel increased the flow of power and there was an audible crack as Ulrich suddenly found himself looking at his backside. His neck broken cleanly in two. Drayel dropped the now lifeless body of Ulrich on top of his brother and began weaving a new sign in the air.

The platform was instantly engulfed in white-hot flames. The platform and bodies were immediately engulfed and incinerated.

It took less than a minute for the entire conflagration to disappear, leaving nothing but ashes behind.

# CHAPTER 12

## SWORDSMANSHIP

ELISA HAD INTENDED ON FLEEING THE COURTYARD THE MOMENT she heard Korin's proclamation. But as she turned for the portal she saw the group of men that had walked past her earlier were lingering there in the archway. Among them was the Warlock Grey Cloak.

Elisa did not wish to encounter that particular individual again so soon. So, she returned to her seat just in time to see Drayel lift the man into the air and snap his neck.

She had let out a short scream before composing herself. She looked over and saw Grey Cloak staring at her intently. Although what he had on his mind, she could not tell.

When the platform went up in flames she'd buried her face in her hands so that she could avoid watching the spectacle.

It hadn't lasted long. Before she knew it the men gathered around the platform had begun making their way back through the archway and into the castle. Elisa stayed seated as they passed. She had to make a conscious effort to ignore the catcalls and rude comments of the men as they walked past her. She normally would have lashed out and put the fools in their place, but despite being called a guest, her status here was tenable at best.

When all of the Warriors had finally left the arena she looked back toward where the platform had stood. It was gone entirely. Only Drayel and Korin remained standing in the courtyard speaking in low but jovial tones. They looked in her direction several times. Korin shaking his head no, and then finally in an approving manner. Both men shook hands then embraced with a friendly hug, like brothers.

When it was clear that they were both coming over to speak to her, Elisa slid off of the cask and met them halfway across the arena.

"Elisa, meet Lord Korin Silver Steel." Drayel said while motioning toward his friend.

Korin smiled and bowed at the waist, not much more than a slight lean forward and a dip of the chin, but a courtesy regardless.

"We've met Drayel." She said hesitantly.

Not sure at all about how she felt about witnessing both men kill someone so flippantly.

"Lady Elisa had a run-in with our good friend Grey Cloak on the way to breakfast. Captain Sandler sniveled his way out of a confrontation with the man. I arrived as Tallon was walking away muttering to himself about fools and the like." Korin said with obvious distaste.

Elisa was picking up on the fact that Tallon Grey Cloak was dangerous, but not held in high esteem within the castle.

"Really? Do I need to have a word with him regarding the treatment of our guest?" Drayel asked almost hopefully.

"No," responded Korin, "He was mostly just putting on a light show for the Captain and company just to remind them he has power. He was not seriously threatening anyone. Had he been serious, then good Captain Sandler would likely have been dead before I arrived."

Drayel nodded. It was true. For all of his posturing and arrogance, Tallon Grey Cloak was the third strongest magic user in the Guild. Well, second now with the death of Maricin.

"Very well. Lady Elisa, keep me apprised of any further interactions with Tallon Grey Cloak. And for your safety, avoid him when you are not in my presence or Lord Silver Steel's." Drayel said sincerely.

Elisa nodded, confirming her understanding of his request.

"Now, you're probably thinking that I brought you here to see the final battle of the tournament, correct?" Drayel asked Elisa.

"Truth be told Drayel, I'm not sure why you brought me here. I did enjoy the fighting. But I was put off by the two men that were...killed."

She had started to say murdered, but as she replayed the event in her mind, it wasn't truly murder in the purest sense of the word. She was still unsure about the day's events, but believed with time she would come to a better understanding of what had transpired.

"I understand Elisa. But you need to understand, war is coming to Tor'Amal. And the deaths you witnessed here today will not be the last to come." Drayel said with certainty.

"So, is that why you brought me here? To start desensitizing me to death?" She asked warily.

"No, I came here to introduce you to Lord Silver Steel, Korin. As he is to be your escort and weapons master for the foreseeable future." He said with a nod in Korin's direction.

Korin smiled and nodded back at Drayel.

"It would be my pleasure." He said with a grin.

"Wait, weapons master? What need have I of a weapons master?" She asked incredulously. "I do not even possess a sword, much less have a use for one."

Drayel just sighed before responding.

"I fear that in the coming days the ability to wield a sword will serve you well. Especially if you intend to continue traveling the roads of Ka'len unescorted. There are bad men on the roads between the Citadel and Tor'Amal." Drayel said sincerely.

"Worse men than you?" She asked without thinking. She threw her hands up in front of her in defense. Meaning to take back the insult.

When she saw Drayel smile and Korin grinning.

"No, Lady Elisa. There are no men worse than us." Drayel said with a smile.

Korin simply shook his head in acknowledgment.

"But that being said, regardless of your decision to side with the Guild or return to the king, you need to be able to properly defend yourself. And until you learn the tricks to maneuvering through my home, you'll find no better escort than Korin. Excluding myself that is." He said, still smiling at Korin.

"So, Elisa, it looks like our dinner tonight may become a standing arrangement for some time." Korin said happily.

Elisa blushed slightly at the big man's exuberance.

"It would seem so, Korin." Elisa said demurely.

Drayel looked at the two of them standing there. Korin grinning like a fool and Elisa blushing at his attention. Drayel felt something rising in his chest. Jealousy? No. Surely not.

"Korin, I leave her in your capable hands. When you are done with her first lesson come see me so that we may discuss the plans for clearing the pass."

With that Drayel spun on his heel and walked quickly across the courtyard and through the stone archway.

Elisa watched him go and was surprised that she felt mildly disappointed that the dark-haired Warlock would not be staying for her training session.

Korin had no reservations regarding Drayel's leaving them. Although he quickly switched his demeanor from infatuated suitor to weapons master relatively quickly.

"Well then, Lady Elisa, let's go find you a sword." He said earnestly.

# CHAPTER 13

## DINNER PLANS

Eʟɪsᴀ ʜᴀᴅ ᴛʀᴜᴅɢᴇᴅ ʙᴀᴄᴋ ᴛᴏ ʜᴇʀ ʀᴏᴏᴍ ᴀᴛ Kᴏʀɪɴ's sɪᴅᴇ. Muscles she didn't know she possessed were aching and sore. She wanted nothing more than to lie down in her bed and sleep.

But she knew she could not rest just yet. Korin had talked about their dinner plans all the way from the training circle to her door. He had been a dedicated taskmaster in the courtyard. He pushed her harder physically than she had ever thought possible. But as soon as the training ended, and he had declared that she was done for the day, he had switched easily back into the cordial and fun-loving Korin that she'd met earlier that morning.

When they reached her door Korin took her hand, bruised and bleeding from busted knuckles, and raised it to his lips to kiss the back of it.

"Lady Elisa, I shall see you shortly before the sun sets this evening. Until then, good day." He smiled politely then disappeared down the hallway back to his own room she supposed.

Elisa closed the door gently and turned to look at her bed longingly. What she saw beside it made her want to cry tears of joy. For where there had been an empty spot on the floor, there was now a large copper tub filled almost to the brim with steaming hot water. A rack of fresh oils, soaps, and other accouterments hung from the side in a thin silver wire mesh basket.

On the other side of the room, where there was previously nothing but a stone wall, now stood a beautifully carved armoire practically filled with dresses, riding pants, shirts, tunics, and, she saw somewhat disappointingly, padded fighting clothes for her training sessions with Korin.

But the training was tomorrow's problem.

She had survived that first torture test and was now going to pamper herself as a reward.

Elisa stripped off her now filthy tunic, boots, and the jeans she'd borrowed from a room just off of the training circle where the Citadel staff washed, dried, and placed the cleaned garments back in the room for re-use.

She'd felt awkward in the very male clothes at first. But she soon grew to appreciate the flexibility provided by the pants and tunic. She realized quickly that had she attempted the training in her normal attire she would have quickly tripped and fallen directly onto her face.

Now the borrowed clothes lay in a heap on the floor. She would take them back tomorrow when she returned for her next training session and retrieve the comfortable robe and shoes she'd left behind.

She stepped over to the tub and raised her left foot daintily to the edge of the tub just as her right leg gave out in a spasm. She crashed to the floor in a very unladylike manner and uttered words that would have made the sailors in Port Ka'len blush.

She was so exhausted from the training regimen that her legs wouldn't support her. Her arms were weak from exhaustion, and she still hadn't slept and recovered from her earlier use of magic. All in all, she was in a pitiful state of being.

It was at that moment, while she lay sprawled naked on the floor, that one of the house maidens barged into her room. The girl was about the same age as Elisa and turned a brilliant shade of red when she saw her sitting on the floor completely nude.

"My Lady, my apologies! I should have knocked. I don't know what I was thinking." She said as she stumbled backward to the door she'd left standing open. She kept her hand over her eyes shielding Elisa from view. Elisa thought, what is it with people and not shutting doors here?

The maiden had almost backed completely out of the room and was about to shut the door when it dawned on her that she DID have a reason for coming into the lady's room.

"My Lady, do you need help getting into the bath? The mistress of the house sent me to aide you. She said she saw you undergoing Lord Silver Steel's training earlier today and thought you might appreciate a hand." She said in an embarrassed rush.

Elisa almost cried, for the second time in minutes, at the offer of help. She couldn't speak due to the embarrassment of the girl seeing her naked, her physical fatigue, and the fact that she would need help just to get into her own bath.

Elisa just nodded yes and braced herself for the coming humiliation.

The maiden shut the door and walked back over to where Elisa sat on the floor. Taking a large cotton towel from the rack on the side of the tub she ran it under Elisa's arms and across her chest. She then wrapped the loose ends of the towel around her hands and rolled it up until her hands were resting against the back of Elisa's shoulders.

The girl placed her feet on either side of Elisa's hips and squatted down behind her.

"My Lady, I will do most of the work, but if you could, try to brace yourself with your legs and lift them into the tub when we get you standing." She instructed.

Elisa nodded her understanding.

With a grunt, the girl straightened her legs and lifted Elisa from the ground as easily as a mother lifting a sleeping child. Elisa found that with the girl supporting her weight she could easily step over into the tub.

The steaming hot water brought instant relief to her aching muscles. To her credit, the girl did not simply drop Elisa into the water but eased her down slowly until she was fully immersed.

Once Elisa was in the tub the girl pulled the now soaking wet towel from under her shoulders and folded it into a square. She placed it across the back of the tub and bid Elisa to lean back against it.

The girl poured some of the sweet-smelling oils into the water, coloring it a brilliant shade of blue that almost matched Elisa's eyes. This also afforded her some modicum of privacy. While she rested against the tub the girl took up a sponge from the tray of soaps and washed Elisa's feet. When she tried to move on to her legs Elisa stopped her.

She could only handle so much assistance. And having the girl bathe her like an invalid was more than she could stand. She gently shook her head no.

"Thank you for your help. I fear I would still be lying on the floor had you not come along." She said with a weary smile.

The girl nodded and smiled back.

"I can wait outside the door my Lady if you feel you may need assistance getting out of the bath." She said.

Elisa considered it briefly.

"I apologize, you must think me very rude indeed. You have been immensely helpful, and I've not even asked your name." Elisa said.

The maiden shook her head.

"No, my Lady, I would assume my name was the last thing on your mind a few moments ago. I assure you, you've done me no wrong. My name is Isabelle. Or Bell. Whichever you like my Lady." She said with a small curtsy.

Elisa raised her hand from the water and held it out to Isabelle. Isabelle's eyes widened at the offered hand. Shaking hands was generally only done by the men at the Citadel. And for the most part, the servants were ignored until they were deemed ready to start their training with Lord Silver Steel. Everyone at the Citadel started as staff before they were allowed to join the Army. Drayel had told them all that humility had never hurt a fighter. And that the ability to serve others was a sign of character and maturity that led to good decisions on the battlefield.

But before you were a Warrior, you may as well not exist within the Citadel walls. Isabelle had grown up in the Citadel. Her mother and father were both Warriors. She had no way of knowing that in Tor'Amal it was perfectly normal for women to shake hands with one another, or anyone else they so choose. So, she was briefly taken aback by the offered hand.

Not wanting to be rude, and offend Lord Drayel's guest, she reached out and gently shook Elisa's hand.

"Bell then. I'd ask one more favor of you, Bell." Elisa started. Isabelle nodded agreeably.

"Bell," Elisa continued, "Drayel does not stand on titles, and I do not wish to do so either. Please, simply call me Elisa. You really do not have to call me Lady."

Isabelle nodded and simply replied, "Yes, ma'am."

"Thank you for offering to help me out of the tub Bell, but I believe I will just lie here and soak until it's time for my dinner...meeting...with Korin. I would not want you to simply stand outside the door waiting for me while I rest. I believe that after I recuperate in the bath I shall be perfectly fine. I cannot thank you enough for your help, Bell. But I should be fine from here." Elisa said honestly.

Bell nodded. And turned to go. As she opened the door she stopped and looked back over her shoulder at Elisa.

"Elisa," using the Lady's proper name felt odd to Bell, "should you need anything from myself or any of the other staff there is a cord on the wall, simply pull it and I will come as quickly as possible to aid you. Enjoy your dinner with Lord Silver Steel."

She said with a smile that did not quite meet her eyes.

Bell shut the door and walked quickly down the hall with a glimmer of tears in her eyes.

# CHAPTER 14

## SUNSET

$E$LISA AWOKE WITH A START WHEN THE WATER TOUCHED HER mouth. She sat up quickly splashing water everywhere as she gripped the sides of the tub and pulled herself up and out of the water.

Once she was back in a fully upright sitting position she noted that the sun had dropped in the sky and had left a bright red sunset across the tops of the mountain range visible from her window. Isolde!

She'd fallen into a deep and comfortable sleep in the steaming hot water and almost missed the promised dinner with Korin.

She noticed with pleasure that the tub, or water itself, had been enchanted and was still as hot as it was when she'd climbed into it hours before. Her body had relaxed considerably in the steaming water.

However, soreness had begun to take root in the heavily used muscles in her legs, arms, back, and core. Everything hurt. She had known that castle life was not physically challenging, but she believed that she'd been fairly fit. Now she knew better. If she were to endure Korin's instruction for months then she'd have to grow stronger.

But again, that was a problem for tomorrow. Now she had to get out of this glorious tub by herself. She looked longingly at the rope hanging by the door and wished she could summon Bell. She cursed herself for sending the girl away. But it had been fair to do so.

Elisa looked around the room and realized for the first time how dark it was. She would have to remember to ask for candles the next time she spoke to Bell. But for now, she needed light to dress by and had to do something about her aching body.

Elisa, now fully rested, placed her hands in the water and sent her healing energy streaming into it. She felt the light tingling as the magic worked wonders on her fatigued muscles.

When the tingling diminished she pulled her legs into her chest. The movement was easy and pain free. She smiled and breathed a sigh of relief.

Elisa stood easily from the tub and was again grateful for the heated room. She glanced around and found a clear glass pitcher sitting on the floor beside the tub. Presumably so that she could rinse her hair after bathing. It would work for now.

Elisa stepped out of the tub and wrapped one of the thick, and incredibly soft, towels around her body. She enjoyed the warmth and comfort of the towel as she bent over and picked up the pitcher. Having secured the vessel, she walked over to the desk and set it in the middle.

She'd not had time to learn much from her mother before she'd been shipped off to serve Mannock. She had, however, learned to summon the element of fire. She called upon that skill now and soon had a small inferno burning inside the jar.

She saw her reflection in the mirror as she looked up from her creation and liked the way her eyes glowed a brighter blue when she tapped into her power. The flames flickered and cast alternating light and shadow across her face. She thought it was positively wicked, but kind of liked it.

Now that she had light, Elisa turned to the armoire. The clothes that had been provided for her were of a similar quality and style to what she owned back home. She was glad to have them as she did not wish to spend the entirety of her time here in robes and training clothes.

She picked a black silk strapless dress that fit her almost perfectly. The top embraced and displayed her feminine assets in a way that was pleasing to the eye of males, and Elisa herself. It then hugged her trim waist before extending down below her hips where it flared out to allow her legs freedom of movement.

The dress had a slit along the side from her ankle almost all the way to her buttocks. It was quite scandalous in her opinion. But she did not want Korin thinking clearly tonight.

If she was to learn as much as possible about Drayel, Korin, and the Citadel, then she wanted Korin drunk and distracted. Not sober and focused. She smiled at her reflection in the mirror.

If she was being honest, she did look amazing in the dress. Her hair, however, was a mess. The tiny strap she had used to pull it back earlier had been lost during her intense training session.

She searched the drawers in the bottom of the armoire and found several ribbons, bows, and other items stored there. And shoes.

She let out a small gasp when she saw the assortment provided for her. She had worried she'd be limited to slippers and boots while she was here. To see the high heels, sandals, and other styles made available to her was pleasing to say the least. She chose a pair of shiny black high heels with small black leather thongs across the top to secure them to her feet.

She walked back over to the mirror and looked at her hair. It was sopping wet, and she imagined that Korin would be knocking on her door shortly. She was growing irritated at the situation when she noticed a dark spot on the wall nearest the armoire. She walked over to it and was immediately blasted with hot air from what she now saw, was a vent in the wall.

Her room was connected to one of the main exhaust vents that ran through the castle. The vent was intended to allow hot air into the room and had a sliding cover that would allow it to be sealed off in the summer months. Elisa smiled.

It would warm the room, but it would also serve to dry her hair. Five short minutes later her hair was dried, styled, and had ribbon wound through it making a circlet around her head. The hair was braided along the ribbon and tied together at the back in a ponytail that fell freely down her back.

Yes. That would do nicely she decided. And just in time.

She heard a polite but firm knock on her door just as she was rising from her stool. She felt a brief tinge of fear as she looked at her fabricated lantern. Then relaxed when she remembered she was in the Citadel, not Tor'Amal. She could use, and practice her magic, here with no fear of discovery. She felt a tiny tingle of excitement at the idea.

When she opened the door Korin smiled appreciatively and unconsciously gave her a quick look up and down. When he realized his gaffe his face turned dark red.

"Apologies Lady, it has been a long time since a woman of your beauty has graced these halls. I forgot myself. Please forgive my crassness." He said sincerely.

Elisa blushed slightly at the compliment. She didn't mind his unintended glance. It played right into her plan of keeping him from focusing. And in her own opinion, she did look amazing.

Korin offered her his arm and she took it willingly. He led them back toward the sitting room and continued down that hallway until he reached another archway similar to the one that led to the training circle. Only this one led to a beautiful open courtyard. The grass was bright green despite the time of year. Several round stone tables with curved stone benches adorned the yard. Each surrounded with gravel of varying colors. The gravel circles were connected to each other by stone paths that served to make the dining area more aesthetic, but also kept the grass from being trampled down.

There was an elevated stone walkway that surrounded the courtyard with ornate glass double doors leading to the rooms beyond. A stone ledge extended from the wall over the walkway to supporting beams and a low wall that ran the length of the walkway providing cover from rain and the elements.

Underneath the stone archway were ornate carved stone supporting beams with arches in between them that served to make private alcoves around the courtyard.

There was also a set of curving stairs leading up to the walkway on each side of the archway that led into the courtyard.

Elisa looked around and found several lanterns using fairy light to illuminate the dining area hung on stylized brass hangers. There were more of the lanterns mounted inside of the alcoves to cast an almost romantic light on the diners.

Fairy light was somewhat of a misnomer. The light came from a flower that featured green, red, blue, or white blooms. When picked or agitated the blooms had a phosphorescent glow to them that was commonly used for lighting. Ka'len lore said that the flowers had been created by the fairy folk centuries before. But no one living had ever seen a fairy, so it was mostly taken as lore alone.

She realized as well that they'd walked outside. In the middle of winter. Yet there was no snow on the ground and it felt like a spring day. Korin grinned as if he could read her mind and inclined his head upwards while tilting his eyes toward the skies. Elisa looked up and gasped slightly again. A barely perceptible green dome extended over the entire courtyard. The falling snow hit the dome and disappeared instantly. It was beautiful.

"Drayel engraved Glyphs into the battlements surrounding the courtyard. They were designed to defend against arrows and projectiles from trebuchets. It did not take long to figure out some of the fringe benefits. We can dine here year 'round with no fear of rain, snow, or other inclement weather. The vents here provide heat for the courtyard at night." He said with an appreciative look around the courtyard. "In the summertime Drayel drops half of the shield, which catches the wind and forces it down here. It keeps it very comfortable and many of us spend our nights here drinking and playing games."

Elisa could see the attraction to the courtyard. It was beautifully designed and would be a very pleasant place to spend her evenings.

Further inspection revealed that two of the alcoves toward the far end of the courtyard appeared to be a tavern style bar. Many of the men she'd seen watching the tournament now stood in the open area in front of the alcoves or sat on the grass drinking pints of meade and other beverages. Korin saw her gaze and grinned.

"Maybe we should eat something before we visit Sandron's?" He suggested.

"Sandron's?" She asked.

"Sandron was one of the best Warriors in the Guild when Drayel first joined. He was injured in a battle shortly after that claimed one of his legs from the hip down. His other leg was damaged severely and could not be restored to full mobility. Sandron would not hear of leaving the Citadel. It was young Drayel that suggested that Sandron could open a bar in the courtyard. Many of the men were venturing into Tor'Amal, or going south to Port Ka'len, to relax and drink. That usually ended up in a lot of drinking followed by the men relaxing in the constable's cells after destroying the taverns in brawls with the locals." Korin recounted.

"The head of the Guild at that time, a lesser Warlock named Orious, was growing weary of expending the Guild's funds to have the men released. So, he was quick to approve Drayel's suggestion. Sandron has been serving the men and women of the Citadel for 10 years now. He's a cornerstone of this place. The members of the Guild love him and he treats everyone like family."

Korin gestured toward one of the stone tables in the middle of the courtyard. That was not ideal for Elisa. She wanted to cultivate the romantic aspect of the date and persuade Korin to continue talking about Drayel and the Citadel. It turned out that she did not need to coerce the man to talk about his friend. Once they were seated he began talking non-stop.

Whether he was simply nervous, or he just liked to talk, he began regaling her with his story and how he'd met Drayel Shadow Walker.

"My father sent me to join the King's army when I was only 12 years old as a page to the King's knights. It did not take me long to realize that Mannock's knights were subpar fighters, and subpar humans. I had to ride along with the supply wagons whenever there was a battle so that I could tend to their wounds. I watched them kill women and children at will. Then they would simply laugh and say, it's war. People die. That, I could not stand. So, I fled Tor'Amal and joined up with various mercenary groups over the years. One benefit of all this was I learned the fighting techniques and swordsmanship skills of several different countries as the mercenaries took in vagabonds from places I'd never even heard of. Not to brag about myself, but swordsmanship came naturally to me. I'd handled blades from the time I could walk, helping my father in his shop. As my skill progressed I began to gain a certain notoriety in Ka'len. It was then that Orious reached out to my father and offered to buy me outright." He said with a forced grin.

"Buy you?" Elisa said incredulously. "Slavery has been outlawed in Ka'len since before Mannock. How could he buy you?"

"Well, as much as we try to avoid the practice, in our world the buying and selling of fighters is quite common. And it's not so much that you're buying the person, but purchasing their skill set and loyalty. In my case I agreed quickly. I had not yet reached my 18th birthday and my father's shop was not doing well. For all of his effort my father's blades were mediocre at best. The king's men bought them from time to time, but truth be told, my father was close to losing his shop." Korin closed his eyes briefly as he thought back on the past memories.

"So, when Orious approached my father and I, it was not a hard choice for me to make. I would join the Guild and serve Orious for a period of 10 years. In return he gave my father enough gold and silver to keep his shop open for the same time period. I would continue living as I had been, fighting and training, my father would keep his shop, and all would be right in the world." Korin said matter-of-factly.

Elisa nodded and took another bite of her fish. A servant had brought their plates and drinks out to the table shortly after they'd sat down. She'd seen Bell across the courtyard and waved at the girl. She was almost certain Bell had looked at her, but the girl did not acknowledge seeing her and did not wave back. Elisa assumed she hadn't seen her.

"So, here I am, seventeen years old, and on my way here to the Citadel. Orious had left days ahead of me and allowed me to take some time to pack my things and say goodbye to my father. I'd been on the road for a full day when I stopped at a small tavern to get a room for the night. You may have seen the place on the way here. A small place with two stories, a pair of swinging doors, and a metal rooster on the roof that spins with the wind?" He asked.

She nodded. The place was now run down and had several unseemly looking men sitting on the porch when she'd rode by. She'd been tired but had no desire to stop in such a place by herself. She'd camped by a creek bed a short way down the road from the tavern. She'd felt safer hearing the wolves howling in the distance than she would have with those characters outside of her door.

"So, I went inside and sat down to order a pint and some food when I heard a commotion behind me. Some of the men there were king's guards, as well as a few knights. They recognized me as a deserter from the king's army. The largest one, a knight I had paged for named Elard, was the first one to approach me."

Korin paused and took a drink of cool water from one of the mugs the servants had brought out with their food. He sat the mug down and continued.

"I'd made the mistake of picking a table that butted up against the exterior wall of the tavern. And I'd worsened my position by placing my back to the room. I had been hoping to get to the Citadel without being recognized by anyone, much less the king's men." He said with a sigh.

"So, there I am, king's knights behind me, and at both ends of the table, with their swords already in hand. There were four more king's guards standing behind them in a loose circle, also with swords in hand. I was in trouble and I knew it. I was sitting there, cursing myself for a fool for putting myself in such a vulnerable location, when I hear this arrogant sounding kid two tables over tell the knights that they should go outside and practice falling down. That as soon as he finished his meal, he'd come outside and join them." Korin smiled at the memory.

"So, of course the knights tell the king's guards to keep an eye on me while they deal with the upstart. They would soon regret that decision. Drayel Shadow Walker had passed his 18th year several months prior. His power had came along quickly, as had his mastery of it. His master had died during Drayel's training after exerting himself too much. The Warlock had been old when Drayel had found him years before. Warlocks, unlike witches, humans, and other beings, can feel their power growing years before their 18th birthday. Drayel had came from a village in the west of Ka'len and was from a long line of moderately powerful Warlocks. So, when he felt the power building in his 15th year of life he'd sought out the Old One. At that time the Old One's name had been lost to time, but he was the most powerful Warlock in Ka'len. He took an immediate liking to Drayel and could sense the power lurking beneath the young Warlocks skin. So, he trained him in basic spells, potions, archaic writings, glyphs, everything that he could use before his power came in. As well as how to focus his power using thoughts and will once it began. During one such training session the Old One succumbed to time, as all things do." Korin paused for a minute as if trying to figure out how to continue.

"It was shortly after the Old One's death that Drayel's eighteenth birthday passed and he came into his power. He'd lived in the mountains at the Old Ones cabin. He stayed there for months practicing the control measures that the Old One had written for him in his Grimoire, and had passed on to Drayel upon his death bed. Drayel had been a natural. He'd gained control over the massive power at his disposal quickly and easily."

Korin took another drink of water and found his mug was empty. He wondered if it might be getting close to time to start walking toward Sandron's. Not yet he decided.

"Drayel had decided that he'd gained enough control to move on from the mountain. So, the last night there he'd packed his things and prepared to leave the next morning. He didn't know where he was going, he just did not want to continue living alone on the mountain. So, he lay down that night to sleep when he was suddenly pulled from his rest by a feeling of yearning. He climbed out of his bed and found a white light glowing brightly behind a book shelf built into the wall. The Old One had never mentioned anything being behind the shelf. But there was definitely SOMETHING there. Drayel had looked for the release to open the bookshelf but could not find it. But whatever was back there was pulling him to it. Drayel had summoned his power and destroyed the book case. When it was gone it revealed a huge cave entrance where the cabin met the mountain. The cave was so brightly illuminated Drayel had to shield his eyes to even enter it. Once he did he let whatever was pulling him guide him through the cave. It opened into a large cavern. The floor of the cavern was a huge emerald that had been flattened and smoothed to walk upon. It stretched the length and width of the cavern. The walls were made up of diamonds of various shapes and sizes. And hanging from the ceiling, like a giant stalactite, was a chandelier made entirely of jade. But that wasn't what caught his eye. In the middle of the floor on a pedestal made of gold, silver, jade, and emeralds, was a medallion. It lay there on top of the pedestal waiting for him to pick it up. It was from this medallion that the white light illuminated. Drayel had been shocked to realize that he'd found, or been led to, the God's Eye Medallion." Korin finished with exuberance.

Elisa could tell that he enjoyed telling his friend's story. And she was enjoying hearing it. A cave full of diamonds and other precious stones, left unguarded in the mountains? Mannock would love to know about that little detail.

"Lady Elisa, I find my cup is empty. If you're finished with your meal, perhaps we can continue the story on the way to Sandron's for something a little stronger?" He asked hopefully.

Elisa smiled and rose from her bench. She looked up at the sky and found it was completely black now. The night time stars glistened like diamonds in the sky. She'd become engrossed in his story and time had passed quickly.

Korin stood and again offered his arm. She took it and they began walking slowly toward Sandron's together.

"So, where was I?" He asked quizzically. "Oh yes, the medallion. So, young Drayel remembered the lore of the medallion and how it sought out the most powerful magic user alive to wield it. He'd known he was powerful, but he soon found that he could not maintain a constant flow of magic through the medallion. He could use it in short burst, but the medallion had been designed for a God with limitless power of his own. Drayel, while powerful, was not inexhaustible." He said. Elisa stored that tidbit of information in the back of her mind.

"So, after another month on the mountain mastering his ability to channel power through the God's Eye, he set out on his own again. He had traveled awhile and was leaving Tor'Amal to visit Port Ka'len when he stopped in a crappy little two story tavern to have a pint and rest for the night. He'd been watching to the King's guards and knights harass the serving girls there. And he'd heard their bragging about their less than glorious adventures in this skirmish or that one. They'd bragged about killing wizened men and women, children, and having their way with the women in the village. Then a lanky teenager with a long sword strapped across his back had walked in. Drayel heard Elard angrily whispering to his cohorts. He'd been following my exploits since leaving the King's service. And now he meant for him and his cronies to murder me where I sat." Korin recounted.

That didn't sound right to Elisa. She'd met Elard and he'd always seemed nice enough. A little coarse, but she had attributed that to his being a knight. Although she had been told he had fallen in battle, no one could ever tell her when and where this battle had occurred.

"Knights from every land have a code of honor that prevents them from taking the cowards way in a fight. Ambushes and assassinations are seen as less than honorable, and are grounds for the loss of knighthood. If a knight has cause to fight someone then that person should be afforded the opportunity to defend himself. Stabbing a man in the back shows no courage and is the epitome of cowardice in the eyes of a warrior." Korin said with more than a little vitriol in his voice.

They arrived at Sandron's and acquired a mug of cold meade for Korin and a glass of red wine for Elisa. They walked together to one of the private alcoves under the walkway and sat in the glow of the fairy light as Korin resumed his tale.

"Drayel was not a warrior in the sense that he'd spent years on the battle field, but his parents had raised him with honor, and the Old One had instilled a sense of duty in the young Warlock. He knew he could not allow these men to simply murder me where I sat. So, he intervened." Korin said with a grin.

"So, I'm sitting there looking at this dark haired boy, roughly about my own age, who is about to fight three of the King's knights empty handed. I thought the boy was a fool or suicidal. But I wasn't going to let the opportunity to engage the Guards by themselves pass by. Guards aren't knights. They are poorly trained, even more so than Mannock's knights, and four on one shifted the odds heavily to my favor in my opinion. If the kid, Drayel, ran and survived long enough, I would go back and help him. I need not have worried about that. Before I could turn from my stool and draw my sword the three knights were thrown across the room and out of the tavern's door by this burst of green and white light. I look back at the kid and he's just covered, head to toe, in this shield of white and green light. The four guards looked at each other before they went to rush him all together. I didn't know if they would be able to take him, but I knew I wasn't sitting out of a fight either. So, I tripped the one closest to me as he ran by, sending him sprawling face first into the table in front of him. I spun as I rose and drew my sword just in time to catch the sword of the next guard, leaving two for Drayel. I defeated the guard quickly and looked over to see the other two guards already on their knees and being choked with that green light." Korin hesitated before continuing.

"Lady Elisa, you have to understand, Mannock's armies had

marched through Drayel's village when he was a child. He witnessed the atrocities that those men committed. And now he'd just sat and listened to them talking about raping and murdering innocent people. They'd harassed the waitresses. And they'd attempted to murder a kid with his back turned to them. I didn't know that at the time, but it shocked me when he twisted his hand and their necks snapped." Korin said solemnly.

"It was at that point that Drayel and I heard Elard screaming for me to come out and face him. I assumed that when he said face him, that he really meant face him and the two knights with him. But at that point I did not care that there were three of them. I just wanted Elard." He said.

Elisa could hear the anger in his voice as he recounted the events of that day.

"I walked outside and found that the two knights with him had retrieved crossbows from their mounts and were aiming at me the moment I stepped outside. The man had absolutely no honor to speak of, and still intended to simply assassinate me instead of facing me in combat. I was certain that I was about to take at least one of those bolts before I could get to cover and re-engage when they fired. However, the bolts, suddenly glowing green and white, turned around in the air and slammed into the knights hard enough to knock them back into their mounts. They received several stomps from the frightened animals before they came to rest. Drayel walked the rest of the way outside and told Elard that if he wished me dead, he would have to be man enough to do it himself. Elard had fumed and raged, but more from fear than outrage. I drew my sword and met him halfway across the yard. The battle was over quickly, and when it was done Elard lay dead at my feet." Korin smiled bitterly as he finished his story.

Elisa sat quietly, sipping her wine, and thinking about his story. Could that really have been how Elard died? If so, how much more of Korin's story was true? Was Mannock really that cruel, or was it just his armies? She had much to think about. But for now, she'd listen.

"At that point we looked up and saw a patrol from the King's army coming down the road toward the tavern. Drayel did not wish to engage them there. It was a poor battle ground to fight an entire patrol from. So, we both saddled up and rode away. We began talking along the way. He asked where I was headed and I gladly told him. He decided along the way that he would join the Guild when we arrived and stay there until he decided what his future held." Korin took a long pull from his mug of meade and sat it back down on the table with a clunk.

Elisa sipped her wine. It was a very good vintage, and potent. She felt her head starting to swim from the drink. She would have to pace herself.

"In the end there's really not that much more to tell. In the Guild strength and power are valued above all else. Orious was under the King's boot heel and was no fan of battle. The Guild has to continue to grow, to amass strength, lands, and wealth. That's our one goal in this life. And Orious bowed before the king and refused to engage with the other Lords of Ka'len. Worse, Mannock feared our Warriors being hired out as mercenaries to fight in other country's wars. He did not like our Warriors getting that type of experience on the battle field. Orious was holding the Guild stagnant. We were running low on funds and the men grew restless. So, when the time came, to prevent open rebellion and the self-destruction of the Guild, Drayel called for a vote for a change of Guild Master. Surprisingly it was an even vote. So, following our laws, Drayel called Orious out to battle for the position. It was a quick affair. Orious conceded the fight before it could begin and fled Ka'len. It was shortly after that Drayel declared that he would rule all of Ka'len, or none of it. And so, the war began." He said almost happily.

"Korin, you say that as if it is a good thing. I do not mean to offend you, or Drayel, but why did the war have to begin? Why does Drayel have to have the King's throne? If the Guild hates the king so much, what makes them any better? Are you not killing men in Drayel's name the same as the men in Mannock armies? Since Drayel does not bow to the king, could you not just continue on as you have in the past? Hiring the Warriors out to foreign lands as mercenaries? Charging Lord's to train their personal guards?" She asked tentatively. She thought she might anger Korin with this line of questioning. But no, Korin's expression showed no sign of anger, merely stoicism.

"Lady Elisa, I understand your point of view. But the answer is no. We're not the same and we can not simply continue on as we did before." Korin answered.

He took another long pull from his mug and frowned at the empty container when he sat it down on the table again.

"I know that you say Mannock has calmed over the years, but it's still true that he keeps men and women imprisoned under his castle for having the ability to manipulate magic. And I know you lived in fear of being discovered. I saw your impulsive glance back at the fireball you contained in the water pitcher. Impressive by the way." He said with a grin.

Elisa opened her mouth to argue and deny his claim about her use of magic when she saw him staring at her with a look that dared her to rebuff his claim. She thought about how quick she'd been to deny her use of magic. And how she'd wait until she'd almost froze in her room before she ignited the cold, wet, wood that the staff always put in the "guest" rooms. Had it not been for her fire summoning skill she would have long since frozen in that tiny little room. But she always waited until the moon was at its highest point for fear that someone would see the glow from her window and inquire where she had gotten the instruments to start a fire, and where they were now. Maybe Korin had a point about the King's fear of magic users.

"I thought so." He said. "But have no fear. While you are here, feel free to practice your magic and hone your skills, whatever they may be."

"That would be refreshing. I haven't had a chance to use my....abilities... freely since I was a child. To be perfectly honest, I'm not even sure what all I am capable of conjuring. I was sent to Mannock at an early age. I'd only learned two, we call them crafts, not skills, before I was sent away." She said solemnly.

She did not have to add moroseness to her voice. She truly regretted being sent away from her mother and coven mates before she'd learned all of her abilities.

"But I digress, Lady. I will save many hours of discussion and simply say the king must fall for his misdeeds. He prohibits magic and cages its practitioners. Drayel would return the freedom to practice it. He took away the Cor Sanctus' lands and forced them to leave them. Whenever the Guild conquers another Lord's territory they are allowed to stay on the land and pay a small tax to the Guild. And to be fair we only attack the Lords that are rumored to be cruel to their serfs. He does not keep his armies in check. Drayel does not allow the rape of women, nor the murder of the wizened or children. The king allows the ransacking of Ka'len for his own personal gain. He allows the people of Ka'len to starve in the streets while he spends wagons of gold building onto his castle. Drayel would see all taxes annulled except for the minimum to maintain roads, security, and water. Everything else would be left to the people. So, you see Lady, Drayel is not a monster. He isn't heartless and unnecessarily cruel. He just wants a better Ka'len and doesn't see a way to make that happen with Mannock on the throne." Korin took a deep breath before continuing.

"However, I will say the stories that you've heard about Drayel in battle are all true. The man does love to fight. He's second only to me with a sword, and his magic is unmatched in Ka'len. He will not back down from a fight and actively seeks his next one."

Korin picked up his empty mug and tried to take another drink. Korin cursed colorfully before he realized he was still in the company of a lady.

"Apologies Lady Elisa. I forget myself. Would you care for a second glass?" He inquired. He gestured to her empty flute. Elisa realized with chagrin that she had drained the tall long-stemmed flute long ago. She nodded yes.

"And a glass of water as well please Korin." She said.

She watched Korin walk back over to the bar and shoulder through the crowd good-naturedly. The men starting to say something rude to their assailant until they saw their grinning weapons master looking back at them.

Everyone liked Korin. And so did she. Despite herself, she decided that she enjoyed the company of the muscled Warrior. He was an interesting story teller and had an easy way about him that made it relaxing to talk to and listen to him.

He returned a short time later with their fresh drinks. Elisa took both of hers gratefully. She had taken advantage of the time he was gone to determine her next line of approach. Korin did not see that Drayel was only slightly better than the king in his methods. And that the only way forward was to get Drayel to call off his attack on the king and seek peace. It was the only way to save innocent lives and bring Ka'len out of this war. She knew that even after Drayel won the day, and he would win, that those loyal to Mannock would continue to skirmish, burn crops, and reek general devastation throughout the land for years afterwards. No, it must be stopped now she decided.

"Korin, has Drayel discussed the terms that the king had me present to him on my first day here?" She asked purposefully.

"No Lady, Drayel dismissed the king's offer out of hand. And had it been the messenger that came to our gates last time, he would have sent his head home tied to his mounts saddle. He really did not like that wormy little man." Korin chuckled.

Elisa realized that Korin was starting to feel the effects of the strong meade. That was good. It meant he might be more amenable to listening to her. She started again.

"Mannock offered to return the Omni plains to my people, give him a lordship over half of Ka'len, and grant him a seat on his council. He feels that if he is doing such a terrible job ruling this country, then maybe Drayel's educated insight could help steer him in a direction that is best for everyone involved. Drayel dismissed it out of hand. It's true, the Guild will take Tor'Amal when the snow melts and the pass clears. That much is certain. But to what end Korin? The people of Tor'Amal have lived under Mannock's rule for over fifty years now. And his son,

Prince Alasander, has been preparing to take over his father's throne for years now. There is a line of succession to the throne, and the people of Tor'Amal will not just sit idly by and let Drayel come in and change their entire way of life in one fell swoop." She said passionately.

"You have to understand, these people have been raised and taught that magic, and magic users are evil. And that paying tax to the king is honoring their debt to the Gods. They have been told this their entire lives. So yes, Drayel will seize the castle. And yes, he will attempt to implement all of his grand ideas. But the people of Ka'len will see him as little more than a usurper that used his power to take the throne. Why not take the King's offer? Take the seat on the council and slowly implement the changes that Drayel desires?"

She asked honestly. She had seen Korin open his mouth to argue with her halfway through her comment, but in the end he had sat silently, sipping his meade, and considered what she was saying.

"Drayel could simply enforce his will. Once he sits upon the throne there would be no-one that could remove him." Korin said quietly.

"That is true, Korin. But the people would resist for a long time. Citizens of Ka'len would die for years skirmishing with Guild Warriors. And the common mortals would seek out and kill every magic user they could find for fear of them gaining power and lording it over them. Humans are easily frightened animals, and when they feel cornered they will attack." She let the last word hang in the air ominously before she continued.

"But, if Drayel takes the king's offer. If he slowly starts introducing magic back into the country, maybe using healers at first, he could change the people's opinions on magic over time. The king has offered to give back my people's lands. Once we are together again we would be more than happy to send emissaries across the land to show the power of our healers, and that there is nothing to fear from us. And taxes, the king has sat on the throne with nothing but yes men surrounding him for decades. It would do him good to have Drayel there to correct his misguided ideas on taxes and other policies. Don't you think Korin?" She asked hopefully.

If she could get Korin on her side, then perhaps the two of them could persuade Drayel to take the king's offer and start a new and better era in Ka'len.

But it all hung on what Korin decided to do.

"Lady Elisa, I believe it is time for me to escort you back to your room. Sandron's meade is his own brew and particularly stout. I don't believe that I am in a decent state to think about such things. I will wait until tomorrow to give you my decision on whether or not I wish to help you change Drayel's mind, or have you put in the dungeons." He said sincerely.

Elisa attempted to laugh off his last comment, but there was no humor in Korin's eyes as he stood to go. He offered her a hand when she attempted to stand up from her chair, but he did not offer her his arm as he had on the way to dinner. And he did not speak to her until they reached her room. He had simply watched her walk inside, said good night, and disappeared down the hall.

# CHAPTER 15



**D**RAYEL WOKE LATER THAN USUAL. HE HAD JOINED THE MEN AT Sandron's before dinner last night. He had been having a wonderful time with the men when she had walked in. He was on his second mug of meade when Elisa had walked in on Korin's arm. She had looked stunning in the clothes that he had procured for her use.

He hadn't told her that he was responsible for the bathtub or armoire that now adorned her room. Or that he had enchanted the water to keep it hot and clean. It was obvious that she had put both the tub and the clothes to good use. Drayel caught himself, along with several Guild Warriors, watching her walk toward the table she would share with Korin. He shook his head and took another long pull from his mug.

Why was he so infatuated by her? She was gorgeous, yes, but she was also a servant of the coward king. Although she did seem to hold some resentment toward him. So, maybe there was hope that she would join him and put her healing powers to use.

He felt like he could use her powers right now. Gods. He'd lost count of the mugs he had drained with the men last night. It seemed that every time he saw her smile at Korin he had ordered a fresh drink.

And the headache that he had pounding behind his eyes was proof that he'd taken it a bit too far.

He rolled out of the comfortable king size bed that graced his chambers and stumbled to his feet. He crossed the room and set down heavily in the high back chair in front of his desk. He opened the drawer in front of him and took out a few small pieces of the white-wood tree bark that he so often used for pain relief. He reached for the small glass that he kept on the desk for just this reason and grimaced as he focused hard enough to fill it with water.

He popped a few pieces of the dry, bitter, wood into his mouth and chewed it into a paste before swallowing it with the cool water he had summoned.

He lay back into the chair and closed his eyes while he waited for the medicine to take effect.

He must have dosed off again because he was startled awake by a banging on his chamber door.

"Enter." He shouted.

He was relieved when his head didn't respond to his shout with a throbbing cadence behind his eyes.

The door opened and Korin Silver Steel walked in. He was adorned in his fighting gear from the training sessions that he held every morning. Drayel looked out the window to see the sun high in the air. They must have halted training for the noon meal. Korin bent slightly at the waist and declined his head in Drayel's direction. As close to a bow as Korin would ever offer any man.

Drayel nodded back and stood slowly, still testing his level of fitness after his medicine and nap. He felt better, but would not be drinking tonight.

"How goes the training today, weapons master?" Drayel asked his friend. Korin smiled before he replied.

"The men are doing well. They are proficient in the battle drills and are sparring like true Warrior's should. The Lady Elisa, however, is so sore that she was most unwilling to engage in anything overly strenuous this morning." He said with a laugh.

Drayel did not laugh. He walked over to Korin and stared at his weapons master. The look said everything.

"Well, maybe when I return, I should impart the importance of today's training and her improved skill with the blade." Korin said almost sheepishly.

He realized that allowing Elisa to rest and not engage fully in the training would not help her become the best she could be, but he also did not consider her a Warrior of the Guild. He hadn't forgotten their conversation the night before and was still mulling it over.

And, if he was honest, he wasn't sure he wanted to invest much effort into someone that might soon be a guest of Drayel's dungeon.

"No, I'll go." Drayel said stoically.

Korin was surprised to hear that Drayel was volunteering to go the training circle. It was normally akin to pulling teeth to get the Warlock to venture into the rings.

And now he was volunteering to go just to help motivate a slacking student? Korin felt there was more to this story. He looked down at his feet to give himself a second to determine the best way to question the Warlock. When he looked up Drayel was gone.

"Gods. I hate it when he disappears like that." Korin said with feigned disgust.

He turned around and walked back toward the training circle, fully confident that Drayel's "conversation" with the Lady would be over long before he arrived back at the circles. Ah well, might as well swing by the kitchens and grab some lunch on the way, he thought. So, instead of making a left toward the arena, he went right toward the kitchen and the smell of frying meat.

# CHAPTER 16

TRAINING

**D**RAYEL REAPPEARED IN THE COURTYARD JUST BEYOND THE CURVED archway that served as the entrance to the training arena. He found Elisa sitting on the same wine cask that she'd chosen for her perch during her first visit here.

She was finishing eating a small portion of baked chicken, steamed vegetables, and a small platter of cookies that the staff had brought out to the Warriors and Elisa for their lunch.

Elisa saw Drayel walking toward her and smiled. A smile which faded away when she saw the angry glower on his face. He was not happy about something, and she was not at all sure she wanted to know what had placed the Warlock in such a foul mood.

He stopped about ten feet from her and placed his hands on his hips with his feet spread apart approximately shoulder width. He looked every bit the angry Lord about to address his subjects she thought.

"Elisa, Korin tells me that you are too sore to participate in the days training. Is that correct?" He asked in a sickly sweet manner.

Elisa looked at the thin sabre that she had haphazardly leaned against the wall next to the wine cask she now sat on. Truth be told she was not sore at all. She'd healed all of her injuries in the bath the night before. She simply did not wish to exert herself to the point that she could not get into the copper tub by herself again. So, she'd been holding back and not fully participating in the training believing that she would simply get stronger as the days went by.

"No, Drayel, I may have exaggerated my soreness slightly. But I see no need for me to go all out again until the point of exhaustion. I was so tired yesterday I had to be aided into the bath in my room. I would prefer to get stronger gradually so that I do not injure myself in the process. You understand I'm sure." She said matter-of-factly.

Drayel nodded and smiled. It did not meet his eyes. With a movement quick as a viper he drew his rapier like sword, dull on the edges but sharp as a razor on the tip, and slapped it against her plate, scattering the remainder of her meal and sending her rolling off of the barrel. She attempted to dodge to his left and he lunged with that razor sharp tip leading the way to bury into the wooden beam right beside her face. She fell back onto her rear and found she was sitting next to her sabre.

"Always go for your sword first." He counseled. "You can't protect yourself if you're not armed. Sword first. Always."

He waited all of a second before re engaging her. Elisa had been climbing slowly to her feet while listening to the seething Warlock. She was not moving fast enough for Drayel. He sent a wide arching swing toward her exposed backside which she was barely able to block with her own sword.

Now standing and facing off with an angry Drayel she managed to pull her sword up in front of her into a ready position.

Seeing that she was now prepared Drayel launched into his attack.

He lunged and jabbed straight for her midsection with that razor sharp tip. Elisa saw it coming. Korin had showed her how to watch an adversary's shoulders and eyes allowing her to anticipate the move.

She stepped semi gracefully to the left while dipping her sword and knocking his rapier out wide. Drayel nodded and retracted his sword. This went on for almost a quarter of an hour. Drayel making simple one step attacks and Elisa blocking or moving out of the way. He started out fairly slowly, giving her time to reset after each attack. Drayel gradually increased the tempo until Elisa was having to block, feint, and move constantly. At the end of the hour Elisa was sweating profusely, her formerly clean hair now hung lifelessly down behind her shoulders. She was nicked, bruised, and bleeding from several spots on her body, and her breath came in gasp.

Drayel on the other hand had barely broken a sweat and appeared to have started enjoying the training. His smile faded when Elisa dropped her sword point toward the ground and went down to one knee with her hand held in front of her asking for a break.

Drayel leapt forward and slashed straight down. Elisa grinned and rolled her wrist bringing her forearm and sword up into a familiar looking high block, surprising Drayel and catching his rushed cut with the guard of her sword before deflecting it off.

Keeping her momentum going Elisa swung her left leg around in a half circle to build up power before driving her elbow into the stunned Warlocks stomach.

It was the move that Korin had been drilling her on all morning. She hadn't been very interested in it during the training, but it came almost naturally to her now. She stood and paused to enjoy the look on the Warlocks face. She shouldn't have.

Before she realized what had happened Drayel had knocked her sabre wide and had that deadly point at her throat.

"Don't gloat. Never assume the battle is over. ALWAYS finish your opponent before you stop." Drayel realized he was barking orders at her.

He looked at her face and saw the hurt there. She was not one of his Warriors. She was not bred for battle and this was all new to her. He realized that she had expected praise from him for the well executed move. Instead he was berating her like a common Soldier. His tone softened slightly.

"Elisa, you must take this training seriously. It could save your life. The soreness, the small injuries, the heat, the cold, sweat, and blood are all part of it. You've sparred with me for much less than an hour and you are completely exhausted. Your last move, as well executed as it was, seemed to be the last move you were capable of making. I, on the other hand, have barely begun to sweat." He said matter-of-factly.

He'd stepped closer to her as he spoke and he was now very close to her. He could feel the heat radiating off of her body and feel her breath on his neck. Elisa herself was suddenly very aware of the Warlocks presence. She found herself looking up into his glowing green eyes and found herself quickly lost in them.

At that moment Korin walked through the archway into the courtyard with a mug of water in one hand and an apple in the other. He grinned when he saw the compromising position his friend had been caught in.

Korin politely cleared his throat and grinned devilishly at his old friend.

Drayel snapped his head toward the weapons master and gave him a searing look. Korin barked a short laugh and raised his hands in front of him in surrender. Korin walked toward the other side of the arena to check on some of the other fighters, leaving Drayel and Elisa to finish whatever it was that he had interrupted.

Drayel's mind whirled. What had just happened? He had transported himself here to berate Elisa for not taking part in the training. He planned on forcing her to fight until she could no longer stand. But why? Why did it matter to him that she was able to protect herself? Was she not just a pawn of the king? The realization slammed into Drayel like her elbow had earlier.

She was not just a pawn. He was shocked to realize that he was beginning to like and care for this woman. It was not wise. It was not an intelligent move.

He did not care.

Drayel looked up from his contemplation and found Elisa still staring at him wide eyed and mouth slightly opened. She looked so innocent in that moment that Drayel felt the pull toward her clearly. When he spoke next it was in a softer voice than he had used in years. The voice was his. Drayel. Not the leader of the Guild, not the all powerful Warlock, the arrogant lord, just Drayel.

"Elisa, this training is important. Not because I need to control your movements around the castle. But, because I need you to be safe." He paused and watched her for her reaction. He could see the confusion there in her eyes.

"In the coming days, when the snow is gone and the pass is cleared, we will go into battle. Whether with you at my side, or not, I need to know that you will be safe. I will train you to use your magic to its fullest, while Korin trains you in physical combat. But please, train. Learn what you need to defend yourself from whatever threat you face."

He stopped and watched her for a moment before spinning on his heel and walking away from her. He did not see her raise her hand to stop him or the words forming on her lips as he strolled quickly back into the castle.

# CHAPTER 17

## NEW BEGINNINGS

ELISA HAD STOOD THERE SHOCKED AT DRAYEL'S PROCLAMATION. Had he truly meant that he wanted her by his side? Or did he simply mean that he wanted her skills as a healer?

Was she crazy to believe that he had just almost openly admitted that he had feelings for her? And as far as that went, what was SHE thinking?

When he had been standing in front of her, she'd lost herself in his eyes as if he had cast a spell on her. And Isolde, the way her body had responded to his closeness. The heat from his body, his smell, everything about him called out to her. She had wanted to reach out and touch him. His face, his hair, anything.

Korin's untimely arrival had been the only thing that interfered with that. Wait, interfered or saved her from making a mistake? What was happening here? She pushed the emotions and thoughts down for the moment when Korin called them all back to the training circles.

Drayel had asked her to train. Not commanded, but practically begged her to train and learn to protect herself. She decided she would.

The next few hours flew by. She found herself pushing harder than she had the day before. She asked questions and paid rapt attention to everything the weapons master showed them. And at the end of the day she was even more depleted than she had been the previous day.

Korin walked her back to her room. He made small talk but thankfully stayed away from the subject of the awkward position he had found her and Drayel in.

To his credit, the big man did not seem to be jealous of her and Drayel's interaction. On the contrary he seemed pleased that his friend was finally opening up to someone. Although they did not discuss it, his demeanor, his jovial attitude, and his wide smile told Elisa that all was well between the three of them.

When they arrived at her room Korin opened her door for her and kissed the back of her hand.

"Elisa, if I may, I know that it might be too early to discuss this, and that there may be nothing to discuss, but know this. In all of the years I've known him, Drayel has never opened himself up to anyone like he did with you this afternoon. I do not know what, if anything, you feel toward Drayel. But it is very clear to me that for the first time in a decade Drayel has found something that he cares about besides power and strength. He genuinely seems to care about your welfare Lady. And as much as I enjoy your company, I will not stand in the way of my friend's happiness. BOTH of their happiness." He said with a smile.

She had been keeping a very serious look on her face to keep any unwanted emotions from being displayed. She did not yet know what she did or did not feel for Drayel, but she was wary of making any facial expressions that could be misconstrued. But she heard Korin's proclamation that she was a friend.

With that she had smiled and threw her arms around the big man's neck. Squeezing him tightly in a fierce hug.

He returned her hug and then held her back at arms length smiling.

"But friend or no friend Elisa, I will be working you as hard or harder than my Warriors. My lord wishes you safe and well trained, so it shall be. You will be sore, tired, and cursing my name on a daily basis.

But by the time the snow clears and you are free to leave this place, you will be more than a match for any bandit or Soldier you meet along the way. I will see to it." He said jovially.

"I look forward to it, my friend." Elisa said with a genuine smile.

"On a slightly more serious note, Elisa, I can not help you to dissuade Drayel from taking the throne for himself. Your arguments have merit, and I find truth in your words. But Drayel is my friend and the closest thing I've ever had to a brother. I trust his judgment and would follow him into hell itself if he said it was a good idea. So, that being said, I will not ask you to turn aside from your path, but just know that I can not counsel him to turn from his either." He said with a somber look on his face.

Elisa knew that the big man had given it serious thought and that he had not come to his decision lightly. But the fact that he still considered her a friend was enough. She could use all the friends she could get in this place.

She nodded her acceptance and smiled.

"So, friend, dinner again in the courtyard tonight?" She asked with a grin. She was pleased when Korin's face lit up in a bright smile.

"I wouldn't miss it for the world Lady. Until then." He bowed his little half bow and almost skipped down the hall. Elisa heart jumped at seeing Korin so pleased.

She walked back into her room and began undressing. She remembered the candles she needed from the night before, so she pulled the rope by the door before stepping into the gloriously hot water of the bath.

She was ecstatic to find that she was able to do so without much agony this time. She was just starting to nod off to sleep when a sharp rapping knock sounded on her door. She called out to the person to enter and smiled when Bell walked in. Although the smile faded when she saw the perturbed look on her face.

"What can I get you my Lady?" Bell asked flatly.

Elisa knew that she had asked Bell to call her by her name and dispense with the formal titles. She wondered if she had done something to offend the girl or if she was just having a bad day.

"Bell, you told me the last time that you were here that I should pull the cord by the door if I needed anything. Would it be possible to have some candles brought in? It gets quite dark in here in the afternoons and they would be greatly appreciated." Elisa said politely.

Bell spun on her hell and stomped back toward the door.

"Of course MY LADY. Why shouldn't you have EVERYTHING you want?" She said angrily. She was reaching back to close the door that she had left open when Elisa snapped back at her.

"Have I wronged you? What did I do, or say, to deserve this vile attitude? When you left the previous evening I thought we might have become friends some day. Now you are being rude and condescending and I truly have no idea why!" She said with exasperation.

Bell spun back toward her and slammed the door in the process. Elisa was surprised to see tears in the young girl's eyes. Bell's breath hitched at she fought the tears that threatened to stream down her young face.

"Lord Silver Steel! I had hoped to catch his eye and win his affections upon my eighteenth birthday! But he doesn't even know I exist, and would not be able to be with me until I join the ranks of the Warriors! And now I will never win him because he is in love with you!" She half screamed through her sobs.

Bell was shaking as she cried and made her way to the stool by the desk. She sat down and let the tears run freely. She couldn't bear to look at Elisa and have the woman see her crying like a child.

Elisa took a moment to process what Bell had blurted out in her fit of anger. Elisa smiled gently and pushed herself up and out of the tub. She grabbed the soft robe that she'd worn the previous night, it had been cleaned and returned to her room along with her shoes, and slipped it on.

She crossed the floor and stood in front of Bell for a moment, waiting on the girl to realize she was there. Elisa lowered herself down on both knees, thankful for the cushion the robe provided.

When she was settled she looked into Bell's eyes and saw the anger and frustration there.

"Bell, I fear you may have gotten the wrong idea about my, relationship, with Lord Silver Steel. Korin, if you will." She paused to make sure Bell was listening.

The girl had raised her head slightly and was looking at Elisa curiously. Most of the anger starting to fade from her countenance.

"It is true that Korin initially may have had romantic designs in my regard...." She started.

Bell's sharp intake of breath told Elisa that she was preparing to respond with an angry retort. Elisa held up her hand in a wait gesture. Bell, to her credit, held her tongue.

"He may have HAD romantic designs in my regard, but we decided tonight that we are nothing more than friends. Something, unexpected, has come up that necessitates our only being friends." She said with a wry smile.

She could tell now that she had Bell's full attention. The girl had stopped crying now and was sorting through Elisa's words.

"So, if not Lord Silver Steel, Korin, then who Lady.....sorry, Elisa?" She asked.

Elisa rose from her kneeling position and walked back over to her bed. She flopped back onto it and propped herself up on her pillows so that she could both lay down and see Bell.

Elisa wasn't sure how much she should tell the girl. She knew how the rumor mill worked in castles like this. It would take less than a day for everyone to know that there was something going on between her and Drayel. Drayel. His name sent a small tingle down her spine. How could she tell Bell anything anyway when even she didn't know exactly what was going on between them? She decided to tell her parts of the story, but to leave his name out of it for the time being.

"I'd rather not say yet, as it's still very new and I honestly don't know how it will end up. But please, just know that I have no designs on Korin in that regard, and that I will not stand in your way if you intend to pursue him. But if you do have feelings for him, you should tell him now. I haven't known the man long, but I know he is sweet and kind. And if he has any feelings for you in that regard I am certain he would share them with you freely." She said with a smile.

Bell wiped the remaining tears from her eyes and relaxed her shoulders. Elisa could see the tension starting to ease from the girl.

"Elisa, it is honestly not that simple. He is the Master of Arms for the Guild. He is prohibited from having a relationship with a servant in the castle. That's why I must wait until I turn 18. Then I will be classed as a Warrior and will be allowed to have relationships with other Warriors within the Guild. Namely, Korin." She said sadly.

"So, you can't tell Korin because dating him is forbidden right now?" Elisa asked.

"Yes, exactly. It kills me to see him in the courtyard with the other Warrior women. Though there was something different about the way he behaved with you. And I think that is what angered me the most. He looked at you the way I wish that he would look at me." Bell said emphatically. Elisa could see the tears threatening to flow again from the girls pretty eyes.

"He seemed genuinely interested in you and spoke to you at length. Normally he just drinks and smiles at his dinner partners before walking them back to their rooms. As pathetic as this sounds, I know he has not taken a lover these last ten years. I was so afraid that it would have been different with you. The way he acted around you, and the fact that you are undeniably beautiful, in my mind it was a forgone conclusion that he would fall for you and take you as a lover." Bell said blushing slightly.

Elisa blushed a little as well. She took a moment to process all that Bell had said before speaking again.

"Bell, I am new to the Citadel, and the rules here are different from any that I have ever known. But, I will say this again, if you have designs on Korin, tell him. Let him know that you understand the laws of the

Guild. That you aren't asking him to be with you now, but that upon your eighteenth birthday you thoroughly intend to pursue him. I can guarantee that will get his attention and he will DEFINITELY know that you exist afterwards!" Elisa said enthusiastically.

Bell smiled for the first time since entering Elisa's chamber. She nodded happily and leaned forward to wrap Elisa up in a very unexpected embrace.

Elisa let out a little surprised squeak when the girl's muscled arms wrapped around her neck and squeezed. Years of working in the kitchen and doing manual labor had made her grip strong and her body lithe but powerful. Bell truly would make a wonderful companion for Korin she thought.

"So, now that we have that settled, can we be friends?" Elisa asked hopefully.

"Gods yes!" Bell squealed excitedly. "I would love that Elisa. If you can forgive my behavior earlier?" She asked quietly.

"Of course, Bell. There does not seem to be an abundance of women here so having you as a friend would be wonderful. Who else would I discuss men with?" She laughed.

They hugged again, thankfully less forcefully this time. Elisa looked out the window and saw that the sun was starting to go down.

"Isolde! I forgot the time. Bell, I must get dressed. Korin is coming to take me to dinner again, as friends." She added. "I still need to dress and prepare. Could you possibly bring me some candles while I get dressed?" She asked. Bell nodded and rose to leave.

"And Bell, are you done with your task for the day after this? Or is there more you have yet to do?" Elisa asked inquiringly.

"Yes, this would be the last thing I have to do today. I usually end my day just before dinner." She said with a questioning look on her face.

"Wonderful. Come back quickly, I have an idea." Elisa said with a mischievous grin. Bell returned her smile and left the room almost at a run. She didn't know what Elisa had planned, but she couldn't wait to find out what her new friend had in mind.

# CHAPTER 18

## NEW BONDS

**D**RAYEL HAD PRACTICALLY FLED THE TRAINING COURTYARD AFTER his conversation with Elisa. Gods, he had all but told her that he cared about her.

The realization that he had feelings for her had hit him quickly and unexpectedly. And he had promised to teach her magic. He had just bound himself to her for all eternity, if she accepted.

It was the same law that he had used to punish Tallon earlier. If Elisa accepted his offer to train her then he would be responsible for her training and welfare as long as she lived. And what of Korin? It was obvious his friend was at least smitten with Elisa.

He had seemed okay in the courtyard, but he needed to know his friend's thoughts on the matter. He left his chambers and walked quickly toward Korin's chambers. He knew Korin had made plans to eat dinner with Elisa that evening, so he would be dressing and making preparations for the evening. Before he knew it Drayel was standing at Korin's door. He was about to knock when a booming, jovial, voice sounded from the other side.

"Come on in Drayel." Korin said.

Drayel was relieved to hear no tone of anger or disappointment in his friend's voice.

Drayel opened the door and walked in to find his friend dressed in his best evening wear. Clean shaven and smelling of fresh scented oils, Korin was dressed to impress. Drayel felt his heart drop slightly. Maybe Korin did have feelings for Elisa. If so, Drayel would stand aside and support his friend. But there was only one way to find out.

"Korin, I'm not sure how to approach this because I've never found myself in this situation." Drayel started. Korin grinned widely and held his hand up.

"You want to ask me about Elisa right?" Korin asked. Drayel nodded affirmatively.

"The Lady and I spoke earlier this evening my friend. It would appear that, while uncertain, she does feel something for you." He said with a grin.

He continued when he saw Drayel contemplating his words.

"We've decided to continue our relationship as friends for now to give your, whatever this is, time to grow. It may be nothing, but I've known you for years Drayel, and I think there is something there between you two. That being said, I still intend to thoroughly enjoy her company in the meantime. And if I make a few of the Warrior females jealous by spending time with my beautiful friend, so much the better!" He said happily.

Drayel had listened to Korin's every word. He was listening for half truths or disguised intentions. He could find none.

Korin was honestly happy for them and their budding relationship. And he would not be hurt if it turned into something more. Drayel felt something like joy in his heart for the first time in a decade.

He crossed the room and extended his hand to the big man. Korin took the offered hand and snatched Drayel forward into a massive embrace. Drayel had turned a nice shade of red before Korin turned the Warlock loose.

"So, my Lord, what do you say we go to Lady Elisa's chambers and escort her to dinner together. I believe you two could use some adult supervision on your first date." Korin teased.

Drayel punched Korin's shoulder in a friendly manner before nodding his acceptance.

"That sounds like a great idea my friend. Let us go and see if the Lady would be willing to dine with both of us tonight." Drayel said with a smile.

Meanwhile, on the other side of the castle, Bell had returned quickly with an arm full of candles. She'd watched in wonder as Elisa lit half of them with a wave of her hand, casting the room instantly into light.

She had balked when Elisa guided her to the armoire and told her to pick something to wear. Elisa told her that even though she couldn't date Korin yet, she could certainly make sure she was on his mind. They talked as they dressed. Elisa explained that Korin was coming to get her for dinner but that along the way she was going to remember something she "forgot" in her room, leaving Bell alone with Korin so that the girl could tell Korin how she felt. And if she was going to declare her love for him, she might as well give him something to think about during the two months it would take for her to turn eighteen.

Bell was nervous but excited about the idea. One way or the other, after tonight she would know if she had any chance of being with the Weapons Master. They sorted through shoes, fixed their hair, and put on makeup. In the end they both gushed over the others appearance. They looked amazing and Bell felt confident that Korin would notice her tonight. They were giggling and speaking loudly when a familiar booming knock sounded on her door. Elisa looked at Bell and smiled.

"Here we go girl. Are you ready?" She asked. Bell nodded excitedly. "Okay, here we go." Elisa said.

Elisa strolled across the room and swung the door open wide with a mischievous grin on her face. That quickly disappeared into a look of confusion. Because where she had expected to see the broad shouldered and smiling Korin, there stood Drayel looking slightly uncomfortable. After a brief pause, both of them standing there staring at each other, but neither finding the words to say, Korin came to the rescue shouldering past his stunned companion.

"Forgive Drayel, Lady, he is stunned to silence by your beauty. He hasn't had the pleasure of dining with you and building up at least some tolerance!" He joked.

He hugged Elisa and was about to say something else quick witted when he suddenly forgot how to speak himself. For standing behind Elisa was a vaguely familiar face that was almost equally as stunning as Elisa. Not quite as gorgeous as the Lady, but beautiful and with arms showing the beginnings of corded muscles, the person waiting behind Elisa took Korin's breath away.

He stood there stunned until Elisa realized what had stolen his attention so effectively. She smiled slightly and released herself from his hug.

"Lord Korin Silver Steel, I give you Bell....." She started. Korin was nodding and stepped passed Elisa to stand in front of the girl. He bowed his little half bow before speaking.

"Korin Silver Steel, at your service." He introduced himself, although Elisa had already done so and the man required no introduction within the Citadel. Or Ka'len for that matter.

"Isabelle Bone Render, or Bell if you please, at yours, my Lord."

Bell blushed a deep shade of red as she mimicked Korin's bow perfectly.

Korin fumbled about for a moment trying to find the words to carry on the conversation with her. Elisa realized that the man was foundering and threw him a life line.

"Korin, perhaps you would like to invite Bell to dine with us this evening? After all, three is an awkward number, assuming you will be joining us as well, Drayel?"

She asked looking back over her shoulder at Drayel. The Warlock smiled a thin smile. He too had recognized Korin's immediate infatuation with the girl. He nodded in affirmation that he would, in fact, be joining them for dinner.

Korin smiled widely and said in his booming voice,

"It's settled then! Let us continue on to the courtyard for dinner and mead!"

They left Elisa's room, Korin and Bell leading the way, hands touching, but not quite holding. And Drayel and Elisa following a short distance behind to give the two some privacy.

Drayel looked toward Elisa and said quietly, as if afraid the two people ahead of them would hear him,

"You look quite lovely this evening, Lady Elisa."

Elisa was glad for the darkness in the halls of the Citadel. The sconces and candles were being lit at that very moment, but the hall they traveled remained dimly lit. Otherwise the blush on her cheeks would have been immediately noticeable. And she might not have been able to summon to courage to respond saying,

"You look quite dashing yourself Drayel." She waited to see what his response would be.

She was almost shocked when he reached out and took her by the hand. Elisa started to pull away at the forwardness of the gesture, but, she decided she liked her hand in his. So, she held on and they walked together toward the courtyard.

# CHAPTER 19

## RULES, LAWS, & MEAD

Drayel's heart had raced when Elisa opened the door. Every time he saw her he was more convinced that she was the reincarnation of Isolde herself.

The woman was simply stunning. At that moment he had wanted Korin to disappear so that he might have Elisa all to himself for the evening. But, in the end, it had all worked out perfectly when he had made the acquaintance of the young Bone Render. He was pleased that Korin had met someone that grabbed his interest so quickly after ceasing his pursuit of Elisa. However, he didn't look forward to telling the big lug that she was a servant in the Citadel and had not yet achieved her eighteenth year.

But that was a problem for later. Right now the two of them were laughing and flirting and having a grand time. There was no law about socializing with the staff before they became Warriors, but they just could not be more than that. Not yet.

So Drayel pushed that worrisome thought to the side and focused on the blond incarnation of the Goddess sitting across from him.

He was just about to start discussing his plans for her magical education when he heard Korin almost roar,

"What do you mean you aren't in the Warrior class?" as he turned and stomped toward Sandron's with a red-eyed Bell following behind him.

"Elisa?" Drayel asked.

"Yes, about that. Bell is a servant in the Citadel and still has two months to go before she is able to join the Warriors. So, if I understand your laws correctly, she can not officially date Korin until then. However, Bell is completely smitten with our good Lord Silver Steel and I encouraged her to take this opportunity to let him know how she felt about him. And to ask him if there was ever going to be a chance that they could be together." She said truthfully.

"That may not have been wise. It seems to me that Korin is very interested in our young barbarian friend. And having to wait two months to be able to even hold her hand may be more than he can stand. It may have been better to have waited until he could legally court her to make the introduction. But, what's done is done. All we can do now is wait and see if the two of them can work it out." Drayel said sadly.

Elisa took a sip of water from her mug and contemplated the situation. Maybe she had been too anxious to help her new friends get together. Was it a mistake to encourage Bell to tell Korin how she felt?

Elisa was still very new to the Citadel and the Warriors Guild. At that moment she was simply hoping that she had not caused her two new friends any undue stress or displeasure.

"Did I err Drayel? Should I have just left well enough alone and let nature take its course? They are both very kind people. I would not wish any undue hardships on them. I swear I was only trying to help!" She was almost on the verge of tears herself thinking that she might have caused her only two friends in the Citadel pain. Drayel just shook his head.

"No, Elisa, you did not err. The heart will only bind to a similar heart. The way those two bonded so quickly after meeting, I believe they will end up together. They will just have to keep any physical acts of romance in check until she enters the Warriors training. It will be fine, or it won't. Either way, we must let it play itself out." He said, taking a sip of his water.

Elisa looked back toward Sandron's and saw Korin was leading an openly crying Bell to the same little alcove that they had shared the previous evening. He looked less angry now and more concerned that Bell was crying and upset.

"So, as I was about to say before the drama unfolded, we need to discuss your magical training." He said matter-of-factly.

The truth was he was not ready to delve into the subject that he knew they must eventually discuss. So, he would exhaust all forms of small talk before crossing that bridge.

"Okay, fine. I am curious about that. I know you said Korin would teach me swordsmanship and train my body to be that of a Warrior. But you said you would train me to use my magic to its fullest. While that does sound wonderful, I have always wanted to discover my innate abilities, I have also read that when a Warlock takes a student he is bound to that student for life." She said timidly. "Is that something you want?" She asked quietly.

Damn it.

She had circled around to the subject he was actively trying to avoid. Was it truly possible that he knew this soon that she was the one? Had he met and fallen for the love of his life in less than three moons? He took his time answering her. He looked at the lines of her face. The soft curve of her jaw and the sparkling blue of her eyes. He thought of her laugh, her smile, the way she was beginning to move gracefully under the sword. And he knew.

"Yes." He said firmly.

"Yes, what? Drayel?" She prodded gently.

Drayel took another drink of water and paused briefly to consider his answer. He had not been prepared to have this conversation yet. He'd hoped to have a few days to contemplate this entirely new sensation before he discussed it with her. He was relieved to find that she seemed open to the idea of exploring this new relationship, if that was, in fact, what this was.

"Elisa, I find myself in unfamiliar territory. As I am sure our good friend Korin may have told you during your first dinner together, I have not been inclined to form a lasting commitment with any of the consorts I have taken over the last several years." He said plainly. "Truthfully, I have not been with anyone longer than an evening since taking over the Citadel. So, you are something of a mystery to me." He said with a wry smile.

"I will admit only a day ago my intentions were solely geared toward you joining the Guild as our healer. But something has happened since then that has left me open to the possibility of more than that. I find myself concerned for your health and safety. When Korin told me yesterday that you were not fully engaged in the training I became angry. Not because you simply were not learning a valuable skill, but because I would not see you harmed." He said quickly.

He was not at his most poetic here. He silently cursed the fact that he was not on solid footing. He would have liked to have had more time to prepare for this, but he was just going to have to do the best he could in the moment.

Elisa saw that Drayel was having a hard time conveying his thoughts on the matter. He had spent so long being the Guild Master and playing the required roles, that now that he was having to speak simply as Drayel, he was having trouble finding the words. She thought it was sweet that he was at least trying. And brave that he would openly admit his feelings for her. So many men felt the need to play games to cover up their own cowardice when it came to women. So, while Drayel was not winning any points with his prose, he was gaining ground with his honesty. She liked that about him. His confidence was one of the things she found attractive about the Warlock.

Drayel had paused after his statement and was gazing over her shoulder toward Korin and Bell. They were sitting in the alcove, her with a glass of wine, him with a mug of mead, and both of her hands enveloped in his. They were sitting on opposite sides of the table but were leaning across the table toward each other and talking in low and civil tones.

Drayel was certain that when Bell reached her eighteenth birthday that Korin would be announcing their courtship. He was pleased for his friend. He was brought back to his current conversation when he felt Elisa's soft hands wrap around the one not holding onto his mug.

"Drayel, thank you for telling me this. Truth be told, I have also found myself interested in getting to know you better." Her cheeks turned a light shade of pink as she looked down and away from him demurely.

"I will admit that you are nothing like the man the King prepared me to meet. You have been kind to me. Saved my life even. And the way your people adore you, it all came as a surprise." She paused to contemplate how to continue.

She took a deep breath and spoke quickly before she could lose the nerve to do so.

"But not nearly as surprising as the fact that I do believe I have feelings for you, Drayel Shadow Walker. I do want you to teach me to make use of my magic. And I do want to spend much, much, more time with you." Her face was now a brilliant shade of red.

She grabbed her mug of water and took a long drink. And suddenly wished for something stronger. Had she really just blurted all of that out? Isolde! She had never been more embarrassed in her life. If Drayel ran from her now she decided that she would lock herself in her chamber and either die from embarrassment or flee when the snow melted.

When she was finally able to look at him again, she saw he was smiling. An honest smile that was reflected in his eyes. So often his smiles were cruel or false. But this one was fully Drayel. He let go of his mug and grasped her hand in both of his, much like Korin and Bell had done earlier, and squeezed gently.

"Elisa, it would be my honor to be your mentor in the arcane. And I do not claim to know what this thing between you and I will become. But I do know that I am willing to find out if you are?" He accented the last part of the statement, making it a question.

Elisa nodded happily. "Yes, I think that would please me very much." She said, returning his smile.

"Then. May I suggest we follow our friend's lead and make our way to the bar for something stronger than water? I think we both may be in need of a drink." He said jovially. Elisa nodded her approval.

Keeping hold of her hand Drayel rose and assisted her to her feet. They turned and walked toward Sandron's looking very much like a young couple in love.

They did not notice the dark shrouded figure standing at the top of the stairs leading to the courtyard, or the wicked smile that crossed her face before she disappeared into the dark.

# CHAPTER 20

SWORDS & SPELLS

"I CAN NOT DO THIS." SHE GROUSED.

Drayel just laughed and sat the hourglass he had been monitoring on its side.

It had been two months since the night they had declared their feelings for each other. Elisa had continued training with Korin every day and had improved greatly. She now sparred with the male Warriors regularly. She had surpassed the females in training and, at Korin's instance, pushed herself by fighting the stronger and faster male Warriors. She did not win often, but more and more she was fighting the skilled Warriors to a draw. An accomplishment anyone would have been proud of.

Korin himself had taken on a big brother role when he was not training her in the circle. And he often bragged on her to anyone that would listen as his prize pupil.

Usually earning him a punch in the arm from Bell, who was always at the Weapons Master's side in their downtime. Bell showed great promise in the training circles as well. She had only recently joined the ranks of the Warriors, but with her great strength, she stood out among the shield maidens and was well on her way to notoriety among the Warriors of the Guild.

But magic, magic was something different. She had left her coven at a young age and had only a limited amount of training because of it. Her mother had taught her how to channel the healing magic and to summon the fire element. But at a very rudimentary level. And due to the King's edicts regarding magic, she had very rarely practiced her craft within the castle walls.

So, the last few months under Drayel's guidance had been incredible for her. But, her progress was slower than she would have liked. Drayel had been raised in a part of Ka'len where magic was, illegally, still practiced in the open. By design, his homeland was very difficult to reach, and traders did not often make the treacherous journey out of fear of both the land and the Warlocks that resided there. So, he had been immersed in magic from childhood and had the benefit of training with the master known as the Old One.

He had taken the entire first week of their training together and made her read tome after tome regarding the nature of magic. Ways to summon different elements and the risk and benefits of doing so. She spent many long nights completing his reading assignments. It was a wonder that in between becoming a Warrior during the day and honing her craft in the evening, that she had the energy for anything else. But, somehow, she did.

She had dined with Drayel every night. Taken walks along the battlements and spent every waking second she was not in the training circles with him. She was also fully head over heels in love with the Warlock. And he with her.

But on days like today, she wanted to throttle the man. Drayel was attempting to discover her natural abilities to summon different elements. She knew that she could summon fire and the healing magic of Isolde. But being able to control wind, water, and earth was a different thing altogether.

During her reading sessions, she had discovered a chapter in an ancient-looking tome that covered the Cor Sanctus witches ability to fly without Isolde's medallion. It required great control on the witch's part, and the ability to summon the wind element at will. So Drayel had latched on to that particular skill and was trying, in vain, to teach Elisa how to call upon the winds.

She had tried for three days and could not get so much as a hair to blow on her head. Drayel had thought to help her by demonstrating his own ability to summon the winds and levitate from the battlements to the ground as he had the night he had rescued her from the avalanche. He had not flown down but merely controlled his descent. This earned him a rude hand gesture and Elisa sticking her tongue out at the man as he levitated back up to the battlement where she stood.

They had moved back into one of the open rooms in the northern-most spire of the castle to continue. Drayel had asked her to give him an hour of trying to summon the wind. If she could not do it they would move on to something else and come back to the wind later. It had been thirty minutes and Elisa was getting frustrated. She had tried for days before this with no success and was beginning to believe she simply could not summon the wind.

"Elisa, love, you are thinking about this too hard. You know you cannot think it into being. It must be your will, your heart, your soul that commands the wind to come. When you summon your healing magic, you feel it in and around your heart first, correct?" He asked though he knew the answer as they had discussed her abilities at length. She nodded in the affirmative.

"And fire, when you summon it you feel it in the palms of your hands first?" He asked. She nodded again, adding a little frustrated gust of air from her nose just to let him know that they'd been down this path already.

"Bear with me, Elisa. Have I ever told you where I feel the wind element first?" He asked sincerely.

She glanced at his backside playfully and smiled. Drayel, thankfully, had developed a slight sense of humor in their time together. Had she made that little joke three months ago he would have berated her for not taking the training seriously and to pay attention. As it was now he just smiled and shook his head.

Drayel crossed the floor until he was standing in front of her. He reached out and took both of her hands in his.

"When I summon wind, I find it comes to me like breathing. I intake the nature of wind when I inhale, then will it to surround me when I exhale. Then I can feel it all around. It is bound to me, like your fire, and your healing is to you after it has been called. After that, you simply will it to do your bidding. Watch."

And with that, he leaned forward and kissed her softly. As their lips touched she heard, and felt, his intake of air. When he exhaled something awakened within her and she could feel the element of air encasing them. When she opened her eyes he broke the kiss and looked down smiling. They were floating roughly three feet off of the floor. She felt it clearly when Drayel released the element and lowered them back to the floor.

"Do you see now?" He asked hopefully.

"I do, but maybe you should kiss me again to be sure." She said with a wicked smile.

Drayel returned the smile but stepped back away from her, letting go of her hands and earning a little pout in return.

"Fly first, kiss later." He promised.

"I'm going to hold you to that." She said seriously.

Elisa cleared her mind as she had been taught to do. She thought back to the sensation she had felt when Drayel had summoned the element and concentrated on that.

She took a deep breath in, focusing her will on the memory of that feeling. She felt a small tingle in her mouth like a tornado was spinning on her tongue. She opened her eyes to find the room had begun to spin. No, not the room, her. She was about a foot off of the ground and slowly spinning in a circle. The realization shocked her briefly causing her to gasp and lose control of the element. This sent her dropping to the floor and promptly onto her backside. Drayel started to rush over to her when she looked up and smiled, holding her arms out to him.

"I did it!" She exclaimed happily. "Thank you so much!"

Drayel reached for her hands to pull her to her feet. Elisa raised slightly up off of the floor before hooking her foot behind his knee and pulling him down on top of her.

"I believe my Lord said fly first, kiss later? Well, I just flew." She said devilishly.

Drayel grinned and lowered himself down to wrap her in his arms to give her what she requested. They had been actively engaged in doing just that when the door to the tower burst open and Korin, followed by Bell, burst through with faces full of excitement.

"The pass is clear!" Korin half-shouted. Bell stood beside him nodding enthusiastically.

Drayel had looked up in annoyance when the door had flung upon interrupting his and Elisa's fun. Now he returned Korin's smile two-fold.

"Wonderful news my friends!" He exclaimed.

With a glance of regret toward Elisa, he stood up and offered her a hand. Elisa huffed and took the offered assistance.

"Grey Cloak just sent word. He went out with the men this morning to clear the last section of rubble. He reports that the work clearing the pass is complete and that the snow is all but completely gone." Korin said enthusiastically.

Drayel nodded. The three of them, Drayel, Korin, and Bell began discussing troop movements almost immediately. They were so excited by the clearing of the pass that none of them noticed Elisa walk off by herself. Now she stood silently staring out one of the windows in the tower. The view of the mountains under normal circumstances would have been breathtaking. Now Elisa could not breathe for an entirely different reason.

In the previous months, she had been so enamored by Drayel, and occupied learning swordsmanship and magic, that she had completely forgotten about trying to persuade Drayel not to attack Tor'Amal. And now the day had come when he could do so again. Elisa fought a torrent of emotions that overwhelmed her at that moment. She did not know what she would do next, but she knew she could not stand in the tower listening to her lover and her two best friends discussing a war that would cost the lives of countless innocent people. Elisa fled the tower.

As she ran out of the door she heard all three of her friends call out after her but she could not stop. Her eyes filled with tears to the point that she was running almost blind back to her chambers. She knew the Citadel well now. She had traversed every hallway with Drayel as they walked together in the evenings. She'd learned to avoid the magically shifting walkways that led only back to where you started. But only one hallway mattered now, the one to her room.

She crashed through the door not bothering to shut it behind her. Another habit she had picked up in her time there. She grabbed her pillow and buried her face in it and let the tears flow freely. How could she have been so stupid? She had completely forgotten the war. She had given up two whole months' worth of time to convince Drayel to turn his course. Now how many would die?

She was lost in thought and did not hear the door shut quietly or the soft footsteps that made their way to her bedside. She only became aware of the other person's presence when they sat down on the bed and rubbed her back lightly. Elisa turned her head to see Bell sitting on the side of her bed with a concerned look on her face.

"I made the boys wait in the courtyard. I do not know what troubles you, but I would love to help if I could." She said sincerely.

Elisa looked at her friend and saw the concern in her eyes.

She and Korin had been together in secret for a month before her eighteenth birthday. They were deeply in love and Bell credited Elisa with them being together. Korin's honor would not allow him to break the Guild's rules regarding intimacy until her eighteenth birthday, so they had only recently become lovers. And it was commonly known that Korin would soon ask for Bell's hand in marriage. So, Bell regarded Elisa as a sister and would do anything to help stop the tears that stained her pretty face.

Elisa just shook her head in frustration. Where did she begin? She trusted Bell and knew she could tell the girl anything and it would stay between them. But just what SHOULD she tell her? That she had been sent to stop Drayel from attacking Tor'Amal and that she had failed? That she loved him unconditionally and had no desire to ever return to Mannock's castle? That much at least was clear. Her cold little room in his castle was no longer home. She had stopped thinking of it that way long before.

She decided that she would just tell the girl the truth and let the pieces fall where they may.

She recounted her first conversation with Drayel, the King's offer, and everything that had happened since. She told Bell that Drayel trusted her, and she did not want to do anything to damage that trust. She hoped that Drayel would know that she truly loved him and that falling for him was not simply a ploy to get him to do her bidding. Elisa looked at Bell hopelessly before continuing.

"So, you see, I MUST try again to get him to turn from his goal of unseating the King. I could care less if Mannock rules, and I would honestly prefer Drayel to rule Ka'len, but not this way. I would not see Korin or you harmed in battle. I would not see the hundreds of innocents that will be trapped between the city walls and the castle injured when the Guild knocks down the gates and engages the King's Guards. And Isolde, even the Guards. Most of them are just working at the castle to feed their families. They will have to fight the Guild or the King will have his Knights kill them." She had almost called them coward knights. Isolde, she had been around Drayel too long.

"You should try again my sister." Bell said hopefully. "Drayel has changed these last few months. He has more of a heart than he had before. And I mean that in the best way. Maybe, just maybe, our Lord will hear you this time."

"He has." Came the quiet voice standing in the doorway.

The women snapped their heads toward the doorway and saw Drayel leaning against the door frame. They had been so caught up in Elisa's story that neither of them had heard the Warlock softly knock and enter.

"Bell, thank you for attending Lady Elisa. I appreciate it. But now would you be so kind as to wait in the courtyard with Korin while my Lady and I speak?" He asked politely.

There was no anger in his voice, just a kind of resignation. Bell nodded in affirmation and looked to Elisa. Elisa just smiled and mouthed, Thank you, before releasing Bell's hands.

Bell hurried from the room so that Drayel and Elisa could have their privacy. She also had to speak to Korin. He had told her almost the exact same story earlier so he was the only person in the Citadel she could confide in without breaching Elisa's trust. So, it was to him she now ran.

Drayel crossed the room and sat on the stool in front of the desk by the window and looked at Elisa. He just stared at the beautiful witch that had stolen his heart. He looked at the woman he loved. And he saw for the first time the tears and pain that his goal of ruling Ka'len was causing her.

"So, I believe I heard most of what you wanted to tell me, again. I apologize for eavesdropping, but you did intend on me hearing it at some point, so perhaps it just saved us some time." He said quietly.

Elisa propped herself up on her pillows and turned so that she was facing Drayel. This was the longest that he had gone fully clothed in her chambers in months. So, it felt wrong to see him sitting on the stool so far from her and out of reach. She started to get out of the bed and go to him when he raised his hand to stop her.

"Please Elisa, I need a clear head to think this through, and the God's know I can not focus on anything but you when you are near. So please, for now, stay on the bed." He asked sincerely. It stung Elisa that he did not want her near, but she understood what he was saying. She felt the same way about him.

"I know that you have not brought this up again in the last two months. And even though it was not by choice, I appreciate the time I have been given to think it over. And Bell is correct. Somehow I am not the same man that I was even three months ago. My heart has opened to different possibilities, all thanks to you. The man I was knew only hate. And I could only imagine a world with Mannock dead and gone. That was my dream, in addition to the things you already know about." Drayel sighed and looked toward the desk searching for something.

When he did not find it he snapped his fingers and a glass of cold water appeared on the desk beside him.

He drank half of the glass and set it back on the desk where it filled up immediately. He looked back to where Elisa now sat on the edge of the bed, patiently waiting for him to continue.

"I still have no faith in the coward King. I do not trust him to keep his word. I do not trust him to take my advice. And I do not trust him to allow magic to be practiced again in Ka'len. But, I trust you. If you say that you and I can ride openly into Tor'Amal and the King will receive us, then I will go and speak to him." He said. Elisa now had new tears running down her cheeks, but the smile on her face told him that they were an entirely different sort of tears.

"But, Elisa, I also promise you, that even though I am willing to try this the King's way, if he deceives me and tries to harm me, you, or anyone that travels with us, I will kill him and bring his monstrosity of a castle down on top of him. Can you understand that?" He asked directly.

She was nodding enthusiastically. Before he could say anything else Elisa was off of the bed and standing in front of him. She reached down and took his face in both hands before kissing him passionately. Drayel was off of the stool in an instant, lifting her into his arms and taking her back to the bed she had just left. She laughed when she felt a familiar sensation on his breath and a gust of wind blew her chamber door closed.

## DECEPTION

**N**EITHER OF THEM SAW THE RAVEN THAT HAD BEEN PERCHED ON the window sill fly away as they made their way to the bed. The sick-looking animal made its way to the far side of the castle and landed on another window sill.

Tallon Grey Cloak gave the pathetic creature a sliver of the chicken he was eating and sent it on its way. He had overheard everything. He would have to relay it back to Maricin soon. The little jade mirror he now held had been gifted to him by her and was enchanted so that they could speak at will. Usually hers. Together they had spent the last two months finding allies among the Warriors that were dissatisfied with Drayel's rule.

There were not many in the beginning. But Talon put on a false face and made it a point to go out with the men into the pass to work while Drayel courted his blond harlot. He protected the men from the biting cold, provided fires to cook their meals, and generally pretended to be their best friend. All the while bemoaning the fact that Drayel could not be there with them since he could have done so much more than himself. He played on their emotions and soon had a large following within the Guild that liked and respected him.

With Maricin's guidance, he found the Officers that had supported her and made it a point to show that same false friendship to them. And now, thank the Gods, now Drayel was playing right into their hands.

Throughout the cold winter months, the freezing winds, clearing the path, the one thing that kept the men driving forward was the idea of marching into Tor'Amal and unseating the King. And now, he couldn't help but laugh to himself, now that fool and his harlot were going to leave the Citadel and go make peace with the man.

And of course, that big oaf Silver Steel would not allow his precious Lord to travel without him. So, essentially, Tallon was going to be in charge of the Citadel while they were gone. Oh, Gods be praised. This could not have worked out any better. He walked over to his dresser and sat down before running a finger around the outside of the glass, activating the enchantment.

She had left the Citadel after their first meeting and had only come back once or twice over the last couple of months due to Drayel's enchantments inside the castle. It was difficult for her to be there undetected and she did not want to risk discovery until it was too late. The mirror was the safest form of communication. And he did not have to wait long for her to answer.

Tallon repeated everything he had overheard in Elisa's chambers. His raven had been spying on the two of them training in the spire, and in a stroke of brilliance Tallon had the animal follow her to her chambers. Maricin's cackle reverberated off of Tallon's walls. He looked around nervously for a second, afraid someone would overhear, but relaxed when he remembered the enchantment that sealed his chambers from those that might overhear what was discussed behind closed doors.

"Should I let the Officers loyal to us, or rather you, know that you live?" He asked. He could see her shake her head no through the mirror.

"No, not yet. Let the fool make peace with Mannock. When the men find out that the Guild will bow before the King there will be unrest and discontent immediately. THAT is when I shall return to the Guild in secret. That is when we will gather those that are loyal and begin our work to unseat Drayel. Remain strong Tallon. I am almost home."

She said before breaking the connection, the mirror going black immediately. Tallon walked back to his bed and lay down to rest. Yes. He would wait. He would bide his time. And in the end, the most powerful being in Ka'len would be brought down by powers oldest nemesis.

Love.

CHAPTER 22

## THE ROAD TO TOR'AMAL

Korin had been shocked when Drayel visited him in his quarters later that afternoon. Bell had told him about the conversation with Elisa, and Drayel's accidental overhearing of what was said. Although the outcome of that conversation was uncertain. Until now.

Korin had decided long before that he would support whatever his friend decided. Although he never imagined that Drayel would agree to hear the king out. He secretly had believed that Drayel could not be dissuaded from his goal of ruling all of Ka'len.

So, to hear him now speaking of peace with the King and rebuilding Ka'len from the inside came as nothing short of a surprise.

But if that was what Drayel wanted, it would be done.

He did not hesitate when Drayel asked him to ride with him and Elisa to Tor'Amal to meet with the king. The one concession Korin asked for was that a certain shield maiden be allowed to ride along as well.

The next morning the four of them were waiting by the front gate for the sun to rise before they began their journey. Tallon Grey Cloak had surprised them all when he offered to ensure breakfast was brought to them at the gate and to be there to see them off. It was unexpected, to say the least.

Tallon and the page that he was forced to serve in the kitchens appeared shortly before dawn with hot biscuits, sausages, and various fruit drinks for the companions.

Drayel silently mouthed an incantation over the food that would immediately cause it to shrivel and dry if there was anything amiss with the food. He was mildly surprised when everything appeared to be in order.

They ate quietly as they contemplated the journey ahead of them. Drayel pulled Tallon to the side and commended the man on his work clearing the pass. He also told Tallon that he had begun to hear his name used as less of a slur and in much more friendly terms than before. A backhanded compliment, but a compliment, nonetheless.

Tallon had just nodded and smiled. His smile was genuine. He liked that the men were starting to trust him, and Drayel congratulating him on clearing the pass just further proved that the powerful Warlock did not suspect Tallon's true motives at all.

"Keep the men busy. They should not break from their routines while I am gone. See to it that walls of the pass are shored up and rein-forced. And conceal stone tablets with detection glyphs at the begin-ning, middle, and end of the path to alert the Guards should anyone enter the pass. I would not give anyone the chance to sabotage it again." Drayel ordered. Tallon just nodded his head and agreed.

"Make sure that they continue to train in the rings and keep up with their daily activities. It would serve no one for them to become lax while I am away. And finally, keep the details of our journey to Tor'Amal to yourself until we know what the end result will be. It is true that we may not march on Tor'Amal, but I may bring the castle down on his head while we are there. In either event, I want the Warriors to stay ready for whatever lies ahead. Understood?" He asked with just a slight tone of aggression in his voice.

A hint of what would happen to Tallon should he fail. Tallon nodded again.

"Of course my Lord. I shall say nothing and endeavor to see that the Guild's best interest are served in your absence." Tallon said quietly.

Although his version of what was best for the Guild was slightly different from Drayel's.

Drayel took his acquiescence at face value and did not consider the connotations of the man's answer. He thanked Tallon and released him and the boy to go about their duties for the day. They both bowed and disappeared back down the stairs into the kitchens.

Drayel turned and observed his companions. They were finishing up their meals and stowing the last of their gear. They checked straps, water supplies, and food stores one final time before mounting up.

The sun was just starting to peek over the eastern mountain tops when the gates opened and the four companions rode out toward the pass.

Elisa had hesitated slightly before entering the place where she was almost killed months before. Drayel had sensed her discomfort and dropped back to ride beside her. He began discussing the night before, causing her to blush and put her finger to her lips in an attempt to quiet him before their friends overheard the torrid details that he was describing. He made an innocent look fall over his features and raised his hands out to the side in a questioning manner and smiled at her devilishly.

Seeing that she was relaxing somewhat, Drayel changed the subject to her control of the wind element. He spoke to her about it in-depth and before long they were lost in conversation about wind, earth, and water. The three elements that she still had yet to master.

When they finally looked up Drayel smiled. They were well clear of the pass and were halfway to the little two-story bar where Drayel and Korin had first met.

"Korin, what do you say we stop for our noon meal at the place where we first met? It has been quite some time and if I remember correctly, I never had a chance to finish my leg of lamb." He said with a laugh. Korin turned around in his saddle and smiled at his friend.

"I think that is a grand idea. The snow may be melting, but there is still a bite in the air. I think we could all do with a reprieve. Maybe a mug or two of meade for us, and a glass of wine for the ladies?" He suggested.

Elisa nodded her agreement, but Bell scoffed at the idea.

"You drink the wine, my love, I will have a shot of whiskey. I need something to warm my insides. This blasted wind has not stopped blowing since we left the Citadel and I fear my buttocks may be frozen to this saddle!" She said with exasperation.

Her three companions laughed heartily at her statement. When she saw she was not getting any sympathy for her plight she could not help but join in the laughter.

"You know, we have all been cooped up in the Citadel these last few months. And this is the first time any of us have truly been outside for any length of time, horses included. What say you we make this ride a little more interesting?" Korin asked mischievously.

"What did you have in mind?" Drayel asked although he thought he knew what his friend was about to suggest.

"A race. The inn is not too far from here, but just far enough to make it interesting. The last one there buys the first round of drinks. Sound fair?" He asked the group.

They all nodded their acceptance. Elisa was not sure how she would do in this challenge. Her horse was a huge beast, heavily muscled, and bred for battle. She looked at Drayel and Korin's mounts and saw their horses were slightly taller due to longer legs, and while muscled, seemed trimmer than her and Bell's mounts. She thought the men were setting them up to lose.

But she honestly did not care. It had been so long since she had felt the wind in her hair, and had the freedom to run, that even losing the race would be worth the exhilaration of flying across the ground.

The four of them reined their mounts in and came to a stop side by side. Korin raised his arm to the sky and shouted loudly,

"Make ready!" All four of the riders leaned slightly forward on their now nervously prancing mounts. He dropped his arm and shouted,

"GO!"

The four of them took off in a thunderclap of hooves on dirt. Mud flew and hair blew in the wind. Elisa's whoops of exhilaration were lost in the clamor and the noise of the four magnificent animals that now barreled down the road at top speed. As expected Korin and Drayel quickly pulled out to the front of the pack and were playfully bumping into each other to make room to pass each other. Bell and Elisa fell into a comfortable pace beside each other, taking turns pulling slightly ahead and then falling back. Neither of them overly serious about winning this race.

They turned the final bend in the road and up ahead there stood the little two-story inn with the spinning rooster on top. Both men whooped and redoubled their efforts to spur their mounts on. But not before Korin turned in his saddle to wave goodbye to Bell, and by association, Elisa.

The two women just turned and looked at each other incredulously. Had the arrogant oaf honestly just done that? She wasn't sure why, but the dismissal from Korin angered her. So, he wanted to race? Fine. She closed her eyes and concentrated.

She felt her healing magic respond first, so she poured some into her tiring mount, refreshing him immediately. Her pace picked up. She felt her hands warm but had no need for fire. Then she felt the tiny swirl of the wind element that she had unconsciously called. Her mount was heavier than the men's, so it stood to reason he was slower. Elisa focused her will on what she wished and felt the horse surge forward as if pushed from behind. The horse bellowed and lowered his head, making it clear that he did not wish to lose to his long-legged companions either.

As the inn neared Elisa's speed doubled. She neared the men and had to lower her head behind her mount's giant neck to avoid the chunks of dirt they were kicking up. Her horse nickered again and she peeked up in time to see they were almost to the end but still behind the men. Elisa watched and as the two men separated and put their heads down for the sprint to the finish Elisa made her move. She could not help but laugh at the expression on Korin's face as she blew by them and entered the courtyard of the inn seconds before them. The three of them reined in their mounts and practically skidded to a stop.

Followed by a loudly whooping Bell who was cheering Elisa and proclaiming her the winner. The two men just stared at Elisa incredulously.

"What in the…"

"How in the…."

Korin and Drayel said together.

Both men turned toward each other and broke out in huge smiles.

"You cheated!" They shouted together, laughing as they said it.

"I did no such thing gentlemen. I do not recall anyone saying magic was forbidden? Do you Bell?" She asked her grinning friend.

"Why no, Elisa, I do not believe that was in the rules. It would appear, these men owe you, and your best friend, a drink!" She threw her head back and howled with laughter. It was a very loud sound, and for the first time, Elisa could see her friend's barbarian heritage come out in her just a little.

There was a pair of rough-looking men sitting on the porch of the Inn when they had arrived. They muttered something unkind about barbarians under their breaths and walked inside the inn. Unfortunately for them, Korin had heard most of what they said. The big man's face turned red, but not from the cold of the wind.

"Korin, love, I did not hear what the fools said, but we are on a mission to build peace. And busting the heads of two local ruffians will not help sell us as people with peaceful intent." She said softly while placing a hand on top of his. He gripped his saddle horn so hard his knuckles turned white but shook his head in acceptance.

"Fine. I will not address their vulgar comments. I will let it go. This time. But I make no promises if they dare repeat them." He said honestly.

It was the best response she could hope for, so Bell just leaned over and kissed his cheek. Tensions eased and the four companions swung down from their saddles.

A stable boy came running out from behind the inn and took charge of their horses. Drayel tipped the lad well and asked him to make sure their mounts were brushed, fed, and watered before being placed in their stalls for the night. The boy nodded happily and disappeared into the barn with the four gigantic horses in tow.

Drayel led the way into the dining room of the inn. Followed by Elisa, Bell, and Korin, they made their way to one of the larger tables at the back of the room and nearest the fireplace. Korin made it glaringly obvious that he was putting his back to the wall and watching the door and the room. Drayel barked a short little laugh at his friend's display. Earning him a few disgruntled looks from the locals that were dining there.

The serving girl came and took their orders, and payment for two of the best rooms in the inn, and left to get their drinks.

The four of them fell into a fairly quiet and jovial discussion regarding the rest of their trip into Tor'Amal, as well as potential hazards once they got into the capital city and the castle itself. Their food arrived, including Drayel's long-missed leg of lamb, and they drank to each other's health.

After dinner, they scooted their chairs over in front of the fireplace, as the dining room was mostly empty except for the two ruffians from earlier and some friends of theirs that were drinking heavily at a table on the other side of the room. They began discussing what would happen once they made it inside the castle walls when one of the ruffians that had been outside earlier overheard them and decided to place himself into their conversation.

"Eh, you lot dinna need to worry 'bout getting into tha castle. They'll never let that barbarian wench through the bloody gates." He said loudly and rudely. His friends all laughed at his poor joke and bumped their beer mugs into each other in salute of his wit. They drank the remainder that wasn't spilled when the second ruffian turned toward the friends and spoke.

"Aye, why don't you have those lasses make themselves useful and have them go fetch us some more drinks!" He squawked in a loud and high-pitched voice.

Bell could see the rage in Korin's eyes, and Elisa could see the medallion beneath Drayel's shirt beginning to glow. The ladies looked at each other and smiled. They put their hands over the men's and forced their attention.

"Just watch." They mouthed silently, all the while smiling at their two angered lovers. Bell turned and addressed the men, there were six of them in total, in a deep and heavily exaggerated barbarian accent.

"O' My frund und I would ne'er refuse ta serve sooch fine mens as your- selves." She said while fighting to keep a straight face.

Drayel and Korin just looked at each other, neither sure of exactly what was going on, but both more than ready to flatten the men at the other table.

Bell and Elisa got up and met the barmaid halfway across the floor and took the platter of drinks from her hands.

Elisa took two of the mugs from the platter and gripped them tightly. They had been steaming from the cold mead interacting with the heat of the room. The men did not notice the handles of the mugs turning red as Elisa channeled fire into the mugs, instantly heating the meade to boiling temperatures. She set the two mugs down directly in front of the two characters that had started all of the trouble, while Bell sat her drinks down in front of the other four. The two ruffians grinned broken smiles at each other.

"Thank ye wenches. 'Bout time a man taught ye your proper places as it were." The first one said as he took a deep belt from his mug, followed in sync by his companion. Both men screamed instantly and rolled onto the floor clutching their burned throats and gasping for water. Their friends jumped to their feet knocking over the table in the process.

"Oh come nah, der was no need ta spill the meade was it?" Bell asked innocently, still affecting the over-the-top accent.

The four remaining men rushed around the table. The first one to reach Elisa was met by a gust of wind that picked him up and flung him back into his friend that was following him around the table. The one that chose to rush Bell was not so lucky. For as he ran around the corner Bell turned and used the heavy serving tray as a shield and swung it flatly into his face. Knocking him down and instantly unconscious.

His partner jumped over his prone body in an attempt to rush Bell before she could recover from her swing. That was his mistake. He was a very small man. And Bell, Bell was very strong and very angry. She caught the little man by the throat in mid-air. She allowed his feet to hit the ground just long enough to step closer and get underneath him. She then picked him up with that same hand and walloped him in the head with the tray before dropping him to the ground next to his friend.

The two that had rushed Elisa had gotten back to their feet. The first one had screamed something about magic and witches and ran for the door. The second one had not seen what threw his friend, so he remained. Now furious at the women he drew his rapier and kicked the table out of the way. Drayel went to stand when he saw Elisa turn and smile, all the while shaking her head, No.

Drayel sat back down but kept a spell of holding on his tongue. If this went wrong he would stop it. If not, it should be fun to watch.

Elisa let the man get closer and drew her sword. Bell had returned to their table and was currently downing her remaining shot of whiskey while watching her friend prepare to fight.

Elisa assessed the man and found he had a poor grip on his sword, his feet crossed often, and his balance was unsteady. He was most assuredly not a trained swordsman. Elisa smiled.

"Well, I'm not going to wait all day. Are we fighting or not?" She asked sweetly, letting her point drop toward the floor.

The ruffian, thinking he had found an opening, lunged drunkenly toward her, grossly overextending his point of balance.

Elisa simply side stepped and slapped his sword away. She retracted her sword to an en garde position before slapping him on the backside as he passed through where she had previously stood. Drunk and confused, the ruffian took a grand spill into the middle of the room. He recovered moderately quickly and stumbled back onto his feet.

With a roar of drunken defiance and a display of extreme stupidity, he charged her yet again. Elisa again slapped his sword to the side, but this time she followed up by shoving the back of his head toward the ground. The end result was him splayed out on the ground in front of her with his sword clattering across the floor, far out of his reach.

Elisa stepped forward quickly and placed her heavy riding boot on his neck and pressed down. To further her point, literally, she placed her sharp sword tip against the base of his neck. The man froze where he lay, suddenly terrified of the two women he had been insulting only moments before.

"I believe you owe my friend and I an apology." Elisa said.

This time there was no sweetness in her tone. Only deadly seriousness.

The man tried to nod but found Elisa's blade prevented him from moving even an inch.

"I'm sorry. Okay? Now let me up!" He bellowed.

Elisa looked at Bell who now stood off to the side watching and laughing.

"What do you think Bell? Should I let him up?" She asked with a hint of a smile. Bell returned it with a mischievous look in her eye.

"Absolutely, Lady Elisa, please do let him get back on his feet. He is sorry after all." Bell said innocently.

Elisa retracted her blade and sheathed it as she stepped off of the man's neck. He rose to his feet muttering under his breath and refusing to make eye contact with the women. He went to pick up his sword when the group clearly heard the word barbarian and wench among his ramblings. As he reached for his sword a second riding boot stomped hard on the pommel, pinning it to the floor. The man stood straight up and turned to curse Bell when the tray smacked into his face. The man, now unconscious, fell unceremoniously to the floor.

"Now he's sorry." Bell said with a smile. She set the tray down on the nearest table and walked back over to their table where Drayel and Korin were both clearly amused by the entire spectacle.

"Elisa, it would appear that Master Silver Steel's lessons have not fallen on deaf ears." Drayel said sincerely, though still smiling.

"And my love, remind me to never anger you when you have a tray nearby!" Korin said through his fits of laughter.

Elisa grinned at her lover when the two fools that had drank the magically heated beer caught her eye. Both were a startling shade of purple and clearly could not breathe. Elisa rushed to their sides. Bell and Korin shouted, half- seriously, to just let them reap the rewards of their actions. Drayel just watched to see what she would do.

Elisa had spent so long hiding her magic that it felt good to use it in combat, but it felt even better to her to use it now. To heal. She placed a hand on each man's throat and let her healing magic flow through her. She saw the color fade from their faces into a more natural shade as their breathing was restored. The damage repaired, Elisa walked back to her table.

They were the ones that started and escalated the confrontation. From all perspectives, they deserved the treatment they had received. They did not necessarily deserve Elisa's kindness either. Displaying intelligence for the first time that evening, both men rose to a knee while they breathed deeply. Both looked toward the fireplace and the four friends seated there. They noticed the hostility in the men's eyes. And the fact that the women that had so handily defeated them were now seated and had picked up on a completely different topic. They were essentially forgotten. One of the ruffians spoke quietly, gaining the group's attention for the third time that night. Starring straight at Elisa he said slowly, as not to offend, "You are a Cor Sanctus witch." He said almost reverently. Seeing the men rise to their feet quickly, and knocking their chairs to the floor in the process, the man quickly held a hand up in surrender.

"I mean no offense lads. I hold no hate for the Cor Sanctus. One of their kind saved me mother when I was born. If not fer her kindness I'd not be drawin' breath today. Poor sap that I am." He dropped his head as if deep in thought.

"And I suppose I should say the same about you savin' me just now. I heard tell the witch told me mum that she was the matron of that clan, coven, something or the other. I swore I would find a way to repay that kindness and I failed dinna I? Miss, it may not mean a thing in the world to ya right now, and I can nay speak fer me friends, but I am sorry for the trouble we caused you and yers. Not that it was much trouble by the looks of it." He said with a slight grin.

"My name is Orin Fieldman lass, and I swear to ya, I will find a way to repay yer kindness this day." He said solemnly. Orin rose and helped his friend to his feet. With a final nod in the group's direction, the men departed without a look back.

Something that Orin said had stuck with Elisa. The matron of her clan had saved Orin's mother? So, her mom had saved his mom roughly around the same time Elisa had been born, as Orin looked roughly her age.

The probability of her ever meeting the man was very low, but it was proof that there were commoner humans that held respect for the Cor Sanctus witches. That gave Elisa hope.

"Did you hear him? My mother saved his mother, and now I've saved him. Admittedly due to harm I inflicted, but he earned it and understood that. Maybe there are more people that will be receptive to our return." She said hopefully.

Drayel returned her smile and did a good job of making it reach his eyes. Though he was not overly confident that they would find many people that did not fear magic as a whole.

But, maybe.

# CHAPTER 23



*T*HE GROUP RODE INTO TOR'AMAL THE FOLLOWING DAY. DRAYEL was astounded to find the gates standing wide open with only two-bored looking castle guards standing on either side.

Neither of which so much as gazed in their direction as they rode through. Korin and Bell rode side by side, followed by Drayel and Elisa. The city had not changed at all since she had left for the Citadel.

But to Bell, it was awe-inspiring.

She had been born deep in the North Mountains. Her nomad tribe had been raiders and warriors who had the unfortunate circumstance of going up against the Guild after a rich lord retained them to protect his estate.

The barbarians had lost the battle decisively. Her clan, though fierce, was not a loyal one. The survivors had fled as soon as the tide turned.

A Guild warrior had found Bell hiding in a barn tending to her seriously wounded parents. Hungry, scared, and injured, her parents had proven the exception. They had struggled to fight and defend their daughter. The Warrior had taken pity on them and offered them a chance to join the Guild. They had gladly accepted. They had been brought back to the Guild and there she had stayed.

So, now she was seeing the open-air markets, merchant booths, and street performers for the first time. She reached for Korin to tap him on the leg and gain his attention. She wanted to point out a merchant displaying beautiful exotic birds. She smiled when he took her hand in his and squeezed gently. He smiled at her and looked at the vendor, though Bell had forgotten them when she saw Korin's smile. No matter how many times she saw it, it always took her breath away.

The pair rode on in companionable silence as Bell took in the sights and sounds.

Drayel perhaps was the only one of the three that was not comfortable with their situation. His companions were riding through what was basically enemy territory as if they were on holiday. The God's Eye glowed softly beneath his armor. He would not be caught off guard and allow harm to come to his friends because of their complacency. He saw no guards with bows on the rooftops, no Soldiers stealing from street to street to flank them, but it just felt wrong to him to be riding freely down the streets of Tor'Amal.

It did not take long for the castle to come into sight.

The monstrosity was not much bigger than the Citadel, but the gaudiness of the place steered it away from elegance and into foolishness. White marble walls streaked with black lines made up the entirety of the exterior walls. Door frames and windows were lined with gold. The windows were made from polished crystal, and bright gems adorned the battlements and walls in increments. Their sole purpose was to catch the light and cause the castle to glisten in the morning sun. While people starved in his streets, Mannock used precious gems to adorn his throne. Gods Drayel hated this man.

They came upon a cozy-looking inn just a short distance from the Castle. Drayel instructed the group to stop there for the night to eat and rest while he assessed their situation.

"I do not know why, but something about this feels too easy. Why would the King simply allow us to ride through his gates unhindered? The Guards did not have us check our weapons, and there was no escort waiting at the gates to ensure we went straight to the castle. We will eat dinner at the inn, then tonight I will investigate the castle and determine if the king means us harm." The group nodded in acceptance.

Although Elisa simply shrugged. She truly believed that the king had honorable intentions. He would find out.

"While I am gone, please remain on your guard. Korin, monitor the streets from the rooftop. Bell and Elisa, stay in a room together, bolt the door and windows, and do not open them for anyone other than me or Korin." Bell and Korin nodded seriously.

Elisa just smiled at him. Drayel smiled back and took her hand. Then, as a group, they turned and walked into the inn.

It was not much to look at compared to some of the larger offerings in the city, but it offered the benefit of being backed up against a castle curtain wall and made it harder to approach undetected. The four of them separated briefly to their rooms.

Elisa was elated when she saw her tub materialize when she walked into the room. The steaming water, the soaps, and fragrant oils were all a welcome sight after days on the road. Washing away the dust and sweat would be bliss. With a mischievous smile over her shoulder at Drayel, she dropped her bag to the floor and walked backward toward the tub, unbuttoning her soft cotton riding shirt as she went. Drayel shut the door and turned the bolt.

An hour or so later four flushed and smiling faces met up in the dining room below. They ordered their meals and laughed and joked together as the night drew longer. They were just finishing their meal when a troop of the King's Guards entered the dining room.

Drayel was on his feet in an instant, God's Eye Medallion instantly glowing brightly. The Guard's did not reach for their swords and appeared very lightly armored for an assault force. The leader of the group unconsciously took a step away from Drayel and cleared his throat audibly before speaking.

"His royal highness, King Mannock Black Spear, First of his name, request the presence of Lord Drayel Shadow Walker, Lady Elisa Cor Sanctus, Lord Korin Silver Steel, and companion, in his greeting hall this evening. I have been instructed to deliver this message and take you, in his majesty's personal carriage, to the castle should you accept.

Or leave you in peace and request you join him for the evening meal on the 'morrow should you decline." The Guard said.

Drayel looked at his companions. Bell looked irritated at having been simply labeled "companion", but she was not well known to the Crown. Which could play in their favor, later on, should it come to fighting. Korin did not look happy about the armed escort, and Elisa appeared to be ready to dive into the carriage. Drayel sighed.

"Lead on." He said.

The Guard nodded his head and ordered his men outside. He waited politely for the group to walk out of the inn before following behind at a respectable distance. The King's carriage, like the castle, was gaudy and overdone. The king liked to bask in his opulence and wanted all of his subjects to know he possessed immense wealth. Drayel groaned.

Now seated comfortably inside the carriage, the four finally began to realize the gravity of the situation. In moments they would be before the king of Ka'len. The man Drayel had sworn to kill and take his throne.

But now they were going as guest. The events over the next hour would shape the future of Ka'len for the next century. Would it be war or peace? It would come down to the egos and pride of the two most powerful men in the country. And while Drayel could simply kill the king and take the throne, would he? Should he? He was still undecided. It all depended on how he felt about the king after they spoke face to face. If Mannock could convince Drayel that he would listen to his advice and change the way the kingdom was ran, then Drayel would give it a try for Elisa. But if Drayel had the slightest inkling that the king would betray him, Drayel would see his friends were taken outside of the walls, then bring the castle down. He smiled grimly and took Elisa's hand. She returned his smile and leaned into him as they rolled through the gates and into whatever waited ahead.

# CHAPTER 24

## MANNOCK BLACK SPEAR

*H*E HAD WATCHED AS THE CARRIAGE ENTERED THE COURTYARD. Soon the devil from the Warrior's Guild would step out of HIS carriage and walk unhindered into HIS home. How had it come to this he wondered?

Mannock was no fool. He had seen the direction the war was taking and knew it was a foregone conclusion that he would lose. The defeat his army had suffered in the valley that housed the Warriors Guild had been the final nail in the coffin.

He had very few knights and Soldiers left to fight the damned Warlock. His Guards were no match for Guild Warriors. His only hope of holding onto his throne was the witchling doing her job and convincing Drayel to join him. He hadn't held out much hope for that outcome.

He had spent the winter preparing to flee the castle and retreat to his home on the other side of the Mavi ocean. His personal fleet had been moored and loaded down with food stuffs and clothes the week before at Port Ka'len. As soon as the snow cleared the roads, he had intended on climbing into his carriage with his son and fleeing before the Guild advanced on Ka'len.

As much as he enjoyed being the King, he loved his son more. So, if he must abandon the throne to save Alasander's life, he would have done so.

Although Alasander was vehemently against it. The young man had grown up a prince. And in his mind, by rights, he would be the next king of Ka'len. So, when Mannock had told him that they would flee, Alasander had raged.

Mannock tried to explain their dire situation, but the young prince would not hear reason. He had threatened to take the palace guards and storm the Guild himself if it meant keeping the throne.

Mannock had finally dismissed him from the throne room and privately decided that when the time came, he would have the guards tie Alasander's hands and force him into the carriage and onto the ship.

Alasander might hate him for it, but he'd be alive to do so.

It was with no small amount of surprise when shortly after the first melt a very frazzled- looking innkeeper appeared at the gates in the middle of the night. The Guards thought the man was a drunkard because he was rambling about witches and magic. However, at that moment one of the kitchen workers bringing a late dinner to the Guards overheard the man's description of the witch and asked if he had heard her name.

It did not take long for the innkeeper to confirm that he had heard that one called Elisa. He also reported that the Warlock Drayel Shadow Walker and his second Lord Korin Silver Steel were with her and that they were making their way to the castle. Along with some other woman that seemed to be Lord Silver Steel's companion and a fierce warrior.

And while the Guards paid little heed to his ramblings concerning the witch, the other two names earned their attention. They'd brought the man into the castle and plied him with warm food and drinks while they questioned him.

When it became clear that they traveled alone and had been overheard planning to speak to Mannock, the Guard's decided it was worth rousing the King.

Mannock had been irate at being woken before dawn and threatened to have the chambermaid's head for rousing him. But he had thrown on his robe and slippers anyway. He made his way to the throne room where the Guards had escorted the now much calmer innkeeper. He told his story again to the King before being escorted from the throne room and put up in a guest room to rest after his long night.

Mannock had pondered the man's story for over an hour, and after watching the sunrise through the throne room windows, called for the Captain of his Guards.

"Lucian, send scouts out along the road between here and our visitor's inn. Do not interact with the Warlock and his group. Just watch and backtrack behind them to make sure his Guild is not simply following behind him waiting to attack. Then report back here to me immediately." The King commanded.

Lucian had practically ran back to the Guards barracks. The idea that the Guild could be less than two days from the Castle walls spurred him on. He chose four of his best men and his fastest horses. He gave them clear instructions to ride out and stage at intervals along the roadway. They would go in peasant attire so as not to attract any unwanted attention from the Warlock. The one backtracking behind the group would check for followers, then sprint his horse back up to the next man, then so on, until the last man sprinted back to the castle. In this way, they would not exhaust their mounts and the message would get to the king, and Lucian, quickly.

Lucian prayed to all the Gods that the Guild would not be riding behind their master.

His prayers were answered late that evening when a haggard and dusty horse and rider ran through the gates at a gallop. The Guard wasted no time dismounting and running to Lucian.

"Captain, it is as the innkeeper said. They ride alone. Four people, four mounts. Armed of course, but only them." The man said breathlessly.

"I had Tristan stay at the gates. When they enter, he will follow at a distance to see where they go for the evening. He will send a page with the message as soon as he can."

Lucian nodded. He dismissed the tired guard and walked quickly back into the castle and straight to the throne room where the king awaited word.

He had barely cleared the threshold before he king spoke.

"What news?" He demanded.

"Your Majesty, we have confirmed that there are only four of them coming into the city." Lucian said.

Mannock's shoulders dropped, and he leaned back against the throne, tension leaving his body. He had been literally sitting on the edge of his throne awaiting word. And now it was confirmed that the Warlock might truly be considering his offer. Had the witchling done her job? If so, she would be rewarded. Perhaps given a room inside the main halls. But that was something to decide later.

Right now, he had to prepare to receive his nemesis and the people with him. And, for now, surrender half of Ka'len to this man. Gods, he hated him. But given time to study him and plan, Mannock knew that he could find a way to kill Drayel. He just couldn't do it yet. So, he would play the submissive king. He would kowtow to the Warlock and let him believe that he truly wished his advice and appreciated his guidance. It would be a difficult few years, but, he would get through it. And in the end, he would remain king.

"Lucian, you and your men have done well. Have my dining hall prepared to receive Lord Drayel and company. We will serve our best wines from my private stock and a meal fit for a king. Have four of our best rooms prepared and fires started so that they may have a warm place to lay their heads tonight if they so desire. When your man reports their location give them time to settle in. They will need time to put away their things and bathe after being on the road. Then send my personal carriage and a SMALL contingent to extend an invitation to join me for dinner tonight. We have much to discuss. If they decline, and they may, do not attempt to force them to come. I will not have half of my city flattened by Drayel being angered. IF they decline, politely accept, and invite them to attend dinner here tomorrow night. But again, no aggression. Allow them to come to me on their own. Is that clear Captain?" Mannock asked.

Lucian had nodded quickly.

"Yes, your majesty." He said.

Mannock had dismissed him again and sent him about his duties. Tristan had reported well after the noon meal and told Lucian that the quartet had stopped at the Black Kettle Inn for the evening. Lucian thanked the man and sent him on his way.

A short time later Lucian and six of his most even-tempered and disciplined guards had ridden to the inn to extend the King's offer. And now here they were. Coming up the stairs and into the entry hall.

Mannock was waiting at the bottom of the wide marble and alabaster stairs that extended up from the floor before splitting off to the walkway that surrounded the entryway. He could see the Warlock's damned medallion glowing like a beacon through the black cloak he wore. He was wise not to trust the king or walk into this meeting unprepared. His companion Silver Steel's hand rested comfortably on his sword hilt. Normally anyone entering the castle would be disarmed, but in the interest of peace and making them feel safe, Mannock had declared they would be allowed to keep their weapons. Taking a deep breath to pull down the hate and bile rising in his throat, Mannock forced a large fake smile onto his face before speaking.

"Welcome Lord Drayel! I am glad to see you fared well on your journey. You must be starving. If you follow me to the dining hall we will eat while we discuss the business at hand!" He said jovially.

Without waiting for a response, he turned and walked quickly into the dining hall.

Drayel looked at the others. Korin shrugged his large shoulders and made an after-you gesture toward the door. Drayel smiled grimly and crossed the marble floor to the dining hall with the others following close behind. Servants waited patiently on either side of the door. As Drayel and the others entered the hall and took their seats they softly closed the large, engraved oak doors.

And dinner began.

# CHAPTER 25

## DINING WITH THE KING

**D**RAYEL SCANNED THE ROOM AS THEY ENTERED. HE WAS WELL prepared for the king to attack them when he believed them to be at their weakest.

The power roiling inside the God's Eye shown clearly through his thick black riding cloak. With a glance or a word, Drayel could eliminate the king, or anyone else for that matter, in seconds.

Drayel was surprised when he found no signs of assassins lying in wait or guards stationed around the room. It honestly appeared to be only his companions, the King, and the servants in the room.

They made their way to the table. All choose to sit at the end furthest from the king.

A slight that did not go unnoticed by Mannock.

Drayel sat at the end of the table facing Mannock. The seat afforded him a straight shot at Mannock should some plot unfold during the course of dinner. Korin sat in the chair immediately to his right along the side of the table. Signifying his position as Drayel's second.

Bell sat next to Korin, and Elisa chose the seat on Drayel's left with her back to the door. This put her close to Drayel, but also showed trust that she had no fear of being attacked from behind should someone charge through the door and assault them.

So, if no one else did, Elisa at least showed some faith in the King's intentions. This was also noticed by Mannock.

No one spoke a word until the castle servants had poured wine and water for everyone present. That task completed; the servants disappeared back through the large oak doors. The doors slammed with a resounding thud that shook the table slightly.

The king and Drayel sat staring at each other across the length of the table. Neither willing to be the first to speak and allow the other a win, no matter how small.

After what seemed like forever Elisa decided to end the ridiculous stalemate between the men.

"Your Majesty," She began. This earned her a sharp look from Drayel. She just reached across the table and rested her hand on top of his mouthing "Trust me" silently.

He stared at her for a moment before relaxing slightly and nodding for her to proceed.

She squeezed his hand gently and turned back toward Mannock.

"Your Majesty, as you well know, when I left your castle some months ago, I was tasked with delivering a message to Lord Shadow Walker." She said calmly.

It felt odd to Drayel to hear her call him by his official title rather than his name.

He decided he did not like it.

"Initially my Lord did not accept your terms. But, after having time to consider it more in-depth, he has deigned to meet with you this evening." Elisa saw Mannock turn red for a brief second.

She would have to be careful with her wording.

The fragile egos of men could be injured by miswording her introduction. And saying Drayel had deigned to meet with him implied the king was somehow lesser than Drayel. And while Elisa knew that to be true, it would not serve her purposes here tonight.

"Which is to say that he sees wisdom in your offer of peace."

She turned and looked at Drayel, silently begging him not to scoff at the idea of seeing the wisdom in anything the king said. Drayel raised the corner of his mouth ever so slightly, enough for her to see he was amused, but did not speak. Thank Isolde.

"As I remember it, your Grace, you promised Lord Drayel a Lordship over half of Ka'len, a chair on your advisor's counsel, and to return the Plains to my people." Elisa re-counted.

Mannock nodded. He remembered well the terms he had sent her to relay. He knew it was less than he could expect Drayel to accept, but it was all he was prepared to give. And adding the Plains into the deal was merely an incentive to get the witchling to passionately plead his case. He believed she had done exceptionally well, seeing how she was able to bring the Warlock to heel. Mannock smiled. The first real smile of the evening. This was going better than he could have hoped.

Now if he could get them to agree to go to the Plains, his first deception would be complete.

He had sent Guards and Knights to the Plains to determine what was killing the animals there. None had returned. Only mounts, scarred and bloody, had returned to the castle stables.

If the Warlock and his companions went to the Plains and were killed, so much the better. If they killed whatever resided there, well, that was fine too. It was a win for the King either way.

"I did promise all of this. And so it shall be. However, Elisa, you have not mentioned if Lord Drayel will investigate the issue of whatever is killing the animals on the Plains. As it will soon be returned to your family, I would think that you would like to know that your, Coven, is it? Will be safe when they return to their ancestral home." He said before taking a sip of wine. He did not want to seem overly invested in their answer.

Elisa looked at Drayel. He nodded and slowly pulled his hand away from hers so that he could cross them in front of him as he leaned forward on the table.

"You and I have much to discuss." He said firmly.

He did well to control the anger that roiled within him. Drayel would have liked nothing more than to turn the King to dust where he sat. But he had promised Elisa to give the King a chance, and so far, Mannock had held to his word. So, Drayel would as well.

"I think first and foremost you should know that I do not hold to titles. They are man-made and given and as such hold no authority for me." Drayel said.

He saw the King stiffen and knew that Mannock had figured out what he meant.

"I will not be calling you King Mannock, Your Grace, or any other construct of the so-called "noble" class. I will address you as Mannock or Black Spear. You may address me as Drayel or Shadow Walker. Either is fine. Is this acceptable to you?" Drayel challenged.

Mannock knew that Drayel would not be a simple puppet that he could play with like his other council members. He bristled at the idea of this man addressing him by his given name, but he also knew that he must play Drayel's game for the time being. That he must choose his battles and not fight the Warlock on minor details.

"It will take some getting used to, Shadow Walker, but I believe in time I will get used to it." Mannock said calmly.

Drayel nodded.

"Good, that's settled. Next order of business. This problem with the Plains has been going on for years now. While I have no problem riding out and seeing what is living there, I have to ask, why have you not sent men?" Drayel asked bluntly.

Mannock almost choked on his wine. He had hoped Drayel would not ask. Gods.

Well, sometimes the truth will get you what you want faster than a lie. Mannock could tell that Drayel was looking for lies and half-truths. Searching for anything he could use to label Mannock a liar and a fraud so that he could continue his war.

Mannock would not give him that. Not yet.

"Well, truth be told Shadow Walker, I have sent men to the Plains to investigate. I am disheartened to say that none of them have ever returned." He said truthfully.

Although it was more disheartening that he would not be able to use his game preserve for sport than it was for the men lost. But truth is truth isn't it?

Drayel nodded in acceptance.

"Okay, so something nasty is living on the Plains killing Knights and Guards as well as animals. Good to know." Drayel said semi sarcastically.

Implying that he had noticed the King left that piece of information out earlier. Mannnock shrugged noncommittally.

"It would appear so." Mannock said. "When might you and your companions leave to look into the matter? Or will you be waiting for others to join you?" He probed.

Drayel knew the King was trying to ascertain if the rest of the Guild was going to be following him to Tor'Amal. If they were, then the King would expect this meeting to be a ruse designed to buy time for the rest of Drayel's army to arrive. And in doing so might react aggressively and make the mistake of trying to capture, or even kill, Drayel and Korin. Luckily for the King, everything was as it appeared.

"No, Mannock, my army remains at the Guild. Training and ever vigilant." He said with just a touch of warning in his tone.

Mannock was no novice to politics. The implied warning was clear enough. It angered him that Drayel would come into his home, sit at his table, and make veiled threats.

But in a rare stroke of brilliance, he held his tongue and simply nodded his head in acceptance of the news. Drayel continued.

"Now before we discuss our departure, there are a few other matters that we need to discuss. I have heard and accepted your demands. Now, will you hear and accept MINE?" Drayel challenged.

Elisa looked at him sharply. He had never mentioned making any demands of the King. Korin raised his head and looked inquiringly toward him. Elisa was somewhat relieved to know that Korin was in the dark as well. It would have hurt her to know that she was left out of this and Korin was included.

Bell continued eating and sipping on her wine. Though the look on her face clearly showed she was no fan of the grape drink.

Mannock cleared his throat and sat up in his chair before leaning forward onto his clasped hands, mimicking Drayel's posture almost perfectly.

"Demands Shadow Walker? I do not remember that being part of the terms that I offered." Mannock stated flatly.

He looked disapprovingly toward Elisa and saw her shrug slightly, admitting that she knew nothing about this.

Drayel saw the King looking toward Elisa and it enraged him to see him casting blame on Elisa for his actions. She no longer belonged to the King. He just didn't know it yet.

"You can stop looking to Elisa for answers Mannock. She did as you asked. I am here. Your castle stands. And you still have your throne. You should thank whatever Gods you pray to that you had the sense to send her to my door." Drayel said low and quietly.

The threat in his words warned Mannock not to continue harassing Elisa. The Gods Eye pulsed in anticipation beneath the cloak. The power there waiting anxiously to be released.

Mannock could see the line he was approaching. How had he missed it? The holding of hands, the way they looked to each other before speaking. They were in love or at least lovers. And his ire made it clear that Drayel would brook no mistreatment of the girl.

Mannock raised his hands in front of him with palms out in a surrendering motion.

"Continue, Drayel. I will hear your request." Mannock stated.

Drayel looked to Elisa one last time and saw her visibly relax. She had been holding her breath, waiting on the King's response. This meeting could have ended then and there, and badly for the King, had he not had the wisdom to stand down.

"My request are few. In return for my accepting YOUR terms for peace, I expect you to accept MINE. They are as such. First and foremost, Elisa Cor Sanctus is no longer under your domain. As the Cor Sanctus witches will soon be returning to the Omni Plains, and thus your feud with them is ended, so too is the need for her to be here. As of this moment, she is free." Drayel said certainly.

It was clear that he would not be moved and expected no disagreement.

Elisa snapped her head around and stared open-mouthed at Drayel. She had all but forgotten that Mannock would still see her as his property. Her time with Drayel and her friends at the Guild had made her forget her hostage status here. Now Drayel, in one moment, had freed her to do as she wished. Whatever that might be. She closed her mouth and smiled at her lover. Her heart warmed and she felt her affection for the man grow even more.

Drayel did not look toward her or return her smile. Not yet. He was playing a role at the moment. He could not play fawning lover and powerful Warlock Guild master at the same time. So, while he wanted to turn and embrace her, he had more to accomplish first.

Mannock tried to find a reason to deny his request. But, the Warlock was correct. If he was to return the Plains and end his persecution of the Cor Sanctus witches, and witches in general, then he did not have a legitimate reason to keep Elisa. And giving him this small concession might make it easier to refuse whatever request he'd make next. Mannock nodded.

"As you wish. Elisa, while it has been my great pleasure having you here at the castle, your indentured servitude here is released. You may come and go as you wish. You are free." Mannock stated.

He smiled and put on a false face of friendship. Now he would see what else the Warlock would ask of him.

Elisa beamed with happiness across the table at Bell. The barbarian had heard that part of the conversation and looked up from her plate to smile at her friend. Elisa blushed heavily when the Bell looked pointedly at Drayel, who was still locked in a stare down with the King, and with her right index finger made a circular motion around her left ring finger. Bell let out a little snort of laughter at her friend's sudden color change.

Korin reached for Bell's hand and took it, gaining her attention. He was not angry, but he shook his head quickly to let her know that now was not the time for fun and pleasantries.

Bell understood. She dipped her head down to look at her plate again, but not without lifting her eyes and smirking at Elisa one last time from beneath her hair. Elisa grinned quickly at her friend before they both resumed their serious demeanor.

Drayel waited on the women to cease their impromptu communications before resuming.

"Next, the Cor Sanctus witches will be allowed to return home immediately upon our clearing of whatever resides on the Plains now. They will not be made to wait for documents, title changes, or whatever noble nonsense that could prevent them from going home. They will return, immediately." Drayel said.

The King nodded in acceptance.

"Agreed. Done." Mannock said with a true smile.

That one was easy. He was already giving them back the Plains. That is, assuming Drayel did not die trying to remove whatever was living there. And if there was no documentation legally returning the land to the witches, then they could be easily removed again once he was dead.

Drayel nodded and took a deep breath before continuing. These next two requests were really one and the same. And it was the one that would define the future of Ka'len from this day forward.

"My last demands are this. You will release every magic user you hold in your dungeons, immediately, and return them to their families. And you will draft a letter, sign it into law, and make a public proclamation, tonight, that from this day forward all forms of magic, being used for the good of the people, will be legal and will no longer be an affront to the Crown." Drayel finished.

He looked around the table and found the eyes of his companions locked onto his face. They had known that he would eventually try to legalize magic and free the prisoners below the castle. They just hadn't known that he intended on doing it the first night.

Mannock turned scarlet red from the neck up. Even his hands, extending out from the sleeves of his velvet robes had changed color. The King looked as though his heart was about to explode from rage.

"You can NOT be serious Warlock." Mannock said in a voice just short of a shout.

"Ka'len has known great peace for decades. With magic outlawed, men have been mostly equal and fighting is rarely seen in our streets and establishments. My Knights and Soldiers have kept the peace within our borders with little or no problems since they have not had to battle those cursed with magical abilities. You can not truly expect me to release criminals, people who broke the laws of Ka'len, back onto the streets based on your demand alone!" Mannock was breathing heavily.

He had intended on staying calm and rationalizing with the Warlock. But this, this was too much!

"Mannock Black Spear, hear my words. Your fear of magic is unfounded. There are dark magic users within the borders of Ka'len. You have been extremely lucky that none of them have fought back against your morally corrupt Knights and Soldiers. Or targeted you because of your hateful and fearful actions. You have caged good men and women who used magic to help their families, to grow gardens to feed others, and treated all practitioners as if they were evil. This can not stand. I hold the power to bring down this entire Castle upon your head. Yet, I do not. I am here. Trying to bring about peace with you when it is well within my power to take your life." Drayel said angrily.

Drayel saw Mannock stiffen and reach for a tassel hanging from the table. Most likely the signal for his guards. Useless as they would be if it came to a fight. At this point, Drayel cared not. The King would listen and obey, or the King would die. He had tried Elisa's way, but he would not accept all of the King's demands if the King would not, in return, accept his.

"You made your list of, requests, and I have accepted them. Now, will you accept mine as well? To keep your throne and your castle. To effect real change in Ka'len. Will you, Mannock Black Spear, keep your word and listen to my advice? If I am to be your council then this is how you prove the truth of your words. Will you hear me and free your prisoners and remove this ridiculous law?" Drayel asked passionately.

He was breathing heavily. Whatever the King said next would bring about an era of change. Whether with the King and Drayel working side by side or with Drayel ruling Ka'len. Drayel did not intend on using his power to force Mannock to accept his request. If he had to force the man to see reason then he might as well kill him and take the throne. He hoped, for Elisa's sake, that the King would let go of his pride.

He did.

"So be it." Mannock said at last.

# CHAPTER 26

## A NEW KA'LEN

Sleep had eluded them all that night. They had left the castle and returned to their rooms at the inn. The quartet had talked long into the night.

None of them believed how quickly life in Ka'len had just changed.

They'd waited to hear Mannock's proclamation. And true to his word, shortly before midnight, his criers appeared at intersections throughout Tor'Amal. They'd made their way to the many taverns and inns still bustling with people to announce that magic was no longer outlawed, the King's magic bearing-prisoners were being released, and that the Cor Sanctus witches were no longer enemies of the crown.

It wasn't much longer after that when, as they watched from their windows, the four saw a motley crew of over a hundred thin, disheveled, and dirty people making their way from the castle toward the housing districts of Tor'Amal.

With that done, Mannock had kept his word.

They had soon discovered that nervous energy was going to prevent any of them from sleeping. So, they had made their way to the small, but well supplied, tavern on the first floor of the Inn.

They found a table unoccupied in the corner and set about the task of celebrating the results of their meeting with the King. They heard many varied opinions on Mannock's proclamation.

Many people were not happy that magic would be openly practiced in the Kingdom, while almost as many recounted stories of Cor Sanctus' healing their loved ones over the years. So, there was an uneasy tension in the air between the two factions.

But in the end, alcohol and music won the day and everyone was soon drinking, dancing, or singing. Mannock's proclamations were all but forgotten for the night.

As the crowd returned to their revelry the four began discussing plans for what would follow. First and foremost, the Omni plains.

"Well, that went better than any of us expected." Korin announced after the barmaid left. She'd brought three drams of mead for the men and Elisa, and a full glass of whiskey for Bell. As well as some smoked meat, bread, and soup for a second dinner.

Despite the meeting going remarkably well, none of them had eaten much from Mannock's table.

Drayel nodded and allowed a small smile to grace his countenance.

"I can't say it would have been displeasing for him to try to ambush us within the walls, but this, this works too." He said grinning at Elisa.

Elisa took his hand and held it loosely gripped in her own. She returned his smile twofold.

This night had gone far better than she could have ever imagined. Not only had Drayel and the King both left the dining room alive, but they had an uneasy truce. Neither man was truly happy with the terms brokered, but neither man was currently at risk of killing the other in his sleep either.

And she was free.

Drayel had done that for her.

They had not discussed it in depth beyond a few brief sentences when they'd first met.

She had been so concerned with the meeting and how it would play out, that she hadn't even considered her own welfare and situation.

With the fate of the entire nation in his hands, he'd had enough foresight and care for her to form his demand for her release as a non-negotiable aspect of his acceptance of the King's terms.

And now she was free.

She looked at the man that she loved.

He had enough faith in her that he had freed her without then legally binding her to him. She could have walked away and rejoined her coven and neither Drayel nor Mannock would have any choice in the matter.

She looked at Bell and saw the understanding in her friend's eyes.

Elisa wanted to be bound to Drayel, but with a ring on her finger and as an equal. Looking at him now neither woman doubted that it would be long before that very thing came to pass.

They smiled at each other and raised their respective glasses in a silent toast.

"So, now what Drayel?" Korin asked with a grin. "Do we ride out to the plains immediately, or return for the Guild?"

Drayel took a long drink of his mead while he considered the question. He shook his head slowly and sat his mug, now half empty, back on the table.

"Neither really." He said. He saw Korin incline his head slightly in a questioning manner.

He took a quick sip and set the mug back down before continuing.

"Elisa and I will leave at first light and make our way to the border of the Plains. We'll scout the area and see if we can find any sign of whatever lives there now. You and Bell, you will go back to the Guild and gather a Battalion of Warriors. And check up on Grey Cloak. He was friendly enough when we left, but that alone is enough to make me suspect he is up to something nefarious." Drayel finished.

Korin nodded his acceptance. There was a time he would have balked at sending Drayel off on his own. But now he knew well that the man needed no additional protection. The Battalion was not to back him up but to provide security along the border once the witches returned. Korin was no novice to war and political maneuvering. The muttering in the bar about witches and magic had not fallen on deaf ears. There would be mortals trying to sneak into the Plains and attack the witches or try to take their heads for souvenirs.

Drayel intended on providing protection for the witches until they could fully occupy their old towns and villages. As well as set up their own wards and protection spells.

"I imagine that Elisa's kin will want to return to the Plains as soon as possible. They will begin moving back toward Tor'Amal when word reaches them. Iplan on having whatever haunts the Plains disposed of long before they arrive to re-settle." Drayel continued.

"So, for the next few hours, let us drink, eat, and celebrate this night's events. Then tomorrow we shall see what the dawn brings." He raised his glass in a toast.

"To us. May your drinks stay cold, your beds warm, and the sun bright on your face."

Drayel drained the rest of his mug while the others followed suit. Including Bell who downed her whiskey with the same zeal as the others. They slammed their mugs down in unison and began looking for the barmaid for another round.

They'd drank and ate into the early hours of the morning when they'd all decided that they wanted some alone time to celebrate in a much more intimate fashion.

They'd fallen asleep in their rooms and awoke when the sunlight streamed through their windows.

They woke grudgingly and made their way downstairs together.

They'd eaten their breakfast in silence. None of them wanted to admit that they may have overdone it with their libations the previous night.

Now their heads hurt and the bright sunlight stung their eyes.

Elisa grimaced as the large double doors that led out to the street swung open repeatedly with people leaving for the day. After a few minutes of this, she put her elbows on the table and leaned forward to place her head in her hands. Shortly after the group noticed the tell-tale white light begin to emanate from her hands. The groan of satisfaction as the healing magic erased the pain and tension from her head told them that it had worked well.

The three companions just looked at her with playful grudging stares.

Elisa grinned before standing up and walking to Drayel, then Korin, and finally Bell. She healed their aching heads in the same manner as hers. Each of them thanked her profusely for the relief.

It was not lost on the group that more than a few of the people milling around the bar and dining area had stopped to watch the display. To their credit, most of them just observed with mild interest. Only a few appeared angry about the open display, but none were mad enough to approach the group and voice their opinions.

So now, fully rested, healed, and fed, the four made their way to the stables. The boy that had taken their mounts the previous day was sitting on a bench finishing an apple and a glass of water when they arrived. He jumped up from his seat and made his way inside the barn to retrieve their mounts.

In short order he had them brushed and saddled. He led them one at a time out to the waiting companions.

Drayel and Korin made a show of looking over their mounts. Although it was very obvious the mounts had been well cared for during their stay.

Nodding their approval to one another the men each handed the beaming lad a gold coin.

Easily more money than the boy could have expected to make in a year. He thanked them over and over and ran to the stables shouting happily for his father.

Drayel and Korin shook hands while Elisa and Bell hugged and expressed their dislike for being separated, no matter how briefly.

They swung up into the saddles and rode together to the edge of town. Korin and Bell headed south back toward the Guild. While Drayel and Elisa went east toward the Plains.

Drayel and Elisa trotted along at an easy pace. Silent and enjoying each other's company.

Elisa broke the silence after an hour or so.

"So, I've been thinking." She started.

Drayel shifted his eyes sharply to the side and tilted his head humorously. "Oh shut up." She laughed.

Seeing him grin and turn back toward the road ahead she continued.

"When Mannock took the Plains over and expelled my people most of them just began wandering wherever the winds took them. My mother, the Matron of the Cor Sanctus clan, always believed that we'd eventually be allowed to return home. She lives in the foothills of the western border of the plains. If we continue on this road we will pass within a mile of her home." She said.

She looked and saw Drayel nod in understanding.

"So, since she lives near the Plains, she might be able to offer some insight into what is living on the Plains. Meaning we would not be charging blindly into the situation. And, if I'm being honest, I would just like to see my mother again." She said hopefully.

"My Lady had it only been for that I would have happily agreed to your request. Yes. Let us go see your mother." Drayel said with a smile.

# CHAPTER 27

## FAMILY REUNION

*T*HEY RODE FOR THE REST OF THE DAY DISCUSSING WHAT THE future might hold. The sun was hanging low in the sky when they came across the first wards indicating her mother's protection spells.

"There's nothing to be afraid of." Elisa said. "These wards are only to alert her to the presence of people close by."

"I see. I'm familiar with your people's specific brand of magic. I have been scanning for malicious spells since we crossed into the foothills. True, when you left your mother's home she may not have had need of offensive wards. But, who knows what dangers the years have wrought? Between men, and whatever is living on the Plains, she may well have placed a few more aggressive wards along the path to her home." He said honestly.

Elisa nodded. It occurred to her, not for the first time, that it had been a decade since she last saw her mother. How much had her mother changed? Would she recognize Elisa? Would any of her siblings be living with her mother? So many questions. Elisa was suddenly very nervous about going home and questioning the Matron regarding the Plains. Was this a mistake? Her mother had given her to the King to keep the peace. True, magic was legal now and the witches no longer enemies of the crown, but would word have reached her mother already? Elisa's head was spinning with all of the questions and fears suddenly crowding her mind.

As if reading the sudden fear and turmoil behind those exquisite eyes, Drayel nudged his mount closer to hers and took her hand.

His touch alone calmed the storm brewing in her mind. Although it didn't slow her racing heart.

She squeezed his hand gently and their horses continued at a slow walk. They were lost in each other's eyes when suddenly they could not see each other anymore. Or anything else for that matter.

While they were walking, and distracted, one of their mounts had tripped one of the wards. A bright white light exploded into existence blinding the pair and their mounts.

Drayel was in the process of placing a shield around them when their vision began to return. As his sight cleared he saw Elisa staring at something in the middle of the road in front of them.

The look on her face was half wonder and half nervous anticipation. Drayel tore his eyes from Elisa and turned to see what had entranced her so.

He quickly understood.

For there in the middle of the road was a beautiful woman glowing from a harsh white light emanating from her skin and eyes. The medallion hanging from her neck was full of power and called to the God's Eye hanging around Drayel's neck. He felt the God's Eye reach out toward that small white sun. Drayel had felt something like emotion from his medallion before, but this time he felt something like happiness from his artifact.

As amazing as the reaction between the two artifacts was, what shook the Warlock the most was the striking resemblance between this woman and the woman riding next to him. They could have been mistaken for sisters, had Elisa not bowed her head and quietly said,

"Mother."

Matron Varna Cor Sanctus stood with her hands clasped in front of her in the center of her chest. Her head slightly bowed and eyes locked firmly on the two trespassers in front of her.

The glow emanating from her skin did not lessen as she stared hard at the woman that had called her Mother. Elisa saw her mother's eyes narrow as she focused on her face.

They widened slowly as her hands began to unclasp and her lips parted as the matron sucked in a small gasp of air. The recognition hit her like a hammer. Matron Cor Sanctus took a small step toward her daughter and stumbled.

Then she was running. Elisa dismounted fluidly and ran to meet her mother. All doubts washed away when she saw the raw emotion on her mother's face.

They collided in the middle of the road and wrapped each other in a fierce embrace.

Varna grabbed the back of Elisa's head and pulled her tight into her shoulder. Elisa's chest heaved as she sobbed in her mother's arms.

She breathed in the woodsy sweet scent of her.

Overcome by the swell of emotions swarming through them, the women collapsed to their knees in the middle of the road. Still clinging tightly to each other.

Drayel did his best not to smile.

He was happy for Elisa but felt that levity would perhaps cheapen the moment being shared between the women reunited in front of him.

So, he sat quietly and enjoyed the look of unbridled joy on Elisa's face as she held her mother.

"How? Why are you here? Is the King dead? Did you flee?" Varna asked in a rush.

She had pushed Elisa back slightly so that she could look into her daughter's eyes. Elisa could see the concern in her mother's eyes.

"I am free." She said simply.

Matron Cor Sanctus stared back at her with a questioning look on her face, then glanced over her shoulder at Drayel.

Elisa smiled brightly when she saw her mother regarding her lover.

"Matron Varna Cor Sanctus, allow me to present Lord Drayel Shadow

Walker. Lord of the Warriors Guild, half of Ka'len, advisor to the King, and..." She paused briefly while she determined the best way to describe her relationship with Drayel.

"My boyfriend." She finally ended with a smile.

Although Drayel noticed the smile did not quite light her eyes the way it normally would. He had heard the softening of her tone with the final proclamation. Was she disappointed in the fact that he was her boyfriend, or that he was ONLY her boyfriend? Did she wish for more?

He would have to delve into that mystery soon. Because truth be told, boyfriend did not suit his intentions for the woman kneeling in the road before him.

He nodded his head in the Matrons' direction and dismounted smoothly. He walked slowly toward the ladies and ensured the Matron could see the Gods Eye at rest on his chest and his hands open and resting at his side.

True, he did not need the medallion or his hands to cast, but for appearance's sake, he would attempt to appear as non-threatening as he could.

"Well met Matron Cor Sanctus. Your daughter has told me much of you and your Coven. I'm honored to meet you, Lady. And, if I may be so bold, We, " He looked pointedly at Elisa before continuing, "have brought you news that you will find most pleasing."

Elisa beamed at him and stood quickly, extending her hands and helping the Matron rise as well.

When they were both standing again, Elisa moved back to Drayel's side and took his hand.

"Then it seems we should find somewhere more fitting for a long conversation my daughter." Matron Cor Sanctus said with a smile.

She turned and walked back down the trail to where it ended. Or so it appeared.

With a wave of her hand the foliage in front of her began shimmering like a disturbed reflection in a pond. As it calmed and began to solidify, a lovely little cabin appeared where a copse of trees had been moments before.

It was a simple rectangular design. But the enchanted carvings adorning the walls and eaves were obviously not fabricated by human hands. The wood had twisted itself into the images portrayed. The very grain of the wood changed directions as the eaves and arches raised and lowered. A large stonework chimney extended ten feet above the roofline and was heavily imbued with protection spells, warning sigals, and hexfoils.

It would not be an easy task to approach this house without being detected. The Matron turned and waved the young couple forward.

Once inside she poured them all tea from the kettle hanging inside the fireplace. As they took their seats around her small kitchen table Matron Varna Cor Sanctus looked across the table into her daughter's eyes.

Eyes she had feared she would never see again. She had hated herself for the last decade and had struggled with her decision every day.

Giving up Elisa to secure peace with the King had been the hardest thing she had ever done. But, as Matron it had fallen to her to protect the entire Coven from being slaughtered by the King's men.

So, she had done what the King demanded and given him a "token" of her fealty to him. As well as a promise that the Cor Sanctus witches would not fight his men and would flee the Plains.

It had saved her Coven, but it had scattered them to the corners of Ka'len, and worse than that, it had cost her Elisa.

But now she was here in Varna's home. She was sitting across the table from her, seeming very happy and in love, and best of all, she did not appear to harbor much anger toward Varna.

Thank Isolde! the Matron thought to herself. She did not know what twist of fate the God's had played, but whatever it was her daughter was home.

Varna smiled.

"So, Lord Shadow Walker, besides bringing my daughter home, and for that, you have my eternal thanks, what is this other news that you bring?" She asked the man sitting next to her daughter.

She noted that Elisa had held tightly to the man's hand the entire time. She had no fear of him and seemed to lean on his strength. It warmed Varna's heart to see her daughter so in love.

"It is quite a long story Matron. Would you prefer I provide all of the details, or would you rather I simply get to the point?" Drayel asked sincerely.

Varna Cor Sanctus smiled. She liked the young man sitting across from her, she had, of course, heard of Drayel Shadow Walker. Never had she imagined that she would meet the man as a friend and ally. Much less have him sitting at her table for tea. Or that he would be in love with her daughter. But such is life and the will of the Gods.

"Lord Shadow Walker, I have not seen my daughter in a decade. If it pleases you, I would very much like the long version of the story. I would ask you to spare no detail." She looked over at Elisa and saw the tears threatening to spill down Elisa's face matched her own.

"Very well Matron. It would be my pleasure. I would ask one favor of you if you please." Drayel said. Elisa smiled slightly, knowing well what he was going to ask.

Varna Cor Sanctus nodded her head for him to continue.

"As Elisa well knows, I do not hold to titles. If it please you Lady, please, just call me Drayel." He said with his own genuine smile.

Matron Cor Sanctus smiled back. She found herself liking this powerful Warlock more and more. So many men clung to vain and useless titles as a means to make themselves feel more powerful or important. This man knew who he was and did not need a title to validate him. She understood completely.

"Of course, Drayel. It would be my pleasure. But, only if you will call me Varna?" She changed her tone at the end implying the statement was more of a question than anything. Drayel smiled and nodded.

"Of course. It would be my pleasure. So, where to start? How about the day a certain blonde witch showed up at my door, charmed her way past my Guards, and invaded my home?" He said looking at Elisa. Elisa blushed under his gaze. He had been smiling brightly, but as he stared at the woman next to him, the smile faded and he took both of her hands in his.

Drayel spent the next hour recounting his initial distrust of Elisa. How she had gained Korin's trust, and Bell's. And finally how he himself had fallen for her. He spoke of her swordsmanship and magical training. He told Varna how Elisa had talked him into meeting with the King and sparing the lives of the innocent.

He told Varna about their meeting with the King and how he had freed Elisa from him. This brought tears to Varna and Elisa's eyes as they looked across the table at each other. He recounted how he had demanded the freedom of the prisoners and lifting the restriction on magic users. And finally, that the Plains had been returned to the Coven.

Varna Cor Sanctus was not easily rendered speechless. But this man.

This Warlock, which she had heard was no more than a power-hungry monster, had single handidly not only freed her daughter but the entire populace of magic users in Ka'len with a single stroke.

And now he had returned her Coven's land that they might once again live in peace and have a place to call home.

Varna Cor Sanctus let the tears of joy roll down her face. Her amulet glowed softly in response to the emotion flowing through the Matron.

Drayel's God's Eye responded by illuminating ever so slightly.

Through their amulet's connection Drayel could feel the torrent of emotions running through the Matron. So much joy and elation. And, demonstrating the depth of understanding of the consequences of his actions, a little fear.

But mostly, it was joy that radiated from both Matron Varna Cor

Sanctus and her daughter. Drayel enjoyed the moment and watched as Elisa rose and went to comfort her mother and share in her elation.

They held each other tightly and cried on each other's shoulders. Mother and daughter reunited in joy and wonder.

Drayel did not wish to interrupt their long-awaited reunion or the bonding moment between the women, so he rose and poured himself another cup of tea while he waited.

He was sitting in a very comfortable rocking chair soaking in the welcome heat of the fireplace when the two women finally composed themselves and rose to join him.

They had talked into the early hours of the morning. The three of them had sat comfortably in front of the fire while Elisa and Varna caught up on a decade's worth of history. Elisa telling the story of her time in Mannock's castle. Varna, of her and the Coven's separation and her eventual settling in this cabin so near her forbidden homeland.

When it became obvious that Varna wished to speak about the Plains Drayel used the opportunity to segue into the topic of his and Elisa's task of finding and destroying whatever was causing trouble on the Plains.

The Matron's mood changed quickly when he mentioned their intentions of entering the Plains the following morning.

"No, you must not enter the Plains by yourselves! It would be the death of you!" She exclaimed.

Drayel gave her a polite, yet quizzical look, that bade her continue.

"Elisa, do you remember the great stone carvings that adorn areas of the Plains?" She asked her daughter.

Elisa nodded her confirmation. She remembered well the huge grotesque carvings placed sporadically across the Plains. She had always believed that they were placed there by her Coven to scare off any trespassers that wandered into the homeland. Was there more to that story she wondered?

"Well, something we never told the children of the Coven, or anyone else for that matter, is that those are not carvings. A century ago, during the battle between the Cor Sanctus and Cor Renders for ownership of the Plains, the dark goddess, Illyian, sent dozens of those monsters from her dimension to fight us. Our ancestors were not able to kill them. They were, however, able to conjure a spell that froze the beast in time. Over the years the beast became covered in dust and mud. Other elements took their toll and gave the beasts their stonework appearance. It was always believed that some of the beasts escaped the purge after the war and hid among the mountains North of the plains. When our Coven called the Plains home the beast feared venturing out of the mountains. When we left they did not hesitate to return to the Plains and the food available to them there. I have seen the monsters myself. What concerns me, Drayel is that the spell and the talisman my mother used to, shall we say petrify, these monsters has long been lost or stolen. So, you see, there is no way to stop these creatures until I find the spell and instructions to make the talisman that was taken from her Grimoire." She finished sadly.

Drayel could tell from her tone that she held little hope for ever finding the missing information. He understood her fear and frustration at, what she believed, was an insurmountable object between her and her Coven returning to their home.

He also knew that although her fears were valid, a century ago THEY could not kill the beast, he smiled slightly as he said,

"Varna, a century ago your ancestors could not kill these creatures. But, a century ago they did not have ME."

## CHAPTER 28

THE ROAD HOME

*K*ORIN AND BELL HAD RIDDEN AT A STEADY PACE AFTER LEAVING Drayel and Elisa. They'd stopped again, much to the displeasure of the owner, at Roosters Inn where Bell and Elisa had fought the drunkards.

They had paid the owner handsomely for the damages before leaving, but the owner was still wary of a repeat performance.

Thankfully the night had passed peacefully. The dining hall had been empty and the only locals that wandered in for a few mugs of mead had stayed to themselves.

Korin and Bell had rested well and started out early again the next morning. It did not seem like a very long ride back to the Guild from the Rooster.

They had laughed and joked the entire ride, thoroughly enjoying each other's company.

They were almost disappointed when they cleared the pass and saw the Citadel in the distance.

Korin smiled when they were met less than halfway to the gate by a contingent of Guards. Well, at least Gray Cloak can follow orders when he wants to, he thought to himself.

Drayel had instructed the lesser Warlock to install wards along the pass to alert the Guards if anyone should pass through. And the wards worked well. This was demonstrated by the Guards that had come thundering toward them before slowing to a trot upon recognizing Korin and Bell.

Captain Sandler bowed from his saddle in Korin's general direction.

"Well met General Silver Steel. And good afternoon Miss Bone Render." Captain Sandler had pronounced Korin's name with reverence but had put a slight sneer on his pronunciation of Bell's.

It was no secret that the Captain thought it was inappropriate of the General to have taken a lover so far beneath his rank. Although there were no specific laws preventing it, the Captain believed that couples within the Guild should be of the same rank. Or at least close to it to prevent the misconception of favoritism amongst the Warriors.

The slight did not go unnoticed by Korin. The smile had vanished from his face and was replaced with a stern visage that had sent many a seasoned fighter scurrying away from the weapons master.

Captain Sandler blanched. The blood drained from his face and he turned so white as to stand out clearly against the darkening sky behind him.

The voice he spoke in was one Bell had never heard Korin use in the time that they had been together. Few still breathing had. The voice he used now was cold, stern, and promised nothing if not a swift death.

"Captain Sandler, I would suggest that if you are fond of your ability to draw breath that you address Miss Bone Render with the proper respect going forward. Do you agree?" Korin finished as his hand dropped to the hilt of the wicked sword that hung casually at his side.

The challenge was obvious. Captain Sandler made a point of gripping the reins tight enough that his knuckles turned as white as his face. He did not even glance in the direction of his own sword.

"Of course General. I, I...I meant no disrespect to your companion." He stammered. Ignoring the snickering of the Guards around him, two of which had subtly moved their mounts to block what appeared to be his impending retreat, he turned back to face Bell.

"Forgive me, Miss Bone Render, I did not intend to disrespect you in any way. If I did so I sincerely apologize." He muttered.

He was scared of Korin, but becoming angry and embarrassed at having to apologize to a Warrior with less than a year under her shield. But, embarrassed or not, he would not be crossing blades with Lord Silver Steel over it. He was angry, but not a complete idiot.

Korin was still staring at the man as if he were already dead. Bell had shaken off the thrall she had found herself in due to Korin's tone. She reached out and oh so gently touched Korin's hand that still held the reins. He snapped his head around and his visage softened immediately. The look of concern on her face was enough to calm him and bring him back from the deadly line he was still contemplating crossing in her defense

"General, the good Captain has apologized for what I am quite sure was a simple slip of the tongue. I am neither injured nor offended by his error. His apology is good enough for me." She said as she held Korin's eyes.

Korin had slipped back into his natural jovial state for the most part, though some anger still clouded his eyes. Bell knew how to fix that.

"Besides, had he truly offended me, I would have had him join me in the ring so that I could break him in half, General." She said sweetly while batting her eyes in Sandler's direction.

Sandler's face flushed red with anger as the men around him, as well as Korin, roared with laughter.

Bell's reputation had been built quickly and honestly. The woman was incredibly strong and viscous when it came to the ring. She was not scared to fight and was most likely more than capable of carrying out her joking threat.

Sandler raged inside. But seeing Korin laugh, and the deadly situation diffused, Sandler thought it best to take the insult and move on.

Besides, General Silver Steel would not always be around. And Bell was still technically below Sandler. So, as soon as he got the chance he would have her cleaning the privies for making that comment.

Sandler smiled and laughed as if all was well.

"Fair play Miss Bone Render. Fair play." Korin said.

He looked back at the now calm Captain.

"Captain Sandler, ride ahead and tell the Captain of the Guard that I will need a Battalion ready to ride out in two days' time. They should pack for an extended stay in the field. I'll provide more details later this evening." Korin did not wait for the Captain to salute and acknowledge the order. He simply expected it would be obeyed. And it was.

Sandler turned his horse and rode quickly back to the Guild, cursing that barbarian wench and the General that she had so ensnared.

Korin and Bell had taken their time riding back with the remainder of the Guards. They turned their horses over to the stable hand and secured their bags before walking hand in hand back to Korin's room to bathe and change out of their riding clothes.

Korin had gone first and had the servants come in and change the bath water for Bell while he reclined, covered only in a soft white towel, on the bed.

Once the steaming hot and clean water had been poured in the tub Bell came out from behind the changing screen that sectioned off a corner of his rooms.

She did not have a towel. The incredulous look on Korin's face made Bell laugh out loud as she slid down into the hot, relaxing, and cleansing water.

Korin rose slowly from the bed and ensuring his towel was well cinched around his waist, made his way over to Bell.

He pulled up a stool behind the tub and removed a washcloth from the rack hanging on the side. He took his time washing her shoulders and her back before grabbing the soap bar and washing her hair.

He was still running his fingers through her hair, working the soap all the way through it, when she finally spoke.

"You know, my Lord, I have never heard you use that tone before."

She started. She felt the weapons master's hands tighten up as he braced for what she would say next. She knew he had thought he may have scared her when he used that tone on Sandler earlier, but no, in fact, she loved hearing that dangerous tone in his voice. And seeing him prepared to go to battle over her honor had resonated with the young barbarian warrior.

"I can honestly say, I quite liked it." She looked up over her shoulder with a mischievous grin. Korin relaxed and resumed cleaning her hair.

"But, I would ask a favor of you, Korin." She said hesitantly.

"Ask away my Love." Korin said easily.

"I like that you were willing to protect my honor and stand up for me. As a man should. But, I would ask you to keep in mind that, I too, and a Warrior of the Guild. In the future, if any man or woman slights me, please allow me to handle the situation unless it is clearly beyond my means. Is that fair to ask?" She looked back up over her shoulder again and saw the big man was smiling.

"Of course that is fair. Far be it for me to steal all of your fun. Miss Bone Render." He said with a slight joking inflection on her name.

Teasing gently and daring her to come out of the tub and fight him then and there. Bell blushed slightly at the image of her and Korin battling nude through his chambers.

She was contemplating doing just that when she noticed the look on his face had changed from joking to contemplative.

"What is it, my love?" She asked seriously, her face now matching his.

Korin rose from the stool behind her and walked across the floor to the stand beside his bed. He took something out of the drawer there and walked back over to the tub.

He hooked the stool with his foot and dragged it around until he was sitting on her left side and slightly in front of her. Still with an almost anxious or nervous look on his face.

He reached into the water and took her left hand in his.

"You know, it occurs to me, Miss Bone Render, that although I would never deny you your fun in battle, that you would receive far less disrespect from Sandler or anyone else, if your last name was Silver Steel." He said quietly.

He raised her hand gently while bringing his right hand up from the edge of the stool where he now held a gorgeous white gold ring.

He held the ring in two fingers and moved to put it on her hand. Just before the ring touched her finger he paused and looked to her for an answer.

The man unconsciously held his breath waiting for her answer. He had faced down and defeated skilled swordsmen and assassins countless times over the years. And he had never been as nervous as he was right now.

The matter of seconds seemed like an eternity before a now teary-eyed Bell hitched a sobbing and ragged breath before happily shouting, "YES!"

Korin practically slammed the ring onto her finger before reaching into the tub and lifting her out and onto his lap.

Bell rewarded him with a long and lingering kiss. Broken only by her sobs of happiness and her occasionally holding his head back to look at his face, his eyes, his mouth. Just HIM.

Bell kissed him again with renewed vigor. It was not long before Korin could not take it anymore. He lifted Bell easily and carried her to the bed where they celebrated their impending nuptials in the most intimate way possible.

# CHAPTER 29

## CAPTAINS BRIEFING

$K$ORIN AND BELL HAD MADE IT DOWN FROM HIS ROOM JUST IN time to eat dinner before he had to brief the Captains on their impending mission. They had eaten quickly and vowed not to tell anyone their news until they had told Drayel and Elisa.

They wanted their friends to know before anyone else. So, they'd eaten in relative silence. They'd talked about riding back to the Plains the next day, the food they were eating, plans for the evening. Everything except for what they really wanted to talk about!

They had walked to Sandron's and had a glass of wine to celebrate privately. Then, seeing that it was time for him to meet with the Captains, Bell kissed him again and essentially ran to her room from the courtyard. Smiling all the way.

Korin watched her leave the courtyard and made his way to the Captain's barracks. The Warriors had a hierarchy like any other military. And the higher- ranking Officers received better accommodations than the rank and file.

One benefit of this was a large oval table in the middle of the barracks. The Officers, and Korin, held briefings here. The acoustics were good, so he did not often have to raise his voice to be heard clearly. And the table allowed him to see everyone's face. That way he could ensure they were paying attention and not drifting off or daydreaming.

When he arrived all of his Captains had assembled, along with their seconds. The lieutenants did not warrant a chair at the table. They stood quietly behind their Seniors with hands crossed behind their backs and listened attentively. Should their mentor miss some minute detail it was their job to hear it.

Seeing that everyone was present and seated Korin took his place at the head of the table.

When he was in position all of the Captains stood in unison and saluted. Korin returned their salute and bid them be seated.

Formalities concluded Korin began.

"Gentlemen, I am certain by now that you have heard that our Lord Drayel Shadow Walker left to meet with the King." Drayel started.

The quiet murmuring among the Captains confirmed it.

"Gentlemen, as you well know, when we joined the Guild we took a vow. A vow to serve our Lord Drayel Shadow Walker. In all things. We do not pick and choose which of his decisions we will decide to honor on a given day. So he speaks, so we do. Agreed?" He asked while staring around the table. Daring any of them to challenge him or speak out of turn. None did. Though several of them looked angry and not at all pleased with this meeting and its subject matter.

"Moving on, it is my duty to inform you all that during this meeting our Lord has not only negotiated the lifting of the ban on magic, but he has also freed all of the prisoners held in Mannock's dungeons." He let that be fully understood before continuing.

A few of the Captains that were previously angry-looking now only appeared interested. Korin knew well that those men had family in the dungeons. And they might just now have learned of a loved ones release thanks to their Lord. That would go a long way to smoothing things over with the men as well.

"In addition to these great actions, our Lord has secured the freedom of our Lady Elisa Cor Sanctus. Now a free woman." A few of the Captains smiled and clapped lightly.

The Lady had made quite a few friends among the men during her time here. Her skill with weapons was well known, as well as the fact that she was their Lord's consort. Though none would dare call her that to her, or Drayel's, face. So, his Lady it would be.

"He has also freed the Omni Plains from the King's grip and returned them to the Cor Sanctus' that called them home for centuries." He finished.

The Captains seemed less interested in that. The Plains themselves held little interest to the Guild. There was no money to be made there. No battles to be fought. No valor to be had. What did they care about the large expanse of grass, lakes, and streams?

Beyond hunting for deer for the winter months, the place meant nothing. And since the false King had prohibited everyone but himself from hunting there they had not been there in a decade. It simply wasn't worth the trouble. Korin read all of that in their faces. Their expressions bored and disinterested.

"Our Lord commands two Battalions of Warriors to load wagon and horse in preparation for a deployment of no less than three Moons." The Captains all grumbled to themselves.

It would remain cold and bitter for the rest of this Moon. By the time this was over they would be in the cold and rainy season just before everything turned green again and the days stretched longer.

As far as timing for a deployment living in tents out in an open field went, it could not be much worse. But at least the snow was gone, so that was something.

Korin had been through enough of these briefings to understand what the men were thinking. He allowed them to work through the problems and complications amongst each other for a few moments. When the conversations began to stray from the topic at hand he took control yet again.

"Gentlemen, in addition to the cold, rain, wind, mud, and other myriad of gripes and complaints you have all voiced, you should know that there is a good chance that we will see SOME type of combat on the Plains." He said.

He smiled when he saw the young Lieutenants, and most of the Captains, visibly perk up at that news.

"During the meeting with the King, it was revealed that someone, or someTHING, has been killing off the livestock and game kept there. Whatever is there has also killed several of the King's knights..." He had to pause as the Captains cheered and laughed at that bit of news. Korin himself smiled before continuing. "..and as pleasant as that news is to us, we can not allow the peaceful Cor Sanctus witches to return to their home while that threat exists. We will end that threat." He concluded.

Most of the Captains agreed. The ones that did not were smart enough to not voice their opinions in the open. In the end they all nodded and agreed to ride out shortly after sunrise the following day. They would spend the night packing wagons and prepare for the trip North using one of their purpose built trails.

They would go to the Plains, kill whatever was plaguing that land, then provide security along the borders until the Cor Sanctus' had all returned to their homes and settled in.

It was not a normal operation for the Warriors Guild. They would get paid from the Guilds coffers obviously. But most of the seasoned Captains wondered where this altruistic Drayel had come from. Doing this with no expectation of reimbursement, and at a great financial cost to the Guild, was not something he normally would have done.

They could not help but wonder if maybe Lady Elisa had swayed Lord Drayel in this wasteful direction. But whatever the reason, upon the 'morrow they would ride for the Plains.

# CHAPTER 30

THE OMNI PLAINS

**D**RAYEL AND ELISA HAD SLEPT SOUNDLY AFTER FINISHING THEIR conversation with Varna. The Matron had shown them to a small, but comfortable, room concealed in the shadows behind the fireplace.

Varna had bid them good night and left for her own chambers on the other side of the sitting area.

They were both exhausted from the travels and the excitement of the day. They had fallen asleep in each other's arms almost immediately.

The sun did not disturb their slumber in their little nook of a room. There was no window for the offending light to make its way through.

So neither woke until the smell of frying bacon and eggs wafted around the corner. Elisa grudgingly opened her eyes and looked up from where her head lay on his chest.

He smiled at her and her heart lifted. She smiled in return before pushing up with her feet and rising on her arms to kiss him quickly before springing out of the soft warm bed.

Drayel groaned playfully and swung his legs off of the bed to rise with her. Elisa led the way, dragging him by the hand, out from behind the fireplace and into the seating area where she froze and gave an excited little squeal.

It was perhaps the most "girlish" thing that Drayel had ever heard from his Lady. But a quick peek around her revealed the reason.

Sitting on the couch, now rising to their feet quickly, were three witches roughly Elisa's age and favoring her heavily. They were so similar in fact that only their red, brown, and silver hair clearly distinguished them from each other and Elisa.

"Cousins!"

"Elisa!" They shrieked in unison. The four women met in the middle of the floor and enveloped one another in a warm embrace.

Varna had stopped her culinary duties long enough to enjoy watching her nieces reunite with her daughter. She saw Drayel looking in her direction and smiled at the Warlock.

He nodded and smiled in return before taking a seat in the recliner he had made his personal refuge during her and Elisa's period of reacquaintance the night before. It appeared that he would do the same for Elisa again this morning while the girls caught up.

Elisa paused briefly when the subject turned to men, with a questioning look from all three cousins in Drayel's direction. Elisa realized to her chagrin that she had failed to introduce Drayel to her cousins in her excitement.

She blushed ever so slightly from embarrassment before turning to her lover.

"Ladies, I give you Lord Drayel Shadow Walker. Leader of the Warriors Guild, and several other things, but most of all, my boyfriend." Elisa did not put the same disappointed-sounding emphasis on the boyfriend label this time.

Perhaps she did not wish her cousins to take note of her slight dissatisfaction and question her in-depth about it.

But Drayel knew the woman well. And he saw the longing look in her eyes when she glanced back at him. Yes, they would have to have a very important conversation soon.

He inadvertently glanced in Varna's direction and saw the Matron smiling at him and giving him a knowing look. So, her mother knew his plans now? Gods. This was going to be a long trip he thought, laughing to himself.

He nodded back to Varna before rising to greet each of the three witches.

He found that the red-haired witch was named Torin, daughter of Varna's sister Alisandra. The brown-haired one was Sabrina, daughter of Miriam, and the silver-haired witch was Cassandra, daughter of Sahnin. Their mothers had all left the Plains to seek a new place to live across the ocean years ago. The cousins had all elected to stay behind in Ka'len for now.

Once they had gotten word of the Plains being returned to them they had rode through the night to Varna's home to tell her the news.

Only to find their long-lost cousin, and boyfriend, asleep in the spare bedroom and a fully informed Varna waiting for them by the fire.

When they heard that Elisa and Drayel were the reason for the return of their homeland it was all Varna could do to keep the girls from rushing into the room and piling on top of the sleeping couple.

So, they had waited, however impatiently, on them to rise. Sabrina had suggested that perhaps her cousin might be hungry and that the smell of breakfast might help rouse them from their slumber. She was correct.

Introductions complete, they made their way into the kitchen to the long bar top table that sat in the middle of the floor between the kitchen and the seating area. Varna handed out plates and utensils and began passing around bowls of eggs, bacon, chopped fruits, biscuits, and butter. Once everyone had fixed their plates and settled the conversation began anew.

Elisa recounted the story of how she and Drayel had met. Her mother listened with rapt attention as if she hadn't already heard the story the night before. She had discussed her weapons training and the meeting with the King.

Elisa noticed that when she had recounted her magical training with Drayel, Cassandra, who asked to be called Cassidy for short, had quietly scoffed beneath her breath.

Her story complete Elisa turned and faced Cassidy in her chair.

"Cousin, is there something wrong?" Elisa asked.

Cassidy shook her head and gave a mischievous smile.

"Why no, Elisa. Of course not. But, one wonders, just how much could your Warlock have taught you about OUR magic? Can you truly use it to good effect? Or is it just smoke and mirrors, similar to Warlock magic?" She asked with a playful grin.

Elisa saw the humor drain from Drayel's face as he took on his role of Lord of the Warriors Guild. Elisa did not wish to see Drayel angered. She recognized Cassidy was teasing the Warlock, and her, but meant no harm. Elisa would have to deflect the conversation before her cousin took things too far.

"You know Cassidy, I think it would be fun to find out just how effective my Lord's training has been. Shall we go outside and test the validity of his instruction?" Elisa asked sweetly.

The cousins all nodded their agreement. The only hold outs being Varna and Drayel.

As the other girls all rushed outside to clear the ground Drayel took Elisa's hand and looked at her questioningly.

"She meant no harm Drayel. Witches tease roughly. And I remember as children we used to duel using whatever magic we knew to practice fighting the Cor Renders should they ever invade again." Elisa explained.

Varna cleared her throat politely to garner their attention.

"That is true Elisa, but forgive me, these girls have been on their own for the last ten years. Cassidy is known for her prowess with casting. Torin is almost as dangerous. And Sabrina? Sabrina infiltrated the Cor Renders for the better part of five years. She traveled with their raiders and learned their dark magics to be better prepared for combat with them should the need arise. She is absolutely lethal. The duels were a game when you were children. But now, not so much. If you intend on showing Cassidy what you are capable of then you should hit as fast and hard as you can. Do not give her a chance to strike first OR second. My healing magic is strong, but pain is pain and if you underestimate your cousin you will get to experience it." Varna said seriously.

Elisa looked at Drayel with wide eyes. This was more than she had expected. As children, they were not able to hurt each other beyond minor irritations. It had not occurred to her that since they were older the danger would increase as well. She realized too that she would not have called her cousin out for a duel had she known there was a risk of either of them truly injuring the other.

"Elisa, you will be fine." Drayel said quietly. "As your mother said, you must simply strike first. If you do not wish to harm your cousin, or for her to harm you, then you must take away her ability to do so. You have mastered fire and wind. Now you need to combine them." He said with a smile.

Varna looked at the Warlock and smiled, clearly understanding where he was going with his instruction. Elisa stood watching the exchange between her mother and Drayel. How had they bonded so quickly that they could speak without words? Elisa found it slightly aggravating. But was pleased that they had become fast friends. It could have been worse.

"Forgive me for interrupting your moment, but apparently I'm the only one here that has no idea what you are talking about my love."She said to Drayel.

He smiled at Varna before turning to face Elisa. He walked closer and leaned in to whisper in her ear. He knew well that witches could enhance their hearing and did not want Elisa's one advantage to be taken away.

Her eyes widened as he explained what he wanted her to do. It would be a true test of her abilities, as well as curtailing any chance her cousin would have to strike her.

Elisa nodded her agreement and turned to walk outside where her cousins waited.

The air was crisp and cool when she walked out of the front door. The leaves on the trees around her were just starting to turn green and the sky above a brilliant blue. The breeze was soft and still smelled of the snow still covering part of the Plains.

Elisa saw the ground in front of the cabin had been cleared down to the very dirt by one spell or another. The cleared area was circular and about 30 feet in diameter.

The familiarity of it helped calm Elisa's racing heart. It looked just like the circles they used to duel in as children. Though this had been cleared by magic and not four girls with straw brooms.

Standing in the center of the circle was Cassidy. Torin stood on the west side of the clearing looking excited about the upcoming duel. Sabrina stood on the east looking positively bored.

Elisa did not know if she was relieved or worried by the fact that both girls had a shimmering white glow encasing their hands already. They stood ready to render aid, but also clearly anticipated someone getting hurt.

Had this duel been with swords, Elisa would have been infinitely more confident. But her grasp of magic, while much better than before she had met Drayel, was still only competent at best. And she had never dueled an adult Witch either. Drayel had promised to teach her offensive techniques when she had mastered all four elements. As it was he had only taught her defensive spells.

She had practiced some on her own, but what Drayel had told her to do to Cassidy would be a great test of her control over the two elements she could now summon.

Wind and Fire.

Elisa knew that as soon as she stepped into the circle that the duel would begin. And she expected Cassidy to strike hard and fast. She did not believe that her cousin would kill her, never that. But she would attempt to assert her dominance over Elisa.

Witches received rank and honor among the Coven by great deeds, mastering new spells, direct combat, or in peacetime, dueling.

Elisa knew that Cassidy would not allow her, an essential newcomer, to win. She would come out swinging. So, Elisa would swing first.

Elisa felt the little tornado of air spinning on her tongue as she called the fire into her hands. Binding the two was something that she had never tried before, but she found that her mastery of the two elements allowed her to bend them to her will easily.

With a smile, she stepped into the circle.

The conflagration was immediate. It surrounded the stunned Cassidy in a swirl of wind. Elisa's construction was a beautiful blend of fire and wind. A veritable tornado of fire surrounded Cassidy. Not touching her but effectively blinding her to Elisa's position and keeping her from being able to draw a deep enough breath to whisper the spell she had planned to attack with. She raised her hands and threw bolts of lightning in the direction she had last seen Elisa. The wind and fire grabbed the bolts and threw them harmlessly into the air.

Thinking quickly, the veteran dueler summoned the earth element that she was so very familiar with. With a twist of her hands, the ground inside the circle suddenly turned to mud.

She had hoped to sink Elisa to her chin in the quicksand-like ground. It would break her concentration and free her from this blasted tornado. But it did not work.

Cassidy found breathing was getting harder as the fire expended all of the oxygen inside the center of the funnel.

She sank to her knees as she struggled to understand why the mud spell had failed. She was just starting to lose consciousness when the fiery vortex around her dissipated.

She looked over to the west side and found Elisa hovering there a good foot off of the ground, much to the amusement of Torin. She understood why her mud spell had failed now. She wanted to be angry at the defeat, but could not help but be impressed by Elisa's quick thinking.

"Elisa, perhaps there is more to your Warlocks teachings than I gave him credit for." She said with a wide smile in Drayel's direction.

Sabrina simply turned toward Elisa and clapped politely for her cousin. As did her mother and Drayel.

The duel now over, Cassidy turned the mud back to solid ground before hopping to her feet and bounding over to Elisa. She hugged her cousin tightly before stepping away from her, still smiling.

"So, now that the fun's over, shall we go see about the beast on the Plains?" She asked everyone.

Elisa grinned broadly at her cousin. Glad that the duel had not caused any hard feelings between them.

Drayel took her hand as the group walked past her mother's cabin to the round pen on the other side of the residence.

"Well done." He whispered quietly.

Elisa smiled and squeezed his hand gently.

They turned the corner and found the horses waiting quietly. The hillside and the house created a natural alcove to protect the animals from the weather. And the thick foliage overhead created a natural overhead cover.

They saddled their mounts in relative silence, each one focused on the task in front of them. It would not do to be unseated due to a loose strap or broken buckle.

Once mounted the group followed the Matron out of the pen and onto a lightly worn trail leading directly east to the Plains.

As they rode, the cousins began discussing everything that had happened over the last ten years. They all agreed that they would send word to their mothers to return home now that the Plains were theirs again.

As the Matron and the cousins lost themselves in conversation Drayel quietly urged his mount on just enough to place himself out front.

He understood that the Witches were all excited to see each other again after so long, but he also knew that they were riding toward an inevitable battle with at least one Illyian sent demon.

They would not fair well if one of the beasts ambushed them while they were distracted. And Kyran knew that any beast of Illyian's would be a handful. If two or more decided to attack them together, then the battle would turn deadly instantly.

They had ridden for less than half an hour when the Plains came fully into view. They broke through the trees and looked out at the vast valley that stretched out for as far as the eye could see.

The Witches all reigned in their mounts and sat quietly staring at the place they had dreamed of for the last decade. It was there in front of them, quietly waiting for their return.

The younger Witches all turned and looked to their Matron for instruction.

"Drayel, I would like to see White Hill again. It has been too long since I have seen my home." Varna said sincerely.

The younger Witches nodded their agreement.

White Hill was the home of the most prominent members of the Coven. Whenever there was a tribunal White Hill was where it would be held. All of them had fond memories of the place, so it would be as good a place to start as any.

And being as it was the only hill in the middle of the Plains, it would make it relatively easy to see any of the beast approaching their location.

And easy for the beast to see them heading there.

They rode in relative silence for an hour. The Witches taking the time to enjoy the fresh air and the generally pleasant feeling of being back in their homeland. Drayel was not as happy to be there. While the Witches were sightseeing and discussing how nice it was to be home, Drayel was noticing the fact that there were no deer, rabbits, or other animals wandering the Plains.

After ten years of not being hunted by humans, the land should have been inundated with game animals. But no. There was the occasional hawk flying overhead, but as far as ground dwellers, there was no sign. This did not sit well with Drayel.

Even with two or three of Illyian's beasts, Vorgan, they were called, the game should not be so completely devastated. How many of the monsters were roaming these Plains he wondered?

It occurred to him that Varna had mentioned Illyian sending dozens of the beast to fight the Witches. It would be beneficial to know how many of them had awoken and were now wandering the Plains and surrounding hills.

He looked up ahead toward White Hill, now less than a mile away, and found he may not have to wait long for his answer.

For charging toward them from both sides of the valley was a vast herd of the Vorgan.

Thankfully there was nothing between the group and White Hill. If they could make it to the town then the Witches could find a position to either hide or fight.

Drayel needed no such place. He would find the highest building and place himself atop it so that he could see the beast that now charged toward them.

He looked back over his shoulder and saw the look of sheer terror on the faces of the Witches.

With the exception of Elisa and Sabrina. Those two appeared angry and ready to battle the entire herd on their own. Drayel smiled.

Elisa would not have been capable of this response when she first met him. Now, fully trained in combat, and moderately trained in magic, she had the confidence to stand up against a herd of vicious, and supposedly invulnerable, beasts.

Sabrina. Sabrina remained a mystery. Matron Cor Sanctus had spoken highly of the young Witch. He hoped she would live up to the Matron's praise. He would need someone to help protect the three that now rode toward White Hill as if it was their only salvation.

He just hoped he could convince Sabrina and Elisa to stay out of the fight and protect their counterparts while he battled the main body.

They reached White Hill with only a few minutes to spare before approxi mately twenty of the Vorgan reached them. Drayel dismounted quickly and slapped his horse's rear end, sending it running on past the village and out across the Plains.

The mount would return when the dust settled or it was called. Whichever came first.

His riding companions followed his lead and sent their mounts to the relative safety of the Plains.

The Witches gathered around Drayel, looking for him to assume leadership of the coming battle.

He did so with practiced ease.

"Matron Varna Cor Sanctus. This was your home for many years, so you know it well. Where is the tallest structure with a view of all approaches to White Hill?" He asked sternly.

Varna thought quickly and pointed toward the center of town. There was a steeple with a bell tower that would provide flat-footing and a perfect line of sight for him.

He nodded his approval.

"Do you have a building with walls and a gate? Somewhere that can be fortified?" He asked next.

He could see Elisa and Sabrina stiffen at his question, anticipating where he was going with it.

Varna thought about it briefly before responding.

"Assuming it still stands, the Covenstead was built to withstand errant spells and castings. And it has a thick barrier wall surrounding it to defend against Cor Renders incursions." She said excitedly.

Drayel turned and took in the faces of those standing around him. Three ready to flee to the Covenstead, and two looking as though they wanted nothing more than to fight.

Drayel knew that he would not get Elisa to leave his side willingly. And if he forced her to go with her mother and cousins it might cause a rift between them that he could not repair. He would have to trust her and find a way for her to help. Sabrina glared at him as if daring him to order her to flee with her aunt and the others.

Drayel smiled grimly and sighed.

"Matron Cor Sanctus, take Torin and Cassidy to the Covenstead and secure the gates. Place a spell of holding on the gates, windows, and doors surrounding the building. Do not attack the Vorgan. Your magic can not harm them and would only serve to enrage the beast. I want their focus on me, not you. Should you get into trouble send a blast of lightning straight into the sky where I can see it. I will come to you as soon as I can. Understood?" He asked.

Matron Cor Sanctus nodded. Angered that he was ordering her around in her village, but understanding that they would not be able to harm the beast, she nodded and turned to look at Sabrina and Elisa.

"And my daughter and Sabrina? What of them Lord Shadow Walker?" Varna asked.

Drayel read the concern and fear in the woman's eyes. It would be hard for her to know that her daughter was placing herself in harm's way so soon after getting her back.

But it was clear that the sweet little girl that she had sent to live with Mannock was not the same person as the armed and determined Witch standing beside the Warlock in front of her.

"Elisa will go with me to the tower. She can keep an eye on the Vorgan that are approaching from the rear and advise me if too many get to the Covenstead. Sabrina, your Matron speaks highly of your skills. What aide might you render in the coming fight?" He asked Sabrina sincerely.

"Lord Shadow Walker, my Matron is correct. The Cor Sanctus Witches magic was useless against the Vorgan so many years ago. However, no one has ever asked how the Cor Renders fared." She said with a wicked grin.

Matron Cor Sanctus snapped her head toward her niece with a questioning look.

"Forgive me Matron, but the subject has never come up, and was pointless to discuss while Mannock claimed the lands for his own. I had no wish to rid the land of these beasts simply so that old fool could hunt it!" She said with a completely vicious smile.

"To answer your question simply, Lord Shadow Walker, I intend to kill every last one of them." She said sweetly.

Although the look on her face, and the fire burning in her eyes, was anything but soft and loving.

Drayel smiled back at the determined young Witch before turning toward the Matron one last time.

"Quickly, prepare yourself and the Covenstead. Elisa with me. Sabrina, may the Gods watch over you." He said quickly.

"Watch over me Lord Drayel? They should watch FOR me." She said.

With a flash of dark red and black flames, the Witch was gone.

# CHAPTER 31

## MARCHING FOR THE PLAINS

**K**ORIN AND BELL HAD RISEN WELL BEFORE DAYLIGHT. KORIN HAD warned Bell that the day would be frantic and fast-paced, so if she desired a leisurely breakfast then they would have to rise before the others.

Bell had agreed happily. If they were to set out on a forced march then they would be eating hardtack and fruits for the next day or so. Korin had told her that there was a very good possibility that they would make it to the Plains that evening.

Whereas Drayel and Elisa's road to the Plains meandered North for a few hours before turning east to reach her mother's home, the Guild would take their Southern Road that went straight to the old trading post called White Hill.

Before the King had taken the place over, the Guild had frequently visited the Cor Sanctus witches to heal grievously wounded or sick Warriors. They had several of these "roads" all across Ka'len that expedited their travels. Most were little more than wagon trails that had been cleared of trees and rocks, but all offered much faster passage across

Ka'len than the well-kept Kings Roads. Scouts had reported back in the early hours of the morning that the Southern Road was dry and easily passable.

It had been an easy decision. The shorter route would be a faster pace for the men but would save a day of traveling. When the pair arrived in the kitchens, it was too early to eat in the courtyard, they found Grey Cloak grumbling and banging around pots and pans in the sink as he washed away whatever remained stuck inside of them.

And shockingly, the Warlock SMILED when he saw Korin walk into the kitchen.

"Lord Silver Steel! Welcome. I did not expect anyone at this early hour. The Warriors will not begin to rise for at least another hour!" He said brightly.

Korin did not know how to take this happy and cordial Talon Grey Cloak. It was odd. But, Bell was hungry, and so was he.

"Well met Lord Grey Cloak. My lady and I would like to take a moment before the day's activities begin to enjoy a hot breakfast before taking to the saddle. Is that possible?" He asked.

Talon smiled again quickly.

"Of course, General. The sausage and bacon are ready, I will simply have to fry a few eggs and you should have a meal fit for a king. And a queen of course." He said with a smile in Bell's direction.

Bell narrowed her eyes and stared hard at the Warlock. This was not the man she knew. Why was he being so damned friendly she wondered?

Korin took her by the hand and shook his head, indicating to her to let it go for now. He led her over to the pans filled with bacon and sausage. He grabbed them both a couple of biscuits and poured Bell a glass of apple juice while he chose the orange juice.

They were preparing to walk outside to one of the small staff tables by the back door when Talon arrived with their eggs, fresh from the skillet.

Korin thanked the man and he and Bell stepped outside to enjoy their breakfast.

They hadn't been there long when a few of the Captains meandered in, seeming to have the same idea as Korin and Bell.

The Captains sat down at a table adjacent to theirs and began discussing the movements to begin shortly. Korin soon found himself engaged in the conversation. He looked over briefly and saw Bell with her elbows on the table and head in her hands giving him a look that clearly reflected how she felt about having their breakfast interrupted. Korin barked a small laugh and turned back to his Captains.

"Gentlemen, we had best rouse the men and get on the road, otherwise my fiance' here is likely to kill us all for interrupting our meal!" He said jovially.

His Captains all began rising to their feet when they paused and looked at their General in unison.

"Fiance'?" They shouted happily.

Korin and Bell found themselves surrounded by the Officers and were soon wrapped up in various embraces, claps on the back, and expressions of well- wishing from the men.

All of them were excited for their General, and Bell, and made multiple promises of pints at Sandron's when they returned.

It did not take long for the word to reach the men. Bell and Korin were greeted repeatedly by well-wishers and people swearing to help with the wedding however possible.

The news put pleasantness into the air. Men that had been grousing and moving slowly due to the early hour and long ride ahead of them were suddenly moving with a renewed vigor.

Laughter and good-humored shouting filled the predawn air.

The horses were harnessed to the wagons that had been filled the night before and in what seemed like record time, the Guild was on the way.

They rode through the pass and turned off of the King's road into a field owned by the Guild. The rutted road appeared to be nothing more than a field road for horse carts, but if someone on the path ever cared to notice, the road had almost no curves. And if not for the small hills along the route, a mounted person could almost see the mountains surrounding the Plains.

The Captains were truly happy for their General, but being Officers, they intended to get the most from the Warrior's good humor. They began making a game of the march, having the men push their mounts and compete for who could cover the most ground.

The route would normally have taken them until late in the evening to arrive at White Hill. But as it was the Guild arrived at the top of the southern most mountain just as dusk was starting to set.

They were greeted by the sight of a huge battle in progress. The tell tall sight of green and white lightning streaking from a bell tower told Korin all he needed to know. Drayel was engaged in battle with....what the hell were those things?

The great monstrosities surrounding White Hill were the size of elephants. Some had furry bodies, while others had skin that looked like leather. All appeared to have long claws and snouts of various lengths with sharp teeth.

They moved fast and, as they soon saw, died quickly. Korin and the Captains that had ridden up with him gasped as a woman suddenly appeared in the air over the back of one of the beasts. The red and black flaming sword she wielded buried into the base of the beast's skull as she rode it to the ground.

The men gasped as two of the monsters turned and raised their massive front paws into the air before slamming them down onto, nothing. The woman had vanished in the same flash of flames. All the beast succeeded in doing was smashing their friend's skull into pieces.

Korin stared hard at the beast below. He had seen them when he was a child. But then they had been statues. How had they come to life? And why were they attacking White Hill and Lord Drayel?

It mattered not. If Drayel was fighting them, they were an enemy. And the Guild knew what to do with those.

Drayel looked to his Captains and shrugged. The men smiled back.

This should be fun Korin thought.

With a wave of his hand, the Guild charged down the mountain.

# CHAPTER 32



**D**RAYEL AND ELISA RAN FOR THE TOWER. DRAYEL WASTED NO TIME with the stairs and levitated up the side of the building. He cursed when he realized he had gotten lost in thought and had not grabbed Elisa on his way up.

He looked down and smiled as he saw Elisa right below him. She was using the erratic structure of the tower to find hand holds in the bricks to stabilize herself as she levitated up right behind him.

They reached the top just in time to see Varna slam the gate of the Covenstead. The three Witches took each other's hands and quietly chanted. A soft blue glow illuminated the entryways in the walls and building. Only the casters could pass through easily now.

Once complete the three Witches entered the building. And in short order could be seen peeking out of the upper windows of the building.

Elisa visibly relaxed, seeing her mother and cousins relatively safe. They looked around for Sabrina and were shocked to see her laying in an old rope hammock strung in between two trees on the edge of the courtyard.

Elisa suddenly remembered that hammock. Sabrina had put it up there for use during the hot summer months ten years ago.

That same day the King had banished the witches and taken Elisa.

Sabrina had never gotten to use the hammock. She appeared to be making up for it now.

When the first of the beast arrived at White Hill it roared down the main road straight toward the seemingly unconcerned Witch.

With an almost lazy ease, Sabrina rolled from the hammock and began walking unarmed toward the lumbering beast.

Elisa squeaked a small noise, like a choked scream, before looking to Drayel to help her cousin.

Drayel nodded and threw back his riding cloak revealing a glowing green and white Gods Eye Medallion. Sabrina noticed the sudden green glow of the bell tower and glanced upwards. She saw Drayel raise his hands and just smiled and shook her head no.

Drayel paused and just stared at the Witch. She was walking unarmed straight toward a killing machine that was lumbering toward her faster than most humans could run. But instead of fear, she had smirked and told him not to interfere.

So be it.

Elisa looked at him incredulously.

"Drayel! Help her!" She shouted although she could not take her eyes off of the scene unfolding below them.

No sooner had she shouted at him, Drayel saw the beast lower its head and turn its neck to snap at the tiny woman that...wasn't standing in front of it anymore.

The Witch had vanished in that same red and black burst of flames.

When she reappeared she was sitting on its neck and holding a sword made of the same flames she had disappeared into.

Sabrina smiled as she sank the blade home. The beast cried out once as the flaming blade severed its spine, dropping it to the ground. Sabrina smiled up at them before disappearing into yet another cloud of flames.

Drayel smiled at a very confused-looking Elisa.

"It's a totem, my love. She holds a relic that was rumored to have been stolen from Illyian herself by the Matron Celeste Cor Render. It was thought to have been nothing more than a child's tale. It appears that is not so." He explained. "Your cousin may be in possession of the one item on this plane of existence that can easily kill these beasts. What is created by evil can also be destroyed by evil. Or more simply, like kills like." Elisa nodded.

"I understand that. But, if it takes dark magic to kill these things, how will you kill them? Isn't the Gods Eye given by Kyran? Is he not considered a God of the Light?" She asked hurriedly. More beasts were coming. She knew the time for talking would soon be over.

"It is Kyran given. And he is a God of the Light, as it were. But, Kyran is also the God of God's. He did not bow to his brothers and sisters. And his power was the greatest of them. It was his will that created all of the medallion Artifacts that were gifted to man. So, while the God's Eye does not use Dark Magic, it can clearly see through the dark."

And, as if by way of explanation, he let loose a stream of green and white lightning from the glowing medallion.

The lumbering Vorgan that had been storming down the street toward its two confused companions was suddenly standing perfectly still in the middle of the street. It had a confused look on its face before it simply fell over dead.

The two Vorgan standing below them looked up in unison to see where the green and white light had come from.

Drayel grumbled quietly to himself. So, the things were sentient and intelligent enough to work out where they were. That could slightly complicate things.

As if in response to his thoughts the beast stood up on their back legs and began slamming their front feet down on the walls of the tower.

Plaster, dust, and wasp nest fell from the rafters overhead. The building would not take much more of this. Drayel leaned out over the tower and sent twin jets of white and green lightening down into the faces of the beast below. They fell together and landed on their sides directly in front of the building.

This gave Drayel an idea.

When the next few Vorgan came barreling down the road Drayel waited until they were beside the first one that Sabrina had killed.

He stopped them directly beside the first and used their massive bodies to create a barrier wall in the middle of the road. The creatures approaching from that side would have to move, or climb over, those three to get to the tower.

Drayel looked out across the Plains and saw the sun was slowly beginning to set. Low light would not be beneficial as it would make the Vorgan harder to see and increase their chances of getting to the tower. He preferred to be done with this long before dark.

As if in agreement, a flash of red and black came from out on the Plains just outside of town. Drayel watched as Sabrina appeared over the back of a Vorgan and downed it instantly. He watched as its two companions turned and tried to stomp on the Witch.

But, as he thought, she disappeared long before they could land their massive feet and claws. He was enjoying the sight of the two beasts that were now fighting each other after missing the Witch. He did not speak Vorgan, but clearly one blamed the other for the miss and vice versa.

His smile disappeared when he saw another large dust cloud in the distance. It was coming down the mountain and across the Plains at break-neck speed. Gods! The Guild had made great time getting to the Plains. But they had picked the worst time to arrive. Korin and the Warriors would fight very bravely against the Vorgan.

And they would die quickly. Human blades, magic imbued or not, could not penetrate the hide of a Vorgan.

Sabrina's blade was made of the same magic, and the same hands, as the Vorgan's. She held the only blade that could kill these monsters. Korin and his men would be slaughtered if they engaged now.

Drayel cringed as he saw several of the beasts take notice of the easy meal riding toward them. Kyran!

He could not reach the beast. They were too far out of his range and Sabrina was on the other side of the village battling the dozen or so Vorgan that were trying to flank them. Elisa too saw the beast now lumbering toward the approaching Guild Warriors.

She understood the situation and the grim look on Drayel's face. She also knew that Korin and Bell would be in that group. She could not allow them to die.

"MOTHER!" She shouted across the courtyard to the Covenstead.

She was relieved to see her mother's face appear at the window immediately.

"The Guild approaches from the Southern Mountains! There are Vorgan charging them. They will be slaughtered if they fight them! Please, fly to them and warn them to flee back to the mountains where they can defend themselves until Drayel can get to them!" Elisa begged.

Her mother, the Matron of the Cor Sanctus Clan, possessed the Isolde's medallion. It was the only way for Witches of this age to fly. It would allow Matron Varna to focus her power enough to fly to the Guild and warn them. The bearer of the medallion did not HAVE to have an item to ride on per se. But it was known that a broom, branch, or other long skinny item made channeling the power and controlling the flight that much easier.

Varna nodded.

Elisa saw her turn and talk to the two girls that had taken refuge with her. They nodded and all three quickly disappeared. Elisa saw movement on the top of the Covenstead and Matron Varna appeared through the doorway leading from the steps to the rooftop.

With a nervous smile, Matron Varna Cor Sanctus mounted the broomstick she carried and called to her medallion. The white glow illuminated the Witch and made her all the more lovely in her daughter's eyes.

Varna was slightly afraid. She had not flown in a decade. And now she had to fly out over a horde of angry Vorgan toward a fully armed contingent of humans that may or may not take her for a friend.

Either way, she was risking her life.

But she would do this for her daughter. With one last glance toward Elisa, she threw her leg over the broom and commanded it to lift.

She rose unsteadily into the air, death grip upon the shaft of the broom, as she struggled to keep her balance and stay aloft.

Once airborne the nerves subsided and it began to feel natural again.

The medallion beat against her chest. Calming her and relaxing her frozen muscles. Varna smiled and leaned into the broom. And she was soon soaring over the treetops. She was well out of reach of the monsters below and traveling much faster than them.

She allowed the medallion to glow bright white as she approached the men riding toward their deaths.

She hesitated for only a moment when she saw the riders in the front yell something unflattering and raise their bows.

If they shot her then at least she would die doing something for Elisa. For her, to make up for what she had done to her by giving her to the King, she would do anything.

She was waiting for the thrum of the bowstrings when she heard a loud, clear, and commanding voice call out.

"Bows down! All stop!" yelled the rider.

A large man with a shining silver sword drawn, and accompanied by the strongest woman Varna had ever seen, rode out to her with no fear.

"Matron Varna Cor Sanctus I presume?" Said the large man as he swung down from the saddle. Though, not without an anxious look over his shoulder at the still approaching Vorgan.

She nodded in the affirmative.

"I am Korin Silver Steel. My companion is Bell Bone Render. Well met Matron." He said with a smile.

Varna found she liked this man, but now was not the time for pleasantries.

"Lord Silver Steel, Elisa bid me fly to you and tell you to flee to the mountains and defend yourselves!" She said in a rush, turning to look back at the quickly approaching horde of monsters.

"Matron, I thank you for your concern. But we are the Warrior's Guild. We will not run from a battle. Especially one that our Lord is engaged in at this very moment!" He said seriously, but still with good humor.

"Lord Silver Steel, I do not question your, or your Warriors, valor or skill with the sword. The Guild and Cor Sanctus have long been friends. So, I tell you now as a friend, your weapons will not harm these beasts. You can not kill them. Your Lord Shadow Walker, and as I have only recently learned, my niece Sabrina possess the only means to kill these monsters. If you engage them here and now you and your Warriors will die." Matron Cor Sanctus said in a rush. "You need to retreat to the mountains. Now. Your Lord commands it."

A small white lie. But Elisa had told her to warn them and tell them to flee to the mountains, and Drayel had not contradicted the order. So, it was basically true.

Korin issued a torrent of colorful words. Varna looked at the Bone Render girl to see if the man's language had offended her at all. The big barbarian girl just stared with adoration at Korin and smiled when he looked her way.

"Gods." Korin groused one last time.

He looked at Varna and nodded a quick acceptance.

"Captains! Turn them around! Now! We have to get back to the cliff at the top of the mountain to hold these things off until Lord Shadow Walker is able to get to us! Our weapons won't harm these beasts, so do not engage directly! Fend them off and form a barrier at the top of the pass! Move out! Quickly!" Korin yelled.

There was no panic in his voice, just clear and calm commands.

Nor did he push his way to the front of the line as some of the Captains did under the pretense of "leading them up the mountain." Korin stayed with the rear Guard to protect the men as they retreated back the way they came.

He tried, unsuccessfully, to get Bell to move to the front of the column, but the shield maiden was not having it. She politely suggested that he could kiss the part of her that made contact with the saddle if he thought she was leaving him without a shield.

Korin smartly decided it was safer to fight the Vorgan than to fight Bell Bone Render.

So, with the Guild turning and making all haste to get back up the mountain, Varna took to the skies.

It was much more natural this time. The feeling of flying came back to her as if she had done it every day for the last decade. She was streaking across the skies back to the Covenstead when she saw a flash of red and black in her peripheral vision.

Sabrina appeared in the midst of four of the Vorgan. The beasts were panicked and slamming violently into each other as they tried to find a place to hide from the deadly green and white lightening that was decimating them so easily.

Sabrina grinned as she saw an opening in the confusion and moved to take it. She appeared over the back of one of the larger beasts and dropped easily unto its back. She was about to bury her blade into its neck when the closest Vorgan saw her sitting there. The larger Vorgan slammed into the one she was mounted on and knocked it into the one standing beside it, pinning her leg and knocking the artifact from her hand.

As the sword fell from Sabrina's hand she let go of her grip on the beast she had mounted and fell to the ground to retrieve the device. Without it, she was dead anyway.

Varna watched in horror as her niece fell under the feet of the now angry and aggressive beast surrounding her. Without a thought, she turned and streaked toward her niece.

Now surely dead.

Varna felt a lump growing in her throat as she fought back the tears and emotions that threatened to overwhelm her. She lost her concentration for a moment and her flight faltered, almost unseating her and dropping her in the midst of the turmoil below her.

She gasped with relief when she saw a familiar black and red glow emanating from underneath one of the beasts.

She crowed with joy when she saw Sabrina roll out from under the now dying beast and use its back to catapult herself onto the next behemoth. She stabbed the monster and pulled the artifact free.

Varna knew what would happen next, Sabrina would disappear into the flames and come back out over the next unsuspecting Vorgan. Except for this time the flames did not appear. They began to materialize, then flickered and went away, about the same time that Sabrina collapsed onto the back of the Vorgan she had just killed.

It was then that Varna saw the blood running in a crimson river from the young Witches hair and down her back. She had been injured in the melee earlier. Now she had succumbed to blood loss and was too weak to stand or summon the magic needed to teleport away.

Varna saw Sabrina look into the sky and reach for her.

She would not allow the girl to die. She was the Matron. It was her job to protect the Coven. She had failed to do anything when Mannock had taken the Plains away from them. She had allowed her daughter to be taken as a hostage. She was done giving in. She would not allow Sabrina to be killed while she did nothing.

Varna summoned her will and forced it into the Isolde medallion. Like a streaking comet, she fell from the skies.

The bright white glow from the medallion lit the darkened sky like the sun rising in reverse. The two Vorgan that remained could not stand to look into the bright radiance that now descended upon them. They turned their heads away and roared.

Varna landed beside Sabrina and lifted the girl over her shoulder. It was no easy task. The Matron was much older than the girl, and Sabrina was solid muscle and dead weight in her unconscious state.

But somehow she managed.

The Matron summoned the power of flight again and began to take off from the back of the beast. It was much harder to stay stable carrying the injured girl. And she did not bolt into the skies as she had hoped. She was much slower than she had expected.

So slow that one of the Vorgan, that had been slowly backing up to them, was able to swing its long tail around and strike Varna.

Between the strain of holding onto Sabrina, trying to maintain the glare of the medallion, and staying in flight, the blow was too much for Varna. As she crashed toward the ground her only thought was to get as close to the bell tower as possible.

If they could make it there then maybe Drayel could keep the beast off of them long enough for her to get Sabrina to safety.

Varna tuned the broom hard and steered toward the bell tower. She was fighting to maintain consciousness. The stress and strain of expending her magic, along with the injury from the Vorgan's tail, was too much. She felt something hot and sticky running into her eyes and knew that Sabrina was not the only one that had been injured.

She leaned forward and used the hand that was holding the injured girl to wipe the blood away. She was staring at the blood on her hand. She knew there was something else she should be doing but it wouldn't come to her. She was still staring at her hand when they crashed into the ground.

## CHAPTER 33

SUMMONING

**D**RAYEL HAD JUST FINISHED OFF THE LAST OF THE VORGAN ON THE North side of the hill when he heard Elisa scream. He turned just in time to see her leap over the rail of the tower and glide to the ground.

He wanted to stop long enough to appreciate her new found control of the Wind element but found that the remaining Vorgan were converging on....her mother and Sabrina.

He realized quickly that he would not be able to get to the women in time to save them from the final group of Vorgan.

There were five of them in all. Two barreling toward the prostrate women, and three from the west that had fled the North side he had been so handily decimating.

Gods.

Elisa must have seen the same scenario and decided to go to her mother and cousin. Drayel did not know what the woman planned to do. She did not possess any spells that could hurt the Vorgan. But yet she went anyway.

Drayel felt his heart ache with admiration for her bravery and the woman she had become. He could only hope that he would be able to stop the two closest to the women lying on the ground and hold the other three at bay until Elisa could do whatever she planned on doing.

So again he summoned the power in the God's Eye. He could feel his own power waning. He hoped he had enough left to do what she needed him to do.

If not he would go to Elisa and try to help her get the women to the Covenstead. That stronghold would be their only safe place. But he was not sure that the building would stand much abuse from the remaining Vorgan.

Elisa looked back once to make sure Drayel had seen her hasty exit from the tower. He had. When he saw her looking in his direction he simply nodded. Suddenly the sky above her was alive with green and white lightning streaking toward the two Vorgan charging her mother and cousin.

Elisa did not like that neither woman appeared to be moving. She had acted irrationally jumping over the rail. She had no plan. No magic to stop the beast. She had merely panicked when she saw her mother and Sabrina crash into the ground. Now she could only rely on Drayel to keep her safe while she figured out how to move two unconscious adult women a hundred yards to the Covenstead.

She gave a silent cheer to herself when she saw the two charging Vorgan become enveloped in Drayel's power and fall to the ground not moving. That gave her a very small window to get to her family and move them.

Elisa ran. In the beginning, she had cursed and railed against all of the hours spent in the training circle with Drayel and Korin. Now she praised the men for the excruciating physical training they had put her through while making her a Warrior.

She sprinted the remaining distance to them and was pleased to find she was not breathing hard at all.

Now, how to move them?

Elisa took her mother's arm and rolled across her prone body to come up with her draped across her shoulders. Okay, one down she thought mirthlessly. She shuddered when she saw the blood-soaked clothing and hair of Sabrina.

She did not have time to try to heal the girl, so she would have to be moved.

Elisa looked around for something to put the girl on and drag her but found nothing. Looking back to the girl once more, Elisa saw a blood-covered sash tied around her waist.

Suddenly she had an idea.

Bending her knees she slowly lowered herself until she was kneeling at Sabrina's side. Elisa took the sash off and was happy to find it was a thick material. Sabrina would not enjoy the next part of her plan but, if it saved her life, Elisa felt she would forgive her for any injuries sustained.

Elisa pulled Sabrina's hands together and tied the sash in a figure eight between her wrist letting the two tails of the sash hang loose in front of her. As she went to stand again Elisa saw Sabrina was still clutching a small black and red onyx rod. About the size of an artist pencil, it fit in Sabrina's hand perfectly and extended beyond her closed fist about an inch or so.

This must be the source of the flaming sword and flames the young witch had wielded so efficiently Elisa realized. She knew Sabrina would not forgive her if she lost that particular artifact, so Elisa gently pried it from the girl's hand.

Placing the rod in the pocket of her pants for safekeeping, Elisa took up the two loose straps and stood back up with her mother, now a familiar weight on her shoulders.

Elisa turned to see one of the remaining Vorgan was down and lying permanently still. The other two, however, had redoubled their efforts and would be upon her in minutes.

She turned and looked back toward the tower to see Drayel raise his arms and fire out a blast of green and white lightning. The beams streaked through the air toward the infuriated Vorgan and slowed the leading beast, but did not stop it. Elisa began jogging backward, dragging Sabrina by the hands across the courtyard toward the Covenstead.

She was only about halfway there when she tripped over a cobblestone that had lifted up higher than the surrounding steps.

Sabrina's weight was the only thing that kept her from slamming her rear into the ground and dropping her mother onto the stones.

As she landed Elisa rolled to the side and slid her mother off of her shoulders as easily as she could. She was exhausted. All of her training had built her into a very powerful physical version of herself, but dragging her cousin while carrying her mother in these circumstances had drained her. The adrenaline and fear alone would have been taxing by themselves. But coupled with the actual physical exhaustion, Elisa did not think she could pick her mother up AND drag Sabrina the rest of the way. She just could not do it.

But neither could she choose between her mother and the cousin that had been like a sister to her. WAS a sister in Coven terms.

Elisa looked up to assess her situation. She was sitting out in the open in the middle of a muddy courtyard. Exhausted, two unconscious family members relying on her to save them, and she found the two remaining Vorgan had somehow managed to stay alive despite Drayel's efforts.

Speaking of which, at that moment a familiar green and white light flew over her head and struck the lead Vorgan.

The beast bellowed and stumbled, but did not fall.

The second blast that followed was significantly smaller and did not affect the beast at all. It kept coming.

Elisa realized with horror that both of the massive enraged beasts would be on top of them in minutes.

Elisa felt a single tear run down her cheek. Her fire and wind magic would not help them.

She did not know how to use Sabrina's artifact, and Drayel had reached the limits of his magic.

Elisa sat down on the ground and crossed her legs. She had never thought about how her time would end. But sitting in a muddy court-yard with her injured mother and cousin was not a possibility that she had ever considered. She was saddened that Drayel would not be able to save them. But she did not blame him. He had done everything she had ever asked of him. He had changed Ka'len for the better by meeting with the King. He had freed the magic users, including her Coven. The Omni plains belonged to them again.

And she had her freedom. That was enough.

She would die having made peace with her mother and having known love. Perhaps her greatest regret at that moment was that she had never gotten the chance to marry Drayel and see what their children would have looked like.

She laughed softly as she imagined a miniature version of Drayel running around the house blasting things with green fire.

Well, if she was to die here she would not do so sitting on the ground and feeling sorry for herself. No. She was a Warrior of the Guild, Drayel Shadow Walker's lover, and the future Matron of the Cor Sanctus coven. If she was going to die then she would die well.

She drew her beloved sword and held it to her side. She would make her stand here.

But she was not alone. As she stepped back into a fighting stance she felt a hand on either shoulder. Thinking Drayel had come down from the tower to stand beside her she turned to tell him to run. If she was to die then she wanted him to stay safe so that he could recharge his magic and return to kill these final two beasts.

She was shocked to see Torin and Cassidy standing there behind her. The two girls smiled at their cousin and shrugged.

Elisa let the tears flow freely down her face. She would not die alone here. That was something. She looked at her cousins and did not see fear there. She saw determination and pride. They wished to fight as well. So be it.

The two girls stood on either side of Elisa, moving forward to put themselves between the Vorgan and the injured witches.

Cassidy struck first. Using the same mud field attack she had attempted on Elisa earlier, the Vorgan beast suddenly found themselves buried to their chest in mud. Their progress greatly slowed but still moving.

Torin struck next. Still holding onto Elisa's shoulder, as was Cassidy, the Witch mumbled a spell quietly and quickly to herself. She suddenly thrust her hand out in front of her and was rewarded with a blast of freezing air that engulfed the struggling Vorgan.

The beasts froze where they stood. The mud around them turned into glacial ice.

The witches cheered when they saw the beasts frozen in place. They had time now to rescue their Matron and sister.

Cassidy turned and took up the straps around Sabrina's hands while Torin struggled to pick up the Matron. She had almost succeeded when there was a loud cracking sound.

The girls all looked at each other in horror before turning to look behind them.

The massive Vorgan beasts were breaking free of the ice and had taken the first step in their direction. And were moving faster. Isolde! Thought Elisa. Would these beasts never stop?

A strange tingle rushed through Elisa at the mention of the God's name. She looked over at her mother and saw the medallion glowing brightly. And calling for her.

It was not an audible calling, but she heard it clearly in her soul.

Elisa looked at her cousins for their thoughts. They had both clearly un- derstood what she was asking. They nodded quickly and gestured hurriedly toward the medallion.

Elisa nodded and rushed to her mother's side. She could see Drayel in the distance. He was running down the outside stairs of the tower. So he was well and truly out of power. She prayed she would be able to stop these beasts with the medallion before they killed them all.

She lifted the chain from around her mother's neck. Her hair conveniently floated out of the way to make it easier to remove. Elisa was glad to see her mother was still breathing soft and evenly.

As she held the medallion up in front of her it glowed brightly and called to her yet again.

Elisa slid the chain over her neck and allowed the artifact to rest against her chest.

Power flooded through the young witch. She had used nothing but physical strength for this battle. Her magic was fully charged and the medallion drew on that power until it was fully charged as well.

Centuries of magical knowledge suddenly opened up for her. She could see and feel all of the wonderful healing magic stored in the artifact. She could feel warmth emanating from the medallion, like the love of Isolde herself. At that thought, the medallion pulsed brightly and seemed to confirm her errant thought. Elisa smiled.

For not only had the White Heart medallion shown her that Isolde was with her, but it had also revealed to her how to call upon the two remaining elements that she had not yet mastered.

When Cassidy had used her muddy earth spell she had still been holding onto Elisa's shoulder. Much like when Drayel had taught her the feeling of Wind, without the kissing, the contact helped pass on the key to controlling that element. The same with Torin's ice-wind. It had also been a combination attack like Elisa's wind and fire. Only Torin's held wind and water.

The Witches had inadvertently awakened those elements inside of Elisa. And now the Heart Medallion told her how to call upon them. And so she did.

The Vorgan had been slowed by the mud and ice. Elisa would see how they would fair against all four.

With a smile in their direction, Elisa stepped in front of her Sisters. She saw Drayel drawing nearer with his sword out and ready. She did not think he would get a chance to use it.

Elisa closed her eyes and surrendered her consciousness to the medallion. The feeling was warm and welcoming. When she opened her eyes the irises were glowing bright white with the power now contained in her.

Isolde was the Goddess of Love and healing. But she was also fiercely protective of her followers.

If her sister had made these beasts, Isolde would surely end them. The Goddess and Elisa at that moment were one and the same. Both shared power and felt love for one another.

They held no love for the beast in front of them. Dark, evil, and full of hate. There was no good to be salvaged from these monsters. So, they would send them away. Together.

Elisa raised her hands in a stop motion. A wall of fire suddenly appeared in between the Witches and the Vorgan. With another word, the ground around the beast suddenly gave way to mud yet again. The beast sank while bellowing their displeasure. Angry eyes focused through the flames on the girl before them.

When they had sunk up to their shoulders in the mud Elisa whispered a command slowly and sternly. The wind suddenly picked up and enveloped the beast in a freezing gale.

Ground and beast froze solid. Only their hate-filled eyes could be seen moving.

Elisa walked forward until she stood immediately in front of the closest beast.

Without a word she lifted her hand and placed it on the monstrous head in between its eyes.

She spoke a word and those eyes went wide with sudden pain and understanding of what was about to happen to it.

Elisa rocked back on her heels slightly, pulling her palm off of the beast's head a fraction of an inch before slamming her weight forward and pushing her palm hard against its skull. Power flowed from the Witch. The beast's eyes glowed bright white and literal steam roiled from its nostrils and ears as it was cooked from the inside out.

The beast was dead before she could remove her hand.

The second, and last, beast now struggled against the icy prison holding it fast. It had seen its companion being dispatched with no more than a touch and wanted no part of the girl now walking toward it.

But it could not flee. So the beast stared at the advancing, shining, girl and growled as loud as it could. And died shortly after.

As the last of the power needed flowed out of Elisa and into the beast she dropped to her knees in front of the frozen, and now lifeless, beast.

She felt strong arms lift her from the ground and smiled when she saw Drayel's worried face staring into hers. She lifted her hand and ran it through his hair gently before smiling and succumbing to the sleep that called her.

# CHAPTER 34

## HOMELAND

**D**RAYEL WATCHED ELISA SLEEP. HE HAD EXHAUSTED HIMSELF trying to stop the Vorgan from the bell tower. Unable to summon the power to levitate, he was left with no choice but to run down the winding staircase. Halfway down he had become light-headed and was forced to stop before he fell headlong down the stairs. He called upon the Gods Eye one last time and found just enough power left there to bolster him. He remembered running the rest of the way to where Elisa had stood with her hand on the frozen Vorgan.

He had watched the entire display as he ran. With the white aura that sur rounded her and the glow from her eyes, she had seemed the very incarnation of Isolde herself.

She was able to summon all of the elements as well. Something that had previously been beyond her. Her mother's medallion must have awakened those abilities within her.

He watched in awe as she stopped the Vorgan then disposed of them easily. But then she collapsed.

He knew well that it was simply from the expenditure of vast amounts of energy. But still, it was Elisa.

He knew well before then that he loved the woman. But seeing her fall had wrecked the man.

He was a veteran Warrior that had no fear of standing before vast armies and cutting them down. He had fought demons and monsters of all shapes and sizes. But seeing that lithe frame fall had driven a spike of fear into the Warlocks heart.

He knew that he would not wait very long after she awoke to ask what he needed too. But for now, she slept. The Heart medallion still glowing softly against her skin.

He turned and watched as Torin and Cassidy tended to their Matron and Sister.

Torin had been very concerned about Sabrina's condition. She had lost a lot of blood. But between her and Cassidy's efforts the blood flowing from her scalp had stopped and the color had begun to return to the young Witch's face. Their mother was in less serious condition. She had become fatigued from expending magic to sustain flight and blind the Vorgan. And the blow that had knocked them from the sky had been glancing at best. Elisa's mother would be fine.

Although, a conversation would have to be had between Elisa and Varna to determine who would be Matron. As it seemed the medallion had chosen a new host.

Drayel was not fluent in Coven politics. He knew the Matron held the medallion, but he did not know if she HAD to hold it to be the Matron. But that was a problem for later. They would all live.

They had been in the Covenstead for about an hour when a familiar horn sounded outside of the sealed gate.

Drayel smiled. Korin had arrived.

He looked over to Torin who nodded and folded her hands in front of her. Looking almost like she was in prayer, she whispered an incantation that removed the blue glow from the windows, doors, and gates. Once completed she looked at Drayel and nodded again.

"Thank you, Torin." Drayel said.

He rose from Elisa's side, and with a final glance at his sleeping lover, went to let in his General.

The man standing on the other side of the gate was not happy. Drayel did his best to hide his smile from Korin. The man was irritated at being forced from a battle. He would be a long time getting over it. But, like everyone else, he lived. Drayel was fine with him being angry as long as he was alive to BE angry.

Drayel released the lock on the inside of the heavy steel gate and swung it wide.

"Really Drayel?" Korin admonished. "You have me saddle up half of the Guild and march them to the Plains, only to have me turn them around and run AWAY from the battle?" He groused.

Drayel understood. His friend was upset about being excluded from the fight. But, and he appreciated this, Korin was also upset that Drayel had been in danger and he hadn't been allowed to help.

"Trust me, friend. This was not a battle you, or the men, would have wanted any part of." He said sincerely.

Drayel saw the doubt in his friend's eyes. Korin had looked him over from head to toe when he walked out of the gate, searching for injuries. His concern was touching.

"Walk with me, Korin." Drayel instructed.

Without waiting to see if he would follow, Drayel knew he would, he walked the short distance to the bell tower where a dozen of the Vorgan lay dead.

"Stab one." Drayel instructed calmly. Not angry, but a simple request. Korin said nothing but drew his fine blade from the scarab. With a look in Drayel's direction, he lunged forward and stabbed the beast. Or tried to.

Korin Silver Steels' sword was the sharpest and finest in the Guild. It had cut through blades, armor, and virtually everything else it had ever come in contact with.

But as the fine point made contact with the skin of the dead Vorgan it did little more than push the skin inwards slightly. When he retracted his lunge he found no injury to the hide of the dead beast.

With a grunt, he was still determined to prove he could have aided in the battle, he walked to the beast's head. With a sharp exhale of breath, he stabbed his blade into the beast's eye. Or would have if his blade had not been deflected as if striking stone.

He looked back at the now openly grinning Warlock.

"Okay, so I couldn't kill the cursed thing. But we could have harried them and kept them distracted for you." He said finally.

"I know you could have. But, I will never put you, or the Guild, in harm's way when there is no need. I sent you back up the mountain to protect all of you from the monsters. You should know that Lady Elisa's cousin, Sabrina, is responsible for killing the Vorgan that were attempting to pursue you up the mountain." Drayel said gravely. "She fell during the battle, but is being tended to by her Coven."

Korin paused to think about the events from earlier in the day. They had turned and moved with all haste back up the mountain. Korin had seen two or more of the beast coming after them. When he entered the tree line he lost sight of the pursuers.

When they arrived at the top of the mountain he ordered the men to quickly set up the wagons in a defensive perimeter. He dispatched archers to the tops of the rises surrounding the cliff and deployed brave scouts back down the path to warn of the beast's approach.

But the warning, and the monsters, never came.

Instead, the Guild Warriors, along with a very anxious Korin and Bell, had watched a green and white lightning storm develop in the valley below. There was an occasional flash of red along the edges of the battlefield, but they were too far away to distinguish the source.

So that must have been this Sabrina striking the beast down. But how? He looked at Drayel who instantly understood the question.

"Magic. The young witch held an artifact that created a flaming sword and a doorway that allowed her to move around the battlefield at will. Quite useful truth be told." Drayel said.

Korin had to agree. Though it stung his pride, her having a blade that could cut something his could not, he appreciated the fact that the witch had most likely saved their lives.

Drayel and Korin sat on a bench in the courtyard while the Captains dispersed the men into a tight circular defense around the town. The Vorgan may have been dispatched, but they did not want any unknown threats sneaking into the town unseen.

Drayel recounted the entirety of the battle for Korin. His friend listened with rapt attention as Drayel told him of striking down the Vorgan, Sabrina falling, the Matron being knocked from the sky, and Elisa taking the medallion to defeat the last two and save her mother.

"Gods," Korin exclaimed. "do you really think that Isolde appeared?" Drayel shrugged and sighed.

"I honestly do not know. All of the Artifacts have different properties. They are all sentient devices. So, is the presence they are imbued with simply the years of magic contained with them, or is there something of the Gods themselves? It is a question that has never been truly answered." Drayel contemplated the question before continuing. "I have, on several occasions, been able to communicate with the Gods Eye without saying a word. And I can feel its desires clearly, as it feels mine. Is it the medallion I communicate with so clearly, or the spirit of Kyran? I can not say. "He said honestly. "What I can say is that when she bonded with the Heart medallion the Gods Eye reached out for it. It woke up as fully as it does during battle and began recharging on its own. I did not have the power to provide a charge sufficient enough for it to reach that level. But somehow it reached capacity in mere moments."

Drayel unconsciously reached for the artifact hanging around his neck and held it loosely in his hands.

The men sat in silence. Both contemplating the events of the day and trying to determine where to go from there. Neither man spoke for quite some time. Content to rest on the bench and enjoy each other's company.

They listened to the Captains barking orders and watched as

wagons bearing men and supplies left the Hill for the various Guard post that had been planned the night before. Soon no one, or nothing, would entire the Plains without the Guild, and the Witches, knowing about it.

The Plains were, for all intents and purposes, secure.

Drayel smiled a thin smile.

He had now accomplished everything that he had promised Elisa. Magic was no longer outlawed, magic users were freed, and there was peace with the King. And the Plains. They were once again safe and in the possession of the Witches.

Drayel determined that he and Elisa would stay there for a moon. That would give her time to catch up fully with her mother. They could decide the Matron issue, and Elisa could speak to Coven members that she had not seen in a decade. And, if all went well, they could have their wedding here at White Hill. After that, they would plan the rest of their future.

He was turning to tell Korin all of this when he noticed his friend beaming at him and rocking back and forth in anticipation. Korin knew him well enough to not interrupt him when he was in deep thought, so it must have been painful for the jubilant man to wait for Drayel to come out of his contemplation.

"What is it Korin? You look like you do when the kitchen announces it is serving steak and potatoes for dinner." Drayel teased lightly.

Korin snorted when he laughed at Drayel's comment.

"No, much better my friend. Much better." He said joyfully. "I have asked Bell to marry me and she has accepted. We are to be married within the year." He announced gleefully.

Drayel smiled fully. It pleased him to see Korin so thrilled. He did not wish to take away from his friend's moment but felt that his news would only add to Korin's excitement.

"That is wonderful Korin. Though it took you long enough to propose." Drayel said with a smile. Korin responded with a certain dirty hand gesture, but the huge smile on his face proved it was all in jest. Drayel laughed and put his arm around the big man.

"So, it is a bit premature, but I too may soon have similar news. Kyran permitting." He said happily.

Korin leaned away slightly so he could turn and face his friend.

"Really? That is wonderful news!" Korin beamed at his friend before leaning back in and returning Drayel's hug. Drayel was quickly patting the big man's back and breaking the hold. Korin was a great friend but his hugs could smother a bear if he squeezed hard enough!

"Have you already asked her? What did she say?" Korin asked. He read Drayel's face and garnered the answer to his own question. "When she wakes then?" He asked in an optimistic tone.

Drayel nodded.

Korin smiled and squeezed his friend one last time before letting him go. Drayel made a point of exaggerating his inhale of breath when he was released. The men smiled at each other one last time before standing.

They had just risen to their feet when Bell came riding up to them on her wheat-colored stallion. The girl was beaming as she swung down from the saddle.

She walked quickly over to Korin and grabbed his head in both hands and kissed him fiercely.

"Been wanting to do that all day." She said with a mischievous grin. One Korin returned immediately. Drayel cleared his throat softly and made a point of looking at the sky in the opposite direction. Bell and Korin laughed.

"Apologies, my Lord." Bell said semi sincerely.

She knew Drayel was not even remotely offended, but she knew she probably should have at least greeted the Guild Master before kissing his General.

"I sometimes get overwhelmed when I see this big lug standing there. But, I come bearing good news. Lady Elisa is awake and asking for you my Lord." She said with a grin.

Drayel nodded and smiled.

"Thank you, Ms. Bone Render. Though I hear it may not be Bone Render much longer?" He said teasingly. He grinned when she blushed heavily. "Congratulations Lady. You shall make a fine Warrior bride for my General. He could not have chosen a better companion."

Bell turned an even deeper shade of red at the compliment. Korin smiled and took her by the hand, pulling her close to his side.

"Thank you, my Lord. Korin and I appreciate your blessing." She said sincerely.

"It is my honor. Korin is my oldest friend. And you, Bell, have been nothing if not loyal to myself, my Lady, and the Guild. I could do no less than blessing this union." He said honestly.

Korin and Bell smiled at each other and gazed into each other's eyes.

It was clear to Drayel, and anyone that cared to see, that the two of them were deeply in love.

Korin suddenly redoubled his grin. He turned and looked at Drayel before continuing. Drayel understood and nodded.

"So it would seem that you and I may not be the only two getting married soon." Korin said with a glance in Drayel's direction.

Bell cocked her head to the side as she contemplated who Korin was talking about, for a fraction of a second. Bell squealed with excitement loud enough that her horse startled and stepped away from them.

"Bell, you must not yet say anything to anyone. As I have not yet asked Lady Elisa for her hand. And I would not be so presumptuous as to assume anything on my Ladies part, you understand?" He asked.

Bell nodded enthusiastically. Although Drayel could tell it would be a test of her will to keep this news to herself very long. He knew he must ask quickly lest Elisa hear the news from someone else before he could even ask the question.

"On that note my Lord, you probably are not helping your chances standing here talking to us while she waits on you." Korin said with a laugh.

Drayel smiled and extended his hand to his General. Korin clasped his hand in a firm grip while pulling Bell close against his side.

Drayel released Korin's hand and turned for the Covenstead. It was a short walk across the courtyard to the building. He climbed the stairs and found himself growing nervous as he approached the landing. He smiled and shook his head. He had handled every challenge ever presented to him. He could handle this one as well.

He opened the door and stepped inside to see all of the Cor Sanctus witches were now awake and sitting in a loose circle around the room. Varna waved him into the room and gestured toward Elisa.

He turned and walked toward a smiling Elisa. It appeared all was well. Varna was awake and smiling, Sabrina was propped up on some pillows, but awake and smiling as well. Torin and Cassidy were sitting side by side on another cot and looking very pleased.

Drayel sat next to Elisa and took her hand in his. He leaned over and kissed the top of her head, breathing in her scent.

"Lord Drayel Shadow Walker, I Matron Varna Cor Sanctus, wish to thank you on behalf of the Cor Sanctus clan. You selflessly put yourself in harm's way to help free our homeland and return it to us. You have freed magic for use in Ka'len, freed the Plains from the Vorgan, and freed my daughter from the King. The Cor Sanctus clan will forever be in debt to you, Lord Shadow Walker. Though we do not have much to give, is there any way that we could repay your kindness?" Matron Cor Sanctus asked sincerely.

Drayel looked around the room again and saw the witches were no longer smiling but had adopted the same solemn and sincere look on their faces.

"Matron Cor Sanctus, Sisters of the Coven, I did not free the Plains from the Vorgan alone. I had help battling the monsters. Lady Sabrina, your efforts, and skill in battle were impressive and invaluable today. I thank you." He said, nodding to Sabrina.

Sabrina sat up a little straighter on the pillows and returned his nod, smiling tightly through the pain still present in her head. She gripped the artifact Elisa had returned and laid back against the pillows, still smiling.

"Torin and Cassidy. You came to my Lady's aide when she needed you. Your efforts slowed the remaining Vorgan and helped Elisa to defeat them." He said rising and walking to the girls. He took one of their hands in each of his and bowed his head slightly. "Thank you for your help." He said earnestly. The Witches squeezed his hands slightly before returning his nod.

"Matron Cor Sanctus, your warning saved the lives of many of my Warriors today. And your actions saved Sabrina when she was injured in battle. For that, I thank you." He said to the Matron.

Who he now saw once again wore the Heart medallion. He was glad that had been settled relatively quickly.

"You are most welcome Lord Shadow Walker. Now, what can we do for you? Had you not brought my daughter home, and engaged in the battle, the Plains would not have been free for quite some time. Now, thanks primarily to you, my Coven can return to their homes as free citizens of Ka'len. What would you have as your reward?" The Matron asked.

Drayel turned back toward Elisa and saw her smiling up at him from her seat on the edge of the cot. He walked across the floor and knelt down on one knee before Elisa and took one of her hands in both of his.

"Matron Varna, you talk of my freeing the lands, the people, and magic. You spoke of my freeing your daughter. But in truth, all I truly desire is to bind her again." He said quietly. The Witches all looked toward their Matron, not yet understanding the implications.

Varna smiled brightly as she caught on quicker than the younger girls, Elisa included. She just stared at Drayel, mildly confused.

"Lord Shadow Walker, I believe you have a question you would like to ask? So, ask it." The Matron said happily.

The realization spread around the room quickly as all of Elisa's sisters took their Matrons meaning. They all began to smile and leaned forward to take in the events before them.

"Lady Elisa, I have spent the last few months of my life getting to know you. I have taught you to fight with your hands and with your magic. You have earned the trust and respect of my nearest and dearest friend. And you have won my heart, Lady." He paused briefly as he tried to think of an eloquent way to pose the question. He looked into Elisa's now tearful eyes. She had figured out where this was leading and was smiling with tears running openly down her face.

"When you first came to my door you gave me a list of demands from the King." He saw her wrinkle her nose in displeasure at the statement, Drayel held up his hand slightly to ask for patience. He saw her nod and lean forward, bidding him continue.

"I never took those demands to be from the King, but more from you. The words might have been the Kings, but they were things that YOU truly desired as well. You wished magic freed. You wished peace for the kingdom. YOU wished for your homeland to be returned. And so, it has come to pass. I did free magic in Ka'len. I did meet with Mannock and broker peace. I did come with you to the Plains and help free them for your Coven to return. And yes, I did free you from your contract with Mannock. But that last part I did not do solely for you." He said quietly. Elisa looked slightly confused at the last statement.

"Lady Elisa, I freed you from your contract with the King for my own selfish reasons. For though you are free of one binding, I would bind you again, to me. Nothing would please me more Lady than to have you by my side for the rest of my life, however long that should be. So now, I Drayel Shadow Walker, in the presence of your Matron, your sisters, Kyran, Isolde, and the other Gods, ask you Elisa Cor Sanctus, will you marry me?" He asked reverently.

Elisa sobbed as she inhaled a deep breath and blew it out forcefully. She forced herself to get her emotions in check as she looked into the face of the man she loved. She flung herself forward off of the bed and into his arms, tackling him and taking them both to the floor, all while yelling, "YES! GOD'S YES!!" at the top of her lungs.

They rolled to a stop in a tight embrace as Elisa kissed him firmly on the lips. A small cheer went up around the room as Elisa's Sisters jumped to their feet, except Sabrina who simply clapped and cheered as best she could through her throbbing head!

"It is settled. Lord Shadow Walker, your request had been accepted, most willingly it would seem. Welcome to the Coven, Drayel." Matron Varna said happily.

Drayel and Elisa smiled at her happily before returning to their embrace.

# CHAPTER 35

## WEDDINGS AND OTHER UNIONS

*T*HE NEXT FEW WEEKS FLEW BY ON THE PLAINS. BELL AND ELISA had unanimously decided that their weddings would be on the same day.

It would be difficult to pull the Warriors off of their post for two elaborate weddings, so the women had decided that they would be married in tandem.

Since Drayel was the groom, he could not be the officiate. So the pairs asked Matron Cor Sanctus to be the one to read the vows. She had happily agreed.

The women planned the wedding and arranged for Korin's father to be brought to White Hill.

While the women worked on wedding plans, Drayel and Korin made plans for the continued security of White Hill and the Plains in general.

White Hill was one of several settlements scattered across the Plains and in the foothills. So far the Guild Warriors had encountered very few people trying to cross into the Plains with malicious intent. The few that had truly believed the Guild would support their ill conceived hatred of the Cor Sanctus witches. They were wrong.

The Warriors soundly thrashed the trouble makers attempting to breach their lines and sent them back to Tor'Amal, or wherever they were from, limping and bleeding.

There had also been a huge influx of Cor Sanctus returning to the Plains. They came at all hours of the day and night. Some having traveled hundreds of miles across Ka'len just to come home. These were welcomed and allowed entry unobstructed.

The towns quickly began to fill up. And to a one, the Witches made their way to White Hill to pay homage to Matron Cor Sanctus, the Witches that had fought the Vorgan, and Drayel Shadow Walker. All swore allegiance to Varna and pledged to stand beside Drayel and the Guild if he ever had need of them again.

And so it went. The outpost were built up and patrols cut paths through the woods so as to better secure the Plains for the Witches that now called them home again.

The settlements grew into small towns. Crops were planted, and homes were made.

Drayel was pleased to see the contentment and joy in Elisa and her mother's faces as they observed all that was occurring.

As the end of the Moon drew closer Elisa and Bell forced the men to cease their travels to the outpost and other settlements so that they could focus on their upcoming nuptials.

Neither man liked being pulled away from their duties. Mainly because they were familiar and they knew the routines of the Warriors well. Weddings?

They knew almost nothing of weddings, or how to conduct them. They had secretly hoped the women would plan everything and then just tell them when and where to be, as well as what to wear.

But now they were sitting in hardback wooden chairs at a table in the kitchen of the house Bell and Korin had been given to stay in at White Hill. On the table before them were a multitude of flowers in various shapes, colors, and fragrances. All of which, to the men, looked and smelled fine. However, the choice of decorations seemed to be the decision that would determine the fate of Ka'len according to their soon-to-be wives.

So the men sat and stared at the flowers. Drayel imbued the God's Eye with power and felt for an answer from the artifact.

It chose to stay out of it as well.

After much quiet deliberation between the two, all of which was not so secretly eaves dropped upon by the women, the two of them settled on some beautiful silky-looking purple flowers that smelled like a child's grape- flavored drink, and a second silky petaled flower that was a dark crimson red.

They chose wrong.

In the end, they were informed that the wedding would be decorated in yellow and white because those colors represented the spring time. Which spoke of new beginnings. And were their unions both not new beginnings? How could they not have seen that?

The men were summarily excused from the color selection.

Having been fired so quickly from their wedding duties, the two men determined that their next step would be something that they knew they were capable of doing.

One of the Witches that had returned brought her new mortal husband with her. A nice young man named Alec. He was well received by the Guild due to his chosen profession as a pub owner. It had not taken him long to open an establishment just off of the courtyard in White Hill.

It hadn't taken long because the men of the Guild had formed a line to help expedite the unloading of the barrels of mead, the cask of wine, and the many bottles of various whiskeys from around the world. Yes, Alec was well received.

The two friends happily made their way to The Union. Named for the bonds of friendship built between the witches and the Guild during the last moon.

They walked through the doors and were welcomed by the cheers of their men, and more than a few Witches sitting with them. It appeared the Guild was going to be very tightly bound to the Cor Sanctus coven by the end of the moon. In spirit and blood.

Korin ordered two pints of mead for him, and two pints for Drayel. They took their drinks and walked back outside to one of the tables in the courtyard. It was cooler and much more serene outside.

"So, what's next after the wedding Drayel? Will you return to Tor'Amal or go straight back to the Guild?" Korin asked.

Drayel took a long drink of his mead as he contemplated his answer. If it was anyone besides Korin he would not have been so forthcoming with his answer. But Korin was his best friend and his General. He deserved to know the truth.

"The truth is, I do not know what my future holds at the moment. This time a year ago I had my path laid out in front of me. I was going to dethrone Mannock, take his seat, and free Ka'len from his tyranny. After that, I would have continued making Ka'len a better place. Better water supplies, more farming, bigger ports, and increased security around our borders. But now that has all changed, has it not? I have done only a small portion of what I had planned. I can still accomplish all of the things that I desired for Ka'len, but now I will have to do it at Mannock's side." Drayel physically shuddered at the thought.

How long would it be before the King tried to betray him? And when he did, would Elisa still support Drayel when he was finally forced to kill the King? For he had no doubt that everything Mannock had said and done up to this point had been a small part of a much larger game. But he supposed he would cross that bridge when he came to it.

"So I suppose my answer is this. I will return to Tor'Amal and update Mannock in regards to the Vorgan and their defeat. I will not be informing him of the security measures that we have emplaced. I do not feel that he needs to know that particular bit of information. After that, I will arrange a scrying glass to be kept in the castle for him to contact me as needed. Then Elisa and I will return to the Citadel to resume day-today operations of the Guild while advising Mannock as needed. That is honestly as far as I have gotten." Drayel said morosely.

Korin understood. Ever since Lady Elisa had arrived at the castle things had been changing. Drayel had turned from his course. The Warlock that Korin had known for so long was mostly gone. The power and skill were still there. But the blind devotion to building power and wealth were gone. The old Drayel would have killed Mannock when he sat across from him at that dinner table without a second a thought. But not so now.

This Drayel had chosen a course that was less glorious but saved countless lives in the process. He had found a way to effect the changes he desired, but without killing Mannock. And he loved. Drayel Shadow Walker had taken many lovers in the time Korin had known him. But he had never cared about anything or anyone, other than Korin, in all the time he had known him.

But now, Drayel was marrying Lady Elisa. He was choosing love over power and seemed all the better for it. Korin was happy for his friend. But he feared how the Guild would react to their Lord refusing to take the throne and choosing peace over a profitable war.

And now they would be staying to Guard the Plains for the foreseeable future, without being paid. Korin loved Drayel, but he was concerned for the stability of his friend's position.

"Drayel. You know that I am very happy for you and Lady Elisa. Nothing will please me more than to share the alter with the two of you. But, I would be remiss in my duties as your General, and as your friend, if I did not point out the fact that your choices of late may cause some....contention.. among the men." Korin said earnestly.

Drayel took a deep breath and gathered his thoughts before responding. He was not angry at Korin. His General, no, his friend, was only speaking the truth. He had always been reliable in that way. When others would kowtow when speaking to him, Korin would always be straightforward and honest. If for nothing else, for that, Drayel would always appreciate the man.

"I am aware that some of my choices of late have been, questionable Korin." Drayel started. "However, as you have undoubtedly noticed, I have changed somewhat over the last year. I still desire a free and better Ka'len. But I see now that war and battle are not always the answer to every problem. I was able to sit down with Mannock and achieve most of my goals with no bloodshed. And although I harbor no illusions that Mannock can be trusted, I feel that I can accomplish the majority of my remaining goals by playing his game." Drayel said confidently.

"I understand Drayel. And you have my full support as always. But I do believe that when we arrive back at the Guild we should have a meeting with the Captains to better explain all that has transpired here. It would go a long way to relieving the men's concerns over our actions here and with the King." Korin said matter-of-factly.

Drayel nodded and finished off the mead remaining in his first glass.

"Very true my Lord Silver Steel. What is also true, is that you and I have not yet toasted your impending nuptials. So, raise your glass, Lord Silver Steel." Drayel ordered, although with a smile on his face.

"Long have you been by my side. You say you follow me, Lord Silver Steel, but long have I followed YOU. It was your path that I followed from the Rooster to the door of the Guild. It was you that I followed into the training circle to learn skill at arms. You claim to follow me, Korin, but know this, where you go, I will go. Where you fight, I will fight. You are more than a General. More than a friend. You are my brother. And as such, I pray the blessings of Kyran and the Old Gods upon you and Ms. Bone Renders wedding. I pray for a long and wondrous life for the two of you. Filled with battles to be fought, wealth untold, and love unending. May your children be as strong as their parents and blessed with the knowledge of the Gods. If the Gods ever see it right for us to be apart, just know that I will come when you call. And woe unto them that would do you and yours harm. For as long as I draw breath, I will ever fight your enemies by your side." Drayel finished his speech and took a long pull from his second mug of mead, matched equally by Korin.

When they placed their mugs on the table Korin was smiling broadly.

"Are you sure you can not be the officiate at the wedding? No one could match that speech, my friend." Korin shook his head as he smiled gratefully. "Or should I say, my brother?" He grinned. Drayel laughed and took a second pull from his mug and frowned when it came up empty. Korin laughed and finished off the remainder of his drink as well before going back into the Union for two more mugs.

When he returned he was fairly solemn looking. Drayel wondered what was bothering his friend. Korin sat down heavily on the bench across from Drayel and set their drinks down with a clinking of glasses.

"So, I was trying to think of the words for my toast to your and Lady Elisa's wedding." Korin said slowly. "But I have never been a great orator when it comes to being sincere and heartfelt. I do better when I am joking and having fun. Or barking orders at the Warriors. But words do not come to me so easily when they have to come from the heart. I am a Warrior by trade, so being emotional does not come easily for me. Bear with me as I muddle through this Drayel."

Drayel nodded and kept quiet as Korin tried to find the words he wanted to say. Drayel knew it would not be easy for Korin to speak and as such would put no demands on the man. But this was something Korin wanted to do, so Drayel would sit quietly until he did so.

Korin took a deep breath before continuing.

"You calling me brother is the best wedding present you could have given me Drayel. I have thought of you as family for years. And Elisa, she has become as a sister to me. During the time I have known you, I have come to know that you are a fierce warrior. You brook no disrespect and demand excellence from those around you. While providing nothing less in return. Though the Warrior side of you does not make the whole. You have shown compassion when it was needed. And lately, you have shown a capacity to put others first and to love. Lady Elisa has truly brought out the best in you my friend. It has been an honor, and my pleasure, to know both of you. I too pray the blessings of all the Gods upon your marriage. I pray that your children get your magic and Elisa's looks." Korin smiled at Drayel's smirk and roll of the eyes. "And I swear, by Daigon, and by my word, that I will always fight by your side. And if the Gods should see us parted, I will come to fight for you and yours, wherever you may be." Korin finished.

Drayel smiled sincerely. Korin's speech had been from the heart.

By swearing by Daigon, the Old God of War, he had bound his life to Drayel's. If Drayel demanded it, Korin would leap in front of a sword for him, Elisa, or his unborn children.

But Drayel would never demand that of him. He would see Korin live on. He could sacrifice himself for his family, but never allow another to die in his place. And certainly not Korin.

"Thank you, my brother. More eloquent words have never been spoken." Drayel said sincerely.

They clinked their glasses together and drained them of their contents. Then repeated that action several more times over the course of the evening.

It was growing late when their fiancés came looking for them. They had glared at the completely hammered men, sitting at the same table, and singing a bawdy song of battle a few of the Warriors had started around the bonfire in the middle of the courtyard.

They smiled widely when they saw the women staring at them in anger. The men waved them over drunkenly and yelled for them to join them. Their joy was contagious and Bell and Elisa found that they could not remain angry at the men. After all, they HAD been relieved of their wedding duties, what else should they have expected them to do?

Now reunited, the two Ladies endeavored to catch up to the men in terms of consumption. Truth be told the two of them had been partaking of wine, though Bell would have preferred whiskey, while going through their selections and weren't THAT far behind their counterparts.

The evening quickly turned into an impromptu pre-wedding cele-bration. Matron Cor Sanctus appeared, drawn by the raucous celebra-tion in the Courtyard. She had wanted to see the place used as it once was, full of life, joy, and music. She had joined the group quickly and was warmly received.

She was followed by Torin, Sabrina, and Cassidy, who had all been inside of the Union drinking and dancing with the Warriors. That party had spilled over into the courtyard when the Union became too crowded.

They had drank, danced, and sang into the early hours of the morning.

Daylight found them all with headaches and smelling of alcohol, food, smoke from the bonfire, and Gods knew what else.

Drayel and Elisa rolled out of bed in the room they had been given in the bell tower. They made their way to the washrooms located below ground and found Korin and Bell had beaten them there. Modesty was not common among the Warriors or the Witches, so soon they were all dressed as they had been born and soaking up the hot spring water in the pools that had been dug out for bathing.

Elisa had sent healing magic into the already soothing water and before long the four of them were feeling much better and ready to face the day.

The four of them departed the bathhouse and agreed to meet at the podium that had been built on the North side of White Hill.

Before leaving the night before the Matron had remembered to ask the pairs to meet there before lunch to rehearse their movements and words so that there would be no hang-ups on the wedding day.

Drayel and Elisa had just left the courtyard and were slowly walking toward the podium when they heard Bell call out to them. They stopped and turned to see their friends jogging to catch up. Reunited yet again, the four walked the rest of the way together.

Matron Cor Sanctus was waiting on them, along with Torin, Cassidy, and Sabrina.

Other members of the Coven were there as well, instructing the Warriors that had volunteered to help on where to place chairs, benches, and other decorations.

The Matron asked them what type of Ceremony they would expect her to conduct.

The Coven had a blood-letting tradition to bind newly married couples.

Warlocks did not believe in any sort of "non-sense" and simply believed that two people saying that they were married made it so. No document or ceremony was needed to verify what was in their hearts.

The Barbarians normally had a very violent wedding. Whereas the chosen husband and wife would fight any suitors that laid claim to their respective spouse. If another man wanted the woman, he had to fight the man. The winner would be allowed to wed the bride. The same held true for the women. If another woman wanted the man, she had to fight the bride. And finally, if either of the original pair did not like the outcome, they could fight the man or woman, that was not the original chosen, and if they won they could choose that person again. Though most did not. Strength was highly valued among the Barbarian tribes, so usually if you lost your fight you lost your spouse.

And the Warriors. The Warriors had perhaps the second easiest wedding proceedings. The couple announced they wished to marry. If there were no class objections, both were full Warriors or non-members of the Guild, then it could proceed after Drayel signed a wedding contract between the two.

So, it stood to reason that the Matron needed clarification as to how to proceed with four fairly different traditions. In the end, Drayel came up with the solution.

They would follow the Guilds Law, as they were all members of the Guild, and would sign the marriage contracts between them. On the actual wedding day, they would say their vows, Korin and Bell first, followed by Drayel and Elisa. Then Drayel and Elisa would take Korin's sword and make small cuts on the palms of their hands so that they could clasp hands and honor the Covens rituals. And finally, and this was a minor risk as no one would willingly want to fight Korin or Bell, they would call for anyone who objected to the wedding(s) to come up to the stage and fight for it.

Assuming no one was stupid enough to try to fight any of them for their fiancé's, the four would then give each other tokens of their bonds.

And so it went. Two days later the sun was shining bright in the clear skies above the Plains. All but the minimum amount of Warriors had been pulled off of the outpost security details. Leaving only the junior Warriors to walk the routes. The rest of the contingent had dressed as well as they could and were stationed around the stage and assembly area. While guests at the wedding, the men could not help but position themselves in areas that still allowed them to secure it if need be. Korin had approved greatly.

Cor Sanctus witches walked or rode in from all directions. Hundreds of Coven members surrounded the stage in a giant horseshoe. Seeing all of her Sisters there again had made Elisa tear up, and Matron Cor Sanctus just let the tears roll down her face. She was admonished good-naturedly by Torin, who then spent the next hour fixing the Matron's makeup.

Almost exactly at noon the four of them walked up onto the platform hand in hand.

First Korin and Bell walked to the left side of the stage, followed by Drayel and Elisa who went to the right. Leaving Matron Cor Sanctus in the center where she could address them as one, or individually.

Matron Varna took a deep breath and spoke in a voice that was greatly amplified by the glowing blue pendant she wore around her neck. Though normal in volume to those on the stage, it boomed out across the valley so that she could be clearly heard by all in attendance.

"Hello, and thank you all for being here. This is a joyous day for the Cor Sanctus Coven, as well as the Warriors Guild!" She announced happily.

There was an instant roar of approval and confirmation from both groups. When the noise had settled down she continued.

"Today, I have the honor to join in marriage four people who are very important, not just to me, but to the Coven and the Guild as a whole!" She announced again. The same roar ensued, followed by a few shouts of encouragement from a few random Guild members.

This earned them a slap on the back of the head from their nearest Captains, though they smiled at their charge's exuberance.

"Korin and Bell have become well known to me this last moon. And I am pleased to be part of their ceremony. But my heart soars with the fact that today, after ten long years of being apart, I am once again reunited with my daughter, and am blessed to be able to unite her with her chosen husband, Lord Drayel Shadow Walker!" At this, the Warriors roared with support and good cheer yet again. They were joined by the majority of the Cor Sanctus witches. Elisa thought they would be heard in Tor'Amal. The thought made her smile. She turned and looked at her mother. She was positively radiant in her white wedding attire. And she seemed so happy. It almost made Elisa want to cry. She only held back the tears by thinking of how she would look with ruined makeup on her wedding day!

Varna continued after the cheering finally subsided yet again.

"And now, Korin and Bell, followed by Drayel and Elisa, shall share their vows." She said with a smile.

The couple's vows were completed quickly, as they were mostly dictated by the Guild Contract and did not leave much room for improvisation. Varna nodded when the last lines were spoken and returned to her duties.

"At the request of the wedding party, all aspects of their respective traditions are being honored here today. They have signed the contract in accordance with Guild law." She said in a very official tone.

Torin, Cassidy, and Sabrina had been standing behind their mother. They represented the Coven in the wedding and were symbolic in their positioning. They stood behind her to demonstrate the Coven supporting her, and thus the wedding.

Torin stepped forward and held up the signed contract for all to see.

Matron Cor Sanctus nodded and Torin stepped back into line with her sisters.

Korin, seeing his cue, now stepped back from Bell just far enough to draw his freshly polished and shining silver sword. He presented it, hilt first to Drayel, who took it with a smile.

"In honor of the Covens heritage and practices, my daughter and Lord Shadow Walker will now make a small incision in the palms of their hands that their blood may be joined." The Matron said with just a slight lilt to her tone. As if giddy that her daughter was not only being married but was doing so following the ancient traditions of the Coven.

With a smile in Elisa's direction, Drayel took the exquisitely sharp blade and allowed it to barely make contact with his skin before pulling it backward. The pain was sharp but the incision was immediate and easily made. He spun the sword and held it out to Elisa, hilt first, as blood pooled in his injured hand.

Elisa grimaced at the sight of him bleeding. She decided that she did not like seeing Drayel injured. Though, following tradition, she would soon fix that. She followed Drayel's actions almost exactly. She did not wince when the blade bit into her hand.

The wound was not deep, but it bled quickly and freely. Spinning the sword over she handed the blade back to Korin who wiped the blood from the blade with a ceremonial cloth that he then handed to the Matron.

Drayel and Elisa clasped their bleeding hands together and smiled at one another. They allowed it to flow, their blood mingling, as the Matron covered their joined hands with the blooded white cloth.

As soon as the cloth covered their hands Elisa bid her healing powers flow into their wounds. The towel lit up like a small lantern and the blood stopped dripping from under the cloth.

Matron Cor Sanctus stepped forwards and removed the cloth. She folded it into a triangle shape and gave it to Elisa who put it into a pocket sewn onto the hip of her sheer white strapless gown. This was there shared token and a symbol of their trust and bond for her to keep forever.

They turned and faced the crowd, raising their hands as one. The crowd erupted yet again. Everyone there cheered and called their names, showing support for the newlywed couple.

The two turned and kissed softly, resulting in more cheers and a few catcalls from the crowd. Drayel and Elisa smiled at each other and turned to face their friends. Drayel draped an arm loosely around Elisa's hip and lower back, as did Elisa to him.

Bell nodded. This was the next cue.

Matron Varna smiled and in a gruff and almost angry voice, addressed the crowd before her.

"And now for the final part of the ceremony. In keeping with the traditions of the Northern Barbarian Clans, Lord Silver Steel and Lady Bone Render have a question for you lot!" She finished loudly.

Bell stepped forward with a malicious grin on her face.

"Any of you witches, or slags, wanna take a shot at takin' ma man from me? If so, step up to the stage now and state your claim. Otherwise he's all mine for tha takin' and that'll be tha end of it!" She said with a flourish.

Several of the witches could be seen nudging their friends and gesturing toward the rather handsome Lord Silver Steel. Although none of them wanted any part of the barbarian girl. The look in her eyes showed that she would take great pleasure in causing pain to anyone foolish enough to step onto that stage.

Minutes passed and there were no takers to her challenge. Bell smiled at Korin and stepped back to his side.

Korin nodded at his soon-to-be wife and stepped forward to the edge of the stage. With a mighty grin, he bellowed his query out to the crowd.

"You lot heard the lady. This is your one chance to claim her for your own. Any of you toad kissers or Mannock followers care to fight me for her hand?" He asked boldly.

Toad kissers was a childish dig at the male magic users in attendance, and to be called a follower of Mannock was a crude insult to the Warriors.

Either was considered fighting words and would be more than enough justification for any man that wanted to try to take Bell from Korin.

Several younger and hot-headed Warriors began taking slow steps toward the stage. They stopped when Korin thumbed that razor-sharp Silver Steel sword up about an inch from its scarab. The gleaming polished steel reflected the sunlight and promised pain or death to anyone that challenged him. But no more so than the eagerness in the General's eyes. Not surprisingly the young hotheads suddenly remembered that they had girlfriends back home and would not be interested in vying for the lovely Ms. Bone Renders hand.

Korin smiled when no one took up his challenge.

He turned and walked back to his wife. He took her into his arms and kissed her mightily while leaning back and lifting her off of her feet. He sat her down gently before taking her hand in his. She had moved his ring to her right hand as a sign of her engagement. Korin now removed it and placed it back on her left hand. Bell smiled and removed a simple golden band from a pocket sewn into the silk belt wrapped around her waist. She placed it firmly onto his hand before kissing him and stepping back to his side. This was the Matron's final cue.

"Ladies and Gentlemen of the Coven and the Guild! It is my great pleasure to present to you for the first time, Lord and Lady Korin and Bell Silver Steel, and Lord and Lady Drayel and Elisa Shadow Walker!"

They knew what would come next. While the Warriors raised their blades to the sky and shouted their Lords and Ladies unions, the Witches gathered around joined hands for the first time in a decade. They chanted low and quietly, building tempo and volume as they went. The Matron and the witches in the wedding party joining in happily.

A soft white aura began emanating from the witches.

When the pace and volume reached a crescendo Matron Cor Sanctus extended her hands to her side and clapped them together. A wave of healing power washed across the crowd to the outside edge before turning back towards the stage and the newlyweds. The power eased all of the aches and pains, sore muscles, and other ailments within the crowd.

It left the newlyweds feeling fresh and invigorated. When the power arrived, centered on the Matron, she channeled it into the Heart medallion and raised her hands to the sky.

A beam of light filled the sky, brighter than the daylight. It reached its peak and exploded into millions of small white dots, like snow falling in the spring. All in all it was a beautiful sight to behold.

# CHAPTER 36

## HONEYMOON IN THE CAPITAL

Drayel and Elisa spent the next week sequestered in their bell tower room doing what young married couples do. They came out only long enough to visit the bathhouse below and to eat a meal at the Union.

Across town, Bell and Korin were doing much the same. Though their antics had resulted in the Guild being called to check on them, as items could be heard breaking inside the house and various battle cries and screams could be heard.

The poor Warriors tasked with checking on their General fled the house shortly after entering. Boots, plates, and various other items followed the extremely embarrassed men out of the door. Along with a string of profanities from Lady Silver Steel.

But like all things, the fun eventually had to end. At the end of the week, the four newlyweds left their marriage beds and met up together at the Covenstead. They discussed the topics of the meeting that was about to begin and decided that Drayel and Elisa would meet with the Matron, and Korin and Bell would go secure a table inside the Union for their noon meal.

Elisa led the way to the meeting room. It was primarily used for casting and spell construction. But, as it was now, it was sometimes used for meetings when quiet and secrecy was required.

When Elisa entered she found her mother seated at what would be the head of the round table. A segment of the Pentacle engraved in the table pointed North. That was the symbolic direction of leadership for the Coven.

Her Sisters, Torin, Cassidy, and Sabrina, sat at three of the other four points. Leaving one point open. Elisa knew that was not her place. She would sit at the Southern most Vertice of the pentagram. In that way, she would be directly in line with the Matron. As the future Matron of the Coven, it was the place of honor second only to the Northern point.

Drayel would sit beside her on the right, though he had no specific spot at the table, sitting on her right was still an honor within the Coven.

The chair that belonged to the point immediately to the Matron's right had been removed to prevent any faux pas. That point was reserved for the Matrons second in command, Cassidy's mother, Sahnin.

The Coven had sent word across the ocean to the witches and received word back that they were making haste to return to the Plains. But their travels would take at least a moon to make their way back across the ocean.

It was not yet determined if Elisa and Drayel would be here to greet them upon their return. Which was, unfortunately for Varna, the subject of this meeting.

When everyone was seated the Matron stood and addressed the room.

"I thank you all for being here this morning. It has pleased me greatly having my daughter, her friends, her husband, and my Coven all together here in White Hill. I did not believe that I would see this again in my lifetime. But it has come to pass and I thank you all for your efforts to see it so." She said truthfully. "It saddens me that I have heard rumors from the Guild Warriors and my Coven that all of you, with the exception of Torin, Cassidy, and Sabrina, may soon be returning to Tor'Amal. Have you already made your plans daughter?" She asked Elisa.

Elisa nodded.

"We have mother." She said, looking to Drayel to see if he wished to interject. He shook his head no and covered her hand with his own. She smiled and continued.

"Drayel must return and meet with the King to report on the state of the Plains. Once he has finished that, he will address any other issues that arise while we stay in the city. We will stay for at least a moon in Tor'Amal. There are shops, restaurants, and other vendors Bell and I wish to visit before returning to the Guild. However, Bell and Korin have expressed a desire to stay no more than a week in Tor'Amal as either Korin or Drayel need to be back at the Guild. They have been gone too long and there are a few people there that should not be long left to their own devices. Lest they begin to think that they are running the Guild." Elisa said honestly.

Varna nodded and waited patiently for Elisa to begin again.

"Once a moon has passed in Tor'Amal Drayel and I will return to the Guild where he will resume his leadership duties, as well as advising the King on policy and laws in general. That is as far as we have planned for now. Although we thoroughly intend on returning in the late summer to visit you again mother. Drayel and Korin will have to return in order to change out the Warriors at the Guard post so that they do not become complacent in their duties. So that gives us a perfect reason to return fairly soon." Elisa said happily.

Varna nodded her acceptance.

"I do not relish the idea of you leaving again so soon daughter. I have very much enjoyed the time we have had together. But, I understand that you have your own life to live and that your path is your own. I am very grateful though, to hear that you are making plans to see me again in the future. That pleases me greatly. And with Drayel's permission, and yours of course daughter, I would ask to be allowed to visit you both at the Guild from time to time as well." Varna said hopefully.

"Of course, Matron. Nothing would please us more. With our marriage, the Cor Sanctus Coven, and yourself, are bound to the Guild in friendship and blood now. And I suspect that after the month of springtime we have had while here, there will be more than a few of your Coven bearing Warrior children. And those same Warriors requesting permanent assignment to the Plains." Drayel said with a good-natured laugh.

Elisa could not help but notice Torin's face suddenly matched her red hair almost perfectly. Torin caught Elisa looking at her and held her finger up to her lips as she laughed quietly and shook her head as she silently begged Elisa not to say anything as the others had not noticed her embarrassed blush.

Elisa nodded quickly and turned her attention back to her mother, lest the others take an interest in why she was suddenly smiling so broadly.

Drayel and the Matron had continued talking while she had her silent conversation with Torin. Elisa caught the tail end of the subject as she turned back to her mother.

"... so soon? I had believed you would wait at least another week or so." Matron Varna said dejectedly.

"I understand your disappointment Varna, but it is as it must be. We will leave in the morning for Tor'Amal. We have enjoyed our time here in your lands. And we thank you for your hospitality. But, as much as we would enjoy simply staying here, we must return to our daily lives. Mannock is still not to be trusted. I must be there to ensure he stays the path. And the Guild requires constant attention lest someone decide that they would do a better job than I guiding it and attempt a coup." Drayel said.

He was thinking of one man in particular that had been left unsupervised far too long. It honestly was time for them to get back to the Guild.

"Of course Drayel. And I thank you again for all that you have done for me and my Coven. We will be forever in your debt." The Matron said earnestly.

Drayel nodded. He knew that telling the Matron that the Coven owed him no debt would be pointless. The Matron was proud and would expect to one day return the massive gift he had bestowed upon them. They were safe, and they were home.

Seeing that the meeting was drawing to an end everyone began to rise from the table. Except for Sabrina.

"Lord Shadow Walker, if I may have a moment of your time?" She asked politely.

"Of course Sabrina, what can I do for you?" Drayel asked. Sabrina rose from the table and walked to Drayel and Elisa's end. She sat down on the edge of the table, in between Elisa and Drayel. She looked up at them both and took a short breath and huffed when she exhaled.

"I may as well just get this over with. During the battle with the Vorgan, I came to understand that my wielding of Illyian's Fang was not, exceptional, in its sword capacity. It is rare that I admit that I need assistance, so you'll understand that this is difficult for me. But, your Lord Silver Steel is renowned for his prowess with the blade. This is evidenced by the skill and ferocity with which your Warriors fight. So, though I am not a member of your Guild, I would like to travel back to the Guild and undergo swordsmanship training with your weapons master. If you would allow it?" She asked respectfully.

Drayel looked to Elisa for her response. She smiled widely and rushed in to hug her cousin.

"Then it is settled. I have no doubt that Korin would be pleased to take you as a student. And, if I am being honest, Elisa is quite capable of assisting you as well." Drayel said with a grin in his wife's direction. "Perhaps you can help her develop her Craft while she helps you hone your skills with the blade?" He asked.

Sabrina nodded.

"Of course. It would be my pleasure. So, if you will all excuse me. I have to go break the hearts of several Warriors and tell them I am leaving for now." She said with a wicked grin.

The group went around hugging and saying their general goodbyes. When Elisa got to Torin she leaned in and whispered in her ear.

"Please call upon me when the baby is born. I would love to meet my Sister's child!" She said quietly and happily.

Torin blushed again slightly before nodding yes excitedly.

Goodbyes complete, Drayel and Elisa headed outside to meet Korin and Bell at the Union. Korin had found a table under a large red-leaved tree with beautiful white bark that provided ample shade for them to eat their meals.

Korin waved to the waiter who had been casually leaning against the doorway into the Union. He had been patiently waiting on Drayel and Elisa to arrive before bringing their food out.

Drayel and Elisa sat down across from Korin and Bell. The two were sitting as close as possible on the bench and had their arms wrapped around each other's waist while Bell leaned into the big man's shoulder.

Korin broke the silence.

"So, tomorrow morning Drayel?" He asked semi-dejectedly.

Drayel knew that Korin had been enjoying his time on the Plains and was in no hurry for his honeymoon to be over. But life moved on and they had to get back to normal. Whatever that now looked like.

"Yes. I am afraid so. We will leave at first light and stop overnight at the Rooster. Then make our way into Tor'Amal the following day." Drayel said "We are also bringing along Elisa's Sister Sabrina. She has requested to become a student of the great Lord Korin Silver Steel. I have agreed, but of course, the final decision is yours, Korin."

Korin smiled and looked at Bell for confirmation. Bell and Elisa had spent many hours with all three of Elisa's "Sisters" planning the wedding. Sabrina and Bell found that their personalities blended quite well. So Bell did not hesitate to agree.

"Wonderful. That is settled then." Drayel said.

The waiter arrived with their meals and placed fresh pints of mead in front of them. They sat and finished their meal while enjoying a jovial conversation. Almost an hour later they went their separate ways once more.

The pairs went back to their respective rooms and began packing for the trip the next morning. They all slept well that night and awoke the next morning refreshed and ready to greet the day.

The Matron and Elisa's Sisters were gathered by the stables with the Captains that were there to see their Lord and General off.

Sabrina had her horse saddled and ready to go when they arrived. She waved to Elisa and Bell before walking over to where Varna and the others waited.

"Elisa, I am going to miss you so much, my daughter. It seems like only a day instead of over a moon since you have come back into my life. I will count the days until we are reunited. But, as a parting gift, I wish to give you something." The Matron paused as she reached for the Heart amulet hanging from the thin silver Mithril chain around her neck. Elisa stepped forward and placed her hand on the amulet, pressing it gently into her mother's chest and stopping her from removing it.

"Mother, I appreciate the gesture, and I know it comes from a place of love. But, although the amulet has accepted me as a bearer, it belongs with the Matron of the Coven. I will wear it one day, Isolde willing, but for now, I beg you to keep it." Elisa said earnestly.

"I know you do not covet the amulet daughter. You returned it freely, even after experiencing the power it awakened in you. So, I have no qualms in regards to your possessing it. Will you not need it should the Guild go to battle? Surely such power would be a boon on the battle-field?" Varna asked seriously

"It would mother. But, I have sufficient power to heal most injuries. My Sister, Sabrina, will also be with me, and unless I'm incorrect, the Coven will come to our aid if needed?" Elisa asked happily.

Matron Varna Cor Sanctus nodded and smiled at her daughter and the woman she had become. She felt tears threatening to spill down her face and did not wish the last image of her Elisa saw to be her crying. So she summoned a small amount of power and wiped her eyes, taking away the tension building there. She smiled and hugged Elisa.

"Until next we meet daughter. Be safe and be well. And Drayel?" Varna looked at the powerful Warlock standing next to her daughter. "Please keep her safe." She requested.

Drayel nodded and stepped forward to hug the Matron.

"Of course Matron. I will fall before I ever let harm come to her." He said intently.

Varna nodded, placated, and trusting that the group would fare well in their travels.

A short while later the five of them were on the road back to Tor'A-mal. It was well into the evening when the group arrived at the Rooster.

They stabled their horses and left them in the care of the same stable boy. He remembered them well from their generous tips, and the ruckus these particular patrons usually caused.

Dinner was uneventful. None of the people that they had interacted with before were present. And the atmosphere in the room was light-hearted and jovial.

As the newlyweds left the table to retire to their respective rooms, Sabrina chose to stay and have a drink with a handsome, and muscular, young woodsman that had stopped on his way through to Tor'Amal. She waved her friends away and bid them good night before turning back to the woodsman with a wicked smile that promised an interesting night for both of them.

The next morning they met back in the dining room. Sabrina smiled brightly as she came down the stairs. It matched Elisa and Bell's expressions almost exactly.

They settled up with the proprietor and were soon back on their way to Tor'Amal. They were still an hour or so away when the first of the King's Guard saw them coming down the road.

The man made no attempt to hide and waved in an excited manner. He gave a short whoop and spurred his horse into a run. In seconds he was around a bend and out of sight.

The group just shrugged and continued onward.

They arrived at the gates to Tor'Amal about an hour later and found them standing wide open. A contingent of King's guards, led by Lucian, was waiting to escort them to the castle.

The man genuinely smiled as they approached and rode out ahead of his men to greet Drayel and the others.

"Greetings Lord Shadow Walker. Welcome back to Tor'Amal." He said brightly.

Drayel immediately cast out a sensing spell to determine whether an ambush hid behind that smile. He determined quickly that there were no assassins hiding in the trees or along the battlements. Surprisingly, Lucian appeared genuinely pleased to see them.

Drayel did not think he would ever get used to being welcomed into Tor'Amal by Mannock's men. But these were strange times.

"Well met Sir Lucian. Thank you for coming out to meet us this morning. I assume you are here to escort us to the King?" Elisa broke the silence by greeting the man jovially.

They had a good rapport with the man, and Elisa intended on winning and keeping, as many friends in the court as possible.

"Of course Lady Cor Sanctus. I have had my men out along the main road waiting for your return for a moon." Lucian replied.

"It's Shadow Walker now, Captain Lucian. Lord Drayel and I are married." Elisa corrected cordially.

Lucian bowed his head acknowledging her new status with a respectful smile.

"Of course Lady. My congratulations to you both. "He said to Drayel and Elisa.

Bell, ever the tactful Warrior, announced her new status loudly and with zeal.

"And I'm now Lady Silver Steel. But if any of you lot call me anything other'n Bell I'll throttle ya!" She said with a wide grin on her face. Lucian took the interruption with good-natured humor.

"Well met Lady.....Bell." Lucian said cordially.

Bell saluted the Captain and turned her attention back to Korin who sat watching the exchanges quietly. She did not fail to notice that her husband was actively watching Lucian's men and the people moving around them.

"If you will all follow me, I will take you to the castle and show you to your rooms. Although, I will need a moment to arrange a room for your additional guest. Who is of course most welcome." He said as he nudged his horse toward Sabrina. "Sir Lucian Gold Shield, at your service Lady." He said. Lucian had forgotten everyone in the group except Sabrina, who now had his undivided attention.

"Sabrina Cor Sanctus, of the Cor Sanctus Coven. At no man's service." She said with a teasing smile.

Lucian grinned.

"Well met Sabrina. Well met indeed." He said with a tone that indicated that he was very pleased to have met her. Sabrina just flipped her hair over her shoulder and appeared to be anything but interested in the young Captain. Though when he turned his mount to ride back toward the gate Elisa caught her sneaking a peek at his backside with a raised eyebrow and a smirk. Sabrina saw her Sister watching and smiled as she shrugged her shoulders.

The group urged their mounts on and fell into step behind Lucian and his Guard escort. To their credit, the Guard made no attempts to surround the group and rode easily in front of them.

They made good time getting to the castle. The people of Tor'Amal were used to seeing the King's men riding through the city. They had long ago learned to move out of the way of the mostly viscous and uncaring knights and Guards.

Lucian's men did not appear to be quite as cruel as what Drayel knew Mannock's men to be. They slowed to allow an elderly couple to cross in front of them, and two of them stopped to help upright an over-turned cart driven by a child barely old enough to handle the horse attached to it. Much less place it back on its wheels.

Tor'Amal was just one surprise after another to Drayel.

When they reached the castle Lucian sent his men back to their barracks and personally led the two married couples to their rooms. He spoke briefly with the Castellan and was directed to a room on the same hallway as Sabrina's companions.

Lucian produced a key given to him by the Castellan and opened the thick, ornately carved, dark wood door. He stepped inside and held it open for Sabrina as she sauntered inside.

"I think you'll find the accommodations to your liking, Sabrina. The room was not aired out prior to your arrival, as we did not know to expect you. The bedsheets should be clean and fresh as the rooms on this level are maintained weekly when they aren't occupied. You'll find a fully stocked bar in the alcove by the window leading to your private balcony. Breakfast is served in the dining hall at sunrise. The King has requested Lord and Lady Shadow Walker attend him for the mid-day meal in his private dining hall. And of course, dinner will be served at sunset. So, if it pleases you, I will return at mid-day to escort yourself and Lord and Lady Silver Steel, Bell, to the main dining hall." Lucian said amiably.

Sabrina nodded nonchalantly and turned to survey her room. After ten years living in empty barns, sleeping under the stars, and the occasional bed provided by a friendly family or lover for a night, this was the most eloquent accommodations she had seen in quite some time. It would do nicely.

"Thank you Sir...Captain...exactly what should I call you Lucian? It is my understanding that the knights and the Guards of Tor'Amal are two separate entities. Yet, you introduce yourself as Sir and Captain? Please explain." Sabrina said as if not at all interested but simply wanting to correctly address the man. It would not do for him to think that she was interested in him. Men were much less fun to play with if they knew your intentions from the beginning.

"I'm afraid that is a complex question that would take some time to answer properly. Both titles are mine to hold. I joined the King's service as a squire to the knights before becoming knighted myself. However, after seeing the behavior of some of my brother knights, and the fact that it was never reprimanded, and almost encouraged, I sought to leave the King's service. " He said before pausing to consider his next words.

It would not be to his benefit to have a loose tongue in the presence of someone who was not a supporter of the King. And in this castle, the walls sometimes listened to conversations that would be better off unheard. He took a short breath and blew it out through his nostrils in a short huff before continuing.

"But, I found that leaving the King's service, after being knighted, is not a possibility. It would have been an affront to the Crown. So, after researching all of the options that would allow my head to remain attached to my body, I spoke to a friend in the Guard. He told me there was written law that allowed a knight to take a commission in the Guard as an Officer. I knew well that I could not change the knight's behavior. They report only to the King, and he remained proud of his knights. But the Guard? The Guard reports to the Officers entrusted over them. And the King rarely meets with the Guards and leaves them to their own devices. So, in them, I saw the potential to make a change. The friend I mentioned earlier is the Crowned Shield. The leader of the Guard. He and I share very similar views in regards to how men representing the Crown should comport themselves. So, he and I have been working dili-gently to weed out small-minded and particularly violent men. And we have, for the most part, succeeded. The people of Tor'Amal are begin-ning to see us as kind and seek us out for aide, and the King has begun to call upon me more frequently for liaisons requiring a more delicate touch. Though there are still undesirables left among the ranks, they will be gone in less than a year's time. Gods willing." He said sincerely.

Sabrina nodded again.

"And for all that, you still failed to tell me what I should call you Sir Captain Lucian." Sabrina said teasingly.

Lucian smiled. He had run away with himself. He was passionate about his work with the Guard and the good that he was doing there. But he had completely and utterly failed to answer the Lady's question.

"In private, Lady, you may simply call me Lucian. In public or formal settings, I would properly be addressed as Captain Lucian, as it is the position and rank in which I currently serve the Crown." He said honestly.

"Bold of you to assume that we will be alone together often enough for me to require a separate name, Captain Lucian." She said with a grin.

"One can only hope, Lady." Lucian had replied eloquently.

Sabrina smiled at him wickedly. Where had that bit of charm been hiding she wondered?

Lucian returned her smile before bowing slightly and seeing himself out. He was shutting the door when he saw Drayel, and then Elisa, emerge from their room. Their timing was perfect as it would allow him to escort them to the dining hall, then return for Sabrina. And Lord & Lady Silver Steel he added quickly.

"Lord Shadow Walker, good afternoon!" He said as he approached the pair. The two turned and acknowledged him with a slight bowing of their heads.

Drayel stepped forward and accepted the offered hand. They shook politely and Drayel stepped aside to allow him to greet Elisa as well.

"If I may, it would be my pleasure to escort the two of you to his Majesty's dining hall. Though I'm well aware that Lady Cor...apologies....Lady Shadow Walker is more than capable of getting you there." He said with a friendly smile.

"Lucian, it has been too long. I would like nothing more than to have you escort us so that we might catch up a little." Elisa said honestly.

Lucian nodded and made an after you gesture with his hand. Drayel and Elisa began walking and Lucian fell into step beside Elisa. They were soon well into a congenial conversation. Elisa provided Lucian the broad strokes of her life over the last year or so. She had just begun recounting the battle for the Plains when they turned a corner and almost walked into a man standing in the middle of the walkway as if he owned the place. And in a sense, he did. Lucian made it a point to speak first.

"Well met Prince Alasander." He said with a bow.

A clever way of informing Drayel of both the man's name and position, while greeting him as well.

"Captain Gold Shield. I was told that you would be escorting our Lord and Lady Shadow Walker to meet with my father. I will take them from here, as I would speak with Lord Shadow Walker." He said dismissively.

Lucian did well to bite back the retort forming on his tongue at being so rudely dismissed. But, decorum dictated he not respond to the Prince's curt dismissal, other than to bow and accept it. Lucian did so grudgingly.

"Lord, and Lady, I bid you good day. Perhaps we will speak again at the evening meal?" He asked quickly. The prince would not abide being made to wait.

Elisa nodded, "Of course Captain. We look forward to it."

Lucian appreciated her use of his formal title in the presence of the Prince. The King may have begun to like him, but the Prince, he did not seem to like anyone. He bowed again quickly to the Prince before spinning on his heel and going back the way they had come to go pick up the Silver Steels' and Sabrina. At the thought of her, his pace picked up noticeably.

"Lord Shadow Walker, I regret that I have not been able to introduce myself before now. So, I thought I might take this opportunity to do so now." The Prince said insincerely.

Drayel looked at Elisa for guidance and could read the worry in her eyes. She was afraid that the Prince was going to offend him and possibly put himself at risk of Drayel killing him. But Drayel was learning tact and patience. Two things that had long escaped him. He would allow the arrogant little princeling to think himself superior to him. It would be, perhaps, the best way to learn the child's true intentions.

"Well met Prince Alasander. You know, of course, my wife, Lady Elisa Shadow Walker. Formerly Cor Sanctus." Drayel said gesturing toward Elisa, who the Prince had failed to acknowledge in the slightest.

Alasander turned his head and regarded Elisa, as if for the first time.

"No, I do not believe I have had occasion to meet the Lady Shadow Walker." He said haughtily. He made no attempt to introduce himself and only looked in her direction briefly as if to confirm to himself that he did not know her.

"Actually, Prince Alasander, you and I spent many afternoons playing in the main courtyard when I first arrived here. You were a kind-hearted child in those days, as I recall." Elisa reminded him gently.

The Prince did not look at her a second time. He appeared to be trying to remember the events she spoke of, but in the end, he just shook his head.

"No, I do not recall that. But if we did, I thank you for your service." He said dismissively.

Drayel looked at Elisa and saw that she did not have tears in her eyes from the prince forgetting her. But she did have a red flush in her cheeks from anger. The future Cor Sanctus Matron did not take kindly to being dismissed so abruptly. Drayel wondered to himself if it was truly him that the Prince should be afraid of at that moment. The thought brought a smile to his face. One that earned him a smack on the arm from Elisa who thought he was finding humor in her anger. He shook his head gently and looped his arm through hers. She leaned into him slightly and he could feel the heat radiating off of her. It was a wonderful thing that she had mastered her control over the fire element at a young age, otherwise, the young Prince would have been engulfed where he stood.

"So, Prince Alasander, if not simply to introduce yourself to me, and again to my wife, Why did you desire to speak with me?" Drayel asked abruptly.

Alasander remained silent for another minute or so. Either to focus his thoughts or simply to make him wait, Drayel was not sure.

Alasander stopped just before turning onto the hallway that would take them to Mannock's dining hall.

"Lord Shadow Walker, I believe my father has begun to suffer from a mental decline over the last year. He has made questionable judgments and seems confused as to the state of this country. Specifically the deal, or deals, he made with you. He is the King of Ka'len. In no way should he have kowtowed before you. I believe that magic is inherently evil and should be removed from this country in all its forms. But no. Now it has been legalized and is being practiced openly in the streets. The people, magic users mainly, see this as a great victory. But, what of the wars waged in the time before magic was forbidden? You, and everyone that practices magic, have been so pleased with yourselves being able to practice again that you have forgotten the terror the Cor Renders brought upon this land. The monstrosities that untrained minor wizards and Warlocks released all across Ka'len. The ships lost at sea due to magic gone awry. I have read the history of this land. I know the calamities that are bound to be released upon the people that look to the Crown for leadership. They will not blame you, LORD Shadow Walker, when things begin to devolve and monsters run free. No, they will blame the King. My father will bear the brunt of your foolish demands. So, just know that when the day comes to pass that my father is removed from the throne, and I am King, that I will rescind these laws. I care not what happens to the Plains. Let the Cor Sanctus keep it, but magic will not be practiced there. I want us to be clear on where we stand Lord Shadow Walker. You may be the most powerful being in Ka'len at this time, but times change, and when they do you will be returned to leading your Guild and I will rule Ka'len with no assistance from you." Alasander said with finality.

Without waiting for a response, the Prince turned away and sped away down the hallway toward the King's dining hall, though he passed by the entryway without a second look.

Drayel was seething. How dare the impudent little fool speak to him thus? Only Elisa holding tightly to his arm kept him from following the arrogant prince down the hallway and reducing him to ashes.

Elisa had pulled him tight to her side when she saw the God's Eye flair to life beneath his Mithril chain mail. Its bright glow reflected the anger coursing through her husband. It would not do for him to destroy the prince now. There was peace in the kingdom. No wars were being fought. Magic was free. She would do whatever she could to prevent Drayel from murdering the man. With a word the Prince would be gone and the kingdom back at war. Assuming Drayel did not simply bring the castle down on the King and the prince at the same time.

"Drayel no. Let him go. He is an arrogant child. He has not the means to carry out any threat against you. He is proud and it bruises his ego that his father did not fight to the last man attempting to defeat you. Mannock was much the same when he was younger. And he is now showing at least some wisdom. Allow the prince the chance to grow out of his youthful ignorance and become a better man." Elisa begged.

The green in his eyes had been glowing as brightly as the God's Eye. Drayel had been giving serious consideration to simply obliterating the man. The disrespect he had shown Drayel, not to mention Elisa, had been more than enough to justify his death.

But now Elisa clung to him and begged him not to. Drayel forced the growing power inside of him into the God's Eye. He felt the magic ebbing and his eyes returned to their normal level of glow. He would store the magic in the artifact for later.

Perhaps if their meeting with the king went much the same as this one, someone would be getting decimated. Drayel could only hope.

Elisa released the breath she had not realized that she was holding when she saw the power ebb from his eyes and the amulet go back to a faint pulsing. She had seen it being used enough to know that it only pulsed when charged with power. So, Drayel had not completely released the magic but had stored it for later. That would work. She had spoken of giving the Prince a chance to grow as Mannock had. But truth be told, the Drayel standing next to her had grown in the last year as well. His self-control and reason were much improved over the impulsive Warlock she had met just over a year ago. This was evidenced by the fact that Alasander still drew breath. A year ago he would have been a smoking pile of ash on the hallway floor. Elisa smiled and stood on the tips of her toes to kiss the still angry Warlock.

The soft touch of her lips, and her hand in his hair, did much to take his mind off of fighting and on to other pursuits. Elisa gave him a promising grin and took him by the hand.

"Later my love. Dinner now, dessert when we are through with politics for the day." She said teasingly.

Drayel growled semi playfully and grabbed her around the waist before pulling her tight against him. He kissed her hard enough to take her breath away and leave her longing for more.

"Fine. Dinner first." He said with resignation.

Elisa smiled and led him by the hand the rest of the way down the hall to the King's dining hall.

Drayel remembered the place well from their first meeting. When they entered this time they found that the servants had removed all but three chairs from the room. The Kings, the largest sitting at the head of the table and two slightly smaller, but still extravagant, chairs sitting to his right.

Drayel was familiar enough with the customs of court to know that this was considered an honor. He was to sit at the right hand of the King. It showed trust on Mannock's part, allowing the Warlock so close. And it showed respect to Elisa, Lady Shadow Walker, by having her sit at Drayel's side instead of insisting upon meeting the Lord alone.

This was a much different reception from the first time they had met. Mannock had placed plates and chairs around the length of the table to allow Drayel to choose where he sat. Which was, of course, as far away from Mannock as possible.

Now he would have no choice but to sit next to him. Or insult him by walking out of the room. Only a year ago Drayel would have happily turned and walked out if only to anger the King and provoke a reaction.

But no, this Drayel knew what peace meant to Elisa and Ka'len. So, with an inner sigh, the Warlock walked forward and took his seat at the table.

# CHAPTER 37

## POLITICS AND CHICANERY

*T*HE MEETING WITH MANNOCK HAD GONE SURPRISINGLY WELL. The King had congratulated Drayel, and Elisa, on a job well done. There were no back handed compliments or loaded questions. The King, for all appearances, seemed genuinely happy that the Plains had been freed and the Cor Sanctus returned home.

Mannock brought the pair up to speed on things that had been happening in the capital city since magic had been restored. Several Cor Sanctus had moved into the city and set up temples to Isolde where they were receiving, and healing, the people of Tor'Amal once more.

The people, in general, were accepting of the witches, and magic, being returned. Though there were a few holdouts that had torched a few of the temples and harassed the witches. Though he claimed Lucian's Guards had arrested all of the perpetrators within a fortnight.

Overall, it was a very amicable conversation. It had ended after Drayel and Elisa had declared they would stay for a moon, and send Korin and Bell back to the Guild with Sabrina within the week. Mannock had agreed to it all and requested that they remain in the

Castle as his guest, although he made it clear that they were free to stay anywhere they chose.

In the end, they had elected to stay in the castle. It would do their burgeoning partnership good to show at least some mutual trust.

When the lunchtime meeting concluded Elisa endeavored to show Drayel around the castle that she had essentially grown up in.

They walked around the lush gardens and admired the colorful fish that filled the ponds. Elisa showed Drayel some of her favorite hiding spots under the large boughs of the trees closest to the curtain walls. Some were quite private and the pair took advantage of the solitude to carry on some of what had begun in the hallway outside the King's dining hall.

After wandering the grounds, seeing the Guard's barracks, and visiting the Knights Hall, Elisa took Drayel to her old room in the tower.

Drayel noticed an air of melancholy settle over her. She had been laughing and thoroughly enjoying herself outside in the gardens. But now, walking up the narrow spiral staircase toward her old quarters, all of the joy seemed to be ebbing out of her.

They climbed for what felt like hours but were really only minutes. They arrived at a landing that opened up onto a narrow hallway with only four doors on it. Drayel could tell from the length of the hallway, and the closeness of the doorways, that the rooms were very small. Almost like prison cells.

He watched Elisa walk to the door at the far end of the hallway and reach for the handle. There were no locks on the doors, as the thin material they were made from would not stop an intruder either way. But still, she hesitated. Her hand hovered barely an inch over the top of the rather plain-looking round steel knob.

He watched a thousand different emotions crease her face. Embarrassment, anger, fear, rage, and finally, acceptance.

Drayel watched with pride as she pulled her shoulders back and squared herself. With a final forced exhale of air Elisa gripped the knob firmly and walked into the room.

Drayel followed quietly behind and observed.

He watched Elisa walk to the small rickety wooden table with a worn and weathered-looking stool pushed under it. He saw the small indentations worn into the wood where her fingers rested while she gazed out of the small balistraria window. The window was designed for an archer to shoot an arrow out of, not for a person to look out of.

How many hours had she spent there in that one spot for the wood of the table to have worn enough to fit her fingers perfectly? Drayel shuddered at the thought.

He watched Elisa turn and walk to the bed hidden behind the open door. She had stretched out her arm and allowed her fingers to trail along the warm stone wall. Something he realized she had probably done countless times. He was also saddened to see that it would not take much for her to be able to touch both walls at the same time. A couple of steps to her left and she would be touching that wall as well.

When she got to the small wood-framed straw bed she stood over it looking down. Drayel saw her looking at the thin blanket and pillow that lay neatly folded on the bed. Most likely folded by her before she had departed almost a year ago.

The only other furnishing in the room was an armoire that he guessed held the rest of her worldly possessions from this period in her life.

Still remaining silent, he watched her turn and set down slowly on the bed and lean back against the wall and exhale a breath that she had been holding.

And then she cried.

With her head leaned back against the wall and her arms folded together across her chest she sobbed openly and unashamed.

The magnitude of the time she had lost being imprisoned in this tiny room was just too much.

Seeing the ridiculously worn furniture she was "gifted" by the King, sitting on the hard straw mattress, and breathing the stale warm air reminded her of the sweltering heat of the summer nights, and the freezing cold of the winters she had endured here.

So many years of her life were sacrificed in the name of "peace" with the King that she had defended for so many years. She had never truly thought of herself as a captive during her time here. She had been a child when she came to live here. In her mind, she was doing a noble thing. She had helped keep her mother, and her coven safe. Safe from the King that had held her as ransom for ten long years of her life.

How she hated Mannock at that moment. She had stood up for him, been a liaison for him when he needed a soft touch on a political matter.

She had done nothing but help Mannock, and the kingdom, since the day she had been escorted from White Hill to Tor'Amal by Mannock's knights. And never once had she been treated like anything more than a slave. He had belittled her, talked down to her, forced her to play with his arrogant son.

And this room. No living being should have been submitted to the torture of this room.

Drayel walked over to her quickly and sat next to her. He raised his arm up and over her shoulders as she fell against him. Drayel could feel her hot tears bleeding through his shirt. He could hear the small stifled sobs as she let out ten years of pent-up frustration.

They sat there, backs against the wall, and held onto each other until the sun started to fade from the sky.

Bells began to ring one after another in the courtyard until they had made their way around the curtain wall. Drayel guessed correctly that it was the signal for dinner.

Elisa appeared to be in no hurry to leave, so Drayel just relaxed against the wall and closed his eyes. A moment or two later Elisa pushed herself up and away from him gently.

She kissed his cheek and sat up with a grunt. Drayel saw that she had a very decisive look on her face.

"Drayel, I can not stay in this castle for a moon. I would not wish to stay here for a fortnite. Right now, I want nothing more than to go

HOME. I do not know what this place is, but it was never home. So as soon as you can conclude your business with Mannock, I would like to gather Bell, Korin, and Sabrina, and leave." She said with certainty.

Drayel nodded and smiled.

"Nothing would please me more Lady Shadow Walker." He said sincerely. Elisa smiled at his use of her married name. She found it pleased her immensely to be his wife. Even in this barren room filled with so many bad memories, Elisa's heart filled with love.

In the fading light of the evening, Elisa literally glowed. A faint white light shimmered in the twilight, emanating from her very skin.

Far away in White Hill, the Isolde medallion suddenly flared to life.

The sudden activation of the artifact startled Matron Varna until she realized the feeling coming from the medallion was one of great calm and satisfaction. She did not understand how, but she knew that her daughter was finally at peace. Varna smiled and leaned back onto her couch, fully relaxed for the first time in a decade.

Back in Tor'Amal Drayel and Elisa had made their way down to the common hall. The King would not be there, and the atmosphere was much more relaxed. Drayel was surprised to find the dining hall was much like an open-air market in the city center. There were at least twelve tables, large white oak affairs with six-inch thick tops over five feet wide and at least twenty feet long and set up in rows of three.

And where the King had individual ornate chairs at his table, long white oak benches sat along both sides of the tables.

There were no servants here to bring food and drink. Several tables surrounded the great hall with servants stationed there much like vendors. Each table had a different offering. Drayel saw that they would go to the first table to get their plates and cups, then make a circuit around the room taking bits of meat and vegetables from each station before filling their cups at the final table.

Inefficient he believed, but Elisa was smiling and seemed content after her outpouring of emotion in her old room earlier. So, if she was happy, he was happy as well.

Drayel was startled momentarily when a large meaty hand slammed down onto his right shoulder. He quickly relaxed when he heard the humorous baritone of his best friend.

"So where did you two sneak off too I wonder?" Korin Silver Steel joked good-naturedly.

Drayel smiled at his friend while Bell rushed over and grabbed Elisa's hand.

"If those two are goin' to stand about gabbin', how about you and I go and start our way 'round this gauntlet?" Bell said with a laugh.

Elisa made a subtle "after you" gesture while smiling at the girl. Bell needed no further encouragement and was quickly dragging Elisa toward the plates and cups. Korin just grinned and shook his head.

"Lass is always hungry. I suppose that makes us a great match." He said happily.

Drayel just smiled and mimicked Elisa's earlier gesture. Korin nodded and started following the women.

"So, where DID you two disappear too? Bell and I haven't seen you all afternoon." Korin asked curiously.

Drayel considered how much detail was required to answer Korin's question and not reveal too much of the extremely personal moment that they had shared in Elisa's old room. He decided to be as honest as possible, but would not say anything that might betray Elisa's trust.

"We wandered about the gardens, then she took me on a tour of the rest of the castle. And after much reflection, my Lady has decided that she does not desire to spend any more time than is absolutely necessary within these walls. So, when you and Bell leave, so shall we." Drayel said unconditionally. Korin nodded and smiled.

"That would be fine with us Drayel. As much as I have enjoyed our adventure on the Plains, and staying in the luxurious suite they have us in here, Bell and I want nothing more than to get back to our own bed at the Citadel. We are ready to be home." He said honestly.

Home.

That was what Elisa had called the Citadel earlier. It was funny. For as long as Drayel had lived there, been Master of it, he had never really thought about the Citadel in that capacity. It was where he slept and ate his meals. It was where he returned after battle to bathe, drink, and celebrate. But it had never TRULY been home to him. Until now.

But was it the Citadel he really considered home? Or was it the woman that was now laughing and talking excitedly to her best friend as they made their way from table to table in front of them? Drayel believed that he could be happy living anywhere, as long as he had Elisa.

But yes, for now, the Citadel would make a fine home for them. And having Korin and Bell at their sides simply made it all the better. Drayel smiled and nodded to his friend.

"Yes Korin, let's go home."

# CHAPTER 38

## HOME AGAIN

*T*HE DAYS FLEW BY. IN LESS THAN A FORTNITE DRAYEL AND THE King had met numerous times to discuss his role as the King's advisor. The Warlock had taken on the role with something like zeal. He pointed out various weaknesses in the kingdom's border security, as well as a few of the known pirate coves along the southern coast. The men tasked with Port Ka'len's security were competent at their jobs and were rewarded well for locating contraband. This forced motivated smugglers to find hidden coves in which to dock their ships and unload their prohibited goods.

Drayel did not tell Mannock about ALL of them of course. What if there was something he needed to be brought in without prying eyes seeing?

And he counseled Mannock on the policing of magic. While Alasander was a petulant child, he was not completely wrong to be wary of the possibility of dark magic causing problems within the Kingdom.

Drayel spoke to Sabrina and arranged for her to return to Tor'Amal for a few days every month to train Captain Lucian. There were certain potions and herbs that could be used to incapacitate practitioners that were causing harm or discord within the Kingdom. And it would be a great benefit to the young man to be able to defend himself from those practitioners that would do him, or others, harm.

She had agreed, fairly quickly he noticed, when he had mentioned who it was that she would be training in this particular Craft.

And then they were done. Everything that required his attention had been quickly and competently dealt with. He had agreed to return to the capital on a monthly basis with Sabrina. And although he was beginning to be a little more open-minded, the King would not agree to use magic himself. So Drayel had provided Lucian with a scrying bowl to communicate with them at the Citadel. Shortly after they had packed and embarked on their journey back to the Citadel.

Their trip had been uneventful and they now found themselves exiting the pass back onto the Citadel grounds.

As when Korin had returned earlier, they were greeted by a small contingent of Warriors alerted by the wards in the pass. They were warmly received and were soon back within the walls of the Citadel.

The group had separated at the stables and went their own ways. As they walked Drayel noticed that not all of the Warriors seemed especially happy to see them returned. They were cordial and greeted their Lord.

But there were far fewer smiles and offered handshakes than he was used to receiving after being gone for an extended period.

He had also noticed that only a few of the Captains had made their way to the stable passage to greet him and their General. Odd.

They meandered through the now sunlight-warmed hallways to their room and settled in. Drayel summoned Elisa's copper tub and the pair enjoyed a luxurious bath to wash away the dust of the road.

Following the bath, Elisa elected to lie down and take a short nap while Drayel met with the Captains for an update regarding the Guild's activities during his absence.

Drayel sent a young Warrior to spread the word to the Officers while he went to rouse Korin from his chambers.

Korin had kissed Bell goodbye and soon they were walking side by side toward the meeting hall.

"Korin, am I misreading the situation, or does it appear that some of our Warriors are less than thrilled with our return?" Drayel asked his friend.

Korin, ever the professional Soldier, slipped easily back into his role as the General.

"I did notice that several of the Captains elected to not be present for our return. And more than a few Warriors have been, cold, when greeting myself and my Lady." Korin said solemnly. He lowered his head while he contemplated Drayel's question further.

"It would seem that something has happened to the morale of the Warriors and changed their outlook on you and I." He answered truthfully.

"Something, or someONE, happened. That is certain." Drayel said with a hint of anger.

Korin picked up on the Warlocks intention quickly.

"You think Grey Cloak has been poisoning the men's trust in you while we have been away?" Korin stated more than asked.

Drayel nodded.

"Yes. I do. He was far too helpful and kind upon our departure from the Citadel. I would have been more at ease had he wished us to fall from our horses or meet a bloody death upon arriving at the Plains. THAT I would have believed from him. But, we shall soon see the extent of his influence among our men." Drayel said firmly.

Korin exhaled forcefully and nodded.

They walked the rest of the way in silence and found that only about half of the Captains and Lieutenants had arrived. Another sign of poor discipline and a negative mindset. Before they had left for the Plains, the Officers would have moved purposefully and endeavored to arrive well before their Lord. Now they were wandering in with no sense of urgency.

This did not sit well with Korin. If they were angry or disheartened by something that had been said or done, there were better ways to handle it. This type of insolence was completely unacceptable. Korin stood up from his chair slowly. He would not lose HIS composure in the face of this disregard.

"Gentlemen, for the ones that were here before our Lord and I arrived, I thank you for your punctuality. For those of you that are just now arriving, we will have words after this meeting is over. And I would highly suggest that each Captain here send their Lieutenants to round up our errant Officers. If they are not here before I finish drinking this cup of water, then they will meet me in the training circle and let Daigon decide their fates." The Captains were suddenly very interested in getting their counterparts into the room.

By offering to let his God decide their fates, Korin was basically leveling a death sentence on the men. For Daigon's way of deciding a man's fate was battle. And to fight Korin Silver Steel was to die.

The junior Officers could soon be heard sprinting up and down the hallways yelling for the missing Captains.

Within minutes all of the missing Officers were sitting in the chairs along the edge of the table. Most of the late arrivals huffing and puffing after sprinting the length of the compound to get there in time to avoid Korin's sword. More than a few angry glares were cast in Korin and Drayel's direction, but no words were spoken out of turn. The men might have been angry, but they were not stupid.

Korin stood and looked out across the gathered men. All were present and accounted for at last.

"Gentlemen. I am aware that myself and Lord Shadow Walker have been gone for more than a moon now. But, be aware, NOTHING has changed. He is still the Lord of this Guild. And I am your General. The next time either of us calls you to council you WILL arrive before us. You WILL be seated and prepared to report. And if not, you WILL have your actions corrected by me. Do you understand?" He asked.

The look on his face clearly indicated what would happen to any man that chose that moment to be flippant or disrespectful.

All of the men assembled nodded, with a few mumbled Yes Sirs mixed in. Korin tilted his head slightly to the right and raised his right eyebrow inquiringly.

"Have you lost the capacity for clear speech gentlemen? I asked, Do you understand?" He said low and threateningly. This time the answer was much clearer.

"YES SIR!" Shouted the men in unison.

"Wonderful. Not that we have settled the issue of attendance, I will turn the floor over to Lord Shadow Walker." Korin said cordially. As quickly as he had become angered he had returned to his jovial self.

Drayel had to remind himself to not shake his head and smile at the control his General had over these men. However, their general disrespect was troubling. These men could usually be counted on to follow Korin's orders to the letter. So, their slow response to this meeting was unusual. The more he thought about it though, the angrier the Warlock became. In less than two moons these men, who had been so loyal, had possibly been influenced by a Warlock that previously had been held in very low regard.

Now truly irate, Drayel addressed the men without rising from his chair.

"Now that you have all deigned to grace us with your presence, I would like a report from each of you over your activities these last few months. Starting with you, Captain Sandler." The Captain had been the last one to enter the room, and as such was the closest to the door and farthest from his Lord and General.

Captain Sandler cleared his throat and looked around nervously. The other Captains became very interested in the wood grain of the table, the art hanging on the walls, or looking at their hands as though they had never seen them before.

Sandler placed his hands on the table and rose slowly from his chair. Drayel could see a million thoughts were racing through the Captain's mind. As well as the large beads of sweat that had appeared on the man's forehead. The Captain was very nervous about something he decided.

"My Lord, I am afraid there is not much to report." He stammered as he started.

Sandler paused and chewed on his bottom lip while he tried to think of something to say to the powerful Warlock and his General, now both staring holes through him.

"Go on." Ordered Drayel.

Sandler nodded and took a deep breath. He noticed his fellow Captains were still pretending that he did not exist. He continued reluctantly.

"My Lord, the Warriors have continued training in the circle under the advisement of Lord Grey Cloak. We have not been able to develop any new commissions for our services as most of the Lords and Barrons in Ka'len now know that you sit on the King's council. They feel they have nothing to fear. That yourself and the King will band together to defeat any malevolence directed at them. Our coffers grow thin buying food and supplies for the men, along with paying their wages. Both for those assigned to the Citadel, and the ones securing the Plains and drawing hazard pay on top of their normal wages. In addition, more than a few men are now claiming marriage and housing benefits due to their marriage to Coven witches. Our expenses have doubled these last months, and we have had no active income to replace our expenditures. Lord Grey Cloak has visited many of our usual patrons only to find their gates locked and barred against us, My Lord." He had spoken quickly once he began.

He did not wish to be the one to express what they were all thinking, knowing that it would put an even bigger target on his back.

And judging by the glare General Silver Steel had leveled on him, he was correct to worry. Drayel had folded his hands in front of him and now rested his head on his thumbs as he thought about what Sandler had said.

"So, Captain, you are saying that the reason you, and a large number of your counterparts here today, have chosen to disrespect me and your General, is due to the state of MY coffers?" Drayel asked quietly. His voice was low, but the threat carried across the room well enough that Sandler blanched.

Drayel watched as Sandler stammered trying to find the words to respond. Then suddenly Sandler just seemed to give up. His hands dropped to his sides and he shrugged. It was as if he knew and had accepted his fate.

"My Lord, I can not speak for everyone here. I can only speak for myself. As it seems my fellow Officers are reluctant to express their thoughts anywhere except behind closed doors, the duty would appear to fall to me." He said dejectedly. Drayel sat up a little straighter and leaned forward to listen.

"Go on then." He directed the Captain.

Sandler nodded and stepped away from the table, electing to stand behind his chair and lean on it as if he needed the support.

"My Lord, and my General, I have been a Captain of the Guild since before your Lordship took control of the Citadel. During that time I have seen us prosper, and I have seen us fall on hard times. We are now in a cycle that is leading us to more than just empty coffers. This route you have set us upon will ruin us." Sandler said with something like confidence. Though he would not look at Korin or Drayel as he spoke.

Both men noticed that there were more than a few Captains nodding in confirmation of Sandler's words. Sandler noticed the support as well. He took a deep breath and stood up tall and proud, no longer leaning on the chair, now that he had garnered support from his fellow Officers.

"My Lord, I have long supported you, but with you on the King's counsel, men deployed to secure the Plains, and no income, I have to wonder if it is not time for a change of leadership. During the winter Lord Grey Cloak stood beside us in the pass. He worked to clear the pass that you destroyed while you stayed warm and comfortable within the walls with the woman who is now your wife. Lord Grey Cloak has run the day-to-day operations of the Citadel while you and our General were out securing the Plains, for free. And Lord Grey Cloak has stated that while he would never attempt to unseat you by force, that if he were to be duly elected by a majority, then he would gladly accept the title of Lord of the Warriors Guild. Since he is not on the King's council, and you would not be in charge of the Guild, it is not unreasonable to assume that we would quickly return to a more profitable situation. Respectfully, I hereby call for the council to reconvene in one week's time. At which point, any Guild member may put forth the names of any Warrior, namely Lord Grey Cloak, and vote for the title of Guild Master." Sandler finished confidently.

There were several calls of Here Here and other confirmations of support. Though not quite half of the men seated there were taking part in the confirmation.

Drayel raised his hands before him to call for silence. The room went still as quickly as it had come alive. Drayel had noticed that Sandler blamed him for the destruction of the pass, though that particular nuisance had been caused by the King's men. And he had falsely accused Drayel of sitting idly in the castle while Tallon aided the men. Drayel decided quickly that it would only serve to make him look defensive if he argued those points now. He would let it go for now and address the misinformation at a later date.

"A motion to hold a vote for Guild Master has been proffered. Per our regulations, the motion must be seconded and supported by no less than a third of the council." Drayel said sternly. "Do I have a second for Captain Sandler's proposition?" Drayel asked calmly.

Several Captains looked back and forth at each other before the one directly across from Sandler stood up. Drayel recognized the man. He was often seen sitting and talking to Sandler. Geoffrey. Artemis Geoffrey. That was it.

"Aye. I second Captain Sandler's proposal." Captain Geoffrey said quietly. The man was not nearly as certain as his friend that the proposal was a good idea, but he would not fail him either.

"Motion has been seconded. And approved for ratification. All of those that support Captain Sandler's proposal, stand and be recognized." Drayel ordered.

There was a brief pause as the Captains weighed their options. If they stood now and the motion failed, or Drayel remained Lord, then they would lose favor with him and the damage to their careers would be irreparable. But for the ones that stood, they truly believed that someone had to step up and take Drayel's place. So they stood. One or two at first, then eventually exactly half of the Officers in the room stood. They drew their swords and placed them on the table in front of them.

Drayel took a deep breath and looked at Korin. He almost laughed when he saw his friend had literally turned red from anger. Drayel did not crack a smile though. He would not insult his friend. He appreciated his loyalty and would do nothing to belittle that.

Drayel nodded and stood up to his full height.

"Gentlemen, the motion has passed. In one week's time, we will meet back in this room. The names marked for Lordship of the Guild will be presented and voted upon until there is a clear victor. Should the voting result in a tie, then the challengers and I will meet in the training circle and battle for the position. Until such time, I shall continue the duties of Guild Master. I expect all of you to conduct yourselves as professionals. There will be no retribution to those that stood in support of this vote. Nor will there be any harassment of those that did not support it. I expect you all to continue to show myself, and each other, the respect a member of this Guild deserves. Is that understood?" He asked calmly.

He was relieved when the men answered quickly and unanimously.

"Yes Sir!"

With a nod, he turned the room back over to Korin. Drayel had rarely seen the man so angry. The ice in his voice penetrated the very air of the room as he cast a hard look over the assembled Captains. A few of them taking a small step to put one of their counterparts between them and that stare.

"Dismissed." He growled.

The men scrambled toward the door. The Warriors knew their General. And the absolute rage building behind his eyes was very close to breaking free. None of them wanted to be around Korin should he act on his emotions.

When the room was once again empty Drayel sat back down in his chair. Korin was lost in thought and still staring at the door the men had gone through. Drayel wondered if Korin was about to charge out of the door and cut down the Captains that had stood against Drayel.

Drayel cleared his throat and turned to look at his General, bringing Korin out of his contemplation.

"So, now we know why the men were so cold upon our return. Grey Cloak must have been working on this in secret for quite some time. I did not think the man possessed this level of cunning. I would not have thought something this well thought out and planned was within his means. Perhaps I underestimated the man?" Drayel said questioningly.

Korin grunted.

"Perhaps my Lord. Or perhaps he has had help?" Korin postulated. Drayel thought about that for a minute before responding. It would make sense that Grey Cloak was being guided along this path. But by who? There were a few Captains in Sandler's group of friends that were decent tacticians, but no one capable of this level of intricacy. A group effort perhaps? It bore further research.

"Perhaps." That was all he could say.

Both men sat in silence for the better part of an hour as they contemplated the events and ramifications of the meeting. After a while, they both became aware of the smells of frying meat wafting through the doors and windows of the meeting hall. They both came out of their contemplation and looked at each other as if to verify that it was already time for the noon meal. Both men shook their heads in unison and rose from their chairs.

"Shall we go and find our wives Korin?" Drayel asked his friend.

"If I know Bell she has probably already gone and dragged Elisa from her slumber and found a table in the courtyard." Korin said with a grin.

Drayel did not doubt his friend's assessment, so with an after-you gesture, the two men left the meeting hall in search of their wives and a hot meal.

# CHAPTER 39

## REVELATIONS

Captain Sandler rushed to find Lord Grey Cloak as soon as the meeting had ended. Sweat poured down his face and heat radiated from his flushed red skin. He had never been so nervous in his life. He had been almost certain that General Silver Steel was going to charge across the room and cut him down.

So, as soon as Lord Shadow Walker had released them, he had fled.

Now his hands twitched as he walked. He felt his fingertips brushing against his sword hilt on several occasions and had to remind himself that the General was not coming after him.

He found Tallon's door standing wide open and the man himself pacing back and forth across the room wringing his hands in front of him. His head snapped around as he caught the movement in his doorway. He spun quickly and started to bring his hands up defensively. He paused when he realized it was Sandler and not Drayel Shadow Walker that had entered his room.

He let his hands fall to his sides, trying to appear nonchalant.

"What news Captain Sandler?" Tallon asked as calmly as he could.

Though the tapping of his foot and the slight swaying back and forth revealed the man's nervous state clearly.

"My Lord, I proposed the vote for Lordship to our council and it passed easily! Almost half of the Captains stood with me. The rest may not be so hard to convince now that the vote had passed." Sandler said confidently.

Tallon knew that a large number of the Officers now stood with him. Though it was not enough to make his succession to Lordship a sure thing. Many of the Captains feared Shadow Walker and his General and would not stand against him for a "lesser" Warlock.

If only they could get the God's Eye away from Shadow Walker. Tallon knew that his chances of winning a fight against Drayel were very slim, even without the powerful Warlock having the artifact in his possession. But the Captains did not know that. Their understanding of magic was limited. And Tallon had used that to convince them that if it were not for the God's Eye he could defeat Drayel, if needed.

But the results of the meeting, while pleasing, showed Tallon that something else was needed to win over the remaining Captains. Many of them would still side with Drayel for fear of him defeating Tallon in battle, should it come to that.

It was time to reveal his secret.

"Captain Sandler, if I were to reveal to you a second interested party, one that's magic surpasses my own and Shadow Walkers, do you think your associates would be willing to meet and help persuade the remaining captains to vote for me?" He asked casually.

Sandler shook his head in affirmation.

"Yes my Lord. Anyone that can strengthen your position would be well received by your current supporters, and those that are not yet decided." Sandler said happily.

Tallon smiled thinly. Perhaps this would be easier than he had first believed.

"Captain, summon your most trusted men. But only the ones that are fixed upon my side of the vote. Return here in half an hour's time and I will reveal my, associate, to you all." Tallon said cordially.

Sandler nodded again and practically ran from the room.

Once he was out of sight Tallon's door swung gently shut and a dark figure stepped from the shadows in the furthest corner of the room.

"That went well." Maricin said with a cruel smile. "You are sure that this turncoat Sandler can be trusted?" She asked.

"Yes, my Lady. I have been working diligently with the Captain and his fellow Officers. It has been difficult pretending to care anything about these peasants, but they firmly believe that I have theirs, and the Guilds, best interest at heart. But I wonder if we might be rushing revealing your presence so soon. Should we not wait until after the vote? Should I win, then allowing you back into the Guild would be an official act of the Guild Master. If I do manage to lose then your presence here might be revealed by those seeking the favor and forgiveness of Shadow Walker." Tallon said matter-of-factly.

Maricin chuckled quietly before responding. "Oh dear sweet Tallon. You still have not changed after all this time. Whatever makes you think that I would give them the choice to stand against me?" She asked with a curious look on her face.

"I don't understand, Lady." Tallon said.

"Oh dear boy, should you lose, or should I fear anyone revealing my presence to Drayel or Silver Steel before I am ready, I will simply entrance them and have them do my bidding regardless. You will be Guild Master. And after you have been affirmed you will use that authority to change the title of Lordship to an appointment, rather than a vote. And you will appoint me Guild Master. As we have planned." She leveled her gaze upon Tallon and let it linger there. Her eyes burned through his very soul. Daring him to disagree and searching for hints of uncertainty on his part.

That gaze and power did not cause Tallon to fear. It aroused him, spiritually and physically. Yes. He would do as she asked. He had never cared about being Lord of the Guild. His goal had always been to see

Maricin upon that throne. He dropped to his knee and bowed his head before responding.

"Of course my Lady." He said quietly and with a respectful tone.

Maricin smiled and extended her hand to him. Tallon had always been a faithful toad. And it had not escaped her notice that he was completely in love with her. And while she felt nothing of the sort for him, he was not without his charms. He was strong and handsome enough. He was loyal. And he was the key to her finally taking over the Guild.

Her grin turned wicked as she thought of the most definite way to secure the young fool to her side. She extended her hand to him and helped him rise to his feet. Then instead of releasing his hand she turned and walked to his bed.

She looked over her shoulder coyly and saw the fire in his eyes and knew that he was hers.

Their union was fast and urgent. Tallon had been dreaming of having her in this way for years. She responded to his attentions with legitimate enthusiasm. For after this he would be well and truly hers until she tired of him.

They rose from the bed and dressed shortly before Sandler returned with ten Officers. A mixture of Captains and young Lieutenants that held sway over the other Officers.

They knocked on Tallon's door and waited to be granted entrance. Tallon quickly kissed Maricin's hand before turning toward the door. He had to remind himself to wipe the foolish grin from his face before opening the door.

Maricin chose to sit on the armless couch under his lone window, looking very much like a queen upon her throne to Tallon.

He wiped all emotion from his face and opened the door with a stern look and invited the men in.

He realized that Maricin had produced a veil from somewhere and had it covering her face. Ever the one for theatrics, he realized that she wanted a dramatic reveal when these men first saw her. It would allow her, and Tallon, to read the looks on the men's faces.

Whether they be welcoming or scornful, the truth of the men's dispositions would be quickly revealed.

The Officers filtered in and formed a semi-circle around Tallon and the lady sitting on the bench by the window.

Tallon allowed everyone to find a position in the group and took a deep breath before beginning.

"Gentlemen, I want to thank each of you for being here today. I would like you to know that your support means the world to me. And with your continued support, I feel that we have a very good chance of winning the vote and having me be appointed Guild Master. And for that, I thank you all." He said sincerely.

He allowed the soft and polite clapping to cease before he continued.

"As you know, many of your brother Officers are withholding their support because they fear Lord Shadow Walker's magic or General Silver Steel's sword. And it is true, that by myself, I can not defeat Lord Shadow Walker in open battle while he possess the God's Eye." He admitted quietly. As if it hurt him to admit that he was weaker than his opponent.

He heard the mummers being whispered quietly among the Captains. He clearly heard them saying that the God's Eye was the only way Drayel could defeat Tallon. That he was nothing without it. Tallon had to force himself not to smile.

"Gentlemen, when our good Captain Sandler came and gathered you together to come here, he probably told you that I have someone I want you all to meet. Someone that can help strengthen our position, and possibly, just possibly, relieve Lord Shadow Walker of the God's Eye. Though once revealed, I must ask that you keep her presence a secret from all of those that are not firmly on our side. She is putting herself in danger by being here, but her care and concern for the Guild and our Warriors has never wavered. With her help, should she relieve Lord Shadow Walker of the God's Eye or not, if the voting is tied, I could defeat Drayel in open battle for the Lordship, if it comes to that." He said with certainty.

The Officers all smiled and nodded in acceptance.

Tallon turned and offered his hand to Maricin. She rose gracefully from her seat and walked halfway to the men before stopping. Tallon, sensing her desires clearly, walked up behind her and reached over her shoulders to secure the ends of the veil hanging loosely in front of her.

She tilted her head down as he raised it slowly and draped it back across her hair and shoulders. She waited for him to step back around to her side and take her hand before she raised her face to the Officers.

There were several gasps and startled looks from the men. Though none showed outright hostility, all of them were shocked that the woman before them lived.

To his credit, Sandler was the first to recover. He dropped to a knee before her and bowed his head low.

"Lady Maricin, on behalf of the Officers of the Warriors Guild, welcome home lady." He said with a slight stutter. He, like the others, was still processing the fact that she was alive. As well as what it meant for them that she was there supporting Tallon.

Slowly, as if bolstered by Sandler's actions, the other Officers dropped to a knee and bowed their heads.

Maricin looked at Tallon and smiled.

# CHAPTER 40

## LORDSHIPS AND THEATRICS

**D**RAYEL AND KORIN HAD DISCUSSED THE EVENTS OF THE MEETING with Elisa and Bell in detail. Neither of the ladies was pleased with Captain Sandler's actions. Elisa thought back to the first time she had met Captain Sandler and the interaction that they had had with Tallon that day in the hall.

She found it bewildering that a man that had seemed to hate Grey Cloak could turn on his Lord and support the arrogant little man so easily.

Drayel had explained that Tallon had been manipulating the men while he, and Korin, were away. Tallon had most likely played on Sandler's loyalty to the Guild and made it seem as if Drayel would ruin the Guild, while Tallon, Tallon would save them all.

So, while Drayel was not happy with the Captains actions, he at least understood the reasoning behind it.

Korin was less forgiving. On more than one occasion the idea of challenging Sandler to a duel had been proposed by the General. But Drayel persuaded him not to challenge the man as it would be taken as a sign of dictatorship. That anyone who challenged Drayel's rule would be killed by Korin. Drayel could not afford to be seen in that light at the moment.

They had discussed it. Both with their wives and alone over the next week. Drayel and Korin both spoke with every Officer in the Guild and asked their views and opinions on the upcoming vote. They were surprised by how many men suddenly supported Tallon instead of Drayel.

But something even more surprising was revealed to Drayel during these meetings with the Captains. So, after speaking to Elisa at length, and receiving her blessings, he walked into the meeting room with his head held high.

The room was filled with the Captains and their lieutenants, as well as Citadel staff and Warriors, that lingered outside of the doors and windows hoping to hear the proceedings as they were carried out. Elisa and Bell had negotiated their way to the front of the crowd so that they could stand in the doorway. They were not allowed IN the room, but nothing said they could not stand in the doorway.

As he entered Drayel found Tallon had situated himself at the head of the table. A bold move on the Warlocks part. For if he lost, he would have to walk past everyone in the room in defeat. As well as risking insulting Drayel since most challengers for the Lordship stood at the far end of the table until the voting was over, as a sign of respect to the current Lord. As Drayel himself had when he challenged for Lordship.

But not Tallon. He sat in Drayel's chair as if it was already his.

Drayel smiled. He did not think Tallon was going to like how this ended.

He saw Korin glowering at Tallon from the head of the table. It would not take much enticement for the big man to snap his blade out and take Tallon's head from his shoulders.

But that would have to wait.

Drayel walked to the head of the table and placed his hand on Korin's sword arm. He just shook his head no and led Korin to the other side of the table so that he was on Drayel's right, and Tallon on his left.

"Lord Grey Cloak, Stand and we will begin." Drayel ordered.

Tallon looked as if he would balk at the order but then acquiesced as it was common practice for the two men being voted on to stand side by side.

Drayel raised his hands for silence and the room stilled quickly.

"Gentlemen, one week ago a proposal was made to cast a vote for Lordship of the Warriors Guild. It was accepted. Now we gather here together to see our traditions upheld. Now we begin. Gentlemen, who do you present as a candidate for Lord of the Guild?" Drayel asked in a steady voice.

He saw a few people whisper to each other as Captain Sandler rose from his chair. He was much more confident standing here today than he was a week ago.

"I present for your consideration, Lord Tallon Grey Cloak." Sandler said in a loud and clear voice. Several Officers clapped politely and smiled at Sandler and Grey Cloak.

Shortly after the clapping stopped, Korin stepped forward and announced in a bellowing voice,

"I nominate our current Guild Master, Lord Drayel Shadow Walker!" Everyone seated there clapped out of courtesy for the current Guild Master, though some less enthusiastically than others.

Drayel looked across the room at Elisa and tilted his head in a silent question. A mere moment passed before she smiled brightly and nodded her approval.

Drayel grinned back at her and turned to look at Korin, who was beginning to catch on to the silent conversation between Drayel and Elisa. He looked at Drayel curiously before the Guild Master put his hand on his shoulder and stepped slightly forward.

Drayel smiled and addressed the council.

"Gentlemen, you have nominated myself and Lord Grey Cloak for the position of Guild Master. During the last week, I have taken the time to meet with each of you seated here today, as well as many of our Warriors and staff that are now listening outside these very walls." He said with humor. Those outside the windows and doors could be heard laughing quietly, though it was obvious now they could hear everything being said in the room clearly.

"I thank each and every one of you that have supported me in the past, and that support me now. But, as I said, I took the time to go and talk to the members of this Guild, and one common thing became instantly clear. There is a third option for Guild Master that would be very well received." He said with a grin in Korin's direction.

Korin was not slow by any means, but the shock of what his friend and Lord had just suggested slammed into the man. He looked at Bell in shock and found his wife had both hands over her mouth and was openly crying with joy.

Elisa, he noticed, did not appear surprised in the slightest. This had been planned for a while now he saw. Korin looked back at Drayel and mouthed, "Are you sure?" to his friend. Drayel nodded confidently.

"So, Officers of the Guild, Warriors, and Staff, as my last official act as Guild Master, I decline my own nomination, and hereby nominate General Korin Silver Steel for the title of Lord of the Warriors Guild and Guild Master." The room erupted in cheers and clapping. The same could be heard even louder from outside as the Warriors and Staff cheered their beloved Generals nomination.

Tallon Grey Cloak was silent. His face glowed red and his fist clenched so tightly that his fingertips showed white around the knuckles and nails. This was not supposed to happen.

The vote was supposed to come down to him and Drayel. In that pairing, he had persuaded enough Officers to stand with him. They believed that he and Maricin could defeat Drayel and turn the Guild in a profitable direction. But Korin? Gods curse him.

Everyone loved and respected the General.

Tears of anger and regret threatened to spill from the man's eyes. He had failed Maricin. Neither of them had seen this coming. Gods.

Drayel raised his hands again for silence.

"Officers of the Guild, it is time to cast your lots. If you stand for Lord Tallon Grey Cloak, stand and be recognized."

Sandler, true to his convictions, though now looking less confident than he had before, stood and drew his sword. He placed it upon the table and stood back with his hands folded together behind his lower back. One by one all of the Officers that had met with Tallon and Maricin rose to their feet. No one noticed the small black rings surrounding their pupils.

But in the end, it was not enough to be a majority. They had planned on several more Captains joining them against Drayel. But had not counted on Korin being nominated.

Sandler looked at Tallon and mouthed an apology. Though Tallon did not see it.

He was raging behind his calm demeanor and was not aware of anything that was going on around him. He knew he had lost.

Drayel waited for a few moments to give anyone else that was undecided time to stand up. None did.

"Officers of the Guild, if you stand for General Korin Silver Steel, stand and be recognized." He commanded.

As one, the remaining Captains stood and raised their swords to the sky. The roar from outside was deafening as the Warriors and staff cheered their support for Korin.

Drayel smiled and guided Korin to his spot in the middle, directly in front of the Guild Masters chair.

"Officers of the Guild, Warriors, and Staff, it is my honor to present to you, the Master of the Warriors Guild, and Lord of the Citadel, Lord Korin Silver Steel! "Drayel finished with a flourish.

The roar went up yet again, louder than before. While the Guild cheered their new Master, Tallon raced from the room, thought his departure was barely noticed in the midst of the celebration.

Only Sandler and the Officers that voted for Tallon followed him as he left. After the noise calmed and the men took their seats once again, Drayel removed a smooth black ring made of onyx and engraved with a

W, overlaid with a double bladed sword through the middle, that comprised the symbol of the Warriors Guild.

With a smile, he placed it on his friend's left index finger and bowed his head in acknowledgment of Korin's new role in the Guild.

The reality of what had just happened struck Korin. His eyes welled with tears of joy, with a few slipping down his face before he could get his emotions in check. Though no one noticed. He hugged Drayel and thanked his friend for the expected gift.

Once all of the formalities were completed the two couples met in the courtyard for food and drinks. They downed mug after mug of mead, while Bell matched them shot for shot of Sandron's best whiskey.

"So, Drayel, you must tell me, What now?" Korin asked in a voice that showed he was only about halfway sober. "Where will you go? What will you do?"

Drayel took Elisa's hand and smiled at the woman he loved so dearly.

"Honestly my friend, I have been thinking about this since we last left Mannock's castle. I have no desire to be in politics. And everything lately has been political. I thought that I wanted to rule all of Ka'len and free magic. I've done that. Mannock is keeping his word. And we have Lucian at the castle. Sabrina can get updates for you when she goes to train him every month. And as far as training, I would appreciate it if you would continue to train the girl in swordsmanship as agreed." He stated. Korin nodded his consent.

Drayel continued, "Magic is freely used throughout the kingdom. The witches have returned to the Plains, and now I find myself no longer desiring a life of battle and war." Drayel said truthfully. "What I have found, and I never knew I was looking for it until it found me, is love." He said while looking at the woman now blushing at his side. "Before Elisa, all I knew was magic, fighting, death, anger, and pain. Those were everything my life consisted of. Now I want more. I want a family with my wife and a small place to call our home." He said with a smile.

Elisa's head popped up and she sat her wine glass down on the table with a clink that threatened to break the bottom off of the flute.

"Family my Lord? I do not recall discussing any such thing!" She said with mock indignation. Though the smile stretching across her face did little to aid her false angry facade. "But, if that is what my Lord wishes, I will see what can be done about that." She said with a wicked grin and a playful grab of his knee.

Korin looked over at Bell who was now grinning broadly in his direction and wiggling her eyebrows up and down in a comical display.

"Oh no Lady Silver Steel. We'll not be having any of that. Yet." He said with a note of promise in his voice.

"Oh I'll be holdin' ya to that YET Lord Guild Master Silver Steel. We'll be seein' how long you can hold on to that." She said with an entirely different tone of promise in her voice.

The two grinned at each other and reached across the table to hold each other's hands tightly.

Korin regained his senses long enough to put off her insinuated promises for later that night to get back to the conversation at hand.

"When will you two be leaving? And where too?" Korin asked sincerely.

"We've discussed it, and the sooner the better. The Guild does not need two masters. And it will ease your transition into power not having people thinking that I still hold any authority in the Guild. So, I will remove myself from the picture as quickly as possible." Drayel said before taking another draw from his mug. "Elisa I will leave in two days time."

"Two days! Bah, that's nah time to prepare for a proper journey!" Bell belted out.

Elisa felt bad seeing the tears welling up in her friend's eyes. She knew that the woman would not like the idea of her leaving. Which was one of the reasons she had agreed to such a sudden departure.

"Bell, I know this is all very sudden, but it will be for the best. You and Korin will settle into your roles much easier without having to plan around us. But it is not goodbye forever. We will return to visit from time to time. And we will let you two, if no one else, know where we settle." She said as she took Bell's free hand and held it.

Bell snorted and wiped the tears from her cheeks as she chased her pain and sadness with another shot of whiskey.

"Bah but you'd better!" She said sincerely. "If not I will hunt you two down and drag ya back by yourn ears! That I promise!"

Elisa and Drayel smiled at the look of frustration on Korin's face. It was well earned because none of the three believed that Bell would not do that very thing.

"As far as that goes, you and Korin will be the only two in Ka'len who know exactly where we are. We wish to be left alone and leave all of this behind. So, we can not go to Tor'Amal. We can not go East to the Omni Plains. The Guild and the Witches there would know our every move. North is the mountains. No offense Bell, but your homeland is too cold for us thin skinned southerners." Drayel said with a smile.

Bell just grinned and nodded her understanding.

"So, we'll go west. Back toward my homeland. Most likely slightly North West. I desire the flat-lands, but the home of the Old One is in the mountains. I would like to be close to there as well. It would please me to share that with Elisa and our children." He said with a smile in Elisa's direction.

"Children? As in more than one? This is just getting better and better my Lord." Elisa said with a happy smile.

"So, such as it is, our plan is in two days time we will load a wagon with provisions, ground working tools, and whatever items my love wishes to take with us, and depart north and west. When we arrive wherever it is we are going, I will send you a message in the flames." Drayel told Korin.

Drayel had long ego discovered a spell that allowed him to send images and short messages through one flame to another. It was simple, and best of all, untraceable.

Korin nodded.

"Well, I can not say that I am pleased to see you go, my brother. But, Bell and I wish you and Lady Elisa well. And if ever I, or the Guild, can do anything for you or your family, you have but to ask." Korin said stoically.

The two men stood and embraced in a brotherly hug before patting each other on the back and turning each other loose just in time to see their wives making over dramatic expressions of adoration at the two men's expression of brotherly love.

The men just sighed at the theatrics and shook hands one more time.

"What do you say Korin, one more round before we call it a night?" Drayel asked.

"One, or two..let's just see how it goes." Korin said with a laugh.

It ended up being much more than one or two more rounds. The couples staggered off to bed shortly before the sun rose to start the new day.

# CHAPTER 41

## NEW GUILD MASTER

**T**HE CONVERSATION WITH MARICIN HAD GONE FAR BETTER THAN Tallon could have ever hoped for. He had believed that the witch would have been infuriated by his loss. But instead, she had sat quietly on the couch by the window again. She had been quiet for a long enough period for Tallon to be uncomfortable when she finally hopped to her feet with a smile.

"Not ideal, but we can work with this. The key, sweet Tallon, was getting rid of Drayel. Now he is gone. And by his own hand. So, there is nothing to trace back to us, no misdeeds to be laid on our doorstep. And the fool Silver Steel will be much easier to manipulate than Drayel would have been. And if we can not make him see things our way, we can kill him." She said mater-of-factly.

Tallon let out a breath that he had not realized he was holding.

"So, you are not angry my Lady?" He asked hopefully.

"No, quite the contrary. Drayel has played into our hands and left us a much easier obstacle to overcome. And on that note, have Captain Sandler send down our most ardent opposition two at a time. We will begin expanding our reach immediately." She said with a hint of deviousness in her eyes.

Tallon melted at the intensity in his lover's eyes. Yes, he would help her any way he could. A short time later two angry looking Captains stormed into Tallon's chambers, incensed at having been summoned. They were met by black and red tendrils that pulled them into the room, slamming the door behind them.

Moments later they left quietly, both with small black circles around their pupils.

Meanwhile, across the castle, Drayel and Elisa were just starting to stir from their rest. They woke up heavy-eyed and with pounding heads. Drayel started to rise and retrieve the white wood bark that he had so often used in this very situation. Elisa just grunted and pulled him back down beside her.

She ran her fingers through his hair until she was holding his head in both hands. She leaned forward and kissed him, letting her healing power flow through both of them. All of their ailments instantly went away leaving them feeling fresh and invigorated.

She grumbled under her breath and said,"Good morning." with her eyes closed and forehead resting against his.

"Good morning." He responded with a grin. "You know with that ability I should have married you a long time ago. It would have saved me a fortune on white wood bark." He said teasingly.

She just smiled and said, "But if you had done that you would not appreciate just how valuable I am to have around." She said with a teasing smile.

"Oh Lady Shadow Walker, I know exactly how valuable you are to have around." He said sweetly while running his own fingers through her sweet- smelling hair until he was holding her head as she had done previously. He kissed her passionately while pressing his arms around her back and pulling her tight to him.

They lay there lost in each other until someone pounded on their door. Drayel, flashing back to the days before Elisa, snapped at the knocker;

"What?" He bellowed.

"Is that any way to speak to your Guild Master Warlock?" Boomed a laughing voice from the other side of the door.

"Gods." Drayel and Elisa said together with an exasperated smile.

"Coming LORD Silver Steel." Drayel said with a slight teasing inflection in his tone.

Drayel sauntered over to the entryway in the thin silk pants he preferred to sleep in with no top or shoes on and threw the door open wide.

Korin just stared at his shirtless friend in shock, while Bell just giggled and gave Elisa a thumbs up from behind Korin's back.

Korin saw the thumbs up in the mirror across from Elisa and gave his new bride a playful elbow in the side. Bell just grinned.

"You'll pay for that la'er love. Now you two get some clothes on and let's find some lunch. We been in bed long enough. And if I only have one more day to spend with the pair of ya I'll nay spend it layin' about in bed!" She said semi-jokingly.

The day flew by. Lunch was a blur of plans and discussions of visits and names of children yet to be born.

As the sun grew higher in the sky the temperature began to rise and the infamous Ka'len heat and humidity began to bake the pairs as they loaded a wagon in the stable yard.

"Let's get over here in the shade for a moment." Korin said. As they sat on a bench outside the stables Drayel was deep in thought. They had discussed names for their children, but mostly in jest. But something had struck Drayel when Korin had made his suggestion to take a break.

Shade. It was another name for a Warlock. Not the most flattering, but it also indicated a Warlock of some power and was rightly feared by all.

"Shayde Shadow Walker." He said with finality.

"I'm sorry, what was that my love?" Elisa asked him.

She had been talking to Bell about putting cushions on the bunk board of the wagon and had not heard Drayel's proclamation.

"Our child, if it is a boy, I would like his name to be Shayde Shadow Walker." He said sincerely.

Elisa said the name over and over out loud and silently. They all sat in quiet contemplation until Elisa finally raised her head and looked at Drayel with a grin.

"I like it! Agreed!" She said with a sincere smile on her face.

About that time a stable boy walked out with four glasses of cool water for the pairs. They took them in hand and toasted together.

"To Shayde!" they shouted in unison.

The stable boy didn't know why they were toasting the shade, but he guessed it was better than sitting in the hot sun.

They finished loading the wagon and putting the cushions on the bunk board. Before they knew it dinner was over and they were walking back to their rooms together for what would be the last time.

They all hugged and embraced before going to bed.

Shortly after they snuffed out their lanterns for the evening a shadowy figure snuck down the stairs into the courtyard to where the loaded wagon sat waiting. Long slender fingers untied one of Drayel's saddlebags and placed a stone with a tracking dweomer on it inside. She tied the bag back as it was and slithered away into the night.

The dawn arrived way too soon and the four met in the courtyard for a sunrise breakfast. Then it was down to the stables where their horses were tied to the back of the wagon and two mules were harnessed and ready to go. With one last round of goodbyes, the pair climbed aboard the wagon and rode out through the pass one last time.

CHAPTER 42

## THE ROAD WEST

**D**RAYEL AND ELISA ROAD IN PEACEFUL SILENCE FOR THE FIRST FEW hours of the morning. Drayel had been undecided on the cushions for the bunk board, but quickly agreed that they were a grand decision.

The gentle breeze blowing the cool morning air caused the tall grasses lining the roadway to sway gently. The sun had not risen very far into the sky, so the heat of the day had not yet begun to permeate the air surrounding the couple. They rode along enjoying the cool and calm morning atmosphere.

Riding back toward his homeland caused Drayel to wax nostalgic regarding his former home.

They stopped beside a small clear stream for lunch and he recounted memories of his family and his version of friends growing up.

The Warlocks were not a tight-knit community. Though they lived in small villages together, it was more due to pragmatism than any real need for community. As a group, they could fend off invading barbarians, and the King's men, easily. Alone they were much more vulnerable.

In his village, called Tor'draco, or loosely The Dragon, he had grown up at the base of an inactive volcano. The rifts in the earth around it provided their houses concealment from prying eyes. It also meant that visiting your neighbors was not an easy, or encouraged task.

It was rumored that, if it was ever required, the Warlocks could awaken the volcano and summon the magma below to use against attackers. Though he had never seen that happen.

His father, Argile Shadow Walker, was no great Warlock. He could summon spirits and do simple incantations, but beyond that, he was very common as Warlocks go. He held no rank and commanded no special recognition among their coven.

Drayel had been a difficult child. He ran freely among the rifts and hills. Since his coven showed his father very little respect, neither did he.

He made acquaintances, but no one that he would call a "friend", while he roamed. The boys would get out of sight of the adults and watch the ones that had come into their power practice various spells and incantations that were prohibited by their parents.

It was never so much a game as an open competition. They would not bond with each other because when they came into their power, they would be required, by coven law, to fight to see who was the most powerful.

The winner would be selected to rule the coven when the current ruler died or was killed by another ambitious Warlock.

So, he trained as much as he could with spells that could be worked without his power. Usually causing a fire or other calamity. His mother, a Cor Render witch, Elisa was surprised to hear, had grown tired of his antics. She sat him down and talked to him out of concern for why he was acting so disrespectfully toward his father.

She was not surprised by his answer. The Warlocks were raised to respect power, and his father had very little.

She confessed to Drayel that her and Argile had met when they were children and that she had known his parents. Drayel's grandfather, Selvin Shadow Walker, had been very powerful and ranked highly among the Warlocks in Ka'len. His mother, Athena Cor Render, had believed Argile's power would match Selvin's when he came of age.

It did not.

But by that point they were engaged to be married and Drayel was already on the way. So, she had married Argile anyway and been mostly happy. Despite his less than impressive abilities.

When Drayel first felt his power coming in it had been Athena who had sent him to live with the Old One to learn magic. She sensed that Drayel's power would outmatch his fathers, and she did not want him to be limited by Argile's teachings. Athena had sent him to the Old One and the rest was history that Elisa knew well by now.

What did surprise her was that Drayel had once dreamed of being a simple farmer. He had feared, before his power came in that is, that he would be a weak Warlock like his father. So, in preparing for that sad fate, he had studied the humans that lived in the lower plains of the Warlocks territories. The men farmed the fertile soil and he relished watching the crops grow each year. As a boy, he had experimented with spells that made the crops grow faster and stronger. He had enjoyed it immensely.

Then his power came in and he had absorbed himself completely into magic.

But now? Now that the magic part of his life was less pressing, he wondered if that might be the next stage of the path he was on. To become a farmer as he had dreamed of as a child.

Elisa smiled and lay down on the blanket they had spread out on the soft green grass for their picnic. She rested her head in his lap and stared up into his beautiful emerald green eyes. She loved him more and more every day.

"Drayel, if you want to be a farmer, be a farmer. I care not if you are Lord of the Guild, the King of Ka'len, or spend your days working in the field. I will be there. And I will love you as I do now." She said as he leaned down to kiss her soft warm lips. He lay back against the tree that they had chosen next to the stream for the meal and rested.

He awoke about an hour later, startled to realize that he had fallen asleep so easily. He looked down and smiled as he saw Elisa, her head still laying in his lap and smiling in her sleep. Her breathing was slow and easy as she rested. He sat there watching her rest until a fly came buzzing down and tickled her ear. She swatted at it with annoyance and opened her eyes to see an amused Drayel watching her battle the fly.

She swatted his leg and laughed. A short time later they had the horses and mules, now watered and full of grass, hitched back up and walking easily down the road.

They traveled for two days at an easy pace until the road branched off. One way continued on due west, the other north and west. That was the way Drayel chose.

Later that day they came to the bottom of a tall hill that bordered the start of the northern mountains.

With a wave of his hand, Drayel dropped the glamour that had disguised the stone cart path climbing to the top of the hill high above.

With a little bit of goading Drayel was able to get the mules to start up the long path. It was wide and well made, so there was no danger of falling off the edge.

Once at the top Elisa saw a small house, little more than a shack, built up against the side of the mountain. Time had ravaged the little building. Windows were broken and the door swung open in the breeze.

Elisa knew immediately that this had been the home of the old one. This was where Drayel learned magic and had acquired the God's Eye. She looked up at her lover and could see he was lost in memory.

She took his hand and brought him out of his distant state. They set the brakes on the cart, and hand in hand they walked into the cabin. Drayel looked around only briefly before waving his hand and dropping a second glamour that disguised a pathway into the mountain.

Elisa gasped slightly, she remembered the description of the chamber Drayel had found the God's Eye in. She was about to see more riches than she had ever dreamed of.

They walked in together, Drayel removing the God's Eye from

underneath his Mithril armor. The God's Eye glowed brightly and pulsed with an almost happy energy.

Elisa looked around and saw it was exactly as Korin had described it the first time they had met. The emerald floor, the diamonds on the wall, every detail was correct. And there, in the middle of the floor, was the alter that Drayel had found the God's Eye laying on so many years ago.

Elisa watched with mild concern as Drayel removed the artifact from around his neck and placed it upon the altar yet again.

The God's Eye flared to life, its green and white power flooding the room, blinding them both temporarily before it settled back into a dim pulsing light. It seemed content sitting there on that altar. Almost as if it was home.

"Are you sure love?" Elisa asked him.

Drayel nodded and turned to her.

"It is safer here. If I were to keep it, someone would eventually come to try and take it from me. And I would fight them, and kill them, until one day I could not. I will not keep something that would put you, or our future children, in harm's way. It is my hope that you and I live out the rest of our days in peace, Elisa." He said sincerely.

Elisa walked over and wrapped Drayel in a hug. She knew what the man was giving up for the sake of her and their family. Her heart burned and melted with love for Drayel.

They walked out of the cavern together. When they were back in the Old One's cabin Drayel turned and faced the mountain again.

He drew upon his own power then. It felt odd at first, not sensing the companion power of the God's Eye, but soon enough he felt the familiar warmth of his own magic surrounding him. He raised his hands toward the wall and cast a spell of concealment upon the opening.

Elisa knew enough to understand that the glamour that had been on the wall previously was only to disguise the opening. But the spell Drayel now cast would prevent the opening from being found, or entered, unless it was by someone that met the parameters of the spell. She listened as he cast.

"Only Blood of mine, this seal can break, Until such time, the God's Eye may awake, The one that is called, may entry be earned, And those of lesser power, always be spurned, From prying eyes, this portal conceal, Only to the one that is called, may it be revealed."

Drayel held his hands out wide and slammed them together with a loud CLAP. When he did the hole in the mountain disappeared. In its place was the side of the mountain.

There was no indication that there was any type of entryway there. Elisa reached out and felt for a magical signature and found nothing. This seal was perfect. No one would ever find the God's Eye again unless it was a child of Drayel's, and hers she thought to herself, or the medallion called to them as it had Drayel.

That task being complete they headed back outside. The evening was nearing and the sun had begun to ride low in the sky. Drayel decided that they would camp there for the night. And tomorrow, tomorrow they would find their new home.

## CHAPTER 43

BLACK CIRCLES

*T*HE DAYS FLEW BY FOR KORIN AND BELL. WITH ELISA AND Drayel gone off to find their own way, Korin had spent his days trying to find new income for the Guild. His evenings were occupied by Bell. His new bride was very invested in starting a family with him. So his nights were long and sleep was in short supply.

He had also spent many days in the training circle with Sabrina, teaching her the fine art of swordsmanship. She had done very well and he was confident that she could put her flaming sword to much more effective use now.

She had ridden out with a small contingent of Warriors as escorts a week ago. She would be spending a moon at the castle training Lucian in defensive spells. Though the last time she had gone she did not seem as happy to be back at the Citadel. Korin and Bell suspected that she and Lucian were spending time doing more than training in magic.

But that was none of his business. If Sabrina married Lucian then it would only serve to strengthen ties between the Cor Sanctus and the Crown.

Korin had been to the castle several times over the last year himself.

Mannock had stayed true to his word and the kingdom was at peace. Which was great for the kingdom and bad for the Guild. So, in an effort to raise funds for the Guild, Korin had sought to alter the Guild's role in the Kingdom. They would remain available to peasants that were being abused by their Lords and for hire to foreign Lords that required additional swords, but in addition, the Guild would become the border patrol for Ka'len.

They would build outpost at intervals surrounding the kingdom. An asset long needed, but never able to be put into service due to lack of man power in the King's arsenal. These outpost would greatly increase the kingdom's border security. And since the Omni Plains held the Eastern border, the crown would now be paying for the men stationed there.

Everything seemed to be coming together. But Korin could not help but notice that the more things improved, the colder the Warriors seemed to be. It was odd. A year ago they had cheered at his election to Guild Master. Now a large number of them spoke curtly to him as if it was an inconvenience having to stop whatever task they were doing to speak to him.

The Warriors used to make way and welcome him when he appeared at Sandron's. They bought him rounds of mead, and Bell whiskey, while they all joined in bawdy drinking songs. These days the men sat in the courtyard, still drinking mead, but quiet and almost sullen. He knew something was wrong, but could not put his finger on it.

If he were better versed in tenebris magicae he might have noticed that their eyes looked different. He may have seen the black rings surrounding their pupils, but as it was, he did not.

Meanwhile, across the Citadel, Maricin Cor Render fumed.

"It has been a YEAR Tallon. A YEAR!" She screamed.

In her fury she swung her arms and knocked everything off of the small table at her side, sending vials and other items crashing to the floor. Veins along the side of her neck bulged as she breathed in a great gasp of air. Her face grew red and fury reflected from her eyes.

The Black Heart Medallion in her chest pulsed angrily in time with her breaths.

Tallon Grey Cloak stayed sitting on the edge of the bed. He had discovered that it served no purpose to try to calm his lover when she was this angry.

"Maricin, it can not be much longer. Surely Drayel and his witch have settled somewhere by now. If we are lucky, they may even be dead." He said hopefully.

It did not have the desired effect. She turned and glared at him.

"Fool. They are not dead. The tracking stone I placed in his saddlebag still moves across the Western lands from time to time. I grow weary of waiting for him to send word to Silver Steel and his wench. If I can not get them all together then I may have to kill them separately. Though the timing must be right. I will see you as Master of the Citadel, then you will see ME take your place as planned." She shouted.

Tallon just nodded and laid back on the bed, his head propped up on the pillows while he waited on her to finish the tirade that he had heard more and more frequently as of late.

Maricin paced the floor as she muttered to herself. It bothered Tallon to see the black and red flames of the Black Heart Medallion spread across her chest and trail behind her as she walked. It was growing more powerful by the day. Tallon hoped that it would not grow beyond her control at some point. If it did then anyone near her would find themselves in a bad way very quickly.

She stopped suddenly and turned with a great smile. The smile was off somehow. Tallon decided he did not like it.

"I will go to him." She announced firmly.

Tallon sat up on the bed and swung around to let his feet hit the floor.

"What do you mean, you'll go to him?" He asked quizzically.

"I mean, dear Tallon, that I am done waiting. We have put our plan into motion and I will have it move forward one way or another. Without the God's Eye Medallion, Drayel can not stand before me. I will make him beg for death. Then, after I have finished off LORD Shadow Walker and his little witch of a wife, I will return here and kill Silver Steel and his barbarian wench." She stated as if she were reporting the weather.

"You think it will be so simple a thing? To kill Drayel Shadow Walker with his witch by his side? I know that you are powerful my love, but he was powerful before he possessed the God's Eye, can you truly defeat him in battle now?" Tallon asked.

The concern in his eyes was real. He believed that Maricin was about to get herself killed for her impatience.

Maricin looked at him with fire in her eyes. He waited for her to lash out at him and curse him for a fool. When she laughed. It was an evil cackle that sounded somehow distorted and overlapped with several different tones. It was demonic sounding to Tallon.

The black and red glow in her eyes when she looked at him caused Tallon to back away a few steps before he was able to get himself under control.

"Oh Tallon, Drayel fought and killed the old me. Since I have bonded with my God he can not hope to defeat me without the medallion. You ask if I can kill him?" Something like humor reached her eyes as she stared at him. Though the red and black glow surrounding her made the whole look appear as if she was evil incarnate. "Yes. I can kill him. I can kill Drayel, his witch, Silver Steel....I could kill the King now if I wished."

Tallon took a deep breath to prevent him from blurting out what he was thinking. The King? She had told him that this was all for the leadership of the Guild. Now she was talking about the kingdom. Tallon decided it did not matter. If she wanted the Guild, she could have it. If she wanted the throne, she would have it. If she wanted the world, they would make it so. But for now, he would help her finish what they started with the Guild.

"When do you leave my love?" He asked her with resignation. She scowled. He knew she hated to be called "his" anything.

She was not property. And she did not like to be told he loved her. She had certainly never said that she loved him. Every time he had said it in the past she had gotten out of saying it back by satisfying his base needs and distracting him.

And she would do so again now.

She walked over to him slowly and ran her hands through her hair seductively. She pressed her body into his and pushed him back onto the bed. She fell forwards, landing astride his waist.

"Soon Tallon. Very soon." She whispered against his lips. When he pursed his lips to speak again she kissed him hard. And like magic, all thoughts of talking vanished from his mind.

# CHAPTER 44

## NEW NAMES

*T*HE FIRST YEAR HAD BEEN DIFFICULT. AFTER LEAVING THE OLD One's cabin they had traveled south and west. They stopped well short of Tor'Draco.

It had been a long time since he had seen anyone from the town, but it would not do for anyone to learn of his presence. Lest they think the great Drayel Shadow Walker was coming to take over the coven and try to kill him before he could.

Truth be told Drayel had no desire to see Tor'Draco. He had learned long ago that his father had been foolish enough to challenge the coven leader for the title in a vainglorious attempt to impress his mother. He had died quickly. His mother, no longer shackled to a man that she had loved, but had lost all interest in, had ridden away and rejoined the Cor Renders. She had not reached out to Drayel in decades, so Drayel had not made an effort to find her either.

They found a small farm owned by an elderly human. The house was in poor repair, the barn roof leaked, and the fields were overgrown. And fortunately for them, his eyesight had faded considerably. So, when the pair rode up to greet him while he rocked on his front porch, he could barely tell where the horses ended and the people began.

They had worked out a deal quickly. The old man wished to retire to Port Ka'len so that he might be near his daughters. They would care for him, but he had no money and did not wish to be a burden upon them. He had decided to live out his last days on his ruined farm and pass peacefully in his chair. It was the last good thing he could do for his family in his eyes.

He had come to life when Drayel offered him a small fortune in diamonds, taken from the God's Eye cave before they departed, in return for the deed to the farm and the old man's word that he would tell no one how he had come into such fortune.

The old man had agreed quickly and produced the deed from an ornate armoire beside his large hand-carved oak bed. Drayel and Elisa had helped the old man pack all of his belongings into his one working wagon. Drayel had fed and watered the old man's nag and imbued a small copper circlet with strength and energy for the beast. Without it, Drayel did not think the animal would make the trip.

That completed, the old man rode with them around the property. As it turned out the land the old man had owned was vast. But due to his advanced age and declining health, he had only farmed enough of it to sustain himself, and his wife, before she had passed.

They spent the night in the cabin with the old man and listened to his stories. He had lived an ordinary life, but a good one. He told them of his wife and her passing. His two daughters had married traders and moved to Port Ka'len. He was happy for them. They had nice homes and wanted for nothing. And now he was alone in the world. He had thought to die alone on the farm but was pleased that he could now support himself and live near his daughters. His only request was that Drayel and Elisa not disturb his wife's grave. It was under a large oak tree just off of a path that went down to the river where he bathed and drew water.

They happily agreed. They all went to sleep that night happy and satisfied with the deal that had been made between them.

When they awoke the next morning they found the old man was not in his bed. They looked around the cabin and did not see him. Drayel opened the front door and found the old man. They had risen with the sun.

He had not.

He was sitting in his rocking chair with a content look upon his face. But he no longer drew breath. They buried him next to his wife under the oak tree. Elisa whispered a prayer for him that the Cor Sanctus used for patients that passed under their care.

After seeing him properly cared for and memorialized, they had returned to the cabin and began making it theirs.

That had been almost a year ago. They had lost themselves in each other and the farm. The house now stood with windows repaired, fresh shingles on the roof, and new boards replacing the rotten facias.

Drayel had cleaned and sharpened all of the cultivation tools that he found in the barn. And now there were acres of various vegetables growing in the fields beyond their home. They had adopted the surname of Fieldman, as most peasants in Ka'len adopted the last name of their craft.

Drayel and Elisa Fieldman had become frequent visitors of the towns surrounding their farm. Their vegetables were large and fresh, and the prices were fair. They traded for what they needed and were soon welcomed with a smile where ever they went.

Their work in the fields and on the farm was hard. But at night they lay down in each other's arms and loved the night away.

So, it was no surprise when at the end of that first year Elisa came outside smiling brightly.

"Good morning my Lady. What has you so pleased this morning?" Drayel asked as he walked up onto the porch.

"Oh nothing much my Lord farmer.. Only that vegetables are not the only thing now growing on this farm." She said with a sly grin.

Drayel was hot and sweating from his work in the fields so it took him a moment to glean her meaning. He was wiping the sweat from his eyes with his forearm when he suddenly snapped his head in her direction.

"Do you mean?" He asked hopefully.

"Yes, Drayel. You are to be a father." She said with a slight squeal at end.

Her exuberance overcame her and she leapt into his arms. They embraced and he kissed her happily as he lifted her and swung her around in a circle.

The next week flew by. Drayel had begun trying his hand at furniture making, though it soon became apparent that they would be buying or trading for a crib so that the baby, Varna Elisa Fieldman if a girl, or Shayde Fieldman, if it was a boy, did not get hundreds of splinters in a tiny hand or foot.

It was after one such excursion that Drayel walked into the house and found Elisa sleeping peacefully on the couch in the living room.

Seeing that he was covered in wood chips and sweat, Drayel decided to take a bath in the river before waking her and climbing into bed.

He walked down to the river whistling happily. He had placed fairy lights along the trail giving it a romantic and peaceful glow. He reached the river and stripped down before realizing that he had left his clean clothes on the bed.

Ah well, there was no one for miles around. If he had to walk back to the cabin nude, so be it.

He dipped his head back under the warm flowing water of the river to wash it. When he surfaced again he what pleasantly surprised to see Elisa stepping from the trail into the water.

She walked and swam the few feet out to him and wrapped her arms around him. Their coupling was sudden and urgent. Drayel had never felt anything like this from her but thought that it must have been a side effect of the pregnancy. When they both finished Elisa kissed him on the nose, something she never did, and swam back to the bank, walking nude into the moonlight and back down the trail.

Drayel chuckled to himself. He supposed that he would never know everything his wife was capable of. But he would enjoy learning as much as he could!

When he was finished bathing he walked back to the cabin, naked as the day he was born.

He was slightly surprised to see that Elisa had changed back into her dress and was back on the couch asleep.

Drayel shrugged and smiled. With a slight grunt, he picked her up and carried her to the bed. She awoke while he was carrying her and slipped her arms around his neck. She looked at him as he laid her gently down on the bed and smiled wickedly when she realized he was nude.

Drayel grinned as he read the intent in her eyes. She grabbed his hips and pulled her down on top of her. This time their coupling was familiar and lingering. Drayel could not help but think to himself how lucky he was to have this woman as his wife.

When they were through he lay back on his pillow and, before he knew it, was fast asleep.

It was then that the front door swung open slowly and Elisa walked into the room. Or the figure of Elisa, complete with river soaked hair. As she walked in out of the shadows a black and red glow surrounded her body and the glamour fell away.

Maricin Cor Render walked the rest of the way into the cabin. She walked to the side of the bed and sat next to Drayel, now caught in a deep sleeping spell with Elisa.

"Oh lover, I wondered for years what it would be like to be with you. And now I know. And you will never know this, but I was not disappointed. You are definitely the Guild Master, just do not tell poor Tallon. I suppose this is simply another way he will always be second to you." She said with a laugh.

"But you should know, that this union will bring about a child. I planned it for this week specifically. I have no need of your God's Eye AND my Black Heart Medallion. Illyian has blessed me with power beyond your imaging Drayel. I do need the God's Eye though so that no one will ever be able to challenge me again. So, our child is the answer. I will find the God's Eye. I will teach our child to hate his father. You. And when he is old enough, and his magic surpasses yours, I will give him the God's Eye. And together we will rule Ka'len." She said as she ran her fingers through his hair.

With that, she stood from the bed and began a careful search of the cabin. She checked the armoire, the chest at the foot of the bed, every drawer and cabinet. She knew it was not on Drayel, that had been clear when he walked into the house earlier.

Maricin split her focus. Half of her power kept the powerful Warlock and his bride asleep, and the other half searched the house for signs of magic. She found nothing.

The most powerful Warlock in Ka'len, and not a single magic imbued item in his entire home. Madness.

She left the cabin in a fury. Dropping the sleeping spell so that she could focus all of her power, she sent a red and black wave out across the property. Her heart leapt when her magic pinged an item imbued with magical properties.

She knew she had found the God's Eye. She ran to the barn and followed the red and black tinged fog that drifted to a cabinet on the wall.

With a small shriek of victory, she threw open the cabinet and found, nothing.

Well not precisely nothing, the fog was wrapped around a small copper circlet that had been imbued with strength and stamina.

Maricin howled with anger. Had the barn door not swung shut behind her that scream would have awoken Drayel and Elisa. Rage filled her body to the point of her shaking. She turned to stalk back into the cabin and kill them both where they slept.

She started forwards to do just that when a force that felt very much like the Black Hearts power pulled against her chest, stopping her.

Maricin froze in fear. Her anger was replaced by sheer terror. She knew that her God was there with her. And Illyian did not appear idly. Maricin stilled her breathing and listened hard for the voice she prayed would come.

"Girl, stop. Think. If you kill the Warlock you will never find the artifact you seek." said a sharp and angry female voice.

Maricin quivered, knees shaking, and a cold sweat taking over her body.

"You fear me? Good. Understand this. You are favored among MY children. And I will help you succeed in your plans. But not if you are foolish. You have done well tonight child. DO NOT FAIL ME NOW. As you are mine, I am Kyran's. Only my father's power is superior to my own. You must find the artifact. Only then will you be truly invincible. Do you understand girl?" The voice commanded more than asked.

Maricin was still unable to speak but nodded her head in affirmation. And as quickly as Illyian had appeared she was gone. The release from her pull caused Maricin to stumble forward and catch herself on the barn door.

She gasped and pulled in great gulps of air as her senses returned to her. She dropped to her knees and lowered her head to the ground in front of her. Then she laughed. A great roaring laugh that rattled the rafters of the barn and startled the quail roosting in the rafters.

Her God had said that she was favored. Her God had told her that she was with her.

Maricin would wait. She would give it time. She would have men watch the farm and report back to her at the first sign of the medallion. Yes.

She would wait.

# CHAPTER 45

## NEW BLOOD

Time flew by in Ka'len. As Elisa's belly grew, so too did Maricin's. Maricin deceived Tallon and made him believe that her child was his. It drew him even closer to her. She now had the man solidly in hand.

She watched and waited for any sign of the God's Eye. She sent spies to every corner of Ka'len and interrogated the Warriors that had been closest to Drayel. Except for Korin.

She knew that neither he nor his wench had been in contact with Drayel. So, it would be useless to reveal herself to him just yet. She could not risk approaching Korin while Drayel was still a threat.

So, she waited.

As the days passed she brought more and more of the Warriors under her control. Until finally she had all of them bearing the black circles in their eyes. She ordered them to continue serving Korin, but to report to her any word of Drayel, Elisa, or the God's Eye.

It was almost exactly nine months from her visit to their farm when one of the servants, a chamber maid favored by Bell Silver Steel, rushed to Tallon's chambers.

She knocked on the door urgently and yelled for Maricin and Tallon.

"My Lord! My Lady! Open the door, please! I have news!" She yelled happily.

Tallon grudgingly rolled away from Maricin. He had been laying against her with his hand on her belly, feeling the baby move. It was close time for it to arrive. With an aggravated wave of his hand the door unbolted and flew open, crashing against the wall.

The chambermaid burst in, oblivious to the angry manner in which her Lord had opened the door. It did not matter. She had been commanded to rush to them with any news, and so she did.

"My Lord, My Lady, a fire message came to Korin and Bell's chamber only moments ago. The traitor's child has been born! A healthy baby boy. He has been given the name Shayde. Shayde Shadow Walker or Fieldman, I'm not sure as...." her voice trailed off as Maricin tuned out the rest of her message.

The child was born.

Maybe this was the leverage that she needed. She had waited for almost a year at Illyian's behest. Drayel and Elisa were noble enough that torturing either of them for information would garner nothing. They would both die before letting her have the God's Eye. But the child? If she could simply get her hands on their precious baby boy then neither of them would be able to refuse her the location of the God's Eye.

Yes, she would leave tonight and ride with a contingent of Warriors to take the child. Maricin turned onto her side and rolled up onto her feet. She doubled over in pain almost immediately as her body was wracked with pain and tension. She sat back down quickly, breathing hard and fast.

Illyian!

The baby was coming. Of all the days for the little beast to make its appearance, why today?

"Girl, stop your yammering and fetch the midwife. My child arrives." She said forlornly.

"OUR child arrives!" Tallon corrected happily. Maricin forced a smile onto her face and nodded in mock enthusiasm.

"Yes, ours." She agreed.

She made a shooing motion with her hands and the girl ran for the midwife.

Later that evening Maricin lay back on a pile of soft feather pillows holding the child.

Tallon stood beside the bed watching them. He acted as though he was afraid his sitting on the bed would hurt her or the baby. Maricin let him believe what he wanted. The last thing she wanted was him fawning all over her and the baby.

Speaking of which, a name. What to do about a name she wondered.

She had never had a pet, so choosing a name was not something that came easily to her. Perhaps the mewling puppet standing beside the bed could be of yet another use.

"Tallon my love, what shall we name him?" She asked sweetly.

She thought the man's knees were going to give out and drop him to the floor. She had never called him anything other than Tallon. Dear Tallon, Sweet Tallon, yes, but never MY LOVE. Between that and asking him to name THEIR child, Tallon was overcome with joy.

Fool.

He knelt on the floor and leaned forward with his elbows resting on the bed.

"My Lady, thank you for this honor." He said with tears welling in his eyes. Maricin struggled not to groan and roll hers.

"If it pleases you, my love, my Father's name was Sangre. He died protecting my mother from bandits when I was very young. I never knew him well, but I remember him as a good man and a loving father. And my mother, she did not survive the attack that killed my father. Though he killed the men responsible with a spell called the Deathrage. Among my remaining family, he was called Sangre Deathrage forevermore. So, in honor of him, I would name our son, Sangre Deathrage. If it pleases my Lady." He said sincerely.

Gods. The tears rolling down the man's face were more than she could stand. She would agree to anything to shut him up. She had asked for a name, not a family history.

Feigning a caring smile she nodded.

"Sangre Deathrage it is then." She said with mock enthusiasm.

Tallon nodded. He rose from the bed and turned to the midwife and chamber maids that had assisted in the birth.

"Go, tell everyone, except for Korin and Bell, that Sangre Deathrage Grey Cloak has arrived and is well!" He shouted happily.

Maricin looked down and whispered to the black-haired baby she held. "Well, we will just shorten that to the first two won't we?" She whispered to Sangre.

She could have sworn that the baby smiled as he turned his head into the corner of her elbow and closed his eyes.

For the next moon, Maricin healed and fed Sangre. He grew steadily and she healed quickly. She quickly grew bored of feeding him herself, so she passed that chore onto a wet nurse on the Staff.

And then it was time.

She was healed and Sangre could be left with the wet nurse and staff for extended periods now.

Now she would visit Drayel's little farm and take his child. The Warlock would give up the location of the God's Eye, or his entire family would die.

They were going to die regardless, but there was no need for him to know that was there? She laughed as the thought rolled through her mind.

She summoned Tallon to their chambers and saw him hesitate when he saw the look on her face. But now was not the time for second thoughts. They had invested too much time and effort into this. She would not allow him to fail her now. If she had to ensnare him in the same spell as the others she would. But she preferred for him to help willingly. He would be more effective that way.

"Tallon my love, it is time." She said sweetly.

Tallon took a few nervous steps toward the bed she lay on as he struggled to find the words to express what he was thinking without angering the witch.

Maricin knew and understood exactly what he was thinking.

"Tallon, I admit that when we started this endeavor together that it was all about my being the Lord of the Guild. But now, something has changed inside me." She said softly and hesitantly. She looked up and saw Tallon looking at her with interest. Good.

"Please do not think me weak. But now, now I simply want what is best for Sangre." She looked pleadingly up at Tallon. Every bit of the pathetic mother bent on serving her child.

Tallon rushed to her side and knelt by the bed. He took her hands in his and looked up at her lovingly.

"Tell me what you need Maricin. Whatever you want for our child, I will do whatever it takes to make it happen." He said with fervor.

Maricin's smile this time was genuine.

"We must continue our plan, my love. We will hold the power of the Guild, but only long enough for Sangre to come of age. Then it will all be his. I can think of nothing I want more in this world dear Tallon." She said sweetly.

No suspicion crossed his face as he considered her words. He simply nodded and smiled his acceptance.

"As you wish my love. It will be done." He was positively glowing when he stood up from beside the bed. A man in love. A father setting his son's future in order.

A fool doing her bidding.

With one last longing look in her direction, Tallon left the room with purpose in his step. He headed directly to the Officer's Barracks where he found Sandler sitting with a few others drinking tea.

"Captain Sandler, it is time. Our Lady advises that we are to continue as planned. You and five of your best Warriors will meet me outside of Korin's chambers in half an hour. The rest of your company will move out immediately and surround the traitor's farm. My Lady and I will follow shortly behind after I have completed my task." He ordered.

Captain Sandler nodded his head. He showed no emotion as Maricin's spell would only allow him to do as he was ordered. The men with him rose from their chairs and went to secure their weapons and order the men to prepare to ride.

Tallon waited only long enough to ensure the men were moving and started back toward the Citadel. Silver Steel would meet his end tonight. It had been a long time coming.

He had not balked when Maricin had told him Korin had to die. But when she had ordered him to kill Bell he had a moment of inspiration. While attacking Korin was out of the question with Drayel still a threat, using his wife as a spy, that was a possibility.

So, for the last few months, Bell had been under Maricin's control. She had been ordered to continue on as if nothing had changed. And so she had. When the fire message came she had been the one to tell the chambermaid the news to report. And now, through no will of her own, she would help her husband to be killed.

Tallon went by the kitchen first. He knew from his time there that Korin sent his wench to retrieve them both a late afternoon meal almost every night. He was not surprised to see Bell coming up the stairs from the kitchen carrying a large platter of food in one hand, and two steins of water in the other. She had been smiling and cheerful when he first saw her. When she saw him blocking the stairs the cheer went away. She stopped walking and looked up at him blankly.

"Our Lady commands you to leave your chamber door unbolted this evening. You will keep your husband's weapons far from his reach and distract him in whatever manner you see fit. So long as his attention is away from the door. Do you understand?" He asked sternly. Though he knew she had listened and would have no choice but to obey.

He could see the girl trying to fight the spell. There were tears welling in her eyes, but just as quickly they disappeared as the thin circle around her pupils grew thicker as the spell applied more pressure.

Bell was strong but she would not defeat the power of a God. She nodded her acceptance. Tallon smiled.

"Go then. Do as you have been commanded. Say nothing to your husband. And when the time comes, stay out of the way."

Bell nodded again and stepped past him into the hallway. She was not smiling and happy anymore. But she would do as she was ordered.

Tallon walked slowly behind her and listened from the corner of the hallway as the door clicked shut. But he did not hear the dull thud of the locking bar slamming into place.

That was good. Moments later Captain Sandler, along with five heavily muscled and battle- scarred Warriors appeared in the corridor.

With a wave of his hand, Tallon directed the Captain to burst through the door.

Inside the room, Bell had sat the platter down on the nightstand beside their bed. Korin had noticed that she had failed to bolt the door but thought nothing of it.

What concerned him was the sullen, almost vacant, look on Bell's face as she entered the room. When she had left she had been full of fun and mischievousness. Now she was almost emotionless.

Korin had turned and rolled onto his feet to sit beside her as she stood removing the cover from the platter.

"Bell, what has happened? I can see clearly that something has disturbed you. Tell me, love." He commanded gently.

His heart broke when she turned to look at him with tears welling in her eyes. He could see that she was struggling to speak, but could not find the words. He was reaching for her when the door behind him crashed open.

Korin leaped from the bed and pushed Bell back behind him. He saw Captain Sandler and three familiar Warriors standing in his doorway. He saw two more and that bastard Grey Cloak standing out in the hallway.

He reached for his sword and scarab beside the nightstand and was startled to find it was not there. And Bell was no longer standing behind him.

She had his sword in her hands, still sheathed, and was walking along the edge of the room. She stopped when she was behind the Warriors and Sandler.

Korin stood there in shock and watched as his Bell took his sword and left the room.

He saw the tears streaming down her face. Though her face showed no emotion. Then he understood. She had been placed under a spell.

"Grey Cloak, I am going to kill you for this!" He shouted the promise with everything he had. "By Daigon I swear this."

By swearing on his God, Korin would not be able to stop until he had fulfilled his vow.

The two nearest Korin charged their former General. A clumsy stumbling attack that did not match the true ability of these men. It was as if they were not fighting with their hearts.

Korin looked hard at his men as he ducked and rolled out to the side of them. As he looked he noticed their eyes did not look right. There was a black ring growing larger and larger.

So, that was it. Tallon had them under the same spell as Bell. The more they fought against their master's commands, the stronger the spell pulled on them.

Korin decided that if he could avoid killing the men, he would. But Tallon, oh no, Tallon would die.

As he came to his feet he was met by Sandler's sword stabbing toward his stomach. He noted the circles around Sandler's eyes were much less prominent than the other men's.

Okay, so maybe Sandler could die with Tallon.

With a roar, Korin spun out to Sandler's right side. The spin concluded with a strong right hook punch into Sandler's midsection.

The air blasted from his lungs and the man collapsed to the floor. The two Warriors that had charged in had recovered and were now stalking back toward Korin. One walking around the foot of the bed, and the other walking across the bed itself. Oh, Bell would not like that.

With a renewed battle cry Korin charged the one walking around the bed. As he got even with the foot of the bed his hand shot out and grabbed a handful of the thick feather blanket and snatched it hard. It sent the man flying off of his feet and crashing onto the floor below.

Korin continued his pulling motion and threw the blanket over the man approaching him on the floor.

He spun around and saw Sandler still kneeling on the floor, blood dripping from the corners of his mouth.

Good. He thought. Let the little turncoat suffer.

Korin looked up and had but an instant to dodge to the right as a silver streak of lightning flashed through the spot he had been standing.

He looked up and saw Tallon grinning. He would not lower himself enough to use a sword. So, the Warlock intended on killing him from a distance.

No, Korin did not see that happening.

With a grunt, he picked up Sandler from behind by the belt and the top of his leather armor and ran toward the door using the smaller man as a human shield.

He felt the man shudder as a lightning bolt struck him square in the chest.

Korin supposed that Tallon had been trying to shock him through his contact with the man. Though the leather belt and tunic made poor conductors of power and Korin felt nothing from the bolt.

He blasted through the door throwing Sandler into Tallon and taking both men to the floor. He turned and sprinted for the end of the hallway and the stairs beyond.

He cursed as he felt the bolt hit him.

Gods. It felt like every nerve in his body was temporarily on fire. Korin's knees weakened for a second and almost brought the big man to his knees. He struggled to move forward and shake off the effects of the bolt.

He took a second step and was struck again. This time he fell.

Korin watched from the floor as familiar boots ran to him. He did not resist as strong arms lifted him from the floor and held him up on his knees.

He was pleased to see that Sandler was still laying on the floor and not moving. He hoped the little bastard was dead.

But now that left five Warriors and Tallon to deal with. His Warriors may not be fighting at full capacity but even at half of their capacity his men were worth two of any other Soldiers. Korin breathed deeply.

He bowed his head because it hurt to try to hold it up. He sagged against the arms holding him up and let his body relax as much as he could.

And as he hung there he prayed to Daigon.

In all of his years of serving the War God, Daigon had never answered him. Korin did not know if he would hear him now, but he needed his help.

As he prayed silently Tallon approached him, walking slowly, and with a supremely arrogant look on his face.

"The great General Korin Silver Steel. Brought to his knees by a simple Warlock and a handful of humans. How embarrassing this must be for you." Tallon said mockingly.

He reached down and grabbed Korin by the chin and lifted his head so that he could look into Korin's eyes. Korin could not resist. When Tallon let go of his chin his head dropped uncontrolled back to his chest.

"Pathetic really. I had thought that you would have put up more of a struggle. Although, I must admit that it would have been much harder had your wife not helped." Tallon laughed boisterously.

Korin tried to speak and could only grunt as his words failed him.

"It has been so entertaining these last months. Watching her come and go, with you none the wiser that she was reporting everything directly back to us." He said while knocking the dust off of the back of his cloak from where he had been knocked down earlier.

Us. Who was US Korin wondered?

As if hearing the unspoken question, Tallon continued.

"So, you see Korin, can I call you Korin? I think the time for titles has passed, don't you? Anyway, as I was saying Korin. Since your wife has told us everything there is to know about your movements these last few months, you have known nothing of mine." Tallon said taking a breath and stilling his shaking hands as he relived all of the times Korin had belittled him and treated him, and Maricin, as lessers.

"What you did not know Korin, it that one more powerful than I, or your precious Shadow Walker, has been living within these walls for over a year now. It is her power that controls every. single. warrior. within these walls. Including your wife." Tallon said tauntingly.

Korin listened to every word but could not make the connection. She? More powerful than Drayel? There was no one living who could even come close.

"You can't make the connection can you Korin?" Tallon asked as he squatted down in front of Korin.

He leaned in until his mouth was right beside Korin's ear.

"Let me help you. I have loved this woman from the day I met her. I loved her until Shadow Walker killed her. And I have loved her since she returned." He whispered hatefully into Korin's ear.

The words reverberated inside his aching head. The realization struck Korin like one of Tallon's lightning bolts. He raised his head to look into Tallon's eyes. What he saw there horrified him. Tallon was telling the truth. Maricin Cor Render had been within the Guild Walls for a year and he had not known. She had been behind Drayel losing the title of Guild Master. She had maneuvered all of this into being. And they had played right into her hands.

"And the best part Korin? The best part is still yet to come. As we speak, a full company of Warriors rides for your precious Drayel's farm. They will hold there until my Lady arrives. And when she does she will take their precious baby boy, Shayde, was it? And use him to learn the location of the God's Eye Medallion. After all, it wouldn't do for someone else to stumble across the medallion and try to take the Guild away from us now would it?" Tallon asked. "Of course, once she finds the location of the medallion she'll kill them all anyway. We can not spend the rest of OUR lives looking over our shoulders for one disgruntled Warlock and his little witch, can we? So no, she will kill them all, and together we will possess the most powerful of the amulets and run the Guild in the old way. We will take what we want, and the name of the Guild will be feared and respected again, as it should be." Tallon said with finality.

Tallon rose back to his feet and held his hands together in front of his belt buckle. He let his fingertips touch and formed a space big enough for a small ball to form in between them. Small flames flickered to life there as the fireball formed. While Tallon was busy forming the fireball that would kill him, Korin prayed quietly.

"Daigon, many times I have asked you for strength War God. I have never felt your presence. I have prayed for your protection from harm, and still sharp blades have found my flesh. Every time I have drawn my sword in battle it has been in your name. I have taught men to fight with skill and honor. These men have bathed the earth in blood, in your name. Now one who follows your sister challenges your loyal servant. Will you stand idly by and allow her this victory? Or is she simply too strong for you War God? It is said among her followers that Illyian is the strongest of Kyran's children. That you fear her. I will ask you one final time Daigon. Heal my body. Let your strength flow through me that I might do battle one more time in your name. Help me Daigon. Help me kill this coward before me and the men now holding me. Let me save an innocent child from death at the hands of your dishonorable sister...help me..DAIGON!"

He had whispered the first part of his prayer, but as he prayed, he felt a warm sensation spreading from his feet up through his legs.

He thought it had simply been the blood flow returning to his legs, but then it continued up his back and chest. Suddenly all of the pain in his body was gone and his strength returned. As he finished his prayer and asked for help a final time he felt Daigon clear his mind.

Now feeling stronger than he ever had before, Korin looked up and smiled at the Warlock standing in front of him.

Tallon was looking down at the fireball he was still forming and missed the smile on Korin's face that promised certain death for the man. He looked up as Korin finished his prayer and shouted his God's name.

The power in that scream shook the men holding him and caused the circles in their eyes to fade away for just an instant.

It was all Korin Silver Steel needed.

With a great push of his hips and legs, Korin shot up to a standing position. The way his captors had been holding him had placed the sword of the man on his right precisely beside Korin's hand.

Korin shot his hand over and around the hilt of the man's sword and drew it from the scarab as he pushed the man with his shoulder hard into the wall. The man's head cracked into the wall, knocking him unconscious.

Now armed with one of his own swords, the Guild prided themselves in carrying his blades after all, Korin Silver Steel was deadly. He spun the sword over grabbed the hilt. Just as quickly he swung the sword around and smashed it into the nose of the man holding his left arm. As the man let go and grabbed his now shattered nose, Korin swung yet again and struck the man in the temple, knocking him unconscious as well.

Korin spun back toward Tallon just in time to catch the flaming fireball square in his chest. Korin instinctively brought his arms up and crossed them in front of his chest and face.

But the anticipated burning never struck him. He looked up and saw the fireball hovering in the air mere inches from his skin.

Tallon had launched it perfectly, but the touch of Daigon was still upon the weapons master. No weapon formed against him would prosper.

Korin smiled.

Tallon turned and ran.

The three remaining Warriors were dispatched quickly, and mostly harmlessly, as Korin pursued Tallon.

The Warlock stumbled as he ran. From the route he was taking it was clear he was trying to make it back to his chambers.

So, that's where Maricin was hiding Korin thought. Good. I will deal with her next.

Korin chased Tallon out of the Citadel and to a bridge that crossed over to a curtain wall that would take him back around to his chambers. Or would have.

One of the floorboards in the bridge broke as Tallon stepped on it, sending the fleeing Warlock sprawling out onto the bridge.

Korin caught up to the man and stepped easily across the gap left by the broken board. He leveled that gleaming blade and placed the tip against the Warlocks chest. Tallon started to tremble and tried to get his lips to form the words to beg for his life.

Korin had had enough.

With a shove, the gleaming silver blade sliced cleanly through the Warlock's cloak and out of the back.

Korin let go of the sword hilt and stepped back away from the mortally injured Warlock. He let Tallon look into his eyes before he stepped forward and kicked out with his massive boot, sending the Warlock over the railing and to the ground far below.

# CHAPTER 46

FLIGHT

**K**ORIN RODE HARD TO THE WEST. HE HAD SPENT ALMOST AN HOUR searching the castle for Maricin. His search had been hindered by the Warriors and staff under her spell. They had fought him at every turn.

Daigon had left him shortly after he had fulfilled his vow of killing Tallon. He could only hope that his god would return if had to face Maricin. But for now, he had to get to Drayel before her. He had tried to send a message in the flames but he was unable to summon the magic that it required. He was not an expert in all things magical, but it was clear that Maricin had done something to block communications between the Citadel and Drayel.

It was a long ride to Drayel's farm. He was thankful that his friend had provided excellent directions for him and Bell so that they could come and visit.

Bell.

The thought of her brought tears to his eyes as he rode through the cool night air. He had found her sitting at their usual table in the court-yard. She was still holding his sword and scarab and staring at it as if it was the only thing left in the world.

He had tried to speak to her, but she would not hear. He tried to get her to stand and flee with him, but she would not move. In the end, he had no choice but to take his sword from her and leave.

He knew that the only way to free her was to kill Maricin and break the spell. So he would.

And now he rode. On through the night and well into the next day. His mount was frothing at the mouth and beginning to stumble when he finally allowed it to stop by a small creek and drink.

Korin dropped to his knees beside the animal and drank deeply. He knew he could not rest long. He did not know if Maricin was ahead of him or following behind him, but he could tell from the torn-up road that a company or more worth of horses had passed this way already. The Guild was ahead of him.

That stark reminder had him back on his feet in an instant. He went to swing up in the saddle when he suddenly remembered a gift Drayel had given him before leaving. The medallion that he had imbued with strength and stamina for his hawk was in Korin's saddlebag. Drayel had freed the loyal bird before leaving with Elisa. Its medallion gifted to Korin for his mount in battle.

Well, he was not yet in battle, but he might soon be.

Korin swung down from the saddle and retrieved the amulet from the bottom of the bag. There was a brief moment of fear and dread when he did not feel the amulet immediately. But after some digging, he felt its smooth surface under his fingertips.

"All right big boy. I know I've been pushing you hard. And you have been a trooper. But now I need you to run a little longer. This will help you, my friend." He told his mount. The horse's sides were still heaving and the beast was reluctant to raise its head from the water.

Korin untied the rope that he had slipped through the amulets loop and tied it around Anvil's neck. Anvil shuddered as the magical strength flowed through his body. His breathing slowed and he drummed his feet into the ground in anticipation of the run ahead.

With a snort he lifted his head from the water and turned sideways to Korin, bidding him to mount up.

Korin laughed and patted the massive black horse's flanks. Then with a grunt, he swung up into the saddle. His feet were barely in the stirrups before Anvil broke into a run.

Korin leaned over the saddle horn and held on tight while loosening his hold on the reins. The big horse wanted his head so he could run. Korin gave it to him.

It was dark when they crested the hill that overlooked Drayel and Elisa's farm. Korin cursed and reined the galloping beast in and off of the road into the woods.

Gods. If the Guild had left scouts out this far up the road he would have surely been seen. Korin dismounted and walked Anvil far into the trees to where a river flowed down into the valley and beside Drayel's cabin.

He tied him to a tree with a long lead rope and watched as the horse waded into the river to cool off and drink. The horse whickered happily, but thankfully did not whinny or make much noise.

Korin took off everything that he did not have to have to fight. Knowing that stealth would be key he covered his face in the thick, dark mud from along the river. Then with a final look around he slipped off into the water.

He would not have been able to sneak through the woods. This time of year the leaves would crunch underfoot with every step. And the roads would surely be guarded. He could not spare the time for a fight. So this was the easiest way.

Thankfully the water was warm and the big man almost floated down the river. He put his feet down and found purchase on the smooth river bed when he floated past a beach with a path marked by fairy lights leading back to the cabin.

That would be his way.

The ground around the path had been cleared, so he could walk outside of the lights without making noise or being seen.

Assuming there were no Guards.

A slight movement in the trees gave away the position of at least one bored- looking sentry. The Warriors may have had no choice other than to follow Maricin's commands, but their actions showed that they did not have to like it.

Korin slid through the water silently. He matched his body's movements to the waves lapping gently against the bank. It felt like an eternity waiting for the guard to turn away from the river. When he did Korin moved quickly up the bank and grabbed the man from behind, choking him unconscious.

He took a rope from around his waist and made a harness out of it. Slipping the loops around the man's arms and around his waist was easy work. He then threw the other end over a tree branch and used it to keep the man in a standing position. The end result caused the unconscious man to appear to be resting with his back against the tree.

That way any roving patrols would not be immediately alerted to a missing guard.

Korin could feel time running out. So with increased urgency, he started making his way up the side of the trail, just out of the light.

He hadn't gone far when the lights of the cabin came into view. He relaxed when he saw Drayel pass one of the windows. His movements were slow and unhurried, indicating that the Guild had not yet made contact with him.

Korin looked hard from the shadows. In the moonlight, his sharp eyes caught the occasional glint of light on polished steel.

The Guild was out there in the trees, watching and waiting. Korin had to get to Drayel before the Guild. But how? There was a hundred feet of open field between his hiding place and the back door to the cabin. That was his safest bet as it faced an open field and there would not be anyone out there trying to hide in the bright moonlight. So, how would he...the answer appeared right before him. Or rather, grazed into view.

Both of Drayel's mules walked up in front of him. Blocking him from the Guild's view. He did not take the time to appreciate his luck, or come up with ways to tease Drayel about owning mules, that would have to wait.

He grabbed one of the beasts by its halter and held out a sugar cube that he had kept in his sealed pouch for Anvil. The greedy beast licked it out of his hand and happily followed him as he crouched beside it and walked to the back door. He found a length of rope tied to the back railing of the porch that looked like what they used to tie the door open and allow a breeze to flow through the cabin. He quickly tied off the mule to the rail so that he would be able to use it to escape if needed.

Korin stepped carefully up onto the back porch, all the while hoping that the boards would not squeak and give him away. He grabbed the door handle and turned it slowly.

It would not do to get blasted by Drayel before he could gain entry, nor could he risk any sign of alarm that might alert the men outside to his presence. Thankfully Shayde had chosen that moment to let everyone in the countryside know that he had a dirty diaper. The wails of the infant were loud enough to cover an advancing army. Thanking Daigon for the distraction the big man burst through the door and closed it quickly behind him.

He turned to find an angry Drayel Shadow Walker holding a green ball of energy in his hand and preparing to hurl it at the intruder.

"Drayel, no wait!" Korin whispered as loudly as he could while holding his hands up and out to the sides of his shoulders to show they were empty. It took Drayel a moment to realize that the big, soggy, mud-covered behemoth that had burst through his door was none other than Korin Silver Steel.

"Korin, what are you..." Drayel started to say before Korin held his finger up in front of his lips to shush him. Drayel no longer looked angry, only confused. The ball of energy faded away and he crossed the floor to greet his old friend. Korin stepped out of the light and into the doorway of a dark storage room. He did not want anyone outside detecting a third person in the cabin.

"Drayel, I need another rag, this one is soaked through." Elisa called happily, though disgusted.

"One moment my love. I will be right there." Drayel shouted back calmly. He turned back to Korin. "Not that I am not glad to see you my friend, but why are you sneaking through my back door, dripping water and mud, and looking very much worse for wear? And without Bell?" Korin asked.

The pain that crossed Korin's face was all Drayel needed to know that something was seriously wrong.

He stepped into the storage room, dragging Korin with him.

"Korin, what is it? Has something happened to Bell? Tell me!" Drayel demanded.

"I do not have much time. The Guild is already here and she is on her way." Korin said rapidly.

"She? The Guild? What matter is it if the Guild is here? Are you not the Master of the Guild?" Drayel asked seriously.

"No, not anymore. Listen, we must be quick so I will give you the short version. Maricin Cor Render is NOT dead. Somehow she survived and is back and more powerful than ever. She has entranced everyone in the Guild...even Bell. The only way to break the spell is to kill her, but you will need the God's Eye to do it. You can not defeat her and an entire company of Warriors without it. They are already here, out front. And when she arrives, they will come for Shayde." He said breathlessly.

"Maricin.." Drayel said with disbelief.

It was at that moment that Elisa stuck her head in the door.

"How long does it take to get a clean...." She paused briefly before smiling when she recognized Korin. "Korin! How are you? Where's Bell?" She asked entirely too loudly for Korin's taste.

The look on the two men's faces told her something was amiss.

With all speed, Korin repeated what he had told Drayel. Right up to the part about Maricin wanting to take Shayde.

"So, you see, she will take Shayde and use him to make you reveal the location of the medallion. We must flee. NOW!" Korin said with emphasis.

Drayel was shaking with anger, Elisa was shaking with fear. Maricin Cor Render alive. And coming after their child with a full company of Warriors.

Drayel saw the fear in his wife's eyes and his anger gave way to concern for her.

"Okay, my friend. We will go out of the back door and run for the woods. Once there we can escape to the next town a few miles west. We move quickly across the yard and slowly when we are in the trees. Maybe we can put some distance between us and the Guild before they...." a loud voice interrupted Drayel before he could finish his instructions.

"Drayel Shadow Walker! Come out and face me you coward!" Maricin Cor Render's voice was amplified many times over by whatever spell she had cast to do so.

"Gods help us." Elisa gasped as she held Shayde tight against her chest.

Drayel walked to the front of the house and was stunned to see a full company of Warriors in a semi-circle around the front of their cabin. And in the middle, like a specter of death itself, Maricin sat atop her horse, shouting and challenging them to come out.

Drayel sent a small feeler out to detect any additional magic users amid the group. He detected none other than Maricin. His magic recoiled from the evil emanating from the woman. Where had she acquired so much power? It was as though Illyian herself sat astride the animal.

Drayel looked back over his shoulder at his wife. Elisa sat in the corner holding tightly to Shayde and comforting him with soft words whispered sweetly.

The baby reached for his mother's face with a tiny hand and closed his eyes when he touched her.

Drayel's heart sank.

He knew that he could not defeat the woman now calling for him to come out. Much less the men that used to be his to command. His friends. If he had the God's Eye he could blast them all away, then deal with Maricin if she survived.

But alas, he had given it up in hopes of avoiding this very situation. And now the thing he had feared was at his doorstep.

He turned and walked back to Elisa before kneeling at her side. The tears streaming down her face broke something inside of him. For they both knew there was only one option.

They had to save their child. Shayde must live on.

Elisa shook her head no as she railed against the inescapable truth of what must happen. She cried as she hugged Shayde against her. Drayel rested his head against her chest so that he could look into his son's eyes one last time.

He did not feel the tears that flowed from his eyes but knew they were there when Elisa wiped them away. They looked into each other's eyes and nodded their understanding.

As one they rose.

Korin had not yet figured out their plan. The strategist in him was still working out scenarios in which the three of them could defeat the entire company and the God infused Witch that stood against them.

"Korin." Elisa said in a voice that was breaking.

He was still lost in thought and did not hear her.

"KORIN." They said together. His head snapped up and he smiled thinking that the two of them had come up with a plan to get them all away safely. The smile faded as they walked closer to him. He read the look on their faces and started shaking his head.

"No." He said firmly. Though the tears welling up in his own eyes showed the lie in his determination. "I can not. YOU can not! You are Drayel and Elisa Shadow Walker! There must be another way! I will fight every last one of them. I will kill the witch herself! But no! Not like this....Please Drayel.." His voice broke and the emotion he was trying to hold back broke free in that instant.

Drayel and Elisa walked forward and placed Shayde into Korin's arms. Elisa handed Korin a small bag filled with diapers and other necessities. Korin was still shaking his head no, but he held on to Shayde as if he were the most precious thing he had ever seen.

"My friend, my brother, thank you for coming to try and save us tonight." Drayel said gravely. "But we will not allow Maricin to harm our child. Shayde is the most important thing in the world to us. Through him, we shall live on. "

"Korin, do not weep for us." Elisa said softly. "We have known love and freedom in the time that we have had together. That is more than many others will ever know. If we survive this, we will come and find you both. If we do not, know that Drayel and I loved you like a brother. And we have nothing but faith in you. That you will take care of Shayde and see him grow into the man he is meant to be. Will you do that for us?" She asked.

Korin had stopped shaking his head no. He let his head drop and his chin rest against his massive chest. He stared down at the dark-haired baby now nuzzled against his chest. Dark hair like his father. Piercing blue eyes like his mother. He was every bit Drayel, and every bit Elisa. He could see them both clearly in the child.

He looked up from his contemplation and saw them staring at him with hope in their eyes. He knew that there was no way for them to all escape. If he could save this part of them, he would do so. Or he would die trying.

"So, what's the plan brother?" Korin asked with resignation.

Drayel took Elisa's hand sat down beside her on a small couch next to the chair Korin had settled on.

"Elisa will go with you. She can heal either of you should you be injured. I will.." Drayel started. Elisa turned red and raged.

"I will do NO such thing LORD Shadow Walker. My hair and complexion will shine like a beacon out in that moonlight! And if you think for an instant that I am going to run while you stand and fight, you Sir, do not know how wrong you are." She said defiantly.

Drayel smiled and shook his head. He had known Elisa would not leave his side. But he had to try regardless.

"I understand my love. Elisa will wait in the house while you and Shayde sneak out the way you came in." Drayel said. Elisa started to argue when he held up a hand asking her to wait.

"My love, I need you to heal me should I become injured. Maricin is powerful. More powerful than I could have ever imagined her becoming. She is God-like. If she strikes me, then it is very possible that you will be injured as well. I need you to come to me should I fall. We have to stay alive long enough to distract Maricin and the Warriors. Their attention must remain on us so that Korin may spirit away with Shayde unseen. Do you understand my love?" He pleaded.

Elisa had calmed, though her cheeks still flushed with heat. That was good Drayel thought. She would need to keep that anger to fight with. She nodded her understanding.

Drayel continued. "When I walk out of the door I will create a distraction. I swear to Kyran that all of their attention will be on me brother. As soon as you see the front door shut go out the rear exit and sneak back across the yard, but quickly. I cannot focus my power without the God's Eye. And I have no means to store it for sustained effort. But I do have enough power to get their attention, this I swear." Drayel said forcefully.

Korin nodded and stood to go. Drayel reached for his hand but Korin pulled the smaller man in for a tight hug. He was reluctant to let his brother go, as he knew in his heart it would be the last time that he would see him.

Elisa came around to the other side and wrapped her arms around Drayel, Korin, and Shayde. They stood there in that embrace, their small family together for the first and last time.

Maricin's screeches had raised in pitch and volume. They knew the witch would not wait much longer.

"Goodbye, my brother. May Kyran, Daigon, and all the Gods aid your flight and give you strength." Drayel said.

He looked down at Shayde, sleeping contentedly in the comfort of the big man's muscled arms.

"Goodbye, my Son. You will never know me in this life, but I will find you in the next. Grow strong. Defend yourself and the weak. Be a good man, a better man than I. I love you Shayde Shadow Walker." With that, he turned and walked toward the door.

Elisa stood over Shayde and kissed him softly.

"Goodbye, my Son. You will not remember these words from my lips, but I love you, my child. You are everything your father and I ever wanted. And we go to our Gods with peace and love in our hearts, knowing that you are safe and cared for by your uncle Korin." She said with a forlorn smile.

She turned and sat down heavily on the couch. It would only be a matter of time now. She looked at Drayel and nodded. He mouthed the words, I love you and saw them returned.

"Go now, Korin. It begins." Drayel said as he reached for the handle and opened the door.

# CHAPTER 47

LAST STAND

**K**ORIN WENT OUT THE BACK DOOR AND DOWN THE STEPS TO WHERE the mule was tethered. Keeping Shayde tucked tight against his side he untied the beast and turned to walk across the open expanse of the yard once Drayel had their attention. He did not have to wait long.

"You dare come to my home and threaten me, witch?" Drayel spoke loudly but did not scream. The picture of total control.

"No, I come to your home to take your child as my own, oh, and to have you tell me where you've hidden the God's Eye?" She said as she raised the timbre of her voice to make the last part of the station a question.

Drayel laughed and shook his head.

"Witch, you could never use the God's Eye. You have not the power." Drayel said in an antagonizing tone.

"Oh Drayel, but I do. I have more power than even YOU ever had. But, the God's Eye is not for me to USE. It is to make sure that it is never used against ME. You understand. So, here is my offer. You tell me where the God's Eye is, and I will only kill you. Your witch and the brat may live. What fear have I of a simple Cor Sanctus and her whelp?

What say you…Fieldman…does your entire family die here today? Or just you?" Maricin asked teasingly.

While they were speaking Korin had untied the mule and crossed the yard unseen. Now he hid in the woods. And though he knew he should use the time to get away, he felt he owed it to his friends, and to Shayde, to tell the story of their deaths.

Drayel smiled at the witch's ultimatum.

His arms hung loosely at his sides. With a slight shrug of his shoulders, he curled his hands underneath his forearms and snapped his fingers down toward the ground. He was instantly enveloped in bright green flames.

Korin, along with half of the mounted Guild Warriors, gasped at the display. He knew that it was exceedingly rare for a Warlock to be able to display and control that level of energy without one of the eight medallions of power gifted to mortals in ancient times.

Drayel held onto his smile as he raised his arms and held his hands in front of his chest as though he still held the God's Eye in his hands. The movement was so familiar and natural to him that he was able focus his power through that narrow window.

He unleashed it with a roar. Maricin reigned her mount around and bolted back behind the Warriors that she had bid sit still and protect her. In an instant half of the men were knocked from their horses. Seriously injured, but not dead.

Drayel sank to his knees.

Korin knew that magic always came at a price. It took a toll on its user. And Drayel had just expended more than any mortal man should have been able to.

Elisa had been watching out of the window. She threw the cabin door open and rushed to his side.

Korin saw her body illuminate as she summoned every ounce of healing power she possessed and poured it into Drayel. Her attention was fixed on healing her husband. And he was mesmerized by the glow that surrounded her and the exquisite beauty of the woman as she healed him. Neither of them saw Maricin walk her horse back to the front of the Warriors. The red and black snake-like strands of energy from the Dark Heart Medallion coiled around her arms and emanated from her chest where Korin assumed it still hung. He wanted to scream a warning but knew that it would give away his and Shayde's hiding spot. He was forced to watch in horror as Maricin uttered the last words of her spell and the magic leaped for Elisa. The glow around her faded with the light in her eyes.

Elisa fell gracelessly to the floor beside a stunned Drayel.

"Elisa?" He begged. "Elisa!" He shook her and put his head to her chest praying to hear a heartbeat. But there was nothing.

"Search the house. Now." Maricin commanded.

The Warrior nearest her dismounted and walked past a distraught Drayel. He was rocking Elisa in his arms. He whispered her name over and over into her ear. But she would not answer.

The Warriors came out of the house quickly. They were efficient if nothing else.

"The child is not here, Lady. They must have been warned." Said the Captain nearest to her. Korin recognized him as the one that had supported Sandler against Drayel.

"Really? How inconvenient." She groused.

She looked all around as if willing the child to appear. Korin held perfectly still as her gaze drifted over him and Shayde.

Thankfully she did not see him.

"Where is the child Drayel? Did you hide him with the medallion? I grow weary of these games. I have waited a lifetime for this. I have DIED for this. And I am done playing games. Tell me where the God's Eye is and I will spare your child when I find him. He will grow up as a servant of the Guild, though he will never know who you or that witch were. That sounds fair, doesn't it? I mean, of course, you will both be dead, but the child shall live. That is fair is it not?" She asked haughtily.

Drayel looked up glassy-eyed at Maricin. He nodded. Maricin

grinned an awful smile that revealed all of her teeth and gums. There was no humor in that smile, only pure selfish victory.

Drayel lay Elisa down gently on the porch and kissed her one last time.

Then, quick as lightning, the Warlock summoned every ounce of his remaining energy into a ball and sent it streaking into Maricin's chest. That much power would have killed anyone alive. Drayel collapsed back to the ground where he hugged his knees and tried to get his breathing back under control. The man was finished.

Korin stopped himself from cheering as Maricin was blasted from her saddle and knocked to the ground.

He saw the Warriors around her shaking their heads as if waking up from a long slumber and reaching for their swords!

He had done it! Drayel had killed the witch!

But then as he watched, the witch sat up and the men removed their hands from their swords.

It was not possible. How? There was no way any mortal could have survived that attack. Then he saw it. Korin watched in horror as Maricin removed her tattered cloak and revealed the Dark Heart Medallion embedded deep inside her chest.

Daigon! How? But it mattered not at that moment, for the witch lived and Drayel was finished. He could barely breathe, much less fight.

Korin could barely force himself to watch as Maricin approached the defenseless Drayel. She muttered a spell and once again the power of the Dark Heart sprang from her chest and enveloped Drayel in Black flames, burning him alive.

In an instant, it was over.

Korin stood and walked carefully back through the woods. Back at the cabin, the entire building had gone up in flames. The roar of the fire masked the sounds of leaves crunching under his feet, so Korin ran.

When he reached Anvil he untied the rested horse and swung into the saddle. With a grunt, they were off and thundering down the road toward Tor'Amal.

## CHAPTER 48

A NEW LIFE

Korin agonized over what to do. He rode through the night, bypassing the Guild, and continued straight into Tor'Amal. It was hellish. His arms ached from carrying the child. His back and legs protested from being so long in the saddle.

He almost fell when he dismounted his weary horse.

It was the wee hours of the morning when they arrived at Tor'Amal, so the gates had yet to open.

Korin knew that he would be recognized if he went into Tor'Amal as he was. He had to do something to disguise himself, lest someone recognize him and reveal their presence to someone at the Guild.

So, with a sigh, he removed his knife from its scarab and set about the task of shaving off his beautiful sandy-colored hair. He looked into the water trough and viewed his reflection.

It was not enough. He could still be recognized.

Korin thought of Bell, still being held under Maricin's spell at the Guild. He thought of Drayel and Elisa and the sacrifice they had made so that their son could live.

Could he do any less?

With a groan he brought the blade up above his right eye and pressed the razor-sharp blade into the skin there. He drug it downward, avoiding his eye, it would serve no purpose to be truly blind, and down his cheek to his jawline.

The fresh hot blood ran freely down his face. It mixed with his tears. He did not cry for himself, but for the ones that he had lost, and the ones Shayde would never know.

He fashioned a bandage from a clean shirt from his saddlebags and wrapped it halfway around his head.

When he looked at his image again he did not recognize the man in the reflection.

When day broke and the gates opened Korin walked into Tor'Amal carrying Shayde.

It had broken his heart to lose Anvil. But he could not sell the animal lest it be discovered that a bald-headed one-eyed man had sold the beast.

So, he pointed Anvil back down the road to the Guild and slapped it on the rump.

The horse knew the way home. Home. Funny how that word had changed so quickly.

Korin wandered the streets for an hour or so wondering where to go and what to do. He could not take the child to the Plains. The Warriors there were most likely under Maricin's spell. And if not they might end up that way. And it would put Elisa's family in danger. So that was not an option.

Should he go to the King?

No, if he knew Drayel was dead there would be nothing preventing him from reverting back to his evil ways.

Korin had sat down heavily on a large set of stone steps. Shayde chose that moment to awaken from his slumber. He began to wail and thrash against Korin. The child was wet and hungry.

Korin dug in the bag and found a cloth and fashioned a diaper from it. But there was no food. He had no money. No way to buy milk or hire a wet nurse. What was he thinking running away with the child? Surely he had saved Shayde from Maricin. But would the baby now die because he could not care for it? Korin was distraught and at his wit's end when he looked up and saw the answer right across the street from him.

The matron opened the door after several minutes of pounding from some heavy-handed oaf. Not everyone in Tor'Amal rose with the sun. She looked around and saw no one. She was about to close the door when she looked down and saw two bright blue eyes staring up at her from inside a bundle of blankets. "Oh my. Who are you little one?" She asked no one in particular. She found a note pinned to the baby's outer blanket. It was scrawled hastily but clearly. My mother and father are gone, my name is Shayde. Please take care of me.

"Well Shayde, welcome to Isolde's House. Someone had the good sense to leave you in the care of the best orphanage in Tor'Amal, if not Ka'len. Let's go get you something to eat shall we little blue eyes?" The matron's smile was genuine.

She did not see the matching one from the one-eyed beggar that was sitting on the steps across the street from the gate.

When the gate shut Korin stood up and walked to the building right beside the orphanage and knocked on the door.

A page of the Thieves and Assassins Guild opened the door hesitantly. Though the big man that knocked had a pleasant smile, he was also dripping blood from a fresh wound and looked worse for wear.

"Good morning boy. I hear tell that you lot may have need of a Weapons Master?" He said jovially.

The page nodded and stepped aside and let Korin in. As he waited for the Guild Master he looked out of the window in the parlor and saw a smiling nurse rocking a small blue-eyed baby as she fed him a bottle and sang softly to him. Korin smiled.

Thank you for reading Book 1 of the Shayde series! I sincerely hope that you have enjoyed the story so far. Hungry for more? Shayde: Upbringing is scheduled for release in early January! Maybe sooner for those of you that follow me on social media! So, turn the page and read on for a sneak peek into book two.

Thank you,

*Jasen R Dobson*

# SHADYE: UPBRINGING – BOOK TWO

## CHAPTER 1

"*S*HAYDE! GET BACK HERE BOY!" THE MATRON YELLED AFTER THE headstrong youth that was now running along the edge of the wall between the

Orphanage and the Thieves and Assassins Guild next door.

The Guild Master had asked her repeatedly to keep the children, especially Shayde, off of the wall. But it was no use. The child was strong and fast and climbed like a monkey.

Quick as a flash he was over the wall and dropping into the Guild's training yard. He landed in a forward roll and came up ready to sprint away when a huge hand clamped down on the back of his collar.

Gods.

He looked up and saw the bald-headed weapons master smiling down at him.

"Shayde, did we not discuss this? You are welcome here, but you must start using the front door. There are protocols here for security. I would hate for some overzealous novice to put a dart into you thinking you from a rival Guild." He laughed.

"Kallen, I am twelve years old. No one is going to think me an assassin." Shayde laughed.

"I would not be so sure of that young Master. We start them young here." Korin said with a laugh.

"In that case, show ME how to use a sword! You train Perrin and she's a girl!" He said with mostly mock indignation.

"Just a girl! I'll show you JUST a girl!" Came an indignant shriek from behind them.

A small ball of female fury came running around the weapons master and wrapped Shayde up in a hug before rolling him over her shoulder and onto his back. She finished with a knee in his chest and a smile on her face.

"Perrin Lightfinger, you let that boy up this minute!" Korin said gruffly.

Though both children could tell the weapons master was trying not to laugh at the comical look on Shayde's face as he stared up at the wiry little girl that had so handily taken him off of his feet.

Perrin rolled her eyes and stood up before offering Shayde a hand. He bounded to his feet and knocked the dust off of the back of his pants and tunic. The Matron would have his hide if he came back filthy again. But as she would probably have it in for him jumping the wall anyway, a little dirt was okay.

"Kallen, may Perrin and I go into town to the market? I have some money I earned from chores and would like to go spend it!" Shayde asked the weapons master.

"Yes, you may. Perrin, keep an eye on young Shayde here and make sure he does not lose his purse to one of our Guild on the way to the market." Korin half-joked.

Perrin nodded.

Korin watched the pair disappear out of the side gate. He watched until they shut the gate behind them and were out of sight.

He did not see the second set of eyes that were watching Shayde from across the street. Sitting on the very steps that Korin had set upon twelve years ago, the dark-haired figure watched Shayde running up the street with Perrin.

When they were far enough away, he followed.

# CHAPTER 2

SANGRE

HE FOLLOWED THE PAIR FROM WHAT HE FELT WAS A SAFE distance.

Never daring to come within a stone's throw of the foolish orphan boy that seemed intent on knocking over everything in his path. The bigger threat of discovery lay with the little thief girl that was ever at the orphan's side.

Sangre shook his head in disgust.

His mother, Maricin Cor Render, had told him all he needed to know about the orphan's lineage.

The orphan's father, Drayel Shadow Walker, had stolen the God's Eye Medallion from her before Sangre had been born. He was also aware that, during the theft of the Medallion, the cursed Shadow Walker demon had forced himself on his mother. Their unwanted union had resulted in his conception and birth.

So, even though he was born of an evil act, his mother still spoiled him and treated him as though he were the King of all Ka'len. And he would be. Once he found where the orphan's father had hidden the God's Eye.

His mother had promised to teach him all he needed to know of magic and sorcery once he was of age. How he longed for the day when his powers would manifest.

Sangre stopped suddenly when he realized that while he was lost in thought he had wandered entirely too close to the pair he had been following.

He cursed himself for a fool as the orphan suddenly jumped backwards trying to dodge a playful punch the girl, Perrin he thought, had thrown at him.

The little idiot never minded his surroundings. So, it was no surprise that he didn't see the large stray dog that he tripped over.

The mangy old mutt had probably been brown before it had been coated in mud. But the beast was so dirty that Sangre could not tell what color its coat actually was.

It leapt to its feet as Shayde clumsily tripped over it's back.

Shayde landed on his backside and suddenly found himself facing an enraged cur dog. The beast had its hackles up and lips pulled back baring broken but sharp teeth. The scars on the animals face and legs showed that it was no stranger to pain and violence.

Sangre entertained, for a brief moment, the idea of letting the street dog tear into the orphan's throat. That would end Sangre's mission of following the little fool at his mother's command.

But, it would also end any chance he had of finding the God's Eye.

His mother believed that the Medallion was spelled to only be revealed to one of Drayel's lineage. More specifically, to Shayde.

She would not allow Shayde to die based on the chance that Drayel had keyed the Medallion to reveal itself to Shayde when his powers came forth.

In that case, it was Sangre's mission to be near to Shayde when the Medallion revealed itself so that he could kill Shayde and take the God's Eye for himself.

He had not been ready to begin his false friendship with Shayde yet.

He had hoped to have more time to observe him. And, truth be told, Sangre did not have any friends.

Everyone at the Citadel was cordial to him. Their weapons master trained him every other day, though he was not yet old enough to be a Warrior. His mother being Guild Master had bought him that courtesy.

But there were no children at the Guild.

Sangre had been raised among the Warrior Class and servants of the Guild. He had no social skills to speak of. He could order the staff around, but having a casual conversation, or starting one, was a skill that eluded him.

So, this situation that presented itself played right into the skills he did possess.

Sangre moved forward quickly and faked stumbling into the vendor's stand beside Shayde. As he pretended to fall he casually grabbed the handle of a steaming pot of water, that the proprietor was about to drop a handful of noodles into, and swung it toward the dog as he continued to fake his loss of balance.

He fell to the ground unceremoniously and huffed as his shoulder impacted against the hard cobble stone street.

He watched with satisfaction as the scalding water struck the dog in the hind quarters just as it was about to lunge for the frozen orphan's face.

To her credit, the Light Finger girl had pulled a long needle like blade from her hair and was preparing to throw it at the dog when the water had sent the animal yelping down the street as fast as it's legs would carry it.

Sangre lay there on the cobble stones and waited. He pretended that the breath had been blown from his lungs when he struck the hard street surface. He hoped that one of the pair would come to his aide as he had come to theirs.

Or more accurately, Shayde's.

He was mildly aggravated when Perrin shot passed him to kneel at Shayde's side.

"Oh Gods. That was close!" Perrin exclaimed. "Are you injured Shayde?" She asked intently.

She looked him over thoroughly, as if expecting to see his very life blood running out onto the ground.

Sangre took a deep breath and pushed himself up into a sitting position before leaning back against the cart of the now very angry vendor. The man walked around the front of the cart and snatched the pot out of Sangre's hand. He called them all some very colorful names that one would think an adult would save for people other than children.

Sangre just smiled thinly.

The man reminded him of the foul mouthed weapons master of the Guild.

It was then that the pair sitting across from him finally realized that he was there. Both were staring at him as if he were a wraith or some other unusual creature they had never seen before.

It was Perrin who spoke first.

"Boy, are you okay?" She asked inquisitively.

BOY! Sangre raged inside. Who did this petulant child think she was. He was Sangre Deathrage. Son of Guild Master Maricin Cor Render. Skilled with sword and potions.

And at the moment he must appear to be nothing more than a common street urchin.

Sangre bristled at the idea of pretending to be less than the little thief and orphan sitting across from him.

But he knew he must.

While he contemplated his anger at the situation Perrin brought him back to the moment.

"Maybe he hit his head? He doesn't seem able to speak." Perrin said to Shayde.

Mostly seriously but with a slight inflection of humour in her tone.

Shayde just shrugged and took her offered hand to rise to his feet. They both turned and looked at Sangre.

"I can speak very well, thank you." Sangre said with what he HOPED sounded like mock indignation.

He forced a smile onto his face as he walked over to where the pair stood watching him.

"Are YOU okay, boy?" Sangre asked Shayde.

He was pleased to see the light of anger flare in Shayde's eyes.

He took some small satisfaction in the fact that Shayde would be easy to irritate and manipulate.

Despite his rather poor station and lot in life, Shayde was still proud and arrogant.

An easy combination to exploit.

Sangre's smile this time was genuine.

"I meant no offense my friend. Your friend called me "boy" and I admit I bristled at the comment and used it foolishly to address you. I apologize. I am Sangre. Pleased to meet you both...." he let the last word trail off and used it as an invitation to introduce themselves.

Shayde stepped slightly forward and placed himself between Sangre and Perrin.

A fully unintentional act on Shayde's part, but it told Sangre that Shayde cared for the girl and felt it was his obligation to protect her.

Perrin, apparently, disagreed.

The girl shouldered past the posturing male and extended her hand to Sangre.

"Perrin Light Finger. Apprentice to the Thieves Guild. A pleasure to meet you Sangre." Perrin did not ask for Sangre's last name or Guild. It was commonly known that those without a home or occupation carried no surname.

If Sangre did not offer his last name or Guild, then it would be rude of her to ask.

Shayde pushed up beside his friend and took Sangre's hand from Perrin's before shaking it himself.

Shayde squeezed the other boy's hand hard as he shook it, thinking to intimidate this new person that had called him Boy.

But to his surprise, Sangre's grip was very strong. Shayde would not have believed that a homeless vagabond would have a grip like that. But, then again, life on the streets could be difficult. Maybe that was what had made this boy tough.

Shayde did notice a slight wince when Sangre let go.

That's when Shayde finally saw the thick red line welling up along the palm of the boys hand. He must have injured himself when he fell and knocked the water off of the vendors table.

It might have been an accident, but the boy, Sangre, had saved him from that stupid dog. So, maybe Shayde could let the BOY comment go.

"I'm Shayde. I live at Isolde's Home next to the Thieves Guild. It looks like you were injured when you knocked that pot of water off of the table. Would you like to come back to the Home with me and see one of the priestess of Isolde? They can fix that for you pretty quickly. And it wouldn't cost anything either!" Shayde said in a rush.

Sangre held back his derisive snort. The potions his mother had gifted him would heal him easily enough. But Shayde did not need to know that. And spending time around the air headed followers of the light strumpet did not sound at all appealing to Sangre.

He shook his head.

"Thank you, but no. The wound will go a long way toward garnering me sympathy from the cooks around the square tonight when I go seeking dinner. So, in a way, it will be better if I do not allow it to be healed." Sangre said with what he hoped was an honest tone.

Perrin tilted her head and studied him closely.

He had done well to borrow some of the stable boy's older work clothes to aide in his disguise. Perrin would not be easily fooled by appearances.

Sangre had donned the old rags and walked into the corral at the Citadel where he ran some of the horses in a circle around the training ring in order to get a realistic coating of dust on his face, arms, hair, and clothing. He had refused to bathe for two days prior to coming into

Tor'Amal because he knew that he could not afford to smell of fine soaps and bath oils. That would not help his false image at all.

So he looked, and smelled, the part of a homeless urchin. He hoped.

Apparently satisfied, Perrin looked away and smiled at Shayde.

"Well, if we can not persuade our new friend to return with us to the Home or the Guild, perhaps he would let us buy him dinner?" She asked hopefully.

Sangre looked at Perrin hard. He was trying to determine if there was any antagonization or teasing behind her offer. But no, the softness of her face, and the way she held her chin just slightly down and away from him as she looked back at him from an angle, indicated that she was actually slightly embarrassed at having asked him to dine with them.

The look on Shayde's face was less embarrassed and more aggravated. Sangre could tell that Shayde had planned on eating alone with Perrin. The idea of messing up Shayde's plans was more than he was willing to pass up.

"Of course, Lady Light Finger. I would be honored to be your guest this evening." He said with a slight bow and drop of his head.

Perrin turned slightly red at the very adult sounding Lady Light Finger Sangre had bestowed upon her.

Sangre hid his smile well after seeing Shayde turn an entirely different shade of red.

He made an after you motion and fell easily into step beside Perrin as Shayde grumbled and trudged along behind them.

# ABOUT THE AUTHOR

Jasen R Dobson is a lifelong resident of North East Arkansas.

He is a U.S. Army Veteran that has served in Iraq and spent time in the UK, Guatemala, and various other countries around the world. He currently serves with the Arkansas National Guard in the role of Platoon Sergeant for the Battalion Mortar Section.

Jasen lives in North East Arkansas with his wife of 20 years and their 3 children.

A lifelong fan of Stephen King, R.A. Salvatore, and other authors too numerous to mention, Jasen was finally persuaded to begin writing and share his stories with the reading community. Jasen did so with his first offering, Dark Gate. The first books unexpected success and growing following helped to cement the plans for book two, Angel Fire, as well as the epic series, Shayde.

In his spare time Jasen enjoys running, riding bikes, Martial Arts (he is a black belt in Tae Kwon Do and has training in BJJ and Boxing), and playing guitar. His greatest thrill, and according to him his greatest achievement, is his family. Jasen hopes that he will be successful enough in his writing efforts to be able to be a full time author and spend more time with his family.

https://therealjasenrdobso.wixsite.com/jasenrdobson
https://www.facebook.com/therealjasendobson
https://www.instagram.com/jasenrdobson/
http://www.x.com/DobsonJasen